For Dottie♥!

finally my favorite

R̃
2015

Praise for The Lake Effect Series

"I really enjoyed this book - from the strong start to the character development, it was on point. The characters were believable, the story itself lovely and relatable. Would recommend for the humor alone, but there is so much more to enjoy here!"

~Angela, Goodreads

"IT'S NOT MY FAVORITE is a story of two sisters, one lesbian and one heterosexual. The point of view changes between them so you are getting both of their stories as they interact…It made you think. It made you cry. It made you laugh. It made you want to reach into the book and throttle their mother. The detail is amazing and the story makes you contemplate your own life. I appreciate my life after reading this book…It resonates with you well past when you put the book down."

~Moonbeams Over Atlanta

"This book is undoubtedly chick lit which I normally do not care for. But Rue's writing was delightful. These sisters are so realistic. I laughed, I felt like crying, I detested their parents, I rejoiced for Gwenn and Rachel. Rue's style of writing made me love these sisters."

~Betty, Goodreads

"This is a complex family saga story – not a straightforward romance. The dialogue and banter is strong, along with the descriptive writing and characterization. The author does a great job of showing how life isn't simple and our emotions can be swayed powerfully by events beyond our control.

The author manages the changing points of view well and without confusion. Above all, this is a story about the enduring bond of sisterhood and the complexities of love."

~J.H., Goodreads

"I loved this part, as being from New Zealand myself, I got to experience all the places Gwenn went, too, as it stirred memories from the Huka Falls in Taupo to the Gardens in Hamilton. IT'S NOT MY FAVORITE is a chick lit novel that will have readers wanting to travel and experience the world, as it shows readers that in order to grow, we must discover and take risks in life."

~The Phantom Paragrapher

"A Must Read book for anyone ever born that had a family."
~Andrew, Amazon

"I adored IT'S NOT MY FAVORITE! It starts off with a bang, and I was hooked right from the very start! This book definitely pulled me in. Everything worked together really well and created a lasting impression long after I finished reading this one.
The characters, y'all. They are rich and detailed. I'm a huge character person, and I couldn't get enough of these characters. The development is brilliant and I felt like I got to know all of the characters. Rachel was my favorite, and I really bonded with her!"
~Pretty Little Pages

"Another great family drama/saga book by Rue that focuses on Sisterhood and that no matter what your parents or love life is like, you can always count on your sisters to have your back."
~Paula, Goodreads

"This is a good book about sisters who stick together through it all. The love they have for each other goes above and beyond, and around the globe."
~Give Me Books

I really enjoyed this book. The sisters are delightful and one really cares about their lives. The author draws the reader in, and gradually more is revealed about their relationships with each...I couldn't put the book down.
~Catherine, Goodreads

Rue has written a beautiful story and I'm looking forward to reading more from her.
~Hooked On Books

I really had an amazing experience following Gwenn on her self-discovery... while soaking in the beautiful sights of New Zealand. Rue wrote it so beautifully that I really wished I was there with Gwenn. I did a little happy dance when I saw that this is a series and I might get more of these amazing characters (ahem! ahem! Todd and Flora please)...
~Gateway to a Different World

finally my favorite

The Lake Effect Series, Book 3

RUE

Sittin' On A Goldmine
Productions L.L.C.

Copyright © 2015 by Rue

All rights reserved. Printed in the United States of America by Sittin' On A Goldmine Productions, L.L.C., Arizona. No part of this publication may be reproduced, distributed, or transmitted in any form or by any manner whatsoever, or stored in a database or retrieval system, without the prior written permission of the publisher.

Sittin' On A Goldmine Productions, L.L.C.
info@sittinonagoldmine.co
www.sittinonagoldmine.co

This is a work of fiction. Names, characters, places and incidents are products of the author's imagination or are used fictitiously and are not to be construed as real. Any resemblance to actual events, locales, organizations, or persons, living or dead, is entirely coincidental.

Rue
Finally My Favorite : a novel / by Rue, —1st cd.

ISBN: 978-0-9860627-9-7 (Paperback) / ISBN: 978-0-9860627-7-3 (Electronic Book)
(1. Sisters — Fiction. 2. Wedding — Fiction. 3. Love — Fiction.
4. Lesbian — Fiction. 5. Adoption — Fiction.) 1. Title.

Printed in the United States of America

1 2 3 4 5 6 7 8 9 10

love \\'ləv\ *n.*
A deep, tender, ineffable feeling of affection and solicitude toward a person, such as that arising from kinship, recognition of attractive qualities, or a sense of underlying oneness.

"There is nothing more lovely in life than the union of two people whose love for one another has grown through the years, from the small acorn of passion, into a great rooted tree."
~ **Vita Sackville-West**

Prologue

Rachel ran her hands along Annie's skin. The heat leapt from her fingertips and left a trail of goose bumps and sighs. She released the belt buckle with a flick of her wrist, slowly tugging Annie's jeans out of the way.

Annie moaned and grabbed a handful of Rachel's thick ebony tresses. "Bring that sexy mouth up here, babe."

The jeans plummeted to the floor and Rachel met Annie's lips with hunger and need. The band had been on tour for weeks and Rachel was way overdue for her fix. "I missed you so much. I can't believe you're finally back." She pressed her teeth into Annie's collarbone and growled.

Two T-shirts hit the floor. Two bodies hit the sheets.

Patience vanished. Desire consumed Rachel. She licked her fingers and pushed them, slowly, into Annie's honey pot. She was instantly rewarded with a luscious shiver.

Annie rocked her hips and pulled at the bars of the headboard. "Deeper, deeper."

Rachel happily granted her wish.

A shuddering, moaning Annie wrapped her legs around Rachel.

Something momentarily blurred Rachel's vision. She brushed at her eyes and felt silky tulle. She pulled at the fabric, but it tightened over her face. She felt it twisting around her neck, like a python. She grabbed at the noose with both hands. Her mind raced ahead of her pulse. "I need air!" A ringing in her ears confirmed her oxygen deprivation.

RING! RING!

Rachel threw the covers off her face and gasped for air. The phone rang insistently and Annie dissolved into the dreamland from whence she came.

"Hello?"

"Rache, did I wake you?" In her desperation to speak to her sister Gwenn had not bothered to check the time.

"You simultaneously ruined the best sex I've had in weeks and managed to save me from asphyxiation."

"Whoa, I had no idea you were into that freaky shit!" Gwenn laughed nervously, stopping abruptly when she realized Annie was still on tour with her band. "Are you cheating on Annie?"

"What? Oh, hell no. I was having dream sex. You know, the only kind of sex you ever had, before Daniel." Rachel laughed at her own joke and continued, "Then out of nowhere this bridal veil attacked me and tried to strangle me."

Gwenn stifled a chuckle and scolded her baby sister, "Don't start freaking out about your wedding, already. Besides, when did you decide to wear a veil? WTF?"

"I haven't decided anything, so save your objections for when they'll really count." Rachel rolled out from under her down comforter and slipped her feet into the soft possum fur slippers Gwenn had brought her from New Zealand. "So, you called me, remember?"

"Oh, right. Steven wants to have sex."

ne

Pastor Ed, wrapped in his down jacket, wool scarf and hat, arrived at St. Luke's Hospital before visiting hours. A quick flash of his "Clergy" card gained him access to the Intensive Care Unit. He removed his cold weather gear and rubbed his hands together to restore some of the heat stolen by the fierce Minnesotan winter. He slipped into the familiar vinyl-clad chair beside his wife's bed and pressed his large hand over her frail fingers. They felt icier than the wind knifing across Lake Superior.

"Good mornin', Shirley. I spoke ta the girls last night and I think Gwenn will be coming ta visit ya this afternoon." Ed swallowed and forced a smile to his lips. "Ya look much better today. I think that there new medicine is doin' the trick." He battled with his conscience a little over the white lie, but he justified it by reminding himself he was doing God's work—ministering to the infirm.

The truth was that he barely recognized the corpse-like woman in the hospital bed. Shirley Hutchinson was a high-school beauty queen who had aged gracefully. She rarely had a hair out of place and she never left the house without a fresh coat of lipstick. Ed had grown accustomed to her picture-perfect appearance—in truth he mostly took it for granted. He searched the hollow cheeks and sunken eyes, desperate for a hint of the woman he'd loved since the tenth grade. Helplessness overwhelmed him and he sought assistance from a higher power.

BEEEEEEEEEEEEP!

Ed's head jerked up from its prayerful pose and his eyes shot to the monitor beside the bed. The green line was flat. The monitor was screaming out its terrible news and Shirley's chest was not moving. He scrambled for the panic button as the nurse ran into the room.

He felt strong hands push him away from his wife. His shoulder collided with the door jamb as a doctor rushed past him and into Shirley's room. Pastor Edwin Hutchinson stood mute and motionless as his wife's life ebbed away.

***

One minute Shirley had been listening to Ed's strong, reassuring voice and the next minute she was enveloped in silence. She opened her eyes for the first time in weeks and found it rather odd to be looking down on an old woman in a sterile hospital bed.

She felt so light, almost weightless. No pain, no discomfort. Slowly Shirley examined the body in the bed. The shrunken, unkempt woman was her ugly doppelgänger. She intended to tell the woman that a little hairspray and a bit of make-up would fix her right up, when a doctor whipped open the woman's gown and revealed a twisted scar across her abdomen.

Shirley gasped and reached for her own mid-section. That was how she discovered she was without corporeal form. The woman in the bed was Shirley, and Shirley was dying.

She watched the medical personnel moving with trained precision. She looked at the flat line on the monitor and waited for it to rebound. No jump. No blip. No heartbeat.

The silence was deafening. She screamed at the people on the ground below her, but they refused to acknowledge her requests. *Where in the world is Ed? Why isn't he doing something?* She finally caught sight of his transfixed form, just outside the door. His hands were clenched into white-knuckled fists at his side and silent tears streamed down his face.

Most women would be touched by this display of emotion, but the ever-disappointed Shirley never missed an opportunity to criticize. *Oh fer cryin' out loud Ed, don't just stand there. Call the prayer group! Call my doctor!* Ed did not move a muscle, until he was physically pushed aside to make way for a large white machine.

Shirley assessed the situation and decided she may very well be dying. Once she entertained that possibility—she had a whole new set of complaints. *Where's the bright light? Why aren't there any angels guidin' me into Heaven? I lived everyday fer the Lord. I would expect a bigger welcome.* Shirley pondered her options as a blinding pain in her chest sealed her fate.

Her ears flooded with sound. Her eyes fluttered open.

Beep. Beep. Beep.

She was back.

Ed pushed past the nurses and crushed Shirley's hand in his own. "Thank God. Oh, thank God."

Shirley meant to answer, but intense pain in her throat and a bossy nurse prevented any further discussion.

Two

Gwenn and Rachel sat in the very back room of the Perkins on London Road. Gwenn's copper-brown tresses were scooped up into a high ponytail and Rachel's purple-streaked ebony hair spilled out of a sloppy braid.

"So, the purple is new." Gwenn's hazel eyes twinkled.

Rachel's hand slipped up to her disastrous braid. "Yeah, as the Annie-missing anxiety increases, the 'doing stupid things that I can control' also increases. So I fucked with my hair, you got a problem with that?" Rachel winked at her big sister.

"I wish that was my problem. As I mentioned on the phone my problem involves Steven and the sex."

"Last I checked you were the straight sister, so what's your problem?" Rachel laughed and struggled to fill her dark-brown eyes with a modicum of innocence.

"Oh, hilarious." Gwenn took a gulp of her coffee and held the warm mug in both hands. "I don't think I'm ready."

"What do you mean ready? Are you still hung up on Daniel?"

"Still? You say that like it's been five years. It's been a couple weeks. So yeah, I'm *still* hung up on Daniel." Gwenn twirled her fork in the hash browns on her plate.

Rachel eyed those hash browns with intense desire. "You gonna eat those?"

"No, and neither are you. You've been complaining about putting on a few pounds and I am not going to support your habit."

"Bitch."

"Get used to it." Gwenn was used to absorbing Rachel's food-related angst. It was comforting to know exactly how to handle one thing in her life. "Annie will be back for the mid-tour break soon and I know you want to drop the stress weight before she gets back. So, from now on, I'm your carb counselor." Gwenn pushed her plate to the edge of the table and placed her napkin over the remaining hash browns.

"Damn your stupid skinny genes and your fucking self-control." Rachel pouted for a millisecond and quickly grinned. "Thanks."

"No problem. Now, can we focus on my problem for a half a second?"

"Gee, you have two guys dying to get in your pants. Sounds like straight-girl problems to me. What could I possibly do?"

"Hey, smart ass, you're the one always saying that sex is sex, so don't play the gay card. I need help doing the whole pros/cons thing about the sex with Steven decision." Gwenn retrieved a pad of paper from her over-sized bag.

"Stand back ladies and gentlemen, *The Organizer* has arrived." Rachel snickered at Gwenn's super-prepared rucksack. "Do you always have that with you?"

"I get ideas. Is that a crime?"

"Ever heard of a voice memo?" Rachel waved her smartphone at Gwenn.

"Shut up and help." Gwenn drew a vertical line down the center of the page and labeled the first column "Pros" and the second column "Cons".

"I've got one for the 'Cons' side." Rachel bit her lip to keep from laughing. "Penis."

"Oh, shut up. If you're not going to take this seriously, I will have to call Randy and get a man's opinion."

"I don't know what part of that sentence is funnier. The part that insinuates the flamingly gay Randy has a man's opinion or the part where you think he would have a single 'Con.'" Rachel reached across the table and flipped Gwenn's pad of paper face down. "Let's talk about this like normal people. Why is Steven in such a hurry?"

"Rache, he was a prisoner of war for over six years. The only thing that kept him alive was a belief that he would find his way back to me. In his world, he's been waiting forever."

"OK, but in your world he was the asshole that left you in the middle of a pregnancy scare over a decade ago—and he never bothered to contact you."

Gwenn hesitated, momentarily pulled back in time, before she rallied to Steven's defense. "But, Rache, that's all changed. I mean, he apologized. I explained that I wasn't really pregnant, just a false alarm. He told me all about his regrets and how I'm the most important thing in the world—"

"Sirens! Warning lights! Gwenn, snap out of it. You can't make this a guilt fuck."

"What?"

"A guilt fuck." Rachel placed her hands on the table and looked at Gwenn as though the term was common knowledge. "Don't agree to have sex because you feel guilty. OK, so the image of your face kept him alive, blah, blah, blah...I get it. He didn't know if he would ever set foot in this country again, but he did. He was rescued and he got to come home. Why does that mean he automatically gets back in your pants?"

"It's not like that. He made up for his mistakes. He won me back. We got a second chance."

"Hey, trust me, I can appreciate the second chance thing. I mean, I can't believe Annie and I got another shot—but we both wanted that chance. He appeared out of thin air and—"

"No, Rache, that's not true. I never stopped loving him. He left me and I was shattered. I made a shit load of bad relationship choices because I never got over Steven."

"Was Daniel a bad choice?"

Gwenn stared into her coffee and watched the oils on the surface swirl and disappear. She didn't even realize she was crying, until Rachel reached across the table and handed her a napkin. "Daniel was the only good choice I ever made...now I...he'll never..."

"Never say never, sweetie." Rachel got up and walked over to Gwenn's side of the table. She squeezed into a chair next to Gwenn and swallowed her in a bone-crushing hug.

Three

Daniel opened his mismatched eyes, one blue and one brown, and drank in the pale yellow morning light spilling across his brightly-colored duvet. The brilliant sunlight of San Miguel de Allende brought half a grin to his worried visage. Gwenn had returned to Minnesota a few weeks ago, leaving him to his artistic sabbatical in Mexico. Technically they were on a "break," but her lack of communication was beginning to feel more like a "break up."

Time to call Todd, his ridiculously efficient assistant, and pump him for a much-needed update. "Hey, buddy." Daniel forced an unnatural cheeriness into his voice.

"Sir, I prefer Todd, as we have discussed on several occasions." Todd rolled his eyes and exhaled slightly louder than necessary.

"How are things at the Gallery, Todd?"

"I hate to answer a question with a question, but are you sober?"

"Indeed, Todd, indeed. I have held my binge drinking in check and I have kept my regular phone appointments with Dr. Mountainside. Any other questions, Todd?"

"OK, sir. You made your point. You need not insert my name into every sentence." Todd twirled the tassel on Flora's throw pillow. He wasn't exactly sure how to break the news to Daniel, but at some point he was going to have to come clean about his whirlwind romance with Gwenn's employee.

"So, any Gallery news?"

"Sabina seems to be handling things quite well in Minneapolis. I am currently overseeing the special project we discussed." Todd was banking on Daniel's lack of attention to detail. They had never truly discussed the project; Todd had only mentioned a few broad strokes about a satellite gallery.

"Special project? Did I sleep through another one of your updates?" Daniel laughed. He always felt better when he spoke to Todd. There was a deep bond there that Daniel never took for granted. On the surface he was the boss and Todd was the assistant, but underneath all of that he knew Todd had gone way beyond the call of duty when Daniel's father was killed. In truth, he owed Todd his life. "Seriously, what project are we talking about?"

So, today is the day. Todd knew he couldn't keep the satellite gallery in Duluth a secret forever, however he had counted on Gwenn's superb distractionary skills to keep Daniel occupied until the grand opening. Fate had other plans for Miss Hutchinson. Damn fate. "Perhaps we should discuss all this when you return from your trip."

"If I didn't know any better, Todd, I'd say you're stalling." Daniel allowed the uncomfortable silence to expand. He wanted Todd to squirm a little. "Hey, I just remembered something Dr. Mountainside said."

Todd eagerly pounced on the segue. "Oh, wonderful. What was it?"

"She said you were at the Beargrease Festival. Did I hear her correctly?"

Todd chewed his lip as his brain spun through a myriad of options. A slow smile crept across his mouth and his blue eyes twinkled as a plan unfolded. "Yes, I was at the Festival, but not alone. I've been meaning to tell you something."

"You secretly love sled dogs, and you want to quit and move to Alaska?" Daniel chuckled at his clever quip.

"Oh, you've found me out." Todd allowed himself far more jocularity than the remark deserved, but he was intent on building good will. "Actually, sir, I've taken up with Flora Long." Todd paused and took a deep breath in preparation for the onslaught of questions.

"Flora? Do I know Flora? Is she in the business—a collector? Oh shit, she's not a gallery owner, is she? Are you leaving me for another woman?"

"Would you like me to answer those in any particular order?"

"Sorry, I got a little bit ahead of myself. How 'bout you just fill me in?" Daniel threw back his duvet and swung his long muscular legs over the side of the bed. His feet hit the cool tile and he scrubbed his free hand through his tousled honey-brown mane.

Todd reminded him that Flora managed *The Organizer*, for Gwenn. He went on to extol Flora's virtues, until Daniel interrupted.

"Any news on Gwenn?"

"Sorry? Were we talking about Gwenn?" Todd was mildly miffed that Daniel completely overlooked all the interesting details about Flora.

"I'm an ass. Let me just get that out of the way, then let me say how happy I am for you. Flora sounds fantastic and I wish you two all the best. You deserve it, buddy."

Todd ignored the casual moniker. "Thank you, sir."

"Now, about the special project," Daniel paused to allow Todd to fill in the details.

"Yes, about that." Todd laid out the highlights. "Last year, at your *final* gallery show, you effectually announced your retirement. When you decided to reinvent yourself with mosaic art, I had to come up with a creative re-introduction campaign. I decided to open a new gallery, dedicated exclusively to your neoteric work."

"And that is why you are the highest paid gallery director in North America!" Daniel smiled smugly. He wasn't exactly sure how he had landed Todd, but he was willing to pay whatever was necessary to keep him.

"Not a verifiable fact, but I am grateful for your generosity."

"So how were you able to find another spot on Hennepin? Vacancies are pretty rare in that area. How far is it between the galleries?"

Todd fiddled with a button on his Oxford shirt. "Well, it's about 150 miles."

"What?"

"You see, sir, you have been spending a good deal of time in Duluth, so..."

Daniel exhaled, audibly. "The new gallery is in Duluth. I have to say, you were on the right track. I mean, I thought things were really going somewhere with Gwenn." Daniel flopped down in a chair and let his head loll back onto the pillows. "What the hell happened, Todd?"

"Steven happened, sir. Perhaps you should let this play out. If things fell apart between them before, there's no guarantee it will work out any differently this time."

"That's just it, Todd, I don't want to take that chance. I thought I could give her some space, and all that bullshit, but now? Now I want to put an end to this nonsense and send this Steven punk packing."

"Would you be needing a strategy?" Todd smirked.

"I need a miracle."

"Fortunately, that's my specialty," Todd replied.

Four

"Gwenny, your phone's ringing."

"It's Dad. Should I let it go to voicemail?"

Rachel bit her lip and shook her head. "It might be about Mom. You better answer."

Gwenn fluttered her eyes in annoyance and steeled herself for the inevitable prayer request. "Hi, Ed. What's up?"

The incoherent words mixed with tears which flooded into Gwenn's ear brought her to her feet. She put her hand over the phone and whispered to Rachel, "Get the check. It sounds bad."

Rachel's huge brown eyes widened with fear. She grabbed the check and ran up to the register. In her haste she broke her cardinal rule, "Oldest pays."

When Gwenn passed by on the way out, Rachel grabbed the phone from her. "Dad, we're on our way. Bye."

"I really couldn't understand him, Rache. It sounded like she almost died. We'd better hurry."

They jumped into Gwenn's Jeep and raced to the hospital. Gwenn searched her heart for an emotion, any emotion. She found nothing. Her mother might be dying, and she felt nothing.

Rachel's eyelashes pushed new tears over the edge with each anxious blink. "I don't want her to die, Gwenny. I know she hates me, but I don't care. I just don't want her to die."

"Don't worry, sweetie, I honestly don't think heaven will have her. Only the good die young. I'm afraid we'll be stuck with her forever."

"Promise?"

"I promise, Rache. I promise."

Rachel encircled Gwenn and squeezed. Gwenn struggled to keep the vehicle between the lines. "Rache, I'm driving. Ease up!"

They arrived at the hospital in one piece and Rachel led the way to ICU.

They found Ed perched next to Shirley's bed. His thin grey hair was surprisingly unkempt and his red-rimmed eyes begged for support.

"Dad!" Rachel swooped in and hugged the man who had only recently made amends for turning his back on her and Annie, after the big announcement.

Gwenn hung back and let Rachel handle the emotional stuff.

Dr. Murashige walked in and gave everyone a moment to compose themselves. "Good morning, Mr. Hutchinson, ladies," he nodded to Rachel and Gwenn. "I am sorry to report that your mother's condition has become extremely critical." He looked down at his tablet, swiped left and confirmed the condition.

"I thought she was already in critical condition. The new medication was supposed to help. What happened?" Gwenn stared at the doctor with a mixture of confusion and distrust.

He nodded and glanced down at the chart displayed on the tablet. He scrolled up and replied, "We charted a mild improvement yesterday, however this morning your mother suffered acute renal failure. The hemolytic uremic syndrome reached its ultimate conclusion. Once we were able to resuscitate your mother, we had to place her on dialysis."

Ed shook his head and remained silent.

Rachel cried and covered her face with her hands.

It was up to Gwenn to get the necessary details. "How long will she be on dialysis?"

"Until we find a donor."

"A donor? For what?"

"Your mother's kidneys have failed. She will remain on dialysis until we find a matching kidney donor."

Rachel found her voice. "We'll all get tested. Family is the best match, right?"

Gwenn glared at Rachel. Only a complete asshole would refuse to donate a kidney to her own mother. Now that Rachel had volunteered all of their organs, Gwenn would not have the opportunity to be a complete asshole.

"Blood and tissue samples can be taken in the lab. I'll issue the necessary orders. That is very generous..." Dr. Murashige paused, hoping someone would fill in a name.

"Rachel, I'm Rachel Hutchinson. Shirley's youngest daughter."

"Yes, that is *very* generous, Rache." Gwenn scowled briefly at Rachel and then turned a lovely fake smile on the doctor. "How soon can we be tested?"

"I'll have the nurse escort you to the lab immediately. They will rush the typing test, due to the seriousness of your mother's condition." Dr. Murashige paused and stared at the Hutchinson family. "Well, I will go and compile the necessary orders and return with the nurse." He could not think of a single comforting thing to say. "OK, I'll be right back." His sneakers squeaked on the linoleum as he hurried out the door.

"Dad? Dad, are you OK?" Rachel put a hand on her dad's shoulder.

Ed clenched his jaw and swallowed hard. "I almost lost her. I guess I'm still a bit..."

"You don't have to talk about it, Ed. I'm sure it was difficult." Gwenn did not want to hear any more about the events of the morning. She was far too busy fuming about the blood and tissue tests for which Rachel had just volunteered them both.

"This is Nurse Ania." Dr. Murashige gestured to the shapely blonde woman trailing him into the room. "She will escort you to the lab and make sure your typing tests are processed immediately. She's a force to be reckoned with when it comes to getting quick results from the lab."

Rachel immediately perked up and introduced herself. "Hi, I'm Rachel Hutchinson. We're getting tested to see if we can donate a kidney to my mom." Rachel smiled appraisingly at Ania.

Gwenn gently pulled Rachel back a few paces. "I guess we'll follow you, Ania." Gwenn glanced over her shoulder at Rachel, narrowed her eyes and shook her head in warning.

The sisters left the room and Ed's gaze followed the group. He stroked his chin thoughtfully and his hands shook, almost imperceptibly. The wish of unspoken words clouded his sight.

Five

Steven stood in his Aunt Miriam's living room and stared out the bay window. He puzzled over the fractals of frost that had formed on the inside of the double-paned glass. After years as a prisoner of war in Afghanistan, winter had only meant increased suffering and the constant fear of losing extremities to frostbite. *Could frost be a thing of beauty? Will I ever forget the stinging pain of winter's icy grip?*

CRASH!

The noise triggered instinct and Steven hit the ground. He rolled for cover and crawled silently toward the origin point.

"Oh, hells bells!" Aunt Miriam spewed her version of profanity from the kitchen.

Steven stopped and took a deep breath. "Auntie M, are you OK?" He used the teasing nickname, but his voice bubbled with tension.

"Oh, I'm right as rain, but that matzah ball soup has seen better days." She rounded the corner holding a dishtowel in one hand and the empty 2-quart pan in the other. "Maybe we should go out—"

He looked up, wretched with shame. "Um, hi."

"Steven Benjamin Hays, what in Jehovah's name are you doing on the floor?"

"I heard the crash...it sounded like an explosion...or...I just—"

"Hush, hush. You don't owe anybody any kind of explanation. The fact that you were coming to see if I survived the explosion is all I need to know. Yasher koach, child. Your strength comes from El Shaddai." She wiped her teary eyes with the dishtowel and smiled down at him. "Now stand up so I can hug you. You know your old Auntie can't make the trip down anymore!"

Steven stood and folded his arms around his hunched, tenderhearted aunt. "Let's get the mess cleaned up and then I'll take you to dinner...on one condition." Steven pulled back and struggled to shape his features into a convincingly stern portrait. "You have to help me figure out the best way to propose to Gwenn."

Aunt Miriam made no protest.

They cleaned up the mess. Of course, Aunt Miriam insisted on rinsing off the matzah balls to reuse the following night. "Waste not, want not," she schooled Steven as she placed the doughy spheres into an empty cottage cheese container. Her cupboards were filled with carefully scrubbed and organized plastic containers of all shapes and sizes. She was a woman who lived by her own creed.

Over an assortment of Chinese food, Steven laid out his plan. "I want to take her on a romantic tour of all our old hangouts, cook her a perfect dinner and finally propose to her at the top of Enger Tower."

"Oh, Bubbeleh!" Aunt Miriam pressed the heels of her hands to her forehead and shook her head several times. "Didn't your mother tell you about the will?"

"Whose will?" Steven had pushed his father's death into a dark corner of his mind. He was using all of his discipline to manage the post-traumatic stress of his captivity. He had almost let himself forget the stabbing pain of missing his own father's funeral while he was imprisoned. "Oh, do you mean my father's will? What does that have to do with proposing to Gwenn?"

"Your father was traditional. Nowadays you would probably label him a racist, but we called it traditional. He didn't want his money to be spent by the goyim. He insisted you marry a Jewish girl."

"What do you mean 'insisted'? He's dead, Auntie M, he can't insist on anything."

"But he did, motek, he did. He left you a huge chunk of money—I can't say how much, it wouldn't be proper—but you can only inherit the money if you have a ketubah."

Steven stared in confusion and disbelief. "A what?"

"A Jewish marriage license. The will was very specific." Aunt Miriam loaded her plate with more sweet and sour chicken, and a few more pot stickers. "I say just shtup her, eh? Why marry her if all you want is to shtup her?" She stuffed a pot sticker in her mouth and nodded with finality.

"Aunt Miriam! Do you kiss the rabbi with that mouth?" Steven burst into a fit of much needed chuckling—before he set the record straight. "I want to marry her, not just 'shtup' her. I made the biggest mistake of my life when I ran out on her and I paid dearly for it. I'm not going to make the same mistake again. I'm going to marry Gwenn and if you won't help me plan the perfect proposal I'll figure it out on my own."

Six

Daniel read over Todd's email for the tenth time. Todd's plan was amazingly detailed; not exactly subtle, but it sounded effective. In order to initiate the plan Daniel needed Gwenn's permission—explicit or implied. He was to call her and test the waters. If she talked to him for more than five minutes, if she giggled nervously or if she mentioned anything about their time in Mexico, that was "permission" and he could put the plan in motion. Daniel did not want to entertain failure. He planned on eliciting one thing—permission.

He reached for his phone and shook like the Cowardly Lion. He would call Gwenn, right after he got back from the archeological tour with Señor Diaz De Leon.

Daniel grabbed his Camelbak, filled with filtered water, and walked out to the courtyard of his mentor's sprawling hacienda. The blue agave business had clearly been profitable for Lorenzo Diaz De Leon.

"Buenas días, Daniel!" Lorenzo stood with both hands on his hips, his stout broad chest inhaling the early morning air. "Are you ready for the tour of Cañada de la Virgen?"

"Buenas días, Lorenzo. I am really looking forward to this tour. You said the guide is a personal friend?"

"Yes, yes, Profesora Alberta is a long time family friend. She actually led the team of archeologists on the dig for two years and she has written several books on the architectural structures and artifacts she unearthed."

Lorenzo's private car pulled up and he motioned for Daniel to enter the vehicle first. Daniel nodded and folded himself into the back seat. He was busy arranging his limbs and finding a space for his Camelbak when he felt the seat depress and an arm brush his. He turned to encourage Lorenzo to slide over a bit and was displeased to see Elena's impish grin staring back at him.

"Um, hey there. Your dad didn't mention that you were joining us." Daniel wedged himself against the other door and squeezed his Camelbak between his thigh and Elena's encroachment.

Lorenzo climbed in with a deep chuckle and patted Elena's knee. "Profesora Alberta is the only teacher that could tame you, no?"

Elena whipped her gleaming onyx hair over her shoulder and glared at her father. "I chose to behave because Alberta actually knows what she's talking about, unlike that pompous ass from the Catholic church."

"Elena! Show some respect for the faith." Lorenzo shook his head and crossed himself, in an effort to protect his daughter.

"Your faith, not mine."

Daniel realized he was smiling about two seconds too late.

Elena acknowledged the smile with a wink and a brush of her fingers across his knee.

Damn, this is gonna be a long day. Daniel was busy planning his Elena-avoidance strategy when Lorenzo leaned over and ruined everything.

"Here, let's put that pack in the front with the driver. It's a long drive out to the site and you will be glad for the extra room." Lorenzo grasped Daniel's Camelbak, pulled it firmly and handed it to the driver as Elena's sumptuous thigh pressed firmly into Daniel's.

The ride was only about 40 minutes, but Daniel found it impossible to slide his 6-foot, 3-inch frame away from Elena's touch. She found numerous ways to brush, bump and generally tease his entire right side. His only salvation was Lorenzo's dry recitation of historical facts.

By the time they arrived, Elena's arms were crossed over her chest and she was fuming that her efforts had not enslaved Daniel to her will.

Lorenzo was the first to exit the vehicle, but Daniel spilled out of the other side of the car in a close second.

Profesora Alberta was a tall, elegant woman, with sun-darkened skin and jet-black hair caught in a smooth bun. She embraced Lorenzo in a familiar hug. She did not attempt to hug Elena, however. They nodded appreciatively at one another and smiled.

As Daniel rounded the front of the car Lorenzo extended his arm in welcome. "This is the wonderful artist who is studying with me, Daniel Gregory. Daniel, this is Profesora Alberta."

"Pleased to meet you, Profesora." Daniel extended his hand toward the intelligent-eyed woman.

Alberta grasped his outstretched hand firmly and looked directly into his eyes. "Pleased to meet you, Mr. Gregory, I hope you will enjoy your day with me." She tilted her head, squinting as she searched her memory, "Heterochromia iridium, no?"

Daniel looked lost for a moment and then laughed, "Oh, yes, my eyes, I forget. You know, I rarely have to look at them." He shook her hand over-vigorously and added, "Please call me Daniel."

"Very well, Daniel." She did not encourage him to call her Alberta, but she nodded cordially and continued, "Come, we will load into the tour vehicle and drive out to the site."

Daniel was careful to allow Elena to choose her seat first and then he promptly sat on the other side of the mini-bus.

Alberta stood near the driver, at the front of the bus, and talked about the eccentric German woman who owned all the land surrounding Cañada de la Virgen. "In fact, at one time she owned the entire archeological site, but the Mexican government impressed upon her the need to return this valuable national treasure to its rightful owners. So you will note a fence surrounding the entire site, which is simply in place to remind us all of her largess." She chuckled and encouraged everyone to grab their water bottles as they exited the bus.

"Oh shoot, I left my Camelbak in the car."

"You can share my water, Daniel." Elena looked at Daniel with an innocently wicked gaze.

Lorenzo clapped his hands and shouted, "Perfecto."

Daniel could not begin to describe how un-*perfecto* he found this situation, but he was a gentleman. "Thanks, Elena." He refused to make eye contact.

Whimsical little native flowers, wild horses, and free-range Corrientes cattle populated the site. It was fantastic.

"This is the only site in Mezzo-America to indicate a matriarchal connection. The inhabitants had a lunar calendar, they worshipped goddesses and the only female warrior ever excavated is from this site..."

Daniel could not prevent his mind from drifting to Gwenn. She would love this place. He missed her smile, her laugh and her all-too-sharp wit.

"Thirsty?" Elena sidled up next to Daniel and rubbed her water bottle on his chest.

He ignored the innuendo and grabbed the bottle. He took a quick swig, wiped the top of the bottle off on his shirt and handed it back to its owner.

Elena let her hand brush Daniel's as she took back the bottle; she licked her lips and winked.

Daniel pushed his attention back to Alberta's facts.

"She was buried here around 700 A.D., in full battle regalia." Alberta gestured, "This is the House of the Thirteen Heavens, named for the 13 moon cycles in a lunar calendar."

The rest of the tour was a bit of a blur and Daniel felt a headache sneaking across his forehead. He had avoided any additional sips from Elena's water bottle and was probably suffering a little dehydration. He took several pictures and made a few recordings of the Profesora's lectures. He was anxious to get to the nearby family-owned ranch for the promised lunch of rice, beans, fresh cheese, tortillas, salsa, guacamole, potatoes with eggs, and nopales (cactus).

The meal was more delicious than promised and Daniel was surprised to see that no meat was served. "Profesora, why don't they serve chicken or beef?"

"Ah, good question. On a small family farm like this, the animals are too valuable to eat. Chickens provide eggs and the cattle are sold. It is a rare and special occasion that features meat."

Daniel nodded and began counting the minutes until he got back into a cell phone service area. He was going to call Gwenn, and that was final. He could not stop thinking about her.

Seven

Gwenn sat in her mother's hospital room listening to the steady beep of the machines and staring at the withered woman in the bed. She knew she should feel some kind of sadness or remorse but when she searched the recesses of her heart she only felt pity. Pity for a woman so self-absorbed and self-righteous that she missed out on the wonderful intricacies of her own amazing children.

Gwenn wondered what it would have been like to have a mother she could have called for support when Steven left her. Her mind drifted into the familiar scene. She could hear his roommate say those fateful words, "Gwenn, I'm sorry...he moved back to his sister's in Philadelphia." She struggled to hold onto the memory, but she couldn't conjure the rest of it today. How different would her life be if she had been able to call her mother, divulge the truth and hear loving words of reassurance? An audible scoff escaped Gwenn's mouth and Rachel glanced toward her.

Rachel looked questioningly at Gwenn and pointed past her, at something in the hallway.

Gwenn twisted in her chair to follow Rachel's indication and gasped when she saw Dr. Watkins standing in the hallway beckoning her to join him. Her eyes widened to saucers and she looked rapidly from Rachel to the man in the hallway and back.

Rachel swished her hands at Gwenn, indicating that she should get out of her chair and see what the nice doctor wanted.

She straightened herself and struggled to place one foot in front of the other. Gwenn's heart was racing.

"Hello, Ms. Hutchinson, I'm not sure if you remember me..."

Her mind hurtled back in time and she could feel Daniel's hand cupped protectively over hers as they waited for the DNA results in Dr. Watkins' office. She had found some old photographs that gave her reason to believe her mother had been unfaithful. Her search led her to wealthy artist Daniel Gregory. She had discovered that his father, whom she believed to be her real father, had passed away some years ago. The then-stranger, Daniel, had agreed to DNA tests to see if they were siblings and that had led them to Dr. Watkins. The moment when the doctor had walked into that office and said the test showed no genetic connection was the lowest point in Gwenn's life. So, yeah, she remembered.

"Ms. Hutchinson?"

She looked at him, salty drops of memory already gathering in the corners of her eyes.

"I was saying, I am the Chief of Staff here, and when I saw the transplant order come through...saw your name and the blood typing test...I wanted to..." he paused to take a deep breath, "can we continue this conversation in my office?"

"I have to bring my sister." Gwenn turned robotically and waved Rachel over.

"Hey, Dad, we're going to grab some coffee." *Well, shit. Way to mention the Devil's caffeine.* "I mean, we'll be right back." Rachel scurried out before she could say anything else offensive.

"Rache, this is Dr. Watkins," Gwenn paused and nodded for emphasis, "he wants to talk to me and I kinda wanted you with me."

"Sure, Gwenny, whatever you need." Rachel was searching her brain for a "Dr. Watkins" and could find nothing. She decided to play along until she figured out what was happening.

The muffled intercom, distant cries of pain and constant beeps serenaded them to their destination.

"Please have a seat." Dr. Watkins gestured to the two chairs opposite his desk.

Rachel slipped into a chair and Gwenn stood stock still, staring at the two paintings. One by *her* Daniel and one by his late father.

"Gwenny, you're freaking me out. Sit down." Rachel snatched Gwenn's hand and pulled her into the second chair.

"Ms. Hutchinson—"

"Gwenn."

"Gwenn, as I was attempting to explain, I saw the information come through for the blood and tissue typing and I remembered why you were here last year...I thought you would want to know."

"Want to know what?" Gwenn felt her heart stuttering.

"Last year? Why were you at the doctor last year?" Rachel looked quizzically at Gwenn. "Oh, the Daniel...oh, shit. Oh, sorry Doc."

"This information actually affects both of you, I'm afraid," he paused and needlessly aligned some files on his desk. "Neither of you are a match for the transplant."

Gwenn sighed with relief and her shoulders dropped at least two inches.

"Because of our discussion last year, Gwenn, I ran some additional tests. The reason neither of you are a match is a result of the fact that neither of you are Shirley Hutchinson's biological children."

Her benumbed heart thumped in her chest. Ice-cold tentacles crept up Gwenn's spine. Her deepest, truest wish had just been granted. *Where is the joy? Where is the relief?*

Rachel wiped at the tear trickling down her round cheek. "So who is our real mother?"

Dr. Watkins leaned back in his chair and stared at Rachel in confusion. "Ms. Hutchinson—"

"Rachel."

"Thank you. Rachel, perhaps I should have been more clear. Shirley is not your biological mother and Gwenn is not your biological sister. I can't say how you came to be members of the Hutchinson family, I can only report the facts of the DNA."

"But I saw Shirley come home from the hospital with Rachel. I was four, I remember Rachel as a baby..." Gwenn's voice trailed off as she searched her memory for evidence to support her claim.

"Gwenn, I shared this information with you as a personal favor. I know you were looking for your biological father when you came here with Daniel. I suppose you will need to get the details from your parents...I mean, Mr. and Mrs. Hutchinson."

Rachel's face was frozen in a portrait of disbelief. She stared at Gwenn and swallowed the sobs clawing their way out of her throat.

"I'll leave you two here. If there's anything I can do, please call me. Here's my personal cell number." Dr. Watkins walked around his desk and handed Gwenn one of his cards, with the number handwritten on the back.

She reached out and robotically accepted the number. "Thank you."

Dr. Watkins walked out of his office and thoughtfully closed the door behind himself.

Gwenn turned toward Rachel just in time to see the waterworks unleashed.

"Gwenny! I can't [sob] we're not [sniffle] it's a lie. [sob] It has to be a lie!" Rachel dropped her head into her hands and continued to protest unintelligibly.

"Rache, we've been through this, remember? We're sisters—wholly sisters—always and forever. OK?"

Rachel lifted her tear-streaked face toward Gwenn, wiped her runny nose and engulfed her sister in a life-and-death-type hug. "Promise? Forever?"

"Promise, forever," Gwenn said as she gasped for air. After several minutes of generalized hypoxia she pried herself from Rachel's clutches. "Sweetie, we have to talk about this before we go back into that hospital room."

"Do you think Dad knows?" Rachel blurted.

"Of course, he knows, Rache. He had to help her create the lie." Gwenn turned toward Rachel and gently took her sister's hands into her own. "I was thinking back to the day they brought you home from the hospital and I remembered something strange. Gramma Carlson had to bring me to the house. I had spent all summer and part of that fall at her cabin, because Shirley was having such a hard time with the pregnancy I couldn't come home until after you were born. Gramma Carlson said the doctor put Shirley on strict bed rest...now it makes sense."

"What makes sense?"

"She was never pregnant! They just wanted me out of the house because I was old enough to notice that her stomach wasn't getting bigger. They didn't have that problem when she was 'fake pregnant' with me because they adopted me first..." Gwenn's voice faded away as she absorbed the impact of that word—*adopted*.

"What are you gonna do, Gwenny?" Rachel's bottom lip quivered.

"Nothing."

"Aren't you gonna find your real parents?"

"Last year I would've jumped at the chance, but after lofting my hopes to the heavens only to have them utterly shattered...I can't go through anything like that again. Just knowing that I can't inherit any traits from Shirley is enough for me."

Rachel paused to process Gwenn's change of heart. She thought about her own desire to adopt and immediately made a decision—or two. "I'm gonna find my real parents and I'm gonna have a baby!"

"Adopt?"

"No, I'm not going to adopt. I'm going to take the hormones, find a donor, knock myself up and have my own baby." A huge self-satisfied smile spread across Rachel's face.

"OK, sweetie, I'm gonna encourage you to hold off on any major life decisions until you talk to Annie. Sound good?" Gwenn nodded slowly and encouragingly at Rachel.

"Oh shit! Annie! What am I gonna tell her?"

"Just tell her the truth, Rache. What else is there?"

"Yeah, you're right—the truth it is."

"Now, are you ready to go talk to Ed?" Gwenn squeezed Rachel's hand.

"Oh, hell yeah!" Rachel gave Gwenn's hand a Thelma-and-Louise-style squeeze and smiled through her tears. "Pastor Holier-Than-Thou has some explaining to do."

Eight

Steven had gotten absolutely no help from Aunt Miriam. Suggestions like "take her on a nice chaperoned walk" or "bring her to talk to the rabbi about conversion" were not the romantic gestures he envisioned. His knowledge of the internet was expanding exponentially, so he decided to turn to Google to assist him in planning the ultimate romantic proposal. His list of "musts" was quite short—it *must* be foolproof.

His search led him to believe that the three most important factors were:
1. The Ring
2. The Surprise Factor
3. The Location

The Ring was a lock. He had already taken the little yellow carbon receipt from the back of his *Hardy Boys* book and made a trip to the jeweler.

"Good morning, sir. How can we help you?" The perky brunette behind the sparkling diamonds oozed commission-based compensation.

"I have a strange question." Steven smiled.

"Oh, I've heard everything. Don't be shy. What can I do for you?" She leaned forward slightly and smiled like a pageant runner-up.

"OK. I brought a ring in to be sized a while ago and I wanted to pick it up." Steven thought it might be best to ladle this story out in small portions.

"Well now, there's nothing strange about that." She paused to add a friendly wink to her enormous smile. "Let me have a look at that receipt."

Steven handed her the ancient scrap of paper and held his breath.

She nodded politely and examined the receipt. "Let's see...looks like you dropped this off on...well, that can't be right." She looked up in confusion and blinked unusually fast. "Can you wait just a moment, sir?" The huge fake smile had vanished.

"Sure. It's been twelve years, so a couple more minutes won't matter." Steven attempted a lighthearted joke, but inside he felt panic tingling in his abdomen and anger itching in his throat.

The sales clerk nodded and scurried into the back room. She returned several minutes later with a ruddy-cheeked elderly man enrobed in a long forgotten blend of polyester and possibly wool.

"I can't believe you finally came back! I been tellin' the girls that I couldn't retire 'til I knew the story behind that ring." The old-timer slapped a hand firmly on the jewelry case and added, "I'll get you that ring, but you have to promise to tell me your story."

This disarming man threw Steven off his game. "You still have it? Are you sure it's the same ring?"

"Of course, I still have it, young man. It was paid for and left in my care. I placed it in the safe myself and I take it out and clean it every year. Call me a sentimental old fool, but there was somethin' special about that one..." the man wiped at his eyes and fiddled with his mustache. "I'll get it for you, son."

The use of the familiar "son" stabbed at Steven's heart. His own father would never get to see him married. Steven nodded appreciatively and the rotund little man disappeared.

He returned holding the orange velvet box out in front of him like a priceless heirloom. "And here it is," he announced.

The perky brunette chose this moment to jump back into her sales mode. "Oh, that is just beautiful. What a lucky girl."

The portly purveyor of gems shushed her with a gesture and looked long and hard at Steven. "You promised me a story, I believe."

The ring took Steven back in time and he spilled his story like a hooker at confession. The old man nodded with the wisdom of a lifetime, and his perky sidekick gasped several times.

"So you're the P.O.W. we saw on TV a few months ago?"

"Yes, sir, that was my official 15 minutes of fame."

"Well, I sure am glad I was here the day you came to pick that up." The pudgy man clasped his hands around his belly and sighed with satisfaction. "That's one lucky girl, young man."

"I hope she agrees with you." Steven managed a small chuckle.

Perky brunette placed her hand on Steven's arm, "She'd be a fool to turn you down. Good men are so hard to find." She batted her eyes and smiled coyly. She was clearly comfortable in the role of runner-up, but eager to take over the duties of the "winner," if necessary.

Steven extracted his hand and the ring box. "Thank you both."

The stout old man smiled and nodded his head. "Thank you, and thank you for your service. Let us know how it turns out."

"Will do, will do." Steven had no intention of returning to that store. He had shared his life story—the edited version—with two total strangers. He planned to make sure they remained total strangers.

Now for numbers two and three.

Nine

Ed sat in the stiff visitor's chair next to Shirley's hospital bed with his head resting on the mattress near her shoulder. He had dozed off with his hand still clasping her small feeble fingers.

Gwenn and Rachel huddled together in the hallway screwing up their courage.

"...OK, but I have to call Steven and cancel our dinner plans. Who knows how long it will take to pry the truth out of them." Gwenn reached for her phone and Rachel paced, silently.

"Hi, Steven, it's Gwenn."

"Hey, gorgeous. What time should I pick you up? I have quite an adventure planned." Steven's sexy chuckle was lost on Gwenn.

"I'm so sorry, but I have to cancel." Gwenn was emotionally spent and she did not have time to sugar coat or spoon feed—just the facts.

The intense heat of his anger was out before he could take corrective action. "Are you fucking kidding me, Gwenn?

Enough with the games. You need to keep your commitments."

Gwenn pulled the phone away from her ear and stared at it with shock and disdain. "Hey, don't take that tone with me. I'm dealing with a lot of shit right now and your complete insensitivity is not appreciated. My sister and I need to be with Shirley and you are just gonna have to grow the fuck up!" Gwenn pressed *end* with a ferocious screen-jeopardizing jab.

Rachel, frozen in place, had one hand over her mouth.

"What? He was being a little bitch. I'm in no mood."

Rachel shook her head and pointed into the hospital room.

Ed was sitting bolt upright and his face bore the indignation of the righteous. He had clearly heard Gwenn's "mood."

Gwenn took one look at that face and decided she had finally reached her quota of Hutchinson judgments. She shoved her phone into her purse and stalked into the room.

Rachel followed meekly in the wake of Polar Vortex Gwenn.

"The jig is up, Ed."

He leaned forward as though he intended to get up from his chair.

"Don't bother standing up, Ed. You're gonna want to be sitting down for this next bit." The force of Gwenn's verbal onslaught pushed Ed directly back into his seat. "Neither Rachel nor I are a match for the kidney for Shirley. Do you know why, Ed? Do you?"

Ed stroked his chin and this time his hand visibly shook.

"You look worried? Let me put your fears to rest. Rachel and I just found out we're not a match because Shirley is not our biological mother." Gwenn stopped and pulled Rachel to her side. "When in the hell were you planning on sharing that little nugget with us, Pastor?" Gwenn braced herself for his retort.

His shoulders slumped, his chest heaved and tears flooded from his eyes. His silent sobs smashed through Gwenn's defenses.

Rachel was the first to react. She ran to his side and threw a protective arm around his shoulders. "Don't cry, Dad. It's gonna be OK."

Gwenn paced back and forth at the foot of Shirley's hospital bed. When she saw Ed wipe his eyes and lift his head, she pounced. "Ed, we need to hear the truth. Now."

He reached up and rubbed Rachel's hand as it rested on his shoulder. "I can only tell ya part of the story, yer mom will have ta tell the rest."

She resisted the urge to point out that neither of their "moms" was in the room, but Gwenn held her tongue and nodded her agreement.

"Shirley's real dad left when she was in junior high school, the Grampa Carlson that you two know is Gramma Carlson's second husband."

"Yeah, Rachel mentioned that. What does that have to do with our situation?" Gwenn asked impatiently.

"I'm gettin' ta that part, Trixie."

Gwenn flinched at the irritating nickname. *Is the name Gwenn really that hard to remember?*

"Leonard, Shirley's real dad, was a mean drunk. He'd get blind drunk on payday and stumble inta the house lookin' fer a fight. Shirley had the great misfortune of gettin' her first, um...well...her menstrual cycle on a payday. Leonard came barreling in the house and saw a pile of laundry on the kitchen table. It was Shirley's turn ta fold clothes, but she had gone ta bed early, because of the cramps."

Gwenn slid a chair toward Rachel and took a corner at the foot of Shirley's bed for herself.

Ed wiped his hand over his eyes and swallowed hard. "Leonard stormed inta Shirley's bedroom and yanked her outta bed by the hair. He threw her down on the ground and just started kickin' her in the gut." Ed's fingers clenched into involuntary fists and his voice trembled. "Yer Gramma had ta call the police ta get him off a yer mom."

"That's terrible. Did he go to jail? Was Mom OK?" Rachel wrung her hands and chewed on her thumbnail.

"No one knows what happened ta Leonard, but yer Gramma always suspected the sheriff had somethin' ta do with Leonard's disappearance. She filed fer divorce and then remarried about two years later."

"What about Mom. Was she OK after that beating?" Rachel's eyes were filled with distress.

"No, no, she was far from OK. Leonard had kicked her so hard that he busted up her insides..." Ed swallowed a sob and continued, "Shirley was bleedin' internally and had ta be rushed ta the hospital. They cut her wide open and she lost her appendix, her spleen, part of her intestines and all her reproductive stuff." A ragged breath and a rogue tear escaped his careful control.

"Weren't they afraid he'd come back?" Gwenn's curiosity got the better of her.

"They were. I visited Shirley in the hospital and she told me the whole story. I slept on a couch in the waiting room 'til they released her and then I slept in a tent in her front yard fer at least three weeks." Ed's eyes glazed over as the memories washed over him. "Once the sheriff told 'em Leonard would never bother them again—I ended my vigil."

"So, Shirley could never have children of her own..." Gwenn's voice drifted across the room.

"But why didn't you tell us?" Rachel wiped the tears from her eyes and cast her innocent gaze on Ed.

"I'm afraid that's the part of the story yer mom has ta tell."

 Ten

Gwenn's phone buzzed and she reached in her purse to ignore the call. She could not handle talking to Steven again today. *Daniel?* Her finger hit the ignore button before her brain had time to process the information. Why was Daniel calling? Based on her amazing luck, she imagined he was calling to yell at her about some shortcoming. She'd listen to the voicemail later. Before she could put her phone away a text appeared on her screen.

">I miss you. I crave the sound of your voice. Call me. No strings, just call."

She wanted to call him that very second—to pour her pain and confusion into the phone and hope that he could absorb it all. She wanted to, but she didn't.

"Dad, we're gonna grab some food. We'll come back tonight during visiting hours. Call us if Mom wakes up or anything, OK?" Rachel rubbed her hand on Ed's shoulder and smiled at the man who had so recently become her hero. He loved Shirley the same way she loved Annie.

"OK. We'll see ya girls later."

"You should get somethin' from the cafeteria, Dad. You look a little pale." Rachel waved good-bye to Ed and steered Gwenn out of the hospital room with her other hand.

"Why so pushy, Rache?"

"I saw the look on your face when you checked your phone. It was Daniel, right?"

"What if it was, smart ass?"

"You should call him. Gimme the keys to the Jeep and I'll wait for you in the car."

"When did you get so bossy, Rache?"

"Um, I've pretty much always been bossy. It's just that you're usually even bossier, so you probably didn't notice." Rachel burst out laughing and flipped her middle finger at Gwenn.

Gwenn smacked at Rachel's hand and shook her head. "Why the hell are you in such a good mood?"

"Because Dad loves Mom, like really totally loves her. It makes me feel warm and fuzzy."

"Rache, I think you might be reading too much into his tale. He *loved* her way back in the beginning, but once he got caught up in her web of deceit I think the shine was off the apple."

"Whatever, Scrooge! Don't ruin my buzz with your glass-half-empty bullshit. Now gimme the keys and call Daniel."

"Fine!" Gwenn feigned far more irritation than she felt. She was secretly thrilled that Rachel was forcing her hand. She rummaged through her purse for her keys and tossed them at Rachel. "There. Now go away, ya little shit."

Rachel grinned with satisfaction and walked off toward the elevators.

Gwenn found a quiet alcove and procured her phone. She read Daniel's text five or six times, took several deep breaths and called.

Daniel heard his phone ring and nearly ignored it, thinking it may be Todd checking up on him. He picked it up after several rings and almost dropped it when he saw her name on the screen. "Gwenn?"

"Hi."

"Hi." He let the silence linger. He closed his eyes and called one of his images to mind. *'Morning's Promise, watercolor on linen.'* The memory of Gwenn's cute little ass untangling itself from his sheets the morning he left for Mexico warmed him all over.

Gwenn wanted to spill out the day's news, but her fears forced her to play tough. "You called me, remember."

"I did. And you called me back." He chuckled. "I know we're on a break, or whatever you call this—but I missed you and I needed to hear your voice."

Gwenn heard the cracks forming in the ice around her heart—mournful groaning splinters, desperately fighting to resist the expanding heat. "I missed you, too—especially today."

Check! Permission granted! They may have been Todd's rules, but Daniel was happy to have Gwenn's unknowing buy-in on Operation Send Steven Packing. "Why today?"

"I had a little meeting with Dr. Watkins."

Daniel had a momentary flash of nausea as he worried that Dr. Watkins had made some error on their original DNA testing last year and had called Gwenn to tell her Daniel was actually her brother. *Gross!* "Dr. Watkins? What did he have to say?"

Gwenn filled in the backstory about Shirley's condition and Rachel's generous offer to get tested for a transplant match.

"She volunteered both of you for testing?"

"Yeah, she volunteered me. I don't even think that's a thing, right?" Gwenn laughed out loud and wished she could lay her head on Daniel's chest and listen to his heartbeat. The sound always soothed her.

"OK, so you had to get stuck with needles, which I know you hate, but how did Dr. Watkins get involved?"

"He saw my name on the lab orders, remembered our visit last year and ordered some additional tests."

"DNA tests?"

"Yep."

"And..." Daniel was not sure why he was holding his breath, but he definitely was not breathing.

"And, Shirley is not my biological mom—or Rachel's."

"What the hell?"

"That's what I said." Gwenn leaned up against the wall and listened to Daniel's breath whispering across the mic on his end of the phone. She closed her eyes and imagined his breath on her skin, his lips on her neck, his hands on her—

"What did Shirley say?"

Gwenn blinked and shook her head as reality flooded back. "She's sedated, but we got part of the story from Ed." Gwenn shared the highlights of Shirley's nearly fatal childhood.

"Holy shit! Now what?" Daniel wanted to jump on a plane and fly to her side, but he was determined to wait for her to ask. He would take his white-knight-complex to his session with Dr. Mountainside.

"Rachel and I are gonna grab some food and we'll come back tonight and try to talk to Shirley. I was supposed to go out with Steven but...oops...never mind." *Idiot! I'm sure Daniel really gives a shit about my canceled plans with Steven.*

"Hey, all I heard was 'canceled on Steven' and I have no problem with that." Daniel struggled to keep a brave tone in his voice, but the truth was that he had a huge problem with Steven.

"I'm sorry, that was super stupid of me. I guess my head's not really in the game right now." Gwenn smacked herself on the forehead.

"I hope it's not a game to you, Gwenn."

"Oh shit. I better go before I say something even more idiotic. It was really good to talk to you, but I have so much going on I better not keep involving you."

"I want to be involved, Gwenn. I'm trying to give you space, but I really just want to fold space and be in your bed right now—with you, I mean." Daniel kicked himself a little for the lame ending. He would have to work on his phrasing.

Gwenn laughed, "Did you just say 'fold space' in some nerd-alert *Dune* reference?"

Daniel's rich deep laughter filled the space between them. "Did you just get my reference? Who's the nerd, now?"

Gwenn swallowed the plea she felt forming in her throat. She could not beg Daniel to come to her aid while she was in the middle of reconnecting with Steven. *Could my day suck any more?* "I've gotta go. Rachel is waiting in the car...thanks for the call."

"Anytime, anytime."

"Bye." Gwenn tossed the phone back into her purse and exhaled.

Daniel slipped his phone into his pocket and smiled at the idea taking shape in his mind's eye.

Eleven

Shirley lay in her hospital bed and dreaded her daughters' return. "Ed, get me my make-up case."

Ed retrieved the case and set it carefully on the rolling table. He slipped the extended table arm over the bed and moved it closer to Shirley. "How's that?"

"It's fine. It'll do." Shirley opened the case and shuddered at the reflection staring back at her from the cracked mirror on the inside of the lid. She shook her head in dismay and brushed at her limp hair. "My roots are showin' and you know I hate the grey."

He nodded his acknowledgement.

"Oh, this is hopeless." Shirley dropped the hairbrush on the table and flopped back onto her pillow.

"Would ya like me ta brush it fer ya, dear?" He hesitated to offer, but he couldn't stand to see her so dejected.

"Well, I suppose it can't get any worse." Shirley knew the words described more than her hair.

Ed picked up the brush and gently pulled it through Shirley's thin tendrils. He saw her lean toward him and continued brushing long after it was truly necessary. "Is that OK?"

"Thanks, Ed."

He swelled with pride. "Anything else?"

"Could ya prop me up with another pillow? I need ta put on a little make-up."

"You betcha." He grabbed the pillow from the foot of the bed and lifted Shirley up while he pressed the extra pillow behind her head. "I can fold the bed up, too, if ya want?"

"Just a tad." Shirley adjusted herself and sorted through her case. She rubbed a bit of rouge on her cheeks and dabbed some light pink lipstick on her ghostly pale lips. She blotted her lips together and reached for the eyebrow pencil.

Ed smiled as he watched his Shirley emerge from the patient in the hospital bed.

Shirley took one last look at herself and shook her head in disapproval. "Well, it'll have ta do." She closed the case and pushed the table out of her way.

Rachel was the first to enter the room. "Oh, Mom, you're awake!" She ran to the bedside and hugged Shirley as gently as she knew how, but her gesture was not returned.

Shirley stiffened and something like a whimper escaped her thin lips.

Gwenn stood at the foot of the bed and waited for her heart to stop abusing the inside of her chest. "Shirley, we have to talk." Her tone was civil, but not friendly.

"Now, don't take that tone with me Gwendolyn—"

"I'll take any tone I damn well please." Gwenn's indignation lit a fire of courage in her heart and she raced ahead before it could be contained. "I'm not sure if Ed filled you in or not, but this isn't a charity visit. Rachel and I want to know why you lied to us about our parentage...for decades."

Shirley took offense to the accusation, "I'm not sure if that's an accurate representation, young lady." She leaned back on her pillows and increased the feeble factor at least thirty percent. "I just don't know if I have the strength—"

"Find it." Gwenn was in no mood for Shirley's manipulations.

"Well, I never..." Shirley looked to Ed for support and found none. The day she had dreaded for more than thirty years—had dawned. *Be sure your sin will find you out.* Indeed.

Rachel pushed a chair next to Shirley's bed and looked up at her with love and support. "Please, Mom, we need to hear the truth."

Gwenn admired Rachel's patience and understanding. She felt nothing of the kind. She was seething with vitriol for all the judgments Shirley had handed down over the years, all the hateful words she had spit at Gwenn and Rachel—this ended today. She fixed Shirley with a steely gaze and waited.

"Well, gee whiz, I don't know where ta start..." Shirley looked back and forth between Gwenn's icy gaze and Rachel's hopeful smile.

"Dad told us what Leonard did to you. You must have been terrified." Rachel patted Shirley's arm and added, "I mean, I've had the crap beaten out of me a few times on the playground...but nothing like what happened to you."

"Yes, we know you weren't able to have children of your own, but why the huge lie? Why did you pretend to be pregnant? Why did you hide it from everyone?" Gwenn paced and shook her head in disbelief.

"Things were different in my day, ya know. I wasn't a good student, I was pretty. Pretty girls got married ta successful men and had babies. I couldn't have babies, so I came up with a plan." Shirley looked at Ed and he nodded his encouragement for her to continue.

Satisfied that the train had finally left the station, Gwenn ceased her pacing, sat at the foot of the bed and listened.

"Ed here was the only one, besides yer Gramma Carlson, that knew the truth about what Leo did ta me. Ed wanted ta marry me and said he didn't care about me not bein' able ta have kids."

Ed nodded vigorously and a flicker of the old love showed in his eyes.

"So, ya know, I just couldn't take the shame of it all. My sisters were havin' kids left and right...so I talked ta Ed about adopting. I didn't want my sisters ta know I wasn't normal, like them. I couldn't bear it..." Shirley paused to wipe an errant tear and continued, "I decided ta pretend ta be pregnant. I'd read a story in the newspaper 'bout a woman who had been put on months of bed rest, but still had a healthy baby...that gave me the rest of the plan."

"So how did you find a birth mother?" Gwenn wanted to get to the meat of the story.

"Yer Gramma helped with that part. She went ta Chicago and found a ladies' church group that helped unwed mothers. She said she was helpin' a family at her church and she set up the whole thing. I never even met the girl."

"And by 'the girl' do you mean my mother?" Gwenn meant the words to come out as an angry accusation, but the fire of her fury had been vanquished. The utterance was barely a whisper.

"Yes, yer mother." Shirley cried quiet, modest, lady-like tears. She cried for herself, she cried for Gwenn and she cried for all the anxious years of hiding the truth. The fear of being found out had gnawed at her like rats at a rope.

"What about me?" Rachel leaned forward and placed a reassuring hand on Shirley's arm.

"It was much harder the second time. Ed was a junior pastor then and I just couldn't figure a way ta adopt without someone findin' out about my drunkard father. And of course, Gwendolyn was nearly three and a half when we heard about yer mother's situation. We decided ta send Gwenn ta Gramma Carlson's and try the bed rest story again." Shirley accepted the tissue Ed handed her, blew her nose and continued. "The ladies' group in Chicago had contacted Gramma Carlson 'bout a young girl who had gotten pregnant with the hope of marrying, but the young man flew home ta tell his parents and never came back. I believe his family was from Greece."

"I'm Greek?" Rachel touched her palm to her chest and looked at Gwenn. "I'm Greek."

Gwenn smiled, "Explains your obsession with filo dough."

Rachel smiled for a moment and suddenly furrowed her brow. "Why didn't the girl keep the baby...I mean me?"

"Once there was no chance of a marriage ta hide the indiscretion, her parents forced her ta give up the baby. She was a minor, so they could do that, ya know."

"But why keep it from us? Why didn't you tell us the truth—at some point?" Gwenn felt a tiny bit of anger, but the overwhelming feeling was loss. Her entire childhood had been based on a lie. The gap that existed between her and Shirley was made of fear, shame and regret—not of her own shortcomings.

"Oh, I thought about it lots a times, but each year that passed made it more difficult ta face the truth. So, I guess I kept hopin' you would never find out. I thought I could take my secret to the grave, ya know?"

"You almost did." Gwenn gave a fait accompli gesture to the machines surrounding Shirley.

Ed leaned forward and grasped Shirley's hand, "Ya almost did, Shirl." His eyes reddened with unshed fears. "I think this is better fer all of us." He squeezed her hand and a tiny smile found its way to his exhausted face.

"Well, I'm still going to donate my kidney," Rachel announced.

"Rache, you're not a match—remember? That's how this whole thing started." Gwenn shook her head in exasperation.

"I know, I know. I talked to Dr. Murashige and he told me about a paired donor program. It's like a kidney exchange thing. I can donate a kidney to the bank, or whatever, and then they'll give Mom a matching kidney. It'll speed up the process, a ton! Otherwise it can take years to find a donor kidney." Rachel beamed with pride.

Shirley wept.

Gwenn protested.

Ed gazed on in confusion.

"You would do that fer me? After what I said ta you and that...Annie?" Shirley took another tissue and dabbed uselessly at the waterfalls spilling down her sunken cheeks.

"I love you, Mom. And somewhere in there I know you love me, too." Rachel scooped Shirley into a snug-but-not-life-threatening embrace.

"I do love ya, Rachel. I do." Shirley forgot all her careful rules of decorum and etiquette and sobbed into Rachel's shoulder.

After years searching for the ulterior motives and meanings behind Shirley's actions Gwenn still wondered if these salty drops were truly tears of contrition or simply crocodile tears. "Rache, we should go. Shirley needs to rest and we have a lot to talk about."

Rachel nodded and slowly disengaged from Shirley. "Thank you for finally telling us your story."

"Did I meet you halfway?" Shirley's red, swollen, tear-stained eyes pleaded for absolution.

Rachel shot Gwenn a nervous glance. The reference to that phrase from their first visit to Shirley's bedside gave her pause.

Gwenn jumped in, "Do you remember that visit? Were you conscious for that whole tirade about...about, well about everything?"

"I don't remember it all, ya know, I was pretty out of it. I heard somethin' about Annie, somethin' about that Steven boy and you were talkin' about takin' a bullet fer Rachel." Shirley managed a small chuckle, in spite of her blubbering. "I think life might be too short fer all this fightin' nonsense."

"I think we have a long way to go, Shirley, but something is better than nothing." Gwenn slowly approached the head of the bed and clasped Shirley's vulnerable hand between her own. "It's not halfway, but it's a start."

Twelve

Flora smoothed her dark brown hair, adjusted her signature headband and looked up at the clock one last time before she locked her desk. She had expected to see Gwenn today and was worried that she hadn't. She was the last one at the office. Thea had left early for a client *meeting*—which Flora suspected to be a thin façade for a date—and the latest installment in the parade of interns had been dismissed at three.

A noise in the outer office startled Flora and she froze like a deer-in-the-headlights. It was too early for the cleaning crew...

Heavy footsteps grew closer and Flora imagined she could hear heavy, menacing breathing. She could call security, but if it were the cleaning crew she would look like an idiot. The footfalls were definitely heading toward her. She picked up the phone and—

"How about some dinner?"

Flora gasped and dropped the receiver. "Oh God—it's only you."

Todd chafed at the reaction.

"I didn't mean it like that...I mean...I was...the noise..." Flora smiled innocently, "Sorry."

"I'm the one who should be sorry. I obviously scared the bejeezus out of you." He shook his head, ran a quick hand through his close-cropped sandy-blonde hair and strode across the office to comfort Flora.

"You did. I almost called security," Flora laughed nervously. "I guess I get a little jumpy after hours—all by myself."

Todd's pupils dilated as he stared at Flora's lips. His grey-green irises sparked with need. Need was new territory. He had always been the one to save the day, solve the problem or deliver the remarkable result. He hadn't needed anyone for as long as he could remember—but he needed this woman. Now. Todd pulled Flora up from her chair and clumsily lifted her onto the desk. He pushed her grey pencil skirt up around her waist and slid his hand up her thigh. *I think it's time you and I took some chances.*

"Todd?" Flora pushed back from her desk.

The sound of the chair rolling back snapped him out of his erotic daydream. Embarrassment flooded his cheeks. "Um, yes, what were you saying?"

She giggled and looked away.

"Am I that transparent?" He took her hand and pulled her up next to him.

"No. I was laughing because I think we were thinking the same thing."

"Oh, I doubt that." He kissed her lightly, but she responded with a hunger he had not anticipated. "Maybe I was wrong."

"Let's get some supper and go back to my place. I just need to call Gwenn before we leave. She was supposed to come in today, but I never heard from her."

"Hmmm. When I checked in with Mr. Gregory he mentioned that they had spoken. Apparently, something major happened at the hospital today. Maybe she hasn't had a chance to update you."

Flora slipped her phone back in her bag. "Maybe I shouldn't bother her. I've got everything under control."

"You always do." Todd smiled proudly. "How about walleye and onion rings at Pickwick?"

"OK, but it's usually pretty quiet there."

"That's perfect. I have a bit of a proposition for you." Todd winked and grabbed her coat off the coat rack.

The walleye was delicious and the onion rings were divine. The view of the seemingly endless Lake Superior was hampered by falling snow, but the inviting British-pub style interior was the perfect, relaxing backdrop for Todd's topic.

"I know we talked about working together at the Gallery and decided that you would be happier staying at *The Organizer*, but I had another idea." Todd's hand crept across the table and stroked her fingers.

"What idea?"

"I'm going to ask Daniel to sell me Gregory North, the gallery here in Duluth. Now that he and Gwenn are parting ways I think he'll be anxious to distance himself from the north shore."

"I still can't believe the way things worked out. I've honestly never seen Gwenn so happy. I mean I didn't really know her when she was with Steven, the first time—she was living in the Twin Cities—and based on the ending I assumed..." Flora let the words dissolve into the dark wood paneling surrounding their table.

Todd nodded and brushed his hand over hers. "I was wondering what you would think about moving in together?"

Flora swallowed hard and set down her root beer. She didn't think of herself as a prude, but she had never really considered living with someone. She always pictured herself getting married. "Gosh, I guess I never really thought about it."

"Will you? Think about it, I mean."

She chewed her lip and smoothed her hair with her free hand. "Um, OK. Can I have a couple days?"

"Take all the time you want." Todd made every effort to sound magnanimous but he was more than a little disappointed. He had given his idea considerable thought—it was a practical and mildly romantic solution to their potential long-distance relationship problem. He had expected a more enthusiastic endorsement.

***

Gwenn and Rachel found themselves right back at the London Road Perkins. Neither of them had the energy to come up with a better idea. To add insult to injury they were lucky enough to have Adele, the waitress from Gwenn and Daniel's first sort-of-date, as their server. Gwenn silently hated the world and Rachel was babbling like a loquacious spider monkey.

"I guess I feel some sense of obligation. I mean I know she wasn't always the best mom in the world, but she did kind of rescue us. I'm not going to back out now. I'm gonna donate a kidney to the organ bank thingy and get Mom a kidney. I know she'll be different, now—I just know—"

"Can you stop talking for one fucking minute, Rache? Please?"

"What the hell, Gwenny? What crawled up your butt and died?"

"Rache, today should have been the happiest day of my life. I finally found the truth." Gwenn dropped her head into her hands, pulled the binder out of her hair and raked through her slightly greasy auburn locks. She scraped her hair back into a sad little excuse for a ponytail and secured it with the band. "I'm more miserable now than I was before. Be careful what you frickin' wish for..."

"Why are you miserable? You have a whole new family out there somewhere. I'm gonna find my parents, why don't you look for yours?"

"I told you, Rache, that ship has sailed. I'm done looking for something outside of me to make it all better. I have to make it all better—from the inside out."

"Will you help me find my parents?"

"Actually I think I'm gonna do more than that." Gwenn reached her hand across the table, looked Rachel in the eyes and cried.

"Are you gonna disappear again? Please don't run away. I can't lose you, Gwenny, you're my rock." Rachel squeezed Gwenn's hand and shed a few tears of her own.

Adele picked that exact moment to return with their malts. She saw the tears and the clutched hands and she cataloged every detail. She knew that scrawny redhead wasn't right for that gorgeous man she'd seen her with last time she waited on them. That handsome man was way out of this girl's league, and apparently this girl was playing for a different league all together. "Can I getcha anything else?"

"No, thank you," Gwenn managed.

"All righty, here ya go then." Adele placed their check on the table, turned on her well-worn, grease-resistant heels and scampered back to the kitchen with her juicy nugget of gossip.

Gwenn smiled, in spite of her mood; at least she had brightened someone's day. "Rache, you have a big year ahead of you. You're getting married, you want to find your real parents and you want to have a baby. The last thing you need is a major surgery to donate a kidney for Shirley's sake. You might cause yourself all kinds of potential problems with getting pregnant...I don't know...it's too much."

"But Gwenny—"

"But nothing! I'll do it. I'll donate the kidney."

"What? Why?"

"Because I know I never want to have kids and I can use the recuperation time to get my frickin' head straight." Gwenn leaned back in her chair and exhaled loudly. "I can even work on your wedding plans while you look for your parents. It's a win-win. Right?"

"I can't believe you would do that for Shirley."

"I wouldn't, I'm doing it for you, Rache—for my sister."

Thirteen

Gwenn stumbled out of the elevator and robotically placed one foot in front of the other. All she could think about was crawling into bed and forgetting the pain of this day. The solace of her dream world awaited.

She rounded the corner and came to an abrupt halt. Wedged uncomfortably into the corner next to her door was Steven. He was sound asleep in the hallway, still clutching a huge bouquet of roses. She did not possess enough adrenaline for fight or flight.

She bent down and placed her hand on his shoulder and shook him gently. "Steven. Hey, Ste—"

Instinct took over before his eyes even opened. He grabbed the thumb of his assailant and twisted hard away from his body.

"Aaaah! Steven! For fuck's sake, Steven, it's me. It's Gwenn!" She went limp in hopes that submission would end the pain faster.

"Oh shit! Gwenny, I'm so sorry." Steven immediately loosed his hold on her and shrank back against the wall.

"Fuck this PTSD flashback shit. Fuck." He shook his head and thumped it against the wall behind him. "I'm really sorry, Gwenn. I must've dozed off and you caught me off—"

"It's OK. I'm OK." Gwenn rubbed her hand where the thumb had nearly been wrenched from its joint. "I didn't think it through. I should've known better...after everything that happened to you...I should've known."

Steven grabbed the roses and shoved them at Gwenn. "I came to apologize for losing it on the phone and I thought roses and a thumb dislocation would be the perfect peace offering. Yeah?"

Gwenn laughed. It felt so good to laugh. She reached out to take the roses and Steven pulled her onto his lap. She did not resist. She curled into his embrace and nuzzled her face into his neck.

A door opened into the hallway and a nosey neighbor gulped audibly before hustling away.

Steven snickered and Gwenn smiled into his delicious jaw. "We better take this inside before one of my outstandingly helpful neighbors makes an inquiry." Gwenn reluctantly extracted herself from Steven and searched for her keys.

Steven moved extremely slowly. He got the feeling that he was going to be invited into more than Gwenn's apartment and he did not want to do anything to derail that train.

She opened the door and turned to Steven. "Unceremonious as it is, I guess tonight's the night—big guy." A wearied smile appeared and Gwenn motioned Steven to follow.

He pursued without hesitation. The door closed behind him. The flowers fell to the floor.

Gwenn did not want to give herself time to think, she wanted to be irresponsible and impulsive. She wanted to put her own needs ahead of everyone else's—for once in her life.

He unzipped her jacket and let it drop to the ground. He scooped her up and carried her directly to the couch.

She kicked her boots off on the way and nibbled on his earlobe.

He almost dropped her as the blood surged from his extremities to his necessities. He placed her on the couch and removed his jacket and shirt faster than a Saturday Night Live cast member between sketches.

"Whoa, slow down. I kinda wanted to enjoy the show," Gwenn teased.

"I think we better get something straight. It's been a VERY long time since I've been in the show, so the opening act is going to be a Guinness World speed record."

Gwenn laughed so hard she snorted a little. "Oh crap, you're hilarious. Do you have condoms or should I grab some?"

"I've been out of circulation for nearly a decade and I have a clean bill of health from the U.S. government. I figured I could get latex free access." Steven winked and unbuttoned his jeans.

"Oh hell no, soldier! I don't care what your story is, last time we went down this path," she stumbled over her words and forced a flippancy she did not feel, "I got the scare of a lifetime and you disappeared...so you're gonna glove up or hit the road." Gwenn jumped up from the couch and disappeared into her bedroom. She returned moments later with an entire box of condoms.

"If you insist," Steven joked. He took the box from her and placed it on the coffee table. "I plan to use them all, ya know."

Gwenn had a flash of guilt when she realized one was missing from the box because it had been used last time Daniel was at her apartment. The sooner Steven smothered her guilt, the better. She whipped off her top and slipped out of her jeans.

"Stop. Do not touch another piece of clothing." Steven grabbed both of her hands, firmly, and pulled her close. "I've been dreaming of unwrapping this present for six years. This is mine." He released her wrists and grabbed her ass.

She shivered as his hands flicked the clasp open on her bra and brushed across her nipples.

He kissed her neck and slowly slipped her panties down. He followed their descent and watched hungrily as she was revealed. She tasted so much sweeter than he remembered. Her moans set his blood ablaze. He was embarrassed by the rapid climax of his opening act, but with one touch from Gwenn he was back in action.

She quickly lost track of the places and positions. Steven had definitely expanded his repertoire since their youthful romance. Despite his carnal expertise Gwenn could not get out of her own head. Her thoughts raced. She forced herself to focus on the way his lips caressed her breast, the way his hand pulled her hair, the way his...yet the more she pushed herself to concentrate, the physical sensations would slip away. She would find herself right back in her mind worrying about Rachel's wedding, Shirley's transplant and worst of all breaking this news to Daniel.

"Gwenn? Gwenn, where are you?" Steven brushed a sweaty strand of hair from her cheek and kissed her shoulder. "I'm givin' you my best stuff, but I seem to be coming up short. Any suggestions?"

"I can't shut off my brain. I think I need to take a more active role." She chuckled as she smacked him on the ass.

Steven rose to attention. "I have no problem with that." Gwenn lunged at him and they tumbled onto her bed. She straddled him and pinned his arms beneath her knees. She leaned down slowly, letting her breasts slide across his chest. She blew hot breath in his ear and whispered her desires in moist, tantalizing syllables.

He struggled to free his arms, but she pressed them firmly into the mattress.

"I remember how much you liked me to nibble your ears." She bit playfully. "Do you still like it?"

"If my arms were free I'd show you what I like." Steven knew she could feel the effect she was having. His impatience wasn't the only thing growing rapidly.

Gwenn pressed down onto him—ever so slowly. She could feel him struggling to push back with greater haste, but she was in control. She was totally in her body now, all she could think of was drawing out this moment until Steven begged for release.

The grey light of morning brought an end to their lovemaking before they ran out of condoms—but it was almost too close to call.

Gwenn drifted off to sleep in Steven's arms and enjoyed nearly three hours of blissful guilt-free respite. The insistent ring of her cell phone brought her face-to-face with reality.

"Let it go to voicemail." Steven mumbled in her ear as he pulled her close.

She struggled to loose herself from his embrace. "I can't, it might be Rachel or...there's just too much going on." She found her phone and her intuition had been correct.

"Hey, Gwenny. I was wondering if you wanted to come down to the bakery and have breakfast with me. I gave Nathan the day off, so it's only me and William here and I need to talk to you."

"Um, well..." Gwenn stalled for time as she slipped on her robe and walked out to the living room. "Can we make it lunch? I have some stuff to take care of around here—"

"Is that Smart Ass?" Steven shouted from the bedroom. He actually hoped it was Daniel.

"Who was that? Is Daniel back?" Rachel loved good gossip.

"No...it's Steven." Gwenn braced herself for the shame shower.

"Damn! You are a fuckin' nympho!" Rachel made several obnoxious noises on her end of the phone that ended with what sounded like a high-five. "Did you end it with Daniel?"

"Stop being a little bitch. I don't want to talk about it..." Gwenn lowered her voice, "I can't right now. I'll see you for lunch."

Steven, clad in nothing but war wounds, was standing in the doorway when Gwenn turned around.

"Shit! I didn't even hear you." Gwenn nearly dropped her phone.

"Stealth, a soldier's best friend."

"I'd have thought it was pants, but clearly I was wrong." Gwenn blushed and forced herself to keep her gaze above waist level.

"I'll take that as a hint. It sounds like you have plans for today," Steven threw the last part over his shoulder as he walked to the living room to search for his trousers.

"I'll fill you in over coffee." Gwenn grabbed the grinder out of the cupboard. "Do you still like your eggs scrambled?"

"You got it." Steven returned with his jeans slug low on his hips and his newly rehabilitated six-pack flexing sexily with each stride. "Hey, eyes up here please." He smiled and pointed to his face. "I'm not just some piece of meat, ya know."

Gwenn flushed a deeper shade of red and smirked. "Sorry, it's a lot to handle at this hour." She held up one finger to indicate a need to pause the banter while she ground the coffee beans. "OK Sergeant, I have a suggestion."

"Shoot. Well, not literally, please."

"Let's put our cards on the table. I'll bring you up to speed on the latest Hutchinson disasters and you'll fill me in on the P.O.W. backstory. Deal?"

Last night had gone pretty well and he was anxious to move things to the next level with Gwenn. He didn't want to scare her off, but he didn't want to lose any ground by refusing her offer. *No pain no gain.* "Deal."

Fourteen

Annie sat in the back of the tour bus and fumed. She should be ecstatically happy; her band, The Spanking Machine, was on tour with Prince and she was engaged to her soul mate—but she was miserable. Everyone was paired off and she was all alone—missing the hell out of Rachel. Cass and Mika had finally made up and Bree had hooked up with Prince's hot blonde drummer.

"Annie, quit lickin' your wounds and get up here! You're gonna miss the world's largest ball of string," Cass yelled.

"Fuck off!" Annie was in no mood for Cass's poking and prodding. "I'm gonna try Rachel again." She tapped Rachel's name on her "favorites" list and waited for the call to connect. She was expecting voicemail for the fourteenth time, so she didn't even put the phone to her ear. Luckily Rachel was no shrinking violet.

"Annie? Annie, can you hear me?" Rachel hollered.

"Babe, is that really you?" Annie's stomach did little flip-flops and she felt warm all over.

"It's me! It's been forever." Rachel allowed herself a brief cry. "I miss you like crazy."

"Me too, babe."

"OK, are you sitting down? I have some news that will blow your pants off!"

Annie snickered, "I'm laying down, and what makes you think I'm wearing pants?"

"Oh shit, that's hot. I can picture…no, no, no. I have to get back down to the bakery in a few minutes and I HAVE to get you up to speed." Rachel shook her head vigorously to dislodge the image of a half-naked Annie.

"OK, but you have to call me back, tonight. I need a little somethin' somethin', babe. A girl can only last so long without some dirty talk."

Rachel flushed, licked her lips and squeezed her eyes tight. "OK, I promise. There's so much to tell, I don't know where to start."

"Just jump in like you always do. I'm fluent in *Rachel*." The tension in Annie's neck dissipated and she settled in to hear Rachel's tale.

Blood tests, meetings with doctors, tell-all talks with Ed and Shirley—Rachel rushed through it all.

"But, wait babe. I thought you said you weren't a match because Shirley's not your biological mother, so why are you donating a kidney?"

Rachel explained the paired donor program and added the bit about Gwenn volunteering as tribute.

Annie laughed at Rachel's *Hunger Games* reference. "So Gwenn volunteered to donate the kidney to the program so you could focus on the wedding?"

"Yep, and finding my birth mom—and stuff."

"What stuff?" Annie was indeed fluent in *Rachel*.

"Oh, you know—baby stuff."

"Are you talking about adopting?"

"Sort of...but I think I want to have the baby."

"Have it do what?"

"I mean...like...have it. I wanna get pregnant." Rachel's eyes darted; her breathing was rapid and shallow.

"And now Gwenn's sacrifice makes sense." Annie loved Rachel more than she had ever loved anyone or anything in her entire life. She didn't know much about being pregnant, she'd never planned on experiencing it, but if the woman she loved was going to go down this road—she wanted to be there every step of the way. "Do they have a book on what to expect when she's expecting?"

Rachel laughed and cried and laughed some more. "Thank you! Thank you! I don't deserve you."

"Yeah, you really don't," Annie teased.

Rachel shared a few more details of her plans to find her real mom and possibly her Greek father and ended the call with a series of sloppy kissing noises.

"I love you for all eternity, Annie Nelson."

"I love you, too, babe."

Fifteen

Gwenn took the sandwiches she had procured from the deli to a table in the far corner of the bakery. Rachel had planned to expand the menu to include a couple breakfast sandwiches and a few lunch options, but with all the family drama she had barely been able to keep up with the regular orders since she inherited the establishment.

Rachel waved to Gwenn and finished ringing up her customer. "William, I'm on lunch, OK?"

"Got it," William nodded.

Two steaming mugs of coffee were ferried to the table and Rachel threw her apron over the back of the chair opposite Gwenn. "I finally got to talk to Annie. She's so fucking amazing," Rachel grinned triumphantly.

"Let me get this straight, Annie is amazing? This is shocking news." Gwenn smirked as she grabbed her mug of coffee and wrapped her chilled hands around its promised warmth.

"Oh, ha ha." Rachel shook her head and took a seat next to her sister. "Seriously, she was super supportive. She wants me to look for my real parents and she's totally OK with having a baby." She took a sip of her coffee and winked conspiratorially at Gwenn. "Operation Baby Baklava is a go!"

Gwenn nearly spewed her hot coffee at Rachel's quip. "Please tell me that is an early-stage suggestion and that 'operation' names are still being considered."

"What? I like it. It's better than 'Greece Baby', which sounded kinda racist, I thought."

This time a little coffee pierced the veil and Gwenn had to jump up and retrieve a napkin. She wiped the drops of liquid off her chin as she returned. "So, you're really running with this Greek thing aren't ya?"

"Totally! I think I might even try to find a Greek sperm donor," Rachel grinned foolishly.

"What if Shirley got it wrong? She only said she 'thought' the father was Greek—she wasn't sure. What if you go and get yourself all knocked up with a Trojan baby and it turns out you're Welsh?" Spasms of laughter consumed Gwenn.

"Holy crap, Gwenny. There are so many things wrong with that sentence I can't even…" Rachel shook her head in dismay.

"Rache, I'm just kidding. Lighten up, jeez!"

"I guess you're kinda right, though. I don't even know where to start. How am I gonna find this 'ladies' church group' in Chicago?"

"I've been giving it a lot of thought and I think we should ask Dr. Watkins for help. I bet the 'Chief of Staff' can get a lot more information than you or I."

"Do you think he'd help us?"

"He gave me his personal cell phone number…" Gwenn shrugged her shoulders and feigned a confidence she did not possess. "It's worth a call, right?" She dug for the card he had handed her, pulled out her phone and dialed.

Rachel squeezed Gwenn's hand tightly while she listened to her explain their request to Dr. Watkins. The call ended quickly and Rachel grew concerned. "Did he turn us down?"

"No. He actually sounded a little excited. I don't know, I suppose his job is kinda monotonous some days. He's gonna call his friend in Chicago right now."

"Right now? So, I could meet my mom tomorrow?"

"No freak! He's got some med school buddy who's an Ob-Gyn in Chicago and is married to a Confidential Intermediary."

"A what now?"

"A Con-fi-den-tial In-ter-med-i-ary, dork." Gwenn over-emphasized each syllable. "It's some kind of court-appointed relative locator."

"That sounds completely made up. A relative locator? For real?" Rachel raised her eyebrows.

"Look, I didn't get all the details, but it's a thing. OK? He said he'd call me back as soon as he has more info. I have to talk to Gramma Carlson about rehabbing up at her cabin after the transplant surgery, so I'll try to pry some additional details out of her."

Rachel blinked back tears of gratitude and smiled. "I don't know how to thank you, Gwenny. You're the best. If there's ever anything I can do for you—anything—just ask."

"Can you call Daniel and tell him I had sex with Steven?" Gwenn folded her arms onto the table and flopped her head down onto them like an over-extended invertebrate.

"Um...anything, but that."

Mumbling from her "Heads Up, Seven Up" position, Gwenn replied, "They take deceased donor organs, too, right?"

Rachel reached across the table and smacked Gwenn on the back of the head. "Don't even fuckin' joke about that! That is not funny."

Gwenn sat up and rubbed the back of her head. "Bitch."

"Slut."

"I've got to call him, don't I?"

"Yeah, you said you would be honest with him. You're gonna keep seeing Steven, right?"

"Well yeah, I didn't just slip and fall onto his...you know..."

"Thankfully, I have no idea what a 'you know' is, and I am happy to say I'll never find out."

"You are the most irritating little sister in the world!" Gwenn laughed in spite of her shame-coated guilt. "No matter what else Ed and Shirley fucked up—they got one thing right. Me and you."

"Thanks, Gwenny. I love you, too." Rachel stood up and put on her apron. "Now, I gotta get back to work before William eats all the day old scones." Rachel pointed an accusing finger at Gwenn, "And you have a phone call to make, Miss Whorey-pants."

"You are insufferable!" Gwenn dragged herself out of the chair and happily endured one of Rachel's rib-crushing hugs. "I'll meet you at the hospital tonight, OK?"

"OK. Good luck, sis."

"I'll need it." She hung her head as she exited Rachel's bakery, but oddly Gwenn felt a spark of excitement for the adventures that lie ahead.

Sixteen

Gwenn was not feeling brave or honest. She decided to delay the inevitably horrible task of talking to Daniel and call Gramma Carlson, instead.

"Hello?"

"Hi Gramma, it's me, Gwenn."

"Gwendolyn? Well, how on earth are ya, dear?"

"Oh, I'm doin' OK, Gramma. Have you talked to Ed or Shirley lately?"

"Let's see...I think I talked to yer mom yesterday. Is everything all right?"

"Not exactly..."

"Oh, dear! Do I need ta get down to the hospital?"

"No, no, Gramma. Sorry, I didn't mean it like that. Shirley is stable. It's just...well, it's about...Rachel and me... about our adoptions."

A loud gasp, followed by a deathly silence, set Gwenn on edge.

"Gramma, are you still there?"

"So, it finally happened. Yer mom worked so hard ta keep...how'd ya find out?"

"OK, that's one response," Gwenn mumbled, more to herself than to her grandmother.

"What's that, honey?"

"It's a long story, Gramma. Mind if I come over?"

"Oh, that'd be lovely. I'll put a pie in the oven. It should be ready by the time ya get here. I think I'm all outta ice cream, though...unless ya wanna pick some up on yer way?"

The last thing Gwenn wanted was pie and ice cream. Her stomach was churning from all the "truth" she'd consumed in the last few days. "Is vanilla OK?"

"Oh, that's perfect, dear. I'll see ya in a jiffy."

Gwenn stopped at the Piggly Wiggly and procured a 5-quart pail of vanilla ice cream. She knew that any smaller sized container would be considered an insult, and she definitely needed to keep the mood positive.

Gramma Carlson opened the door before Gwenn hit the salt-covered bottom step of the porch.

"Hello, doll. I saw yer car pull up." She reached for the pail of ice cream and continued, "Let me get that fer ya."

"Thanks, Gramma." Gwenn was perfectly capable of carrying five quarts of ice cream up two de-iced steps, but it was a peace offering and it was important that it served its purpose.

"Now, what's all this about a long story?" Gramma Carlson busied herself re-arranging the freezer to make room for the ice cream. Her coral pink polyester pants had a small hole near the waistband. Each time she reached into the freezer, her "Tarkenton" sweatshirt, with a huge number ten on the back, would ride up and expose the hole and the elastic band of her control top panty hose beneath. She finally crammed the bucket into the frozen compartment, fixed her mussed grey hair and turned back to Gwenn. "Well, go on, dear."

Gwenn carefully laid out the details of Shirley's illness, the kidney failure, the blood tests, the "no match" and finally the revelation of the adoption. She was careful to gloss over the details of the blood tests and she made sure to emphasize the generous role of her Gramma in the adoption process.

"Gosh, that's such a lot fer Shirley ta deal with, ya know." Gramma Carlson wrung her hands and shook her head.

It was quite a fucking lot for Gwenn to deal with, too, but she decided not to point that out at the moment. "Do you remember the name of the church group that asked you for help?" There, make her sound like a saint and that should loosen her tongue.

"Oh my goodness! That was ages ago, Gwendolyn—ages."

"Yes, I know—over 30 years ago." Gwenn's patience was running thin. She thought to herself, for the millionth time, *patience is not a virtue; patience is what prevents progress.*

"Gosh! Has it been that long?" Gramma Carlson put her hand to her face like a great Southern lady enduring an attack of the vapours.

"Yep, it sure has." Gwenn clenched her teeth and felt her jawbone flex under the strain.

"Oh dear! The pie!" Gramma Carlson jumped up from the age-worn kitchen table and raced to the oven. "Well, shoot! The edges are a little dark, but we'll scrape that off and she'll be as good as new."

Gwenn listened to the sound of the knife scraping across the crust as Gramma Carlson banished the burnt crumbs into the trash. She hated that sound. That noise reminded her of poverty and hunger. No piece of toast was ever discarded in the Hutchinson house. Shirley used to stand over the waste bin scraping the burnt crap off of toast on a regular basis. Gwenn could not stave off the wave of self-reproach that washed over her when she thought about the slices of burnt offerings she had chucked into the bin once she was out on her own. *Oh the shame of it all.*

"There, good as new. How big of a slice do ya want?"

It was pointless to answer. No matter what anyone said, Gramma Carlson always cut the pie into enormous slices and covered each slice with insane amounts of ice cream. "Just a sliver for me, Gramma."

She returned to the dining room with two large slices of strawberry rhubarb pie, dwarfed under slabs of vanilla ice cream. "There ya go, dear."

Gwenn took a bite and had to admit it was delectable—pie and ice cream at Gramma's was one of her few enjoyable childhood memories. Somehow Rachel had inherited the skill of baking from a woman who was of no relation. "It's delicious, thanks. So, did you think of the name of that church group in Chicago?"

Gramma Carlson polished off a few more dairy-ensconced morsels of pie before she answered. "Chicago...that's right, it was Chicago. I think it was my second cousin, once removed, Myrtle's church." A few more bites went down the hatch. "Bethlehem Methodist? Yep, that sounds right. I think it was Bethlehem Methodist, honey."

"Thanks. I'm so glad you remembered." Gwenn forced the rest of the pie down and swallowed hard. "I was wondering if I could stay up at the cabin after the transplant surgery?"

"Whaddya mean, dear? I thought ya weren't a match. Why would ya need ta stay at the cabin?"

Shit! The sugar rush from the pie was making Gwenn even more impatient and somehow she had forgotten the big, magnanimous news about the paired organ program. "Oh, I forgot the most important part. I'm going to donate a kidney to this exchange program, so Shirley can get a kidney faster. The less time on dialysis the better, at her age."

"Well, Gwendolyn Hutchinson, I don't know what ta say. That is just about the kindest thing I've ever heard. Ya go right ahead and stay at that cabin as long as ya want, honey."

Success! Now she simply had to extract herself before more food was forced down her gullet. "Thanks, Gramma, I really appreciate it."

"Anything for you, angel."

"Well, I better hit the road. I promised to meet Rachel at the hospital and you know how she worries." It was the lamest line she had uttered all day, but her head was spinning from the dessert overload and she desperately wanted to get some coffee.

Gramma Carlson enveloped Gwenn in a huge hug and shed a couple of actual tears. "You've always been my favorite, dear."

Somehow that line didn't hold the same meaning as it had all the years Gwenn had believed the lies about her birth. She had always assumed her status came from being the first grandchild born *in* wedlock, but now she couldn't make heads or tales of her historical status. "Oh, thank you, Gramma."

Gwenn scurried out the door and drove up to Skyline Parkway. The city sparkled in the crisp, dusky light. She looked down at the Aerial Lift Bridge, the canal and Park Point. She took a deep breath and called Daniel.

Seventeen

Daniel paced back and forth in his room at the De Leon Hacienda. The call he had been dreading had finally come. She had slept with Steven.

A deluge of emotions washed over him. He ignored the painful stabs and went straight for the fury. He threw on a pair of shorts, hurriedly tied his workout shoes and rushed down to the training room beneath the hacienda.

He entered the room with the force of a hurricane, slamming the door into the wall with a blow that chipped a generous chunk out of the stucco.

"Easy, El Espectro!" Elena turned her attention from the heavy bag to the electric force of Daniel. They did not have a training session scheduled and Elena had a wrestling match coming up, so she had taken the free time to get in some extra reps. As a female luchador, she had to work twice as hard as the guys.

Daniel was in no mood for Elena's flirtatious nonsense and teasing pet names. "Get out." He did not yell, he was not rude, but the quiet, even tone of his command left no room for argument.

Elena's flesh sizzled. No one could tame her, no one dared. She had been using her blind determination and visible assets to control her world for years. The tone in Daniel's voice was a challenge. She accepted.

His eyes followed her like a leopard tracking an impala.

She stepped away from her workout and slowly removed the tape from her hands. She grabbed the edge with her teeth and ripped—all the while maintaining an intense eye contact with Daniel.

He felt the heat of his anger writhe down his torso and change into a flame of another kind. He wasn't sure if he had the strength to fight the urges—this time.

She felt the energy in the room shift and she took her cue. Elena looked Daniel squarely in his multi-hued eyes and slipped off her shoes.

His heart raced.

She pulled her sports bra off over her head and revealed her firm, impertinent breasts.

He struggled to slow his breathing.

She turned away with a modesty she did not possess and slowly slipped her yoga pants down—exposing her magnificent ass.

His body made the decision before his mind could protest.

He was across the room in three strides and had Elena bent over the bench press bar before she could react.

She was so thrilled with the result of her conquest she submitted without thinking. However, submission was not in Elena's repertoire.

Daniel's mind was locked in a prison of pain and loss, but his body was behaving like a sailor on shore leave.

She saw her opportunity to turn the tables and get him to focus on her. She turned and pushed him back onto the mat.

He went down without a fight.

She straddled him, released her sleek ebony hair from its ponytail and sunk down onto him. She pressed down hard and lunged for his mouth.

He growled and pulled his head away. He gave no explanation, but he would not allow her to kiss him.

His resistance angered her and she redoubled her other efforts. Harder. Faster.

He didn't like the implication that Elena was in charge. He grabbed her ass firmly and flipped their positions. Daniel stretched her arms above her head and pumped into her with emotional abandon.

Elena's body crackled with pleasure. She forgot about the kisses and met his pounding, stroke for stroke. Her glorious caramel skin glistened with sweat. Her powerful legs pushed her pelvis up to meet Daniel's onslaught and when she finally found her release she forgot he was even in the room. Her quads collapsed, her abs contracted and she saw stars. "Ese fue el mejor sexo de mi vida!"

Daniel, unfulfilled but finished, got dressed. He did not acknowledge Elena's comment. He crossed the room to exit.

"Hey?" Elena, naked and magnificent, jumped up and shouted at Daniel's back, "Hey, I said that was the best sex of my life and you're gonna walk out?"

Daniel inhaled and faced the truth. He had done a stupid, impulsive thing. He did not feel better; he felt worse. Bedding Elena was not going to bring Gwenn back, it only made him miss her more. "Sorry," he mumbled.

"Sorry? Sorry?" Elena marched her bare ass across the room and stood in front of the door. "What the hell just happened?"

"Elena, we both know what happened. You've been trying to seduce me since I arrived. I made it clear I wasn't interested, but I kept training with you. That was my mistake."

"So now I'm a mistake?" Elena's black eyes burned with indignation.

"No, you're a wonderful girl that deserves a man your own age. A man whose heart is actually available for you to possess. I made a mistake by staying here. I knew what you were trying to do and I thought I could resist. Today I ran out of opposition, and that's why I'm sorry."

She flipped her hair over her shoulder and leaned her beautiful breasts millimeters from Daniel's chest. "If you are still here in the morning my father will have the Federales drag you into the mountains and make you disappear."

"Understood."

She turned back to her pile of clothing and walked across the room with the pride of an Olmec warrior princess.

Daniel watched her taut ass one last time before he made his hasty retreat.

Eighteen

Rachel apprehensively paced around the lobby of St. Luke's Hospital. Her gaze snapped to the sliding doors every time they opened. *Where the hell is Gwenn?* The "deceased donor" comment had left her with an uneasy twinge in her stomach. *What if Gwenn did something crazy? Maybe she was super upset after she talked to Daniel...*

The doors slid open and finally revealed the prize Rachel awaited. Gwenn stomped the snow off her boots and shoved her gloves into her coat pockets. She left her hat securely on her head. She rarely wore hats, but if she did they were on for the duration. There was nothing Gwenn hated more than hat hair—except possibly the conversation she had just finished with Daniel.

"Gwenny!" Rachel rushed over and smothered Gwenn in an embrace. "Shit, you had me worried. I was thinking you might have done something desperate...or worse."

"Nope. Only the good die young, remember? I've got decades and decades ahead of me."

"How'd it go with Daniel? Did he get upset?"

"He was utterly stoic. The only word I would *never* use to describe him—so I'm guessing he was furious." Gwenn blinked back the stinging tears. "He politely told me to 'take care of myself' and then he hung up. I sat there and listened to the silence for about 20 minutes."

Rachel put a comforting arm around Gwenn's shoulders. "Should we skip visiting hours?"

"Can we?" Gwenn's visage pleaded for the mercy of escape.

"Sure. What should we do?"

"Honestly, Rache, I think I need to call Steven. I left things kinda weird this morning."

"But what about me? What do I do?" Rachel's selfless moment had passed and her favorite topic was back in rotation.

"Why don't you go home and write a love letter to Annie? It's such a lost art, ya know. I think it would be ridiculously romantic." Gwenn got a wistful look in her eye.

"Why would I write a bunch of nonsense down when I can call her and tell her exactly what I think of her sexy little mouth...and stuff. Omycrap! I forgot, I'm supposed to call her tonight. I gotta go. Call me tomorrow, Gwenny!"

Gwenn watched Rachel race out the automatic doors and into the frosty night. Her own heart felt as cold as the thick layer of ice creaking and groaning across Lake Superior. She crunched her way across the snowy sidewalk to the parking garage. She knew she had to see Steven, but she desperately wondered what Daniel was doing in Mexico.

***

Daniel had asked Raphael, the Hacienda's manager, to call him a cab; he made up a lame story about a family emergency—which wasn't entirely false. It was simply that the family was Elena's and the emergency was his imminent death.

He had trifled with the idea of calling Todd for an extraction, but instantly thought better of it. His own infantile actions had gotten him into this mess and maybe it was about time he got himself out of trouble—for once.

He hastily dressed in jeans and a wrinkled oxford shirt. He threw the remainder of his clothes in his duffle and grabbed his phone—but opted to leave his toiletries behind. He had no idea where to procure a quart-sized bag and he did not want to alert any other members of the household to his departure.

Raphael appeared at his door. "Señor, the taxi is arrived."

"Thanks, I'm ready." Daniel cast a quick glance at the room and realized his swim trunks were drying out by the pool—too late, they were forfeit. "OK, that's everything."

Raphael led the way to the taxi and opened the door for Daniel. "I wish the best to your family, Señor Gregory."

"Gracias, Raphael. Todd will make arrangements to have my mosaic pieces transported to the States. Please thank Señor De Leon, I mean Lorenzo, for me."

"I will, Señor. Safe journey to you." Raphael shut the door and pounded twice on the cab's roof.

Daniel glanced out the rear window and swore that he could see Elena laughing from a darkened portico.

***

Todd walked up to Flora's front porch and noticed the light bulb had burned out. He was not one for omens or portents, but something about that dark stoop gave him a bad feeling. He would definitely call Daniel in the morning.

He knocked softly on the front door and Flora appeared in her flannel pajamas, bathrobe and fur-lined wool slippers. She was practical and Todd loved that about her. There would be plenty of time for sexy lingerie when the damn weather warmed up. Besides, he had purchased a pragmatic space heater for the bedroom.

"Good evening, Miss Long," Todd teased her with the formality.

Flora giggled and kissed him quickly, before she pulled him inside and shut the door firmly behind him. "It's freezing out there. We might have to cuddle." She blushed at her own brazenness.

Todd nodded his agreement before he added his segue, "Your porch light is burnt out. Did that happen recently?"

"Mmmhmm!" Flora chuckled, "I heard it pop a few minutes ago. It scared me a little, but I knew you'd be here any second so I didn't panic too much."

"Hmmm, I have a weird feeling...maybe..." Todd waved away his suspicions and took off his coat.

"Is it about Daniel?"

Todd's eyes darted to Flora. "What makes you say that?"

"I don't honestly know. It's just that when the bulb popped, I ran to the door and my first thought was of you... then I had a weird thought about Daniel."

"That's it, I have to call. Do you mind?"

"Not at all, I'd call too—if it was me."

Todd finished removing his winter gear and fished his phone out of his pocket. He held it tensely and stared unseeingly at Flora while he listened to the unanswered ringing. "No answer. Laptop?"

"On the table." Flora gestured to her small mahogany dining room table.

Todd's fingers flew across the keys. His hands froze above the keyboard and his brain digested the information in front of him. "He bought his own plane ticket..." Todd's fading voice was a mixture of awe and concern.

"Oh gosh, I'm sorry. I know you usually take care of all of his travel arrangements." Flora rubbed Todd's neck and shoulders. "Don't worry, he'll still need you to take care of things."

"No, no, actually this is good. I've been waiting for the right time to talk to him about the gallery up here. I think this is a good sign." Todd closed the browser and lowered the laptop screen. "I'm sure he'll call me in the morning." The *business-y* side of Todd was quite relieved to see Daniel managing some of his own affairs and making way for Todd to branch out. However, the part of Todd that secretly thought of himself as Daniel's friend and confidante was smarting a little from the personal affront.

***

Gwenn didn't want to think about how much she had hurt Daniel. She never meant for any of this to happen. How could she have possibly presaged that Steven would join the Marine Corps and be held captive in an Afghan prison for six years with only the memory of her to keep him alive? She thought the ship had sailed on Steven years ago—but he had magically appeared in Mexico and begged her to give him a second chance. She could never have predicted this outcome.

Their earlier breakfast conversation had given her a better understanding of the torture and neglect Steven had suffered while he was a prisoner of war, but it had left her with murky unsettling feelings about their future together. She wasn't sure she was the kind of woman who could handle his PTSD, but she wished she could see herself through his eyes. He thought of her as his savior, his reason for hanging onto life—his future. He viewed her as an elixir of healing; she had always seen herself as a poisonous draught. They couldn't both be right. She wanted to perceive things differently—possibly better.

Nineteen

Rachel's heart thumped in her chest as she listened to the phone ring. She had promised Annie a phone sex call and she was going to make good on that promise—if it killed her.

"Hey, babe. I was hopin' you didn't forget about me." Annie's voice was husky with sleep.

"Did I wake you?"

"No big. Let me get my coat and step outta the bus so I don't wake everyone up. Hold on, OK?"

Rachel wasn't sure what was going on, but she waited for further instructions.

"Alright, I'm out. What's goin' on?"

"Um, you said to call…about…somethin' about dirty talk…I'm confused."

Annie's laughter poured through the phone. "Oh, sorry, babe. I was only sayin' that in front of Bree, 'cuz she spends half the day readin' me sexts from her new drummer girl."

"Well, that's a relief," Rachel exhaled and snickered.

"I'll bet."

"Can we talk about the wedding?"

"You definitely know how to turn a girl on, babe. I'm wet just thinkin' about all those flowers and ruffles and shit." Annie lit a cigarette and took a long drag.

"Are you smoking?"

"What?"

"Annie Marie Nelson! Are you smoking?" Rachel was *pre*-furious.

"Just on the tour, babe. I swear I'll quit the day I get back." Annie snubbed out the cig on the side of the bus and put it back in the pack.

"You will quit immediately if you know what's good for ya. Both my grampas died of lung cancer! I'm over here planning a wedding and a pregnancy and you're out there murdering my bride and leaving my child with only one parent. What the fuck?"

Annie's blonde spiky hair was not the only thing perking up. "Rache, you know it turns me on when you take charge," she teased, because she knew Rachel was right and she had no good reason to smoke again. It was just a way to get through the lonely moments.

"Why is everyone out to kill me today?"

"No one better lay a hand on you." Annie's protective nature kicked into over-drive.

"It's not like that. Gwenn was hinting around at taking her own life—joking about deceased organ donors and other stupid shit. She just didn't want to face Daniel."

"What'd he do?"

"Not a damn thing. Gwenn took things to the next level with Steven and then she got all freaked out because she had to tell Daniel."

"Straight girl problems."

Rachel laughed, "Right?"

The sound of their shared sense of humor erased the miles between them. They talked about the wedding, the pregnancy and finally about finding Rachel's birth parents.

"Yeah, the doctor at St. Luke's has a friend in Chicago. Gwenn's talking to him and trying to get more info from my gramma."

"Maybe you can come to my show in Chicago? I mean if this guy gets you any good leads by then..."

"When's your show?"

"Friday, at the Aragon Ballroom. It's an epic venue, babe."

"I'll try, I will. Hopefully there'll be more information... that's really fast though...if she didn't want to be found...I mean...it might be a dead end."

"I got faith in you. If you want somethin' you get it. I mean look what happened with the bakery—"

"Annie! Don't say that. I didn't kill Mrs. Lindstrom. She's old, she just died."

"Sure, right after she fired you for being a lezzer—but before she could change her will. Kinda got a karma's-on-your-side feel to it, right?"

"You are the worst! You're gonna burn in hell with Gwenn."

"That's OK by me. Your sister turned out to be a pretty solid chick."

"Yeah, she's pretty much the best. So you're really OK with her kinda being my wedding planner?"

"I'm not wearin' a dress, I'm not goin' anywhere near a church and I get to pick the DJ for the reception. You and Gwenn can do whatever the hell you want with the rest."

"DJ? I thought you would play, I mean I thought The Spanking Machine would play...wouldn't you?"

"At my own wedding? How the hell am I gonna dance with you and play bass at the same time?"

"Oh...yeah. OK, you pick the DJ."

"I love you, babe."

"I love you, too. I hope I get to see you in Chicago."

"Ditto."

Twenty

Gwenn awoke to the buzz of a text on her phone. She squirmed around in her flannel sheets and tried to retrieve the phone without letting too much cold air under the covers.

">can i take u to lunch?"

Could Steven take her to lunch? That was a question for the powers that be. She hadn't slept much and what little she could remember of her dreams involved duels, jousts and other competitions for her love. She had to face the facts—what she had with Daniel was over. What she had with Steven was just beginning. If she didn't get her head in the game she would end up wasting her second opportunity with Steven, too.

">OK. 12:30?" She sent the text and forced herself out of bed. Technically she had at least ten more minutes, but her mind was already racing.

She pulled her cozy robe tightly around her body and allowed herself to reflect on what was developing with Steven. There was a genuine connection, that couldn't be denied. It felt good to be around him and she enjoyed joking and laughing with him, too. His resurrection had the potential to heal some of her old wounds and help her feel more satisfied with herself—if they could be truly honest with each other.

She walked into her closet and aimlessly pushed hangers back and forth. She refused to wear black. She had some beautiful sweaters.

Several outfits later, she acquiesced. She allowed black trousers, but only because she would pair them with an Alexander McQueen jacquard kimono sweater—otherwise known as the consignment store steal of the century!

She trudged along in her warm shearling-lined leather boots and carried her fashionable-but-impractical Phillip Lim ankle boots. She wound her way through the steel and glass skyway passages that crisscrossed downtown Duluth like an elevated, metal cardiovascular system.

A comfortable calm settled over her when she opened the door and saw the ever-reliable Flora walking toward her.

"Good morning, Miss Hutchinson."

"Morning. It's so good to see you here—holding down the fort." Gwenn continued on to her office and stopped to take a second look at Flora. Something was different...she couldn't quite put her finger on it... "Flora, you're wearing a dress! I mean...well, crap...I should've said, you look fantastic. Is that new?" She admired the grey cashmere dress and noticed, for the first time, that Flora had a rockin' body—to use Rachel's vernacular.

Flushed but pleased, Flora turned and walked back toward Gwenn. "Todd says I wear too many pantsuits...um, it's a waste of my legs—he said." Her face was severely reddened by the admission.

"I'd have to agree with him, Flora. You look fabulous. You'll be giving Thea a run for her money, if she's not careful."

"Did I hear my name being taken in vain?" The flaxen-haired Thea rounded the corner in her signature 5-inch platform heels, carefully blotting her freshly-applied lipstick.

Flora nervously smoothed at her hair and blurted, "Gwenn was just teasing me about my dress."

"I was not teasing, Flora. You look gorgeous, doesn't she, Thea?"

"Yes, my Padawan, you look splendid. That Todd fella is doin' you some good." Thea exchanged a knowing glance with Flora and continued to the break room. "Anyone else need coffee?"

Gwenn looked at Flora and smirked. "There's something going on here...but I'll leave it alone, for now."

Flora exhaled with relief.

"I'll take a cup, Thea."

"Sweet and creamy? Like you like your men?" Thea shouted from the break room.

"Of course," Gwenn replied. She looked at Flora and shook her head, "I literally have no idea what that means, but I *need* some coffee."

Thea returned with the coffees, her crystal-blue eyes sparkling with secrets. "Did you tell her yet?" She nodded encouragingly at Flora.

"A new account?" Gwenn queried.

"Oh, I'll bring the Hit List into your office in a—"

"Oh, for cryin' out loud! Todd asked Flora if he could move in," Thea blurted.

Gwenn immediately thought of Daniel and attempted to hide her distraction with an overzealous response. "Wow, that's so great!"

Flora exchanged a knowing look with Thea and opted to downplay the whole incident. "Gosh, it's nothing, really. He just thought it would be a practical solution to live together, since he's going to end up running the gallery..." Flora clapped her hand over her mouth and froze.

There's one in every social circle—the girl everyone tries to protect. Gwenn did not want to be the basket case that forced everyone to walk on eggshells in her presence. "Hey, Flora, I'm honestly happy that things are working out so great with Todd. You don't have to hide your happiness around me. Things didn't work out with Daniel—that's life. I'm getting a chance to re-build things with Steven and that's an opportunity I thought I'd never get...so it all works out...in the end." Her bravery dissolved and she blinked rapidly, while she looked up at the ceiling—an old junior high trick for staving off tears until she could hide in a bathroom stall. "Well, I'll be in my office. Can you bring in the Hit List? Give me about 30 minutes to catch up on emails." She spun around, sloshed a little coffee over the side of her cup and beat a hasty retreat.

"Yeah, she's totally fine," Thea quipped. She made absolutely no effort to hide her sarcasm.

"She'll be thrilled to hear about that big corporate client you landed in Minneapolis. That account will give us all a chance to relax," Flora added wistfully.

"You mean the client I 'bedded', don't you?" Thea laughed at herself, but not for as long as usual. "Oh, he's a good guy. I know it won't last, but it's a great project and the margins on my estimate are ri-DONK-ulous!" Thea winked at Flora and walked back to her office—hips undulating just enough to qualify as interesting, without screaming "trampy."

Gwenn sat down at her desk and grabbed her mouse. She flicked through her emails, trashing most and responding to a select few. The number of junk emails from vendors never ceased to irritate. Her mind wandered, as it was prone to, and she lost herself in visions of Steven. She'd enjoyed rediscovering his body. The tattoos and scars were new, but the lips were just as she remembered—soft, sexy and talented.

She dropped the pretense of reading emails and applied her full attention to the reverie. She could feel his skin under her fingers, hear his rough breathing in her ear and taste the salt on his neck. She saw the aching need in his eyes and recalled how many times they had fulfilled that craving.

"Ready for the Hit List?" Flora beamed.

Gwenn snapped out of her mental dalliance and dabbed at a bit of drool pooling at the corner of her mouth. "Hit List, right...yes...totally ready. Fire away."

Prior to her sexual awakening, Flora would have written off Gwenn's distraction as "boss worries," but now that she had been to paradise she recognized the expression for something else entirely. "I can come back in a few."

"No, it's fine, really. I just have a lot on my mind lately." Gwenn shook her head a bit to clear the cobwebs.

They discussed client projects, adjusted a few priorities and both jumped when Steven walked in with a large vase of flowers.

"How's my girl?" Steven winked.

"I should go...I'll just update this list, Miss Hutchinson... and..." Flora scuttled out of the room mumbling workplace-related phrases as she went.

Gwenn smiled and soaked in Steven's big blue eyes peering over the colorful bouquet.

"She's a jumpy one, eh?"

She nodded her acknowledgment. "Is it lunch already?"

"It is."

"Where are you going to take me?"

"I'd like to take you right here. Does this door have a lock?" He fiddled with the door handle while Gwenn hurriedly vacated her desk.

"It's lunch, not a nooner, ya man-whore." She playfully smacked his firm ass.

"Where was all that—"

Gwenn interrupted before he derailed lunch entirely with his sex appeal. "Are those for me?"

"Why yes, m'lady." Steven bowed and presented the arrangement with a flourish.

"Thank you, sir." She attempted a clumsy curtsy and nearly dropped the vase.

"Never did finish charm school, did ya?" Steven caught her elbow and pulled her in for a kiss and a nibble.

She lost herself in his tempting lips. She felt a sharp tingle in her nether regions and felt the vase slipping through her fingers. "Shit! I practically dropped the damn thing, again." She turned and walked over to her desk, determined to set the flowers on a more stable surface.

Steven struggled to resist the urge to follow her and hoist her up onto the desk alongside the bouquet. "Yep, we definitely need to go to lunch—now."

Gwenn smoothed her sweater and wiped potential lipstick smears from the corners of her mouth. "I actually do have a few things to tell you…I called Daniel last night."

He plucked up his courage and offered her his arm. "Well, it's off to lunch we go." Steven put on a brave face, but all he could think was the sooner this Daniel schmuck was out of the picture, the better.

Twenty-one

Daniel landed at the Minneapolis-St. Paul International Airport and sulked all the way through Customs. He was supposed to feel proud of himself for resisting the bottle, but all he could think about was how much he wanted to drink—and forget.

He waited until he was securely in the taxi before he called Todd.

"Good morning, Mr. Gregory. How was your flight?" Todd kept his tone professional, but he could not resist the chance to steal Daniel's bolt-in-the-night thunder.

Daniel chuckled. "I'd ask how you know that I was on a flight, but that would ruin the enigma that is you. So, I'm back—as you surmised. Can you meet me at the house to discuss damage control?"

"Of course. Two questions: Are you sober? When is your appointment with Dr. Mountainside?"

"Yes, surprisingly, and in 30 minutes."

"Good, on both counts. I'm on my way down to the Cities, so I should arrive just after your phone session with the good doctor. Can I bring you anything?"

"You wouldn't happen to have any spare dignity?" Daniel rubbed his forehead and wished he could wipe away the memory of his "indiscretion" with Elena.

"No sir, I'm using mine."

"Todd, was that an actual joke? What the heck has Flora done to you?" Daniel chuckled with a lightness he wished he could posses. He felt genuine happiness for Todd, but his own life was far from satisfactory.

Todd permitted himself a brief titter—nothing outrageous—but a respectable teehee. "I will see you in roughly 90 minutes, at which time I will fill you in on the details of my situation with Miss Long."

"That's it? No snide remark about how I managed to get all the way back from Mexico—all by myself?"

"I'll save my lecture for the face-to-face."

"That's the Todd I remember. Safe travels. See ya soon." Daniel ended the call and spent the remainder of the cab ride collecting his thoughts and attempting to place events on a linear timeline. In the end he knew he would just spill the gory details and wind up jumping *in medias res* with Dr. Mountainside.

Daniel was glad that Dr. Brenda Mountainside had found a way to squeeze in a phone appointment today. As he searched his contacts for her number he reflected on his catalogued mental picture of her, '*Serenity*, oil on canvas.' An intelligent, compassionate face surrounded by gray pixie-cut hair that added energy and movement to her face, while the elegant lines of her wardrobe complemented the placidity of her office. He even recalled the way the light sieved through her blinds and sprinkled a tranquil glow all around her shoulders. She emanated professionalism.

"Good morning, Dr. Mountainside's office. How may I brighten your day?"

He never got tired of that salutation. "Good morning. I have an appointment—Daniel Gregory."

"Oh, Mr. Gregory, you're timing is exquisite. She's just finished up and I can put you straight through. One moment, please."

He took a deep breath while he was transferred to the doctor.

"Good afternoon, Daniel. I didn't hear from you at our regular Monday timeslot...I had hoped for the best, but it sounds like things have taken an unwelcome turn. Are you still in Mexico?"

Daniel had kept the details sketchy in his voicemail. He had simply mentioned the importance of speaking to Brenda today. "No. I probably should've kept the Monday appointment, I might have had my head in a better place."

Brenda made a few hasty notes and asked Daniel to continue.

"Things kinda unraveled with Gwenn. She called to tell me she was moving forward...had moved...basically she slept with Steven."

"That must have been painful for you to hear. Were you able to discuss your feelings with Gwenn?"

"Uh, that would be a big NO. I just said something lame like, 'take care of yourself.' It was pathetic."

"It was human. Grace under pressure is a skill that rarely surfaces in a breakup. I would encourage you to give yourself credit for ending the conversation before you said anything you might regret."

"I regret staying in Mexico."

"Because you didn't chase after Gwenn and fight for her?"

"Not exactly." Daniel knew he had to confess if he wanted to move past the incident with Elena, but he dreaded the moment of revelation.

"What happened in Mexico?"

"I slept with Elena, my mentor's daughter. Actually, slept is the wrong word. I was angry and Elena was there...things got rough." Daniel looked down at his hand as it squeezed the fabric of his chair—his knuckles were white.

"Did you hurt her?"

"Hardly. She was thrilled; she finally got what she wanted. She said it was the best sex of her life...I just felt disgusted with myself. I'm old enough to know better."

"Again, you were human. We all make mistakes. The best of us regret those mistakes and take measures to prevent them from recurring. Measures like talking to a therapist." Brenda smiled to herself and jotted down a few more notes. "So why did you leave Mexico?"

"To avoid Elena's revenge." Daniel chuckled, in spite of the seriousness of his situation. "She threatened to have her father 'make me disappear' so I grabbed my stuff and got on a plane."

"Sounds prudent." She adjusted her teal cashmere scarf and tapped her pen sharply. "So what's next?"

"I'm going to win Gwenn back. I know she still has feelings for me...I let her down. She wanted me to fight for her and I thought I could prevail by giving her space. What an idiot!" Daniel picked up a magazine from his coffee table and flung it against the wall.

"Everything OK over there?"

"Yes, just one less copy of Condé Naste for my cleaning lady to read."

"What if Gwenn doesn't want to be won?" Brenda chewed on the end of her pen.

"I don't plan to fail, this time."

"Daniel, it is important for you to explore these feelings. Failure may not be your goal, but you have to accept that it is an option. If Gwenn has truly moved on and she is determined to build a life with Steven, how will you handle that?"

"I'm guessing I'll drink my way to the bottom of a few bottles and wait for Todd to straighten me out."

"Interesting. That doesn't sound like the same Daniel that bought his own plane ticket and stayed sober all the way from Mexico. How do you feel about taking care of yourself—being alone?"

"I hate it." Daniel leaned back in his designer chair and kicked his feet up on the custom coffee table. "I hated being an only kid. I felt like shit after my mom died and I spent every minute trying to get my dad to notice me—spend time with me."

"Does losing Gwenn bring up those same feelings of loneliness and abandonment?"

"I guess..." Daniel didn't want to think about the loss of Gwenn. He wanted to focus all his energy on eradicating Steven and resuming his rightful place in Gwenn's life. "If I can just get this Steven punk out of the picture, I know I can fix things with Gwenn."

"Daniel, you asked me to be honest with you at all times—is that still your desire?" Brenda glanced down at her notes and waited for Daniel's permission to continue.

"Yes, honesty always." He braced himself for her next words.

"Steven is not a punk. Steven is a Sergeant in the United States Marine Corps who survived over six years in Afghan prison camps. You can not eradicate him."

"I won't give up. I know...if I can just..."
"Daniel?"
"Yes."

"If you intend to pursue this course of action you will need to think like a man who loves himself first and Gwenn second. This is not medieval court, you cannot fight for Gwenn and you are not fighting against Steven. You need to accept that failure is an option, and then you can formulate a compassionate plan to reconnect with Gwenn."

"You mean brains not brawn?"

"No, Daniel. I mean heart. You will have to show Gwenn your true heart—for better or worse."

"Well, that sounds easy enough." Daniel moaned and rubbed his hand across his face. "I'd rather joust," he laughed.

"Most men would." Brenda chuckled lightly and made some final notes. "That's the end of our time today. Will you need another appointment this week or shall we stick to our Monday morning schedule?"

"It's going to take me a few days to sort out the Mexico stuff with Todd and get re-acclimated. Let's stick with Monday for now."

"You can always call me if something comes up before that, OK?"

"You got it. Thanks, as usual, Brenda."

"You're welcome, Daniel. Be good to yourself this week."

"Will do, g'bye." Daniel pressed *end* and heard the welcome sound of Todd stomping snow off his boots in the foyer. *No rest for the wicked.* Time to bring him up to speed.

Twenty-two

Steven could barely contain his joy. Gwenn had downgraded Daniel from benched to off the roster—this was cause for celebration. "Let me order you a drink."

Gwenn did not share Steven's bliss. She felt a sense of peace with her decision, but not joy. "I have to go back to work."

"Come on, you're the boss. Who's gonna say anything? Thea? I think that girl puts whiskey in her coffee!" Steven laughed and waved over the server. "I'll have a gin and tonic and a Midori sour for the lady."

"Certainly, sir." The server nodded politely and hurried off to fill the order.

"Man, this place has changed." Steven looked around Grandma's Saloon and Grill.

No response.

"Did you hear me? I know it's kinda loud in here." Steven leaned across the table toward Gwenn and smiled.

A steely glare met his smile.

"Uh oh, I know that look. What did I do?"

Pursed lips. No verbal encouragement.

"It's not about the drink, is it? It's one drink...come on, we're celebrating." He reached his pleading hands across the table and opened his palms toward her.

Silence, followed by a spectacular eye roll—finished with arms crossed over chest.

"OK, OK. I'm a bad listener. I get it." Steven slid out of the booth. "I'll go find her and cancel the drink order."

Normally this win would have resulted in a superior pinch-lipped grin from Gwenn, but she was saving her strength for the next phase of the conversation. She had read something on the internet about sandwiching bad news between two pieces of good news to make it more palatable. She had led with the Daniel update, which had obviously thrilled the crap out of Steven. She planned to close with an invitation to a horse-drawn sleigh ride up at Lutsen Mountain. Now she just had to get him to swallow the middle bit.

Steven returned and slid into the booth next to her. "I'm sorry for ignoring your protest. It was insensitive of me to assume that you were as ecstatic as I was about dumping Daniel."

Gwenn flinched at the "dumping" imagery, but she had to play nice. "Apology accepted. There are actually a couple more things I wanted to discuss."

"Shoot. You're the only thing on my agenda today." Steven slid an arm around her shoulder and she leaned in for a minute.

"So I told you about the whole kidney donation thing, right?"

"Yep, totally up to speed on the adventures of Saint Gwenn."

"Spare me the bullshit, OK?"

"Yes, ma'am." He saluted her, acknowledging she was the superior officer.

She responded with a partial eye roll. "After the surgery, I'm going up to my Gramma's cabin to recuperate."

"Sounds romantic. I can make you hot cocoa, cook you dinner and we can do it in front of the fireplace." Steven winked and wiggled his eyebrow.

"I'm going alone. I need some time to clear my head and kinda reset my whole…operation," Gwenn gestured to herself.

"Well what am I supposed to do? Sit around my Auntie M's and get fat eating her kugel?" Steven grinned and played with a lock of Gwenn's hair.

"I actually have a project for you."

"Go on."

"I want you to see a neurofeedback specialist and schedule some sessions." Gwenn had been fastidiously searching the internet that morning and one of her threads led her to a helpful article touting the benefits of neurofeedback in veterans suffering from PTSD.

Steven retracted his arm and turned to look at Gwenn. "You want me to get my head checked out?" His jaw muscles tensed.

"If we are going to move forward together I have to know we are both working on the relationship—"

"I'm working my ass off over here." Steven's tone was defensive and a tad too loud.

Hutchinson 101: Do not make a scene in public. "If we can't have a civil discussion about a very real obstacle in our relationship then I may have misjudged you." Gwenn chose a snarky but professional tone for her response.

"Obstacle?"

"Steven, you can't see what I see. The PTSD has to be addressed; you can't just ignore it and think that it will go away. You have been to hell and back. You are tense, jumpy, quick-tempered and...and I worry that it could get worse."

"I don't want to take pills. I can't do that." He pinched the bridge of his nose with his thumb and forefinger. "I can handle it."

"There are no pills in these sessions, you don't even have to talk about what happened. You just listen to some pleasant tones and watch images on a computer screen. Your brain learns to respond to the tones and begins to create new neural pathways that will help you manage your emotions."

"You learned all this on the internet?"

"I just stumbled across it—but it sounds legit. While I'm up at the cabin you can try a few sessions and see what you think. We'll get a chance to start fresh."

"We are starting fresh." Steven's hand gripped the edge of the table like a vise.

"Not really. You came after me with a head full of enhanced memories and I've been bouncing back and forth between you and Daniel like a tennis ball at Wimbledon. Let's give ourselves the best shot we can, OK?"

Steven took three deep breaths and shook the tension out of his arms and hands. The peak of Mount Everest was in sight, no point in forcing his way through this storm. He would make camp, and prepare himself properly for the final ascent. He knew he would only get one attempt. "You're right, I have been pushing pretty hard. I'll check into this neuro stuff, but if they try to give me some shock therapy crap—I'm out."

"Sounds reasonable. Deal?" Gwenn extended her pinky as homage to the deal they had made in Mexico.

"Deal." He hooked his pinky with hers and shook it.

Twenty-three

Shirley was not pleased with the placement of her venous catheter. She tried on outfit after outfit, but the lump was always visible. "How many times a week do I hafta go in fer the dialysis?"

Ed had wandered away from the wardrobe fiasco and could not hear Shirley's query. "Just a minute, Shirl, I'm gettin' a caffeine-free pop."

"Oh, fer cryin' out loud. What if I was havin' an episode or somethin'? Gettin' a pop, well I never." Shirley cast her eyes heavenward for the thousandth time. She wondered if these earthly trials and tribulations were stacking up her appropriate rewards in Heaven. A flashback of her near death experience temporarily distracted her from berating Ed.

He rounded the corner with a can of soda in his hand and a grin on his face. "So what's the emergency in here?"

"That's nothin' ta joke about, Edwin Hutchinson. I got a serious condition." She fiddled with a scarf around her neck and made several fruitless attempts to disguise the medical device protruding out of her chest. The sooner she got the kidney transplant the better, as far as she was concerned. "I was askin' about that there dialysis."

"Oh, well the doc said ya probably needed ta go in three times a week. Why? Are ya feelin' down in the mouth already?"

"No, I'm just ready to get rid of this confounded catheter. I can't seem to camouflage it." Shirley looped the scarf through one more time and looked in the mirror. "Should I call the doctor and see if there's any news?"

"He said they'd call as soon as they found a match. We'll get the whole church prayin' fer ya—it won't be long." Ed nodded with pastorly reassurance.

***

Gwenn did not recognize the number on her phone. She toyed with the idea of letting it go to voicemail, but in the end she worried it might be about Shirley and answered the call. "Hello."

"Hello. May I speak to Gwendolyn Hutchinson?"

"Speaking." The formality of the voice on the other end of the call made the hairs on the back of her neck stand on end.

"Hello, Miss Hutchinson. I'm the Transplant Coordinator at St. Luke's Hospital. We just received an urgent message from the United Network for Organ Sharing. They found a recipient for your kidney and another paired donor who is a match for your mother. We would like you to come to the hospital as soon as possible. The recipient for your kidney has a narrow window of transplant eligibility."

Gwenn heard the words but her brain had trouble connecting the message with an outcome.

"Miss Hutchinson, are you still there?"

"Yes, I'm here. Sorry, what am I supposed to do?" She could feel the phone tapping against her head. Her hands were shaking uncontrollably.

"Can you get someone to drive you to the hospital?" The well-trained coordinator patiently talked Gwenn through each step.

"Yes, I think my sister can bring me." She forced herself to take deeper breaths. The room looked slanty and the floor was moving. "I need to sit down."

"Would you like me to call your sister?"

"Um...OK. Should I shower?" Gwenn knew she wasn't making sense, but she couldn't stop the words from coming out of her mouth.

"Just sit tight, Miss Hutchinson, and I will call your sister, Rachel. When you get to the hospital the surgeon will explain the procedure and you will be prepped for surgery."

"I'm not ready...I didn't pack...and my employees..."

"When was the last time you had something to eat or drink?"

"Lunch, I guess."

"OK, so you will have a few hours before they will be able to administer anesthetic—that should give you time to put things in order."

Put my affairs in order. This is it; I'm going to die. I'm going to die an unmarried spinster and I don't even have cats. "OK."

"I'll call your sister now and I'll let Dr. Murashige know you are on your way. Do you have any other questions?" The coordinator kept her tone light and cheerful.

"No, I guess not. Thanks." Gwenn heard the coordinator hang up, but she shakily kept the phone to her ear. She lost track of time and rocketed to her feet in a panic when her phone buzzed loudly in her ear. "This is Gwenn."

"No shit, I called you." Rachel completely ignored the raw terror in her sister's voice. "Are you ready to go to the hospital? I'll be there in about ten minutes. Are you packed?"

"What?"

"Gwenny, are you OK?"

"I don't think I can do this, Rache. I can't move. I've been sitting in this chair since the hospital called and I can't move." Soft tears cascaded down her alabaster cheeks. "I'm scared."

"OK, I'll be there in five minutes." Rachel ended the call, bundled up in her warm jacket and ran down her back stairs to the waiting bakery van.

***

Shirley carefully placed items in her overnight bag. She had mixed emotions about the transplant. She looked forward to getting rid of the tube in her chest, but she was severely disappointed in God's timing. She had pictured herself standing in front of the congregation and leading them all in a prayer of supplication—unifying them all in a perfect prayer request for a kidney for the pastor's deserving wife.

"Ya ready ta hit the road, Shirl?" Ed's mood had improved. The Lord sure took care of his flock today. He looked forward to standing behind the pulpit on Sunday and sharing the wonderful news with his congregation. He was sure that a story of God using a wayward soul like Gwenn to perform this miracle would bring a tear to a few eyes.

"Keep yer shorts on, Ed. I'm still packin' my suitcase."

"Well, the doctor said to get there as soon as we could."

"I'm sure he didn't expect me ta race down there without a clean pair of underpants, Ed." Shirley placed a few more items in her bag and firmly closed the case. "Okey dokey, can ya take this out ta the car?"

Dutiful and diligent as usual, Ed quickly responded to Shirley's request. He retrieved the packed bag and transported it to the waiting Land Rover. He returned to see what was keeping his wife. "Ya ready? Do ya need some help or somethin'?"

Shirley had affected the most pious pose she could muster—seated on her bed, head bowed, Bible open.

Ed stopped in his tracks when he saw the tableau. "What's got ya so worried?"

"I just don't know if the Lord wants me ta accept Gwenn's kidney—if she's not turnin' away from her sin."

All the husband and father in him wanted to scold Shirley for her ingratitude and drag her to the car, but the pastor in him took the high road. "Shirley, I think the Lord might be using this whole transplant process ta bring Gwenn back ta the fold. I think He would want ya ta play yer part and help Gwenn see His light." He almost mentioned that she wasn't even going to be getting Gwenn's actual kidney, but he thought better of it.

She slowly closed her scriptures and exhaled dramatically. Her bent head nodded and she patted her Bible. "Thy will be done." She placed the tome on her nightstand and rose to follow Ed.

Twenty-four

Rachel burst into Gwenn's apartment like a force of nature. "Gwenny, where are you?" She soon discovered that her sister was still in a catatonic stupor at the kitchen table. "Hey, what's going on? What's wrong with you?"

The blame-laden question snapped Gwenn out of her tonic immobility. "Wrong with me? There's nothing wrong with me. I don't think there's one fucking thing wrong with having second thoughts about giving our lying, hypocritical not-mother one of my kidneys!"

Words alone would not assuage Gwenn's pain. Rachel encircled her sister in a snug, honest embrace and said the only thing that would bring Gwenn out of the swirling eddy of doubt, "Not-mother, huh? That's quite clever, Sis."

A cascade of laughter released the pent up tears. "Freak!"

"Right again." Rachel squeezed the last bit of anxiety out of Gwenn. "Ready?"

"Never."

"Do you want me to pack your suitcase?"

"Are you insane? I would actually like the contents of my suitcase to be neatly folded, not stuffed in like cornbread dressing up a turkey's ass."

"I would have accepted a simple no." Rachel took this opportunity to pout shamelessly. Her sexy full bottom lip protruded and her perfectly plump rear end tipped out suggestively. Unfortunately, there was not a single woman in the room who could appreciate the view.

Gwenn hastily, but immaculately, packed her bag. "OK, let's do this before I change my mind."

"You know, you're not actually giving your kidney to Mom, right? For all you know you could be saving the life of the first woman president of the United States."

"I would love to live inside your head for a day. Is it all rainbows and unicorns?"

"I've always been a pegasus girl. I think it's a lesbian thing...no horns!"

"Oh, shit, you are the best." Gwenn laughed until her cheeks hurt, wiped some joyful teardrops from the corners of her eyes and picked up her overnight bag. "Bring the car 'round," she teased, in her best British accent.

They were nearing the hospital and Gwenn's intense anxiety was manifesting as control. "Park on Second. We can walk down 10th and hopefully avoid Ed and Shirley completely. If I see her and she says one insanely judgmental word to me I will lose my nerve and never come back."

Rachel knew better than to question *The Organizer*. She compliantly found an open meter on Second Street and pulled the van into the spot. "Do you need to call Steven?"

"The coordinator said I would have a few hours, so I'll call him after we check in."

"OK, but there will probably be a bunch of nurses poking and prodding at you...it just might be kinda...you know."

"Inconvenient?"

"I was going to say 'not private,' but yours works, too."

"Come on, let's get this over—"

Rachel indignantly interrupted, "Hey, you don't have to do this, you know. I was going to donate the kidney and then you jumped in front of me. You can always back out."

Tears sluiced down Gwenn's cheeks. "I don't know what's wrong with me. I want you to be able to track down your parents, I want you to have the best possible chance at a pregnancy and I want this anonymous 'recipient' to have the possibility of a healthy life. I just have so much anger at Shirley...I can't get past it, Rache. I can feel it burning inside me."

Rachel climbed across the van and gently, for once, cradled her big sister's head on her shoulder and rubbed her back in the little clockwise circles that had always been reserved for Gwenn's consoling of her. "Just let it out, sweetie, let it out."

As Gwenn released the tears of anger, resentment and fear, her mind slipped back in time. She remembered the day she got the curse. She had gone to the bathroom at school, pulled down her pants and as she sat down on the toilet she noticed a stain in her underwear. Shirley had never had "the talk" with her, but based on Penny and RayAnne's reports she was fairly certain this was the "period" everyone had been talking about. The only thing she could think of was to go to the office and pretend to be sick.

"Hi, Mrs. Donaldson. I need to call my mom...um, I'm... not feeling well."

"Oh, you poor dear. Come back here and let me take your temperature." Mrs. Donaldson was the receptionist, nurse, playground monitor and substitute teacher in their backwater town. "Have a seat over there, dear."

"I'll stand...my back hurts when I sit." Gwenn was not going to take a chance on staining the office furniture with her blood.

The woman looked at her askance, fetched the thermometer and took her temperature. "Well, that looks normal, dear. Do you just need an aspirin?"

"No, I really need to go home. I think I might throw up," Gwenn added to increase the urgency.

"Let me call your mother." She dialed the phone and manifested a huge smile when the call was answered. "Hello, Mrs. Hutchinson, this is Mrs. Donaldson down at the school...well, no she's not in any trouble, ma'am...she said she was ill...well, I..." At this point Gwenn had watched the defeated woman swivel her chair away and whisper conspiratorially, "I think she may have gotten her period." The comment had been met with precisely the motherly concern Mrs. Donaldson had expected. "She wants to talk to you, dear." The receptionist-nurse-teacher smiled as she handed Gwenn the phone.

Once Shirley heard Gwenn's voice, the sugar coating dissolved. "Gwendolyn, this Donaldson woman says you have the curse. Is this true?"

Gwenn mumbled an affirmative.

"Like Eve before her, Lord," Shirley said to no one in particular. She did not rejoice at the thought of her daughter becoming a woman, she simply acknowledged the fulfillment of the biblical curse placed on womankind since the Garden of Eden. "Yer just gonna have ta handle it, Gwendolyn, don't expect me ta drop everything and run ta yer rescue. Women have been carrying this burden fer thousands of years. You'll be dismissed from school in a couple of hours, we'll discuss it then." CLICK.

The look on Gwenn's face must've told the story of her shock, horror and shame.

Mrs. Donaldson took the receiver from Gwenn's hand and bent down to quietly ask, "Did you get your period, dear?"

Gwenn swallowed and blinked back tears.

"It's OK, sweetie, it's perfectly natural—happens to all of us. Let me see if I have something for you in my purse." She dug through her enormous satchel and pulled out a little floral-print zipper pouch. "There's something in here, dear. Just take it to the restroom and bring back the little purse when you're finished. I think you'll figure out what to do."

Gwenn had walked stiffly to the bathroom, unzipped the pouch and had somehow solved the riddle of the maxi-pad. The wad of cotton between her legs mortified her and she begged Mrs. Donaldson to let her sit in the office until school was dismissed, so she could walk home.

"Sweetie, you live out on County Road 18—that's at least five miles. Isn't your mother coming to get you?"

"No, she told me to take the bus."

"Well, I never..." Mrs. Donaldson grabbed her giant satchel-purse and yelled in to the principal, "Walt, I'm taking a sick student home. So, I'll see you tomorrow."

"Confirmed."

She shook her head, murmured a few "tsk-tsks" under her breath and put a comforting arm around Gwenn. "Let's get you home, dear."

An ambulance raced by, siren wailing, and snapped Gwenn back to her current Shirley-related disappointment.

"Do you honestly think the recipient might be the next female president?"

"I swear."

"I love you, Rache. You're my favorite sister." Gwenn snickered through her tears.

"That's not a super great compliment, you know—I'm your only sister."

"Maybe not, remember..." Gwenn gave her one last squeeze and got out of the van.

They walked, hand in mittened hand, to the surgery center.

Twenty-five

Daniel finished the tale of his Mexican standoff, kicked his feet up on his polished burl wood coffee table and waited patiently for Todd's solution.

"How many pieces do I need to retrieve?"

Daniel chuckled. Classic Todd—no comment about the unsavory Elena situation, just a laser focus on securing the valuable artwork. "I had completed three small pieces and had sketches for six more. I didn't start on the larger pieces...but I do need an armoire from Fabrica la Aurora for one of those."

"Do you have a photograph of the armoire in question?"

"Nope."

"I will contact the manager and get the images. I'll arrange for the finished pieces and the sketches to be properly packed and shipped immediately." Todd tapped his fingers distractedly on the arm of the distressed leather club chair. "Is there anything else, sir?"

"If it's not too much trouble, I really liked those swim trunks...the ones I left out by the pool..." Daniel hesitated, "and, thanks for handling all this."

"It's the least I can do after you managed to extract yourself from the predicament." Todd struggled to keep his tone professional.

"Hey, I knew you would have sent Chuck Norris in to Delta-Force me out of there with one phone call...but it was my mess and I thought it was time I cleaned up after myself."

Todd nodded.

"Trust me, if Elena would have made one step toward her father's end of the Hacienda I would have been on the phone faster than greased lightning."

"Thank you, sir." Todd allowed his chest to swell with a centimeter of pride.

"Although, that Elena could give Chuck Norris a run for his money. Damn, that girl is terrifying!" Daniel ran a hand through his honey-brown mane and smirked.

"Let's put it behind us, sir." Anxious to bring up his own agenda, Todd forced a closure on the Mexican adventure.

"Right. What else is on the menu, Todd-ster?"

Todd despised nicknames. He was eternally grateful to his mother for blessing him with a non-shortenable name. "Sir, you know how I feel about nicknames."

"The same way you feel about hats?" Daniel laughed heartily at Todd's expense. The weight of his Latin fling was lifted and he was filled with optimism for his Gwenn-winning.

"Indeed. There is one more thing I wanted to discuss..." Todd hesitated.

"Anything. What's on your mind?"

"Remember when you said, 'some day you'll figure out what you want'?"

"If you're quitting, I will go directly to the nearest bar and drink myself into the grave." Daniel meant the comment to be facetious, but he could not handle the loss of his closest friend.

"Save your declarations for Gwenn. I actually wanted to ask for Gregory North, the gallery in Duluth. Would you be willing to sell it to me as a sort of franchise?"

"Sell it? No, I would not be willing to sell it to you." Daniel slid his feet off the coffee table, unfolded himself to his full 6-foot 3-inch height and fixed Todd with an unreadable stare.

"Sir?"

"I'm offended that you asked. You have earned that gallery ten times over. Draw up the papers, it's yours." Daniel extended his hand toward Todd.

"What are you...which papers did...are you?" A befuddled Todd grasped the warm outstretched hand of his benefactor and rose to his feet. The meaning of Daniel's words sunk in has he stood. "You're giving it to me, free and clear?"

"Sure. You know this stuff better than me. We'll have some kind of agreement about the artwork and branding, but the gallery will be yours." Daniel released Todd's hand and walked toward his kitchen. "Can I get you a whiskey—to celebrate?"

"Just one?"

"Just one," Daniel confirmed. He returned with a Maker's Mark over ice for each of them. "To the best assistant/director/owner in the biz!"

They clinked glasses and returned to their seats.

Todd's brain was already whirring through enough calculations to burn out a microprocessor. "How long do you think it will take Sabina to get up to speed?"

"Oh no, Sabina can't be my personal assistant. I don't do well with women." Daniel raised his eyebrows and then his drink.

"Oh, OK. I will put her in charge of the Gregory Gallery, on Hennepin, and look for a new assistant for you."

"Looks like you're going to have to settle for a demotion." Todd eyed Daniel suspiciously.

"You're just gonna be my friend, now." Daniel smiled wistfully.

"I've always been your friend, sir."

"Yeah, that 'sir' shit is gonna have to stop." He took another sip of his Maker's and smiled. "You've always been like family to me, Todd. Do you think you could find a way to reprogram your operating system and call me 'Daniel'?"

"I will try, s...Daniel."

It felt strange to finally acknowledge the deep bond they had built over the years. Neither of them could remember the exact moment they morphed from *boss and assistant* into *brothers*—but the truth of it was undeniable.

"Well, you better tell Flora the good news and I better get a fix on this whole Gwenn situation." Daniel jumped up and set his unfinished drink on a coaster. "You wanna stay here tonight and drive back tomorrow?"

"I have an apartment down here, sir...I mean Daniel."

"Yeah, I know, but I think we need to have a guys-night-sleepover-type-thing to seal our deal. We can watch action movies, smoke cigars and talk about chicks, right?"

"I don't think guys have sleepovers, but if you agree to refer to it as a *poker night*, I'll stay."

"Done! Make the call, buddy." Daniel slapped him firmly on the back, nearly dislodging Todd's baby blues, mid eye-roll.

Twenty-six

Gwenn stood in the small lavatory of her hospital room. She slipped off her jeans, folded them neatly and added them to the stack of clothes balanced on the edge of the sink. *What if I pull that emergency cord and tell the nurse I changed my mind?* Rachel's soft but insistent pounding on the bathroom door interrupted Gwenn's escape fantasy.

"Gwenny? You OK in there? Did ya fall in?" Rachel chuckled.

The door whizzed open with more force than necessary and narrowly missed Rachel. "Hilarious. I've heard that joke for over twenty years and it's refreshingly hilarious every time." Gwenn glared at Rachel as she slipped her folded clothes into a plastic bag and fiddled with their positioning in her open suitcase.

"I'm just tryin' to lighten the mood—"

BUZZ BUZZ BUZZ!

Gwenn's vibrating phone interrupted Rachel's excuse-planation.

"Is it Steven?"

"Daniel." Gwenn stared at Rachel and willed her sister to tell her to let it go to voicemail.

"You should answer it. If he can't get ahold of you he'll start calling me and I'll crack like an egg when he puts the pressure on." Rachel shrugged her shoulders in a half-hearted apology.

Gwenn closed her eyes, drew in a deep breath and answered the call. "Hi, Daniel. I'm sorry, but now isn't a good time."

His mind bubbled with thoughts of all the things he wanted to say—all the ways he wanted to push his way back into Gwenn's life, but Dr. Mountainside's words rang in his head, "You'll have to show her your heart." OK, time to put that plan into action. "Hey, is everything OK? You sound... scared." He wasn't sure if that's what he heard in her voice but something he was learning to call his *men-tuition* told him she was afraid.

She blinked back tears and responded factually. "I don't really have time...I'm just about to go into surgery to donate a kidney. I don't have time to go into all the details. I'll be recuperating at my Gramma's cabin for several weeks and I won't be reachable. My apologies, but I don't have time to get into it right now." She looked at Rachel and her gaze pleaded for moral support.

"So, you're saying you don't have time, right now?" Daniel chuckled lightly, hoping to send some softness through the phone.

Gwenn laughed, in spite of her pre-surgical terror. "Thanks, I needed that."

"I won't keep you, I just wanted to see if you could recommend a new personal assistant—but it's a long story and you need to focus. Would it be OK if I call Rachel to get an update? I mean, I don't expect you to call the minute you get out of surgery...but I'll kinda be pacing around until I hear something."

She smiled and nodded as she responded, "Rachel's right here, so she can hear me giving you permission to call and check on my post-surgical status—and *only* that status. Don't pump her for any additional info, she's weak." Gwenn smiled and winked at Rachel.

Rachel whispered, "Bitch."

Gwenn gave her a knowing smirk.

"Your terms are acceptable, Miss Hutchinson. I'd tell you I'd pray for you, but I know that would just piss you off. So...you better come out the other side of this thing or I'll drive up there and...well, just make it, OK?"

"That's my plan. I gotta go, Daniel. Thanks for calling. Bye." Gwenn pressed *end*.

"So what's up with Bachelor Number One?"

"Oh, ha ha." Gwenn climbed into the hospital bed and fussed with her blanket. "Don't joke, OK. Daniel is just a friend now. He was being *friendly* by showing his concern. When he calls just give him the facts about the surgery, don't answer any questions about Steven. Got it?"

"10-4, Captain."

"Time for you to go get a coffee, plebe. I'd like to call Steven without any commentary from the peanut gallery." Gwenn flicked her hand at Rachel, encouraging her to exit immediately.

Rachel took her leave, but not without a wag of her impudent tongue.

Gwenn placed her next call and listened to the ringing. Her mind drifted off to visions of dying on the operating table and she completely missed the beep indicating she should leave a voicemail. When she realized the ringing had stopped she murmured an unnecessary apology, hung up and redialed Steven.

"Hey, Gwenn. You got me worried when I saw the second call. I didn't answer the first time 'cuz Auntie M and I are playing Scrabble. She normally doesn't allow interruptions," Steven laughed.

She could hear his aunt protesting the taunting Wizard of Oz-ish nickname in the background. She knew Steven's Aunt Miriam was a formidable Scrabble opponent—Gwenn had suffered many defeats, back in the day.

"Is there an emergency?"

"I'm at the hosp—"

"I'll be there as fast as I can. Are you OK? Can I bring you anything? Should I call your sister?"

"Steven, sit down." It came out with a harshness Gwenn did not feel, but she had no other ideas on how to stop the locomotive. "Wow! You really do just switch into crisis-management mode, don't you?"

"Yeah, it's hard to shake the reactionary impulses. So if you're OK, why are you at the hospital? You were going to say 'hospital'—before I rudely interrupted you, right?"

"Yes, I am at the hospital. They found a recipient for my kidney, so I'm going under the knife in about three hours."

"Shit!"

Gwenn heard a gasp in the background, on Steven's end of the line.

"Sorry, Auntie M...Aunt Miriam, sorry."

There was a delay and some shuffling noises.

"OK, I'm upstairs in my room. I have complete access to the English language up here. Please continue." Steven's breath came in quick puffs.

The heavy breathing gave Gwenn a mini-flashback to their tawdry romp. She forced herself to focus—worried that any increased heart rate would bring a nurse to her bedside. "The surgery is considered routine. I'll call you when the anesthesia wears off."

"I'll come down and wait. I'd like to be there when you wake up."

"I know, and that's sweet, but we talked about this. I'm going up to the cabin and you're going to schedule some neurofeedback. Remember?"

"No," he lied.

"Well, then, you really do need to get your head checked out. Seems like you may have some short term memory issues developing."

"I remember the taste of your skin. I remember the feel of you sliding—"

"Ahem." Gwenn cleared her throat and fought to hold onto her rapidly evaporating resolve. "Me—cabin. You—sessions."

Steven paced around his room and fiddled with chotskies on his bookshelf. "You're gonna call me, though. I mean you can't expect me to let go of you now—after all I've been through."

"Give me a couple weeks to get past the initial pain and healing phase. I don't want to say something stupid when I'm half-baked on pain meds. I just want to focus on recovering and getting back to work."

"You afraid you might invite me up to the cabin, to play doctor?"

Gwenn laughed, "Yes, that's my greatest fear. Seriously, though, I do need the time. Can you respect that?"

"Absolutely...on one condition."

"You and your frickin' conditions. What is it this time?"

"If you let me come down there right now and give you a good luck kiss, I will promise to be a good soldier and leave you alone for a couple weeks. Deal?"

She looked down at her pinky, wriggled it, rolled her eyes back and agreed. "Deal. I'll see you in—" The line went dead and Gwenn calculated she would see Steven in approximately 12 minutes. She was about to text Rachel the "all clear" when Dr. Watkins' number flashed onto the screen. "Hello?"

"Gwenn, It's Dr. Watkins. Do you have a minute?"

Twenty-seven

Ed held Shirley's elbow as he walked her into the Emergency entrance. She had insisted on walking by herself, but Ed threatened to get a nurse and a wheelchair if she didn't submit to some assistance.

They approached the clean modern desk and the overworked nurse spoke without looking up from her stack of charts. "What's the nature of your emergency?"

"Shirley Hutchinson, we're here fer a kidney transplant." Pastor Ed took offense to the young woman's lack of respect for her elders, but he told himself God would prefer if he didn't make a scene.

The nurse glanced up briefly and returned to her task. "You'll need to check in at Campus A."

Unfortunately for the nurse, Shirley had not heard the Lord's preferences, like Ed. "Young lady?" She waited for the nurse to look up. "I'm sure ya have much more important things ta do than help a dyin' woman find her way around the hospital, but I'm pretty sure there's an expiration date on that there kidney and I wouldn't want ta keep the *surgeon* waiting." She emphasized the word surgeon like he was a personal friend. Shirley exhaled and fell weakly onto the counter. A consummate performance.

"Yes ma'am. Sorry, the night nurse called in sick and I'm just so backed up with charts...let me get a wheelchair and I'll call an orderly to assist you in getting to the surgery center." She picked up the phone, punched in a code and made the necessary announcements over the intercom. "Do you know your surgeon's name, ma'am?"

"Yes, Dr. Murashige." Shirley smiled smugly.

The exhausted nurse had no intention of confronting Shirley with the fact that Dr. Murashige was a nephrologist and not a transplant surgeon—that he simply dictated her care plan and would not even be in the theater. "I'll let him know you've arrived."

The orderly rushed in with the wheelchair.

"Darryl, can you please take Mrs. Hutchinson to the Campus A surgery center? She's here for an urgent kidney transplant. Give her the V-I-P treatment." When Shirley turned to grace the orderly with her smile, the nurse gave Darryl a huge wink.

Ed pretended to miss the entire exchange. "Thank you, we'll be on our way."

Shirley attempted to control the speed of the wheelchair through a series of "slow down" epithets hurled at Darryl.

He never endangered her person, but he got his VIP to the surgery center in record time. He wheeled her up to the nearest nurse and announced, without fanfare, "Kidney transplant." He could hear his VIP sputtering behind him as he casually walked back to his interrupted donut.

Ed arrived a few moments later, huffing and puffing.

Twenty-eight

Gwenn glanced out to the hallway, desperate to hand off this phone call. *Where the F is Rachel?* "Actually they're prepping me for surgery, Dr. Watkins. I'm at the hospital, about to donate a kidney."

"Well, I'm glad I caught you. I have some news for your sister. Should I call her directly?"

Movement caught Gwenn's attention. "She just walked in. Can I put you on speaker phone?"

"Sure." He waited for a cue from Gwenn.

"OK, Dr. Watkins. What did you find out?"

"My friend's wife, Corrine, found Rachel's mother—"

"Holy shit! That's awesome!" Rachel circled her hips in a celebratory dance.

Gwenn took the reins. "What do we do next?"

"It sounds like you will be in surgery and recovery, Gwenn. However, Rachel has been invited to Chicago to meet her mother this weekend, if she feels ready."

"I'm more than ready. What about my mom, though, does she want to meet me?"

"According to Corrine your birth mother has always wanted to meet you. There was something in your file… Corrine will have all the details. Should I text you the contact information?"

"For my mom?" Rachel blurted.

"No, excuse me, I meant for Corrine. She is a licensed Intermediary and she will facilitate the meeting with your birth mother."

"Yes, Doctor, go ahead and send over Corrine's info. Thank you so much for your help, I know we never would have gotten this far on our own." Gwenn smiled at Rachel and reached out for a hug.

"All right, good luck to both of you." Dr. Watkins ended the call.

Rachel squeezed Gwenn until the phone buzzed with the promised contact details for Corrine.

"Should I call her right now?" Rachel grabbed a strand of purple-streaked hair and chewed on it desperately.

"Rache, stop that! You haven't chewed on your hair since you were like nine. It's gross." Gwenn leaned forward on the bed and swatted at Rachel's hand. "Just call her, if she's busy it will go to voicemail."

"I'm so nervous!"

"She wants to help you, Rache. Why are you nervous?"

"What if my real mom is even worse than Shirley? What if she thinks I'm fat or rejects me for being gay?"

"First of all there's no way she's worse than Shirley and second of all you're not fat…you're in winter shape."

"What if she rejects me, though?"

"We don't need any more haters in our life. If she's not willing to accept you—on your terms—then we walk away."

Tears welled up in Rachel's big brown eyes. "I just want her to love me, Gwenny. I can't take rejection…not from her."

"Call Annie, right now. Make sure she can go with you, OK?" Gwenn was furious with the useless technology of cloning. If you couldn't make duplicates of yourself at the drop of a hat—when you definitely needed to be in two places at once—what good was it? "Rache, call Annie, you can't do this by yourself and I'm about to get butchered, so—"

"I made it!" Steven burst into the room a full three minutes ahead of Gwenn's calculations. He looked at the expressions on the sisters' faces and immediately reacted. "What happened? What's wrong?"

"I'm fine, and 'hello' by the way." Gwenn looked at Rachel and gave her one last nudge. "Go call Annie, and get your butt back here before they wheel me off."

"Yeah, Annie...good call." Rachel shuffled off in a daze.

"What's with Smart Ass? She didn't even bear-hug me."

"She just got the OK to meet her birth mother, this weekend...and I can't be there for her. This kidney donation decision has got some serious suck-i-tude."

"What about you? Are you looking for your real mom?"

"Nope. I've got my hands full just looking for the 'real me'." Gwenn was not ready to share the DNA disaster that led her to Daniel—not today, maybe not ever.

Steven grew quiet and shoved both hands in his pockets. He looked around the room, back to Gwenn and fixed his gaze on the floor.

"What? What did I say?"

"No, no it's not that...it's just...well, I have to...I mean, I want to...oh, hell." Steven dropped down on one knee and proffered the memory-fused ring to Gwenn. "Gwendolyn Hutchinson, will you make the hopes and dreams of a broken man come true? Will you give me the only thing in the world that matters to me...will you marry me?"

The abrupt segue and the oddly inappropriate venue threw Gwenn into a tailspin. She could not find her voice. Her heart raced. Her breathing ceased.

Steven jumped to his feet, dropped the ring and grabbed Gwenn by the shoulders. "Gwenn? Gwenn, you have to breathe!" He reached for the *Call* button as Rachel blew into the room.

"What the hell? What's wrong with her?" Rachel saw the open ring box on the bed and leapt into action. SLAP!

Gwenn gasped for breath and fixed Rachel with a dangerous stare. "Fuck! That hurt like a mother...damn, Rachel."

"Swear at me all you want. It worked, didn't it?"

Steven released his hold on Gwenn and clumsily scooped up the ring box.

Unable to let the incident lie, Rachel pounced. "And the award for Most Awkwardly Timed Proposal goes to..."

Fear gripped his chest. He pushed it away and the terror morphed into anger—molten, swirling anger. He threw the ring box against the wall and collapsed into a chair. He was hyperventilating and he could not get control.

Gwenn climbed out of the bed and approached him cautiously. "Steven, can you hear me?"

He nodded, gasping for air.

"Put your head between your knees. Take slow, deep breaths." She put her hand on his back and gently pushed him forward.

He tensed and resisted. Her touch breached the fog and he softened.

Rachel retrieved the ring. "Sorry, I can be mildly oblivious." She handed the ring box to Gwenn, but Gwenn waved it away and gestured for Rachel to put the talisman on the bed.

Steven inhaled deeply, and mumbled from his hunched position, "It's OK, Smart Ass, I'll survive." He would survive. Somehow he always managed to survive, but what he wanted was to thrive. A wife, children, a house—a life.

Gwenn removed her hand from his back and sat on the edge of her hospital bed. "Rache, sweetie, we need a moment. Is everything OK with Annie?"

"It's fucking fantastic. I'll be back in a few." Rachel shrugged her shoulders and mouthed, "Are you OK?" as she backed out of the room.

Gwenn nodded and returned her attention to Steven. "Can you talk?"

"Yep." He raised his head and looked at Gwenn like a dog that had just destroyed a $400 pair of stilettos. "I really threw a boomerang into things, didn't I?"

"A boomerang?" Gwenn couldn't help but laugh. "Sorry, I know I shouldn't laugh, but I think the saying is a 'monkey wrench.' A boomerang comes back to the person who throws it." She laughed even harder as her over-active imagination pictured the boomerang bouncing back.

"That's kinda what happened, though. It came back and damn near knocked me out." Steven found some relief in chuckling at himself.

Gwenn pointed to the ring box. "What were you thinking?"

"I wasn't, I guess. I just thought if something goes wrong...I didn't want to lose you...I wanted you to know how I felt before you went under the knife." His eyes filled with longing and regret.

"That's not a real encouraging sentiment. It's a routine surgery. Try to think positive, for my sake at least."

"It's not like that...I...it's been...shit." Steven closed his eyes, took three deep breaths and shook his arms and hands to release the stress. "I held my tongue too many times. I thought there would always be a tomorrow, but when you are locked in a dark, disgusting cell for years on end—the future is nothing more than illusion."

She nodded, silently. There were no words to explain away his fear, no words to assure his future. She could not accept that proposal because she might die in the operating room—that was not how she wanted to build their relationship.

He was damaged and he wanted her to help him rebuild the life he thought he had lost. He kept pushing, rushing, forcing—failing. A tiny voice in his head told him to respect the boundaries that had been set and find a way to be patient. He hated that voice—utterly.

"I'll call you from the recovery room, OK?"

He stood up, snatched the ring box off the bed and shoved it into his pocket. He gave a small Jedi wave of his hand and said, "These aren't the droids you're looking for...you can go about your business."

Guilt weighed down on her, but she pushed it away and jumped off the bed to wrap him in her arms. She could feel the firm planes of his chest through her thin hospital gown. Warmth surged through her girly parts. "I have so much history with you, all the memories, the call backs, the good and the bad. I need time to figure out if we can build a future. You had all those terrible years in Afghanistan to figure out what you wanted. Can you give me a few weeks up at the cabin to do the same?"

His hands wandered and he squeezed her ass. He knew he wasn't imagining the stiff nipples poking into his chest. He excited her and that made him reckless with desire. "What do you say to one last pre-surgical quickie?"

She struggled to create space between them, but his grip on her ass tightened. She was forced to speak into his neck. "Steven, be serious. This is not happening. Not here. Not now. Release me." She squirmed until he loosened his hold.

"I thought there were some signals," he teased.

"Yeah, there were some signals, but I'm not a sex-in-the-hospital-bed girl. Sorry to disappoint."

"You could never disappoint me—unless you turn down my proposal." He pulled her close and whispered in her ear, "I can be very persuasive."

His hot breath sent sparks of need shooting down her spine. The way the hairs stood up on the back of her neck was so intense it made her shiver. She bit his neck and pressed her body tightly to his. "I guess you better hope for the best in that operating room...I'd hate to cross over and leave you with blue balls."

He chuckled, but nodded in agreement. "Yes, that would be quite unpleasant. There's nothing worse than an erection at a funeral."

"Steven!" Gwenn pulled away and punched him in the shoulder.

"Ow!" He laughed and rubbed the point of impact. "Mercy! Mercy!" He put his hands up in surrender.

"I'll call you, once—but you have to promise to let me have some time to myself?"

"I swear on my mother's kugel." Steven extended his pinky.

Gwenn hooked his pinky with hers and sealed their contract with a kiss.

Twenty-nine

Dr. Andreas looked down at Gwenn and asked, "Did you want to see your mother before your surgery?"

"No." She had answered too quickly. "I mean, no, thank you."

"OK, I will let the anesthesiologist do her thing and we'll get started. So, did you have any more questions for me?"

"The, um, CO_2 gas that you have to pump into my abdomen...will it hurt?"

"The gas itself will not hurt. You may experience some discomfort over the next two weeks as the gas dissipates. Your abdomen will be distended, as we discussed, and some patients have reported stiffness in their shoulders. If you have any unmanageable pain or increased redness at the incision site, you should contact us immediately."

Gwenn could not see the doctor's mouth behind the surgical mask, but she knew there was a warm and patient smile. The confidence in Dr. Andreas' eyes filled her with trust. She was ready to give her kidney to the next female president of the United States. *Rachel, what a nutter.*

"Actually, can I see my sister one more time—before you put me under?"

"Certainly, I understand she is lurking outside the door and refusing to return to the waiting room. I can't allow her into the sterile room, but I'll ask the nurse to have her peek through the window. Sound good?"

"Sorry, thanks."

Dr. Andreas turned her stocky frame toward the surgical nurse and within 30 seconds Rachel's goofy face could be seen through the porthole in the door to the surgical theater.

Gwenn smiled and waved—holding back the tears she knew would bring Rachel catapulting through the sterile barrier.

Rachel waved and planted a kiss directly on the glass.

She watched her sister quickly disappear as an orderly in the hallway most certainly coerced Rachel to return to the waiting area. Gwenn was as ready as she could ever be—terrified, but ready. "OK, knock me out." She clenched her fists and failed miserably at slowing her breathing.

The masked face of the anesthesiologist popped into view and a calm, commanding voice asked her to count backward from 100.

"100, 99, 98, 97..." And she was out.

***

Shirley insisted on praying, out loud, for everyone in the operating room before she would allow the anesthesiologist to put her under.

Two of the nurses exchanged a look, but the surgeon—who was not Dr. Murashige—stepped back from the tray of instruments and nodded his approval.

She folded her hands prayerfully over her hospital gown and closed her eyes. She let a moment of silence lie in the room and hoped it would encourage eye-closing-compliance. "Dear Lord, I submit myself ta Yer grace. I ask that Ya guide this surgeon's hands, that Yer will might be done here, today. I ask that Ya fill each of these nurses with Yer spirit and forgive them if they have sinned against Ya, Lord. We are all here ta serve You, and protect Yer Word on this earth. We're all sinners in Yer eyes, Lord, and we accept the blessed sacrifice of Yer Son, that all of us might serve a higher purpose. In Yer name we pray, amen."

The surgeon, a devout Muslim, nodded respectfully when Shirley completed her supplication. "And now we'll sedate you and begin the transplant, Mrs. Hutchinson."

"Yes, go right ahead."

As soon as Shirley stopped counting backward from 100, the surgical nurse looked at Dr. Bashara and asked, "Why didn't you stop her? That was about ten kinds of rude."

"When a patient is faced with their mortality, it is not my place to prevent them from connecting to the source of their strength."

The nurse lowered her eyes and busily straightened the surgical tools on their sterile blue drape.

"Scalpel." Dr. Bashara had no admonition in his voice. He trusted in the balance of the universe and felt blessed, in his own life, to have been given the gift of healing the sick. He held no ill will toward his patient, or his misguided nurse. He grasped the scalpel, cleared his mind and dropped into the quiet space within—the place from which he performed all of his surgeries.

***

Dr. Andreas stepped back and surveyed her work. "Laparoendoscopic single-port donor nephrectomy, successful." She handed the surgical endocatch bag, containing Gwenn's left kidney, to the waiting nurse. "Let's get this to the recipient. Good work, everyone."

"Nicely done, Doc." The anesthesiologist surveyed the beautiful closure sutures on the umbilicus and nodded. "In a couple months that will be damn near invisible. You are a magician." She made her final check of the patient and released Gwenn to the recovery nurse.

Thirty

Rachel had weaseled her way out of the waiting area and verbally tackled the nurse as soon as Gwenn was rolled out of the surgical theater. "Is she OK? Did the surgery work? Where's her kidney? How long 'til she wakes up?"

"Are you family?"

A few weeks ago Rachel wouldn't have given her answer a second thought. After the strange revelations of the Kidney Chronicles she had to pause. Legally she was Gwenn's sister, technically they were *family*—but genetically...

"Miss, are you a relative?"

"Yes, I'm her sister." Blood might be thicker than water, but choice was indestructible. Rachel and Gwenn had chosen to be in each other's lives. Rachel followed the nurse to a recovery room. "How long till she wakes up?"

"Everyone metabolizes medications differently, but emergence generally occurs in 30 minutes, for most people. However, she may still be groggy from the pain meds. I'll be back to check on her. Can I get you any water?"

"Me? Oh, no, I'm fine. Thanks."

The nurse bustled off to continue her duties.

Rachel stared at Gwenn. She chewed her lip, looked out the window and bounced her foot on the linoleum. She checked the time on her phone. An entire three minutes had passed. She decided to call Daniel.

"Rachel? I hope this is good news." Daniel paced back and forth across the Brazilian hardwood floor in his kitchen.

"She's out of surgery and I guess everything went OK. She's still knocked out, but I thought you'd want an update."

"Yeah, thanks. Waiting is a helpless feeling."

"Tell me about it. The rude nurses kept shooing me back to the waiting room and I kept sneaking back to the surgery area. I just wanted to be close, in case she needed me...ya know."

Daniel swallowed hard, stopped pacing and leaned down onto the granite countertop. "Yeah, I know exactly what you mean." Silence hung between them.

"Hey, what the hell happened?"

"Steven happened, I thought you knew."

"I never would have sent him to Mexico if I thought he had a real chance..." Rachel's words faded as she realized Daniel might not know about her role in releasing The Steven.

"You sent him?"

"He would've found her anyway." She knew it sounded defensive, but she was not about to take the blame for whatever happened between him and Gwenn.

"Maybe, I guess. I thought you were on my side."

"I was...am...was. I told him Gwenn was in a good relationship and that she was really happy. I didn't think he stood a chance. I never...I...what happened?"

"Elena." Daniel pushed himself off the counter and rubbed the bridge of his nose. He opened a polished zebra wood cabinet and grasped an old fashioned glass.

All of Rachel's affair-inflicted wounds winced. She thought of the painful moment when Annie had leaned down from the stage and kissed Blue Bangs. "You cheated? On Gwenny?"

"Not exactly..." Daniel removed his hand from the glass and closed the cupboard. He grabbed a bottle of dry cucumber soda from the refrigerator and rummaged through a jumbled drawer of utensils in search of a bottle opener.

"I'm no expert on breeder sex, but I can't figure out how you could kinda cheat, so you better explain."

He laughed at Rachel's clumsy inquest. "How long till she wakes up?"

"Oh, you've got time. Spin your tale, Canterbury."

"It was Chaucer...never mind." Daniel settled into one of his Safavieh birch wood dining chairs and spilled his guts. He told Rachel about trying to take the high road and give Gwenn space, he told her about choosing to stay in Mexico instead of chasing Gwenn back to Duluth, and finally he told her about his poor use of Elena as an emotional salve, when he got the fateful call from Gwenn.

"Wow. What did Elena do?"

"She threatened to have her father kill me."

"Shit. No wonder you got outta there so fast...oh, she's waking up. I gotta go."

Gwenn turned toward Rachel's voice and blinked hard. She could see Rachel but her brain refused to give her any additional information. She was aware of her body, but she was not in her body. Her fingers would not respond to her urgent need to scratch her nose and her vocal cords refused to vibrate. She stared at Rachel and blinked furiously.

"Gwenny, are you OK? Why are you blinking like a debutante on crack?"

She wanted to swallow, but there was a burning in her throat. Gwenn knew her heart should be racing, but she felt like a wooden doll. She continued to put all her energy into blinking.

"I don't know what to do, Gwenny." Rachel looked around for a poster or pamphlet that would explain how to handle the recently drugged. Nothing. Her eyes landed on the call button and she hastily sent the signal for a nurse.

A blur of lavender scrubs rushed into the room and systematically checked Gwenn's vitals.

Rachel leaned over the bed, determined to understand the actions of the ultra-efficient nurse. "Is she gonna make it?"

No Nonsense Lavender turned and fixed Rachel with an unreadable gaze. "Why did you push the button?"

"She was blinking like a crazy person. She wouldn't move...or speak. I thought she was seizing." The only *Grey's Anatomy* word she could remember.

"She was not *seizing.* She is emerging from anesthesia and muscle control is slowly returning. She cannot speak because she was intubated during surgery and her throat may be in a state of discomfort." No Nonsense Lavender slipped her pen in her pocket and walked toward the door. "Offer her water...there." She gestured to a mauve plastic pitcher and a cup/straw combo. She exited without further explanation.

Tears were leaking out of the corners of Gwenn's eyes. She wasn't sad, she was laughing at Rachel's pseudo medical speak and it hurt to laugh.

Rachel fumbled with the water, spilled a little on Gwenn and finally managed to get the straw in her sister's mouth.

The cool liquid was a balm to her stinging sore throat. She took two long draws on the straw before she panicked. *If I drink, I'll have to pee. If I have to pee, I'll have to get up. I can't get up. I'll pee the bed.* She blinked rapid-fire imaginary Morse code to Rachel.

Luckily Rachel noticed the blinking and removed the straw. "Can you talk yet?"

A scratchy whisper escaped Gwenn's lips, "Freak."

Rachel burst into tears. "I want to hug you, but I know I'll end up breaking something. Oh, this is just the worst." She stood up and walked back and forth.

Gwenn swallowed and attempted a few more words. "Yeah...not hugging...the worst." A raspy gurgle shook her shoulders. "Ow, ow ow."

"Don't laugh. You shouldn't laugh."

"Your fault," she whimpered.

"Me?"

Gwenn pointed to the machines, the IV in her hand and finally at her throat. "No hugs...the worst."

A nose-snorting guffaw held Rachel in its clutches. "Omycrap that was stupid. OK, maybe kidney swiping is worse."

More giggle-induced tears oozed out of her eyes and Gwenn forced herself to stop laughing. The pain was faint, but she knew it was buried under layers of opioids. She didn't want to tear any stitches...or worse.

"I called Daniel to tell him you made it. He sounded super relieved." Rachel decided to omit the details of the lengthy conversation.

"Steven?"

"I think he's been a good boy. I didn't see him skulking around and he didn't try to call me. Should I check your phone?"

Gwenn nodded.

Rachel dug through Gwenn's suitcase.

Gwenn felt her muscles tense as she watched Rachel un-organize her entire bag. She wanted to yell, "It's on top of the notebook in the back left corner," but her recuperating throat would not comply. Eventually, Rachel recovered the phone.

"Found it!" Rachel wiggled the phone at her *emerging* sister. "Only 15 missed calls from Steven. Want me to call?"

"Then I'll talk...water?" Gwenn's throat stung.

Rachel maneuvered the water, sans spill, and let Gwenn get a couple good sips before she pulled it away to call Steven.

"Finally! I'm goin' crazy over here," Steven blurted.

"Hello to you, too, Mr. Hays."

"Hello, Smart Ass. Why are you calling from Gwenn's phone? Is she OK?"

"She's fine...just wakin' up...can't talk much."

"Did they have to intubate?"

"Impressive, were you a medic in the Army?"

"Geez, Rache. That was insulting on so many levels. First of all, I'm a Marine—that's nothing like the Army. Secondly, they're called Corpsman, 'Doc' for short. Now back to our patient, is she all right?"

"Yeah, she's *emerging*, or some crap. She can't move much yet and her throat is sore. She wants to talk to you, but she kinda has to whisper, OK?"

"Understood."

Rachel held the phone to the side of Gwenn's face. "OK, she's listening."

"Are you in pain? I wish I could hold you."

Gwenn didn't have the mental capacity or the verbal acuity to respond like she wanted, so she settled for a muffled, "Yeah."

"I can be there in 10 minutes, if you want me."

"No...thank you."

"OK, I won't push. Thanks for calling. I'll be missing you like crazy, so if you ever get too lonely up at that cabin—you call me, OK?"

"OK." Gwenn shook her head at Rachel to indicate she was finished.

"All right Sarge, that's it, the patient needs to rest."

"Thanks for the call...oh, tell her I'm gonna make an appointment. She'll know what it means."

"You got it. Take care." Rachel ended the call on Gwenn's phone and set it on the bedside table. "He said to tell you he's gonna make his appointment. Make sense?"

Gwenn nodded carefully and mouthed, "Turn it off."

"You afraid he'll get weak and call you back?"

"No, me."

Thirty-one

Ed sat uncomfortably in the small chair next to Shirley's hospital bed. He balanced a Bible on one knee and a notebook on the other—chewing on the end of his pen, deep in thought. This week's sermon was shaping up to be a doozy. He had managed to create a loaves-and-fishes style miracle out of Shirley's transplant and Gwenn's donation. The gilding on the wings would be Gwenn coming back to the Lord, but one miracle was enough for Pastor Ed—on this day.

Shirley stirred and mumbled. She was drifting back to consciousness and her first thought was of her new kidney. She hoped it was a Christian kidney.

"Hey, Dad. How's the patient?" Rachel breezed into the room full of smiles.

Ed ventured a glance toward Shirley and whispered, "No ornerier than usual." He chuckled, folded up his materials and stood up to hug his daughter. "How's Trixie holdin' up?"

"If you mean Gwenn, she came through like a champ. I just came to make sure Mom was OK before I take off."

"Headin' back ta the bakery?" He lowered himself back into the chair. The drain of Shirley's illness and surgery lined his face.

"Not exactly...I'm going to Chicago."

"What takes ya ta the Windy City?"

"I'm going...actually I have an appointment..." Rachel lost her nerve. "Annie is playing a concert there and I promised to show up and support her and the band." The lie tasted better in her mouth than the truth.

Still rather uncomfortable with Rachel's girlfriend situation, Ed opted for a solemn silent nod.

"So my brush with death has done nothin' ta right yer walk with the Lord? You're still plannin' on continuing down this road ta Hell?" Shirley's voice was not loud or strong, but the sting of her words needed no such aid.

Rachel jumped and the hairs on the back of her neck stood on end. It felt like the scene in a movie when the horrible nemesis—who just got shot 50 times—crashes through the window to continue their killing spree. "Mom, I didn't know you were awake."

"Bring me the water, Ed." Shirley coughed and swallowed.

Ed fetched the water and stood by her side while she took several sips.

"That's better." Shirley waved the water away. "Don't let me keep ya from yer date with the Devil." She turned her face from Rachel.

"I just came to make sure you were OK...Mom." Rachel uttered the last word begrudgingly. "If this is 'meeting us halfway', Shirley—don't bother." She turned to leave, looked back and added, "Bye, Dad."

If Rachel had known that would be the last time she would see Shirley alive, she may have chosen a different *adieu*. Unfortunately, there are no do-overs in life. Each moment approaches, passes and is woven into the tapestry.

Todd carried the last of his boxes into Flora's apartment. She closed the door behind him and surveyed his possessions. "Is that it?"

"Single guy, living alone, working 100 hours a week—what would I need?"

"Gosh, I hope you won't be working 100 hours a week up here."

Todd pulled Flora close and kissed her perfectly plump lips. "I'm gonna have trouble working one hour a week if you keep this up."

"Keep up what?"

"Being so sexy."

Flora blushed profusely and her long lashes shielded her eyes from his probing look.

"Don't look away. It's true, you're sexy." Todd pulled her back toward his body and lightly kissed her eyelid. "Let's put a pin in this and get my meager belongings put away."

She swallowed, smoothed her hair and smiled. "OK."

Todd grabbed his two large suitcases and walked up the stairs. He stopped halfway and turned to look back. "Is it OK if I hang some stuff up in the closet? I'll just leave the rest in the suitcase. I have to buy a new dresser, my old one wasn't worth moving."

"Oh, gosh, sure...yeah. I'll come up with you and make some room." Flora scurried anxiously after Todd. She hadn't given the details of living together much thought. It simply had not occurred to her that Todd would have things, and his things would have to fit into her place—with her things.

Todd flopped the suitcases onto her bed and unzipped the older, larger bag. "Not too much stuff, just a couple suits, some slacks and a few oxfords."

Flora looked at the wad of clothes bulging out of the open bag and raced into her closet. She stared at the perfectly spaced wooden hangers, gently supporting a carefully pressed and sorted array of pantsuits—and froze.

Todd happily followed her into the closet with a handful of items on metal, dry cleaners' hangers. He reached up and roughly slid a row of her suits to the left and squeezed his items onto the bar. "Perfect. Just a couple more trips and we can head back downstairs."

Flora pressed her back into the wall and her eyes darted from the perfectly spaced end of the closet to the jumbled, crammed end. She thought she might hyperventilate. She heard him returning with another handful of insipid intruders and she sprang into action. Carefully sliding her clothes down toward the *perfect* end of the closet, she was able to make an adequate opening for the remainder of Todd's clothes.

"Thanks, that looks great." Todd placed his hands on his hips and nodded appreciatively at Flora's handiwork.

"OK, back downstairs. We should have this knocked out before dinner."

The full impact of *thing integration* seeped into Flora's consciousness. She would have to remain on high alert—one step ahead. The precious organization of her eco-system depended on it.

Todd hustled downstairs and grabbed a box of his books. He carried it over to Flora's bookshelf and thumbed through the contents. "Wow, I haven't looked at some of these personal development books in years. Now that I'm climbing into the business owner's seat I better take a refresher course."

An entire box of self-improvement books. Flora tipped her head in wonderment. She imagined Todd voraciously devouring each book, highlighting passages and making notes in the margins. She watched as he grabbed two or three books at a time and squeezed each handful in between the alphabetized books on her shelf. Once again, panic gripped her and she responded.

He pretended not to notice how she grabbed each book he had placed and carefully re-shelved it. He feigned disinterest when she offered to finish putting the books away so he could make them a snack. "So, how about if I make us some cheese and crackers? Any special kitchen instructions?" He lobbed the question over his shoulder as he walked out of the living room. It was an actual question, but not the real question—the one burning in his mind.

"Sounds great, cheese will be in the middle drawer in the fridge—in expiration date order—oldest at the front."

"Got it." Todd applied intense self-restraint and canceled the eye roll queuing up in his orbital sockets.

Flora emptied the box of books and retrieved another box. An entire box of shoes—shiny stinky shoes. *Oh dear!* She decided to stuff dryer sheets into each shoe and come up with a good reason to house the collection in the downstairs coat closet—far away from her precious silk blouses.

By the time Todd returned with the well-plated snack, Flora was down to the final cardboard container.

"Are these records? Like actual vinyl records?"

Todd turned toward the box and smiled softly. His eyes drifted to a distant memory and he slowly exhaled. "Originally it was just my mom's old collection, but over the years I started hitting vintage stores and now about half of those are mine. I have a record player, but I couldn't fit it in the car. I'll grab it in the next week or two when I'm in Minneapolis. I still have three months left on my lease...so no rush."

Flora knew the sacred ranking of the possessions of the dead. She had an entire drawer filled with her departed sister's T-shirts and a shelf full of books they read together, by flashlight. She looked at all the DVDs and Blu-rays stacked under her television. "I can put all those old movies in a box and we could put the records in the TV stand. Is that OK?"

He felt the connection—the respect for lost loved ones. "That would be great." He watched as she packed up the movies and wiped out the stand. He struggled to contain the unfamiliar emotion of deep gratitude and blurted, "My mom would have loved you."

She turned her tear-filled face toward this man who had filled her life with so much more than boxes of things, and replied, "My sister, Laura, would have been crazy about you, too."

"May they rest in peace." Todd raised a cheese-laden cracker and toasted the deceased.

"Never far from our thoughts," she added.

He placed the untouched cracker back on the tray and walked across the room to scoop her up into his arms. He wanted to say, "I love you," but android life forms have their limits. Todd would masticate on that emotion for a while longer before he could put thought into words.

Thirty-three

Rachel's heart was hopscotching in her chest and her face was frozen in a shit-eating grin. She walked down the jetway toward the waiting 727 with a solitary thought thrilling every fiber of her being, "I am going to meet my real mom."

The flight departed on time and the cabin crew made several announcements that failed to penetrate her euphoric haze. When the plane dropped suddenly and surged upward with an audible thud, more than her phone hit the floor.

Passengers were scrambling to tighten their seatbelts. Lights flashed. Bells dinged.

Rachel scraped her hand around under her seat and locked her fingers around her phone like a vice. She shoved the phone down her shirt for safekeeping.

WHAM! The aircraft bucked like a wild bull.

Gasps and a few screams escaped the mouths of fellow travelers.

The head flight attendant's voice filled the cabin and encouraged everyone to remain in their seats with their seatbelts tightly fastened.

Rachel had no intention of moving a single muscle until they touched down on the precious Chicago runway. *I'm never going to meet my mom. I'm going to die in a horrible plane crash. I won't get to marry Annie...or kiss her sweet lips.*

The plane continued to drop and hop like a stone skipping across a pond. Several passengers fished out their phones and sent what they believed might be their final words, out into the ether.

Rachel didn't want to die. She thought about sending a final message to Gwenn to tell her what an amazing big sister she was, but she didn't want to terrify anyone. Her head banged into the seat in front of her as a horrible bounce sent the plane skittering left in the sky.

The pilot's voice echoed through the cabin, "We have requested permission to descend to 20,000 feet and get below this turbulence. Please remain in your seats for your own safety. We should be in clear skies in about five minutes."

The unified sigh of relief was punctuated by the cries of frightened children—and the moans of a few adults who wished they could un-send that last text.

Her plane circled O'Hare International Airport. Rachel anxiously looked out the window and marveled at the mass of freeways, runways and roads below. It reminded her of Gwenn's "off limits" Spirograph set—winding, twisting, confusing. She could not wait for the pilot to land this bucket of terror.

"We've already started our descent into Chicago's O'Hare International airport. We expect to land at 4:30, approximately 10 minutes ahead of schedule. If you want to adjust your watch, it is 4:15 p.m. Central Standard Time in Chicago right now. The weather is chilly, but sunny and the temperature is 50 degrees Fahrenheit or 10 degrees Celsius. We wish you a pleasant stay in Chicago and hope to see you again soon. On behalf of your crew, we know you have a choice when you choose to fly and we thank you for choosing North by Northwest." The disembodied voice was courteous, but emotionless.

Rachel checked her phone, which she refused to turn off, and noticed a missed call from Annie. She fired off a quick text, ">landing luv u". She realized she had less than 15 minutes until she would be kissing Annie's lips. Lips she thought she might never kiss again when the turbulence had tossed the plane around like a hot potato. Warm fuzzies of anticipation filled her insides.

Warm fuzzies quickly turned to icy daggers as Rachel came to the realization that "landing" at O'Hare is entirely different from getting off the plane and walking up the jetway into the actual airport. Her disillusionment found its voice in text.

Rachel: ">OMG first they almost crashed and now we are just sitting on the runway"

Annie: ">glad you lived :-) welcome to chicago"

Rachel: ">fuck chicago! I want u"

Annie: ">i only read fuck"

Rachel: ">i can't even remember how"

Annie: ">happy to refresh ya"

Rachel: ">i am going to pull the emergency slide and run for it"

Annie: ">prolly beat the plane"

Forty-five minutes and innumerable texts later, Rachel finally had her arms wrapped tightly around Annie. "I can't believe you are real. I've been dreaming about you nonstop. And then...today...the turbulence..."

"I missed you too, babe." Annie snuffled and instantly blamed the weather. "Damn cold...makin' my nose run."

"Cold? Are you kidding me? It's like summer here. It was barely above zero when I left Duluth." Rachel squeezed Annie one more time. "This is almost sun tanning weather."

"You got bags?"

"Um, Annie, it's me, Rachel—not Gwenn. This is it." Rachel gestured to her backpack and small rolling bag. "Let's get back to the damn hotel already."

The cavernous glass arched ceiling, floating above huge steel tubes, temporarily distracted Rachel. "It's like piping on a wedding cake."

"Ah shit, you got it bad. Nightmares about strangulating veils and visions of cake...you OK?"

"I'm fine—totally fine." Rachel continued to glance surreptitiously upward.

Annie hailed a cab like an expert and they cuddled together in the backseat. "528 Brompton, The Majestic."

The cabbie nodded and gunned into traffic.

Rachel had never been to Chicago. She wasn't counting her birth, which she assumed was in Chicago. The city was breathtaking—traffic, honking, lights, people, noise. It would take a couple days to get used to all the noise. "Are there any restaurants by the hotel?"

Annie snickered, "Yeah, I figured we'd go to the Pie Hole and grab a slice of pizza after you get settled in."

Rachel cracked up. "I thought we were on our way to the pie hole right now."

"That's my nasty girl." Annie kissed her with all the longing of the road.

"I'm gonna do you in this cab if you keep that up."

"Patience, babe." Annie brushed the hair back from Rachel's face. "I have a few fantasies of my own to share with you."

Rachel shivered with anticipation. "Do you have your own room?"

"I do, for the next three hours," Annie winked.

It felt like decades had passed by the time they pulled up in front of the Majestic. They tumbled out of the cab and Annie pulled Rachel hastily to her room.

Door closed. Lock clicked. Panties dropped.

Annie pinned Rachel to the bed and pulled a nipple between her teeth, licking and sucking until Rachel moaned loudly.

"I missed you like pie misses ice cream." Even in the throes of ecstasy Rachel had an unhealthy pre-occupation with food.

"I heard pie..." Annie slid her hand over Rachel's hipbone, down her thigh and finally her fingers slipped into the dessert she had been missing.

Rachel gasped and rocked her pelvis against Annie. It had been too long, she came in seconds. Her body was tingling and sparks kept shooting through her legs.

"Wait, there's more," Annie teased. She slithered down between Rachel's thighs and lapped up the nectar of her dreams.

The response was intense. Rachel grabbed a pillow and held it over her own face with one hand as she dug the fingers of her other hand into Annie's spiky hair. A muffled scream and a few shudders later, Annie pulled herself back up next to Rachel.

Panting and weak, Rachel breathed into Annie's ear, "I...can't even...move."

"No worries, that was all for you, babe." She brushed her hand across Rachel's breast, "I know you're good for it."

Thirty-four

Gwenn folded the "Kidney Donor" T-shirt and slowly placed it in her small suitcase. She was up and around, but she wasn't planning on running any marathons. The incision pain was minimal, but her *everything* hurt on the inside. She was grateful for the yoga pants and loose sweatshirt; she could not imagine anything with zippers anywhere near her tummy right now.

"Miss Hutchinson, I'll place your discharge orders on the bed. Did someone go over your after-care instructions with you?"

The parade of nurses made Gwenn's head spin. At first she attempted to get to know each new one, but after the first four or five she couldn't keep track. This new one looked about 12-years-old. "Yes, someone from the last shift, I think."

"OK, I'll get transport to bring a wheelchair in and take you down to meet your ride."

"Shit." Gwenn realized that her "ride" was in Chicago.

"Pardon?"

"Sorry, it's just that my sister was my ride...but she...dirty sow." In an attempt to clean up her language Gwenn fell back onto one of Pastor Ed's favorite curses. She certainly did not want him driving her anywhere. Steven was not an option.

"Do you have someone else?" The nurse paused with what appeared to be genuine concern, and waited for Gwenn's response.

"I can call a work friend." Gwenn dialed Flora's number. The hungry tendrils of Hutchinson-instilled guilt wended their way around her heart. "Don't inconvenience people with yer problems, Gwendolyn," one of Shirley's famous refrains. She became a bastion of self-sufficiency and only permitted herself to lean on Rachel—rarely and for extremely short intervals. Flora answered on the second ring and promised to arrive in 30 minutes.

"All set?" The nurse checked the time on her phone and smiled.

"Yes, I have a ride coming in about a half hour. I was wondering if I have time—"

"Did you want to meet your recipient?" The nurse interjected her idea without invitation.

"What? Oh, no, I don't think so. Actually, I was wondering if I could check in on my mom before I leave?"

"Of course. I'll send someone to take you."

"I think I can walk." Gwenn wanted to sound brave.

"Not on my watch," the nurse joked. "Honestly, it's hospital policy. I'll send someone right in." She left the room and Gwenn instantly lowered herself into a chair. Standing was incredibly taxing work.

A few moments later a familiar face popped into her room.

"Randy? What the hell are you doing? Do you work here?" Gwenn was flabbergasted to see her favorite interior designer pushing a wheelchair.

Randy waved his hand in a Broadway gesture, struck a pose and announced, "I'm a candy stripper! It's fantastic, right?" He shimmied his shoulders and flashed his pearly whites.

Gwenn held up her hand in protest. "Do not make me laugh. Do not." She struggled to stifle the giggles and control her breathing. "And, it's candy STRIPER, jack ass."

"Tomato, tomahto. Whatever puts smiles on the patients' faces!" Randy spun the chair around so Gwenn could get a full view of his Giuseppe Zanotti high-top sneakers.

"Randy, those are too much—even for you."

"I'll have you know that I received several compliments today."

Gwenn cautiously settled into the wheel chair. "How many is several?"

"More than one!" Randy rolled her suitcase around in front of the chair. "OK, you push this and I'll push you—like a human centipede."

She groaned, "I don't think that means what you think it means, Randall."

"Where to, Miss Daisy?" He snickered at his own joke.

"Dead girl rollin'."

"No, say it isn't true? Are the Reverend and the Mrs. here—in this hospital?"

"Indeed. Shirley had her kidney transplant surgery the same day I gave up this," Gwenn pointed to her left side, "to some lucky recipient."

"Lucky? I'll say. I can think of a few guys who would like a little Gwenn Hutchinson inside them."

"Oh, shut up. That doesn't even make sense, Randy. The girl bits don't go inside the boy bits."

"I don't claim to be an expert on your freaky hetero nonsense." Randy giggled mercilessly as he propelled Gwenn toward Shirley's room.

"Are you coming in?"

"Hardly. I'm out and proud."

"Oh, shut it. Seriously, I just want to make sure she's breathing—I'm not sure why—and then you can take me down to the lobby to wait for Flora."

"All right, Miss Gwenny, but if the Pastor tries to lay hands on me and pray the gay away, I'll make a run for it and leave you to the wolves."

"Of course you would." Gwenn chuckled painfully. "Here it is. Courage, D'Artagnan."

"Really? I always saw myself as more of a Santiago Cabrera, you know, Aramis?"

"Shhhh, behave now." Gwenn composed herself as they rolled into Shirley's room.

The energy drained from their faces as soon as they saw the solemn Pastor Ed praying in his chair. Randy scooted to a halt and waited for Gwenn's instructions.

She cleared her throat and launched into a greeting, "Hi, Ed, is everything OK?"

"I guess. Lots of nurses in and outta here, ya know. So, she's on quite a bit of pain medicine. She was complainin' about the pain, yesterday..." Ed's voice faded out and he looked helplessly at Shirley.

"Are you getting any sleep?"

"Enough."

Gwenn looked at his sagging shoulders, the dark circles under his eyes, and wondered if Pastor Ed was telling a little white lie. "They're discharging me today, so I just stopped in to say 'goodbye'."

Ed looked at Gwenn and his eyes lit up with remembrance. "Sorry, Trixie, I forgot all about yer surgery. The Lord works in mysterious ways, doesn't he?"

"One would have to agree." Gwenn did not have the energy or the time to debate how or if the Lord worked. A simple, vague response would have to suffice.

"How ya feelin'?"

"Tired and sore, but Dr. Andreas said everything went well. Can't complain." Gwenn heard a small chuckle from her candy striper. "Oh, I almost forgot. Ed, do you remember Randy? The designer I subcontract on big projects?" Gwenn gestured to her chauffeur.

Before Ed could decide whether or not to stand, Randy strode across the room. "Pleased to meet you, Reverend." He didn't mean to curtsy with the handshake, but the nerves messed with his etiquette gene.

Gwenn bit her lip to hide a crooked smile and held her stomach to prevent laughter pains.

"Nice ta meet ya, Randy." Ed raised an eyebrow when he caught sight of the gold-embellished white sneakers.

Gwenn looked up at Randy, "Can you wheel me over by her bed?"

Randy obliged.

Shirley looked like warmed over death. Gwenn had never seen anything like it. No make-up, no hairdo and a shapeless hospital gown. The effect was disconcerting. She took Shirley's cold, fragile hand in hers and gently rubbed. "I'm sure you'll be feelin' better tomorrow. I'm glad the surgery went well. Mine went OK, too." Gwenn stared at this woman who had caused her so much pain. A wave of sorrow washed over her and she wiped a trickle of pain from her cheek. Suddenly self-conscious and uncomfortable, Gwenn fumbled for an exit strategy. "My ride will be here any minute, so...tell Shirley I stopped by to check on her."

"Will do, will do." Ed nodded. "I'll call ya if anything changes." He tapped the phone in his breast pocket. "Got yer number, right here."

"OK. Try to get some sleep, Ed."

"You betcha."

Randy pivoted the wheelchair around and nodded farewell to Pastor Ed.

Thirty-five

Flora was waiting in the drop-off/pick-up area and waved frantically as Gwenn and Randy rolled out of the hospital.

Randy was so excited to see his "Angel," he released his hold on the wheelchair and hurried over to hug Flora.

When Gwenn realized she was ghost riding the wheelchair directly toward the street she panicked. Holding her suitcase with one hand and grabbing a wheel with the other resulted in an unsatisfactory spinning of the chair, which resulted in a painful twisting of her midsection. "Shit! Randy, what the hell?"

"Oh-my-gawd! Gwenny!" Randy flew to her side and apologized profusely. "Did you burst? Are you hurt? Should I take you back in?"

She held her stomach and forced her breathing back to a normal pace. "I think I'm OK, but if I die I will haunt you and make you crave French fries."

"You wouldn't!" Randy put his hands on his hips and sputtered indignantly.

Before her chair could roll away, again, Flora secured the brake and offered her arm to Gwenn. "Let's get you into the car."

"Yeah, before Captain Candy Cane kills me," Gwenn teased.

"That's Captain Candy Ass to you," he replied. He leaned into the car and kissed Gwenn on the cheek. "I'm sorry, Your Highness. Get better," he commanded.

They slowly pulled away from St. Luke's and Gwenn watched in the side view mirror as the waving Randy receded. The queasy feeling in her stomach felt like more than post-surgical discomfort. She decided to chat up Flora and distract herself from the uneasiness. "I just need to stop by my place and grab the 'cabin' suitcase I packed and my laptop, OK? Oh, and how's Todd?"

Flora hesitated. She wanted to tell someone about the move-in drama, but Gwenn was her boss first and her friend second. It didn't seem appropriate, or maybe she was being overly cautious. "He's fine."

Gwenn smiled, understanding the unspoken response. "You can tell me. After last year's Daniel drama and this year's Daniel/Steven drama I think we've sufficiently blurred the employee/employer line. So, how are things with Todd?"

They spent the rest of the drive to Gramma Carlson's old cabin talking about the pros and cons of living with another human being. Both Gwenn and Flora enjoyed having their own spaces.

Gwenn's failed marriage to Bruce and her disastrous fling with Jax had definitely turned her off to the idea of cohabitation.

Flora was filled with the hope of the uninitiated and felt sure that a few bumps in the road were normal.

By the time they reached the long dirt road that ended at Island Lake and the peaceful cabin, they had agreed to disagree.

"Oh, shoot. I should've stopped at the Piggly Wiggly so you could grab some groceries. Should we go back?"

"I don't want to jump to any conclusions, but generally speaking Gramma Carlson can't resist the opportunity to stock the pantry. Let's head inside and take a look around, first." Gwenn grabbed the car door handle and yelped. "Ouch! I keep forgetting how much abdominal effort is needed to open a car door. Can you help me out?"

"Of course." Flora jumped out and hurried around to assist Gwenn out of the car. "I'll grab your suitcases. Can you make it to the door by yourself?

"Yep, I'll just use the old invalid shuffle." Gwenn was thankful for the lack of recent snowfall—putting one foot in front of the other was all right as long as she didn't have to pick one of those feet up off the ground.

Flora jogged around Gwenn, opened the never-locked cabin door and turned on the lights. "I'll turn the heater on and boil some water for tea. Sound good?"

"Sure." The short shuffle had completely exhausted her. She made her way toward the well-worn plaid couch and gingerly settled into a tolerable position. The sounds of Flora bustling around the kitchen took Gwenn back in time.

She remembered Gramma Carlson baking bread. The memory of the comforting smell pulled her deeper into the reverie.

"Fresh outta the oven," Gramma had called. She had handed Gwenn a thick slice of warm bread with butter trickling into the heavenly nooks and crannies.

"Mmmmmm. You make the best bread in the whole world, Gramma."

That had been the summer before Rachel was born—or adopted. Gwenn still remembered the silent canoe rides at sunset, the early mornings catching sunfish for lunch and the evenings braiding fabric for the huge area rug. She looked down at the rug and smiled. Old bedspreads, recycled curtains, she always loved finding the section that contained strips from her favorite sundress. If Gramma liked the fabric—it got added to the rug.

"Here's your tea."

Gwenn looked up, startled to see she was not alone.

"Gosh, did I surprise you?" Flora stood, arm outstretched with Gwenn's tea.

"I don't know where I went...this rug...this place brings back a lot of memories."

"Were you and your grandmother close?"

"I thought so...maybe not as close as I imagined."

"What makes you say that?" Flora tucked her legs underneath her as she took a seat in the faded green easy chair across from Gwenn.

"The adoption, I guess. I mean how could she keep that from me...my entire life?"

"People have strange ways of showing affection. My parents never told me how Laura, my sister, died."

"Really?"

"Yeah, I finally sneaked down to the library and did my own research." Flora smoothed her hair and continued, "I mean, it was an awful car accident. I get why they didn't tell me when I was a kid...but never...we never talked about Laura."

"Never? Do you still miss her?"

"Every day. I don't consciously think 'God, I miss my sister,' but I feel the hole in my heart where she used to be—she was my idol."

"I can't imagine my life without Rachel. The times we huddled together in the dark listening to my parents fight... if I had been alone I know I would've run away. I told myself I had to stay to protect Rache, ya know?"

"Yeah, oddly I do. Laura was older, but she was the one who needed protecting. I was always covering for her. Weird, right?"

"And here we are, organizing the shit out of other people's lives for a living. We make quite a pair," Gwenn smiled.

"I love this job, ya know. Todd wanted me to come and work with him at the Gregory North gallery, but I didn't want to leave *The Organizer*. We're a good team—Thea, too."

Gwenn pulled a hand-knitted throw over her legs and smirked. "Thea. I still can't believe she took the job. We got lucky on that one, eh?"

Flora absently touched her lips, "I'll say." The memory of Thea's kissing lesson made her blush.

"Flora, you're blushing. I knew I sensed something strange in the office the other day. What aren't you telling me?"

Her face reddened to a shimmering crimson and Flora spilled the entire story of her virginity, lack of kissing experience and Thea's exciting lesson.

"I knew it! Only Thea, right."

"Yep." Flora bit her lip and grinned, "She's a really good kisser."

"Should Todd be worried?"

"Oh, no, no, no. He's fantastic...I'd never...I mean...gosh, I think I love him," Flora blushed anew.

"That's great. Have you told him?"

"No way! It's too soon. I don't want to seem desperate."

"You're not desperate. You're a catch. He should consider himself lucky to be loved by you." Gwenn raised her mug of tea in a toast to Flora's awesomeness.

"What about you? Are you in love with Steven?"

The sobering question brought Gwenn face-to-face with the dilemma she came to sort out at the cabin. "I honestly don't know. I came up here to get away from everything and figure out what I want."

"Do you still have feelings for Daniel?" Flora knew Daniel wasn't over Gwenn, but she also knew it wasn't her place to spill those beans.

"Honestly, I do. I burned that bridge beyond repair, though. He was civil to me when I called to tell him about the surgery, but I don't think he'll ever forgive me for sleeping with Steven."

Flora kept herself quiet with a big gulp of tea. *Not my place. Not my place.* Gwenn had enough on her mind.

"Thanks again for driving me out here. I should be set for at least a week. The fridge is full, right?"

"Oh, most definitely. Your Grandmother has you all set up. Can I make you some dinner or anything before I go?"

"I'm exhausted. I plan to take the maximum dose of my pain meds and crash out for 12-24 hours," Gwenn joked.

"All right. I'll let you get some rest. Don't worry about anything at the office—you can count on me."

"I know, I really do count on you. You'd tell me if it was too much, right?"

"It's great. It's what I do...it's what we do." Flora smiled and clinked her mug on Gwenn's. "Call me if you need anything, OK?"

"OK." Gwenn took a sip of her tea and watched Flora walk toward the front door. "Oh, Flora, one last thing."

"Sure, what is it?"

"Tell Todd, life's too short to keep secrets."
"Do you think so?"
"I do."

Thirty-six

Rachel woke up nestled in Annie's arms and immediately pinched herself. "Ow."

"You OK, babe?"

"Just makin' sure this wasn't another dream."

Annie cupped Rachel's breast and pulled her closer. "Feels like a dream to me." She kissed her neck and nibbled at Rachel's shoulder.

Rachel moaned pleasurably.

"Hey, horny bitches, you're not alone anymore. Some of us need a few more hours of shut eye," Cass yelled from under the covers in the other bed.

"Let's go get some breakfast at Ann Sather's. You're gonna love that place—Swedish everything," Annie whispered in Rachel's ear and was rewarded with a bit more moaning.

A pillow crashed down on top of Rachel and she giggled. "OK, OK we're going to breakfast. Bree, you can have the bed."

The shape under the blanket on the sofa did not move. Clearly Bree was not owning up to the missile launch.

Rachel shrugged and pulled on her jeans. She struggled with the zipper and was forced to leave the top button undone. She hurriedly pulled her sweatshirt down before anyone could see the reality of her weight gain. The stress had taken its toll. Shirley's adoption revelation, Annie's tour and Gwenn's surgery—it was all too much. Rachel's anxious fingers had grabbed more than their share of delectable pastries from the day-old case at her bakery. Diets and owning a bakery were less than complimentary life choices. Rachel decided to table that philosophical conundrum until after breakfast. She never thought clearly on an empty stomach.

Annie was right about the restaurant. Rachel audibly hummed as tart lingonberries exploded in her mouth to combine with sweet whipped cream and tender Swedish pancake. She ordered a side of scrambled eggs, Swedish potato sausage and a homemade cinnamon roll—just to check out the competition. The Sather's sweet rolls did not contain the rum-soaked raisins that made her swoon with delight, but they were soft and chewy—both of them.

Annie ate her breakfast in relative silence, carefully avoiding direct eye contact with Rachel's plates of food. She knew the love/hate relationship her partner had with food and she also knew today was not the time to explore the issue. Today held a promise of happiness that Rachel had never imagined. "Are you excited to meet your real mom today?"

Not bothering to swallow, Rachel pushed her answer past the partially masticated Swedish pancake. "I'm terrified. If she hates me I will jump off...the...Willis Tower."

Annie stifled a chuckle and replied, "She will love you, you'll see. When do we meet Corrine?"

"I texted her when we left the hotel and she said she'd pick us up, here, in about..." Rachel checked her phone, "ten minutes. Perfect. I'll get the check."

Annie looked at Rachel's empty plates and said a little prayer for her girl. She would never consider herself religious, but Annie believed in some kind of positive energy out there somewhere that could be called upon with a heartfelt request.

"Ready?" Rachel smiled at Annie and her eyes said all the things her forced grin was hiding.

"She's gonna love you, babe." Annie reached across the table and squeezed Rachel's hand.

Corrine texted that she was circling the block in her blue SUV and would flash her lights as she approached.

Annie saw the signal first and pulled Rachel into the avenue to jump into Corrine's car.

"Hi, I'm Rachel. I seriously hope you're Corrine." A nervous snicker burst from Rachel's lips.

"I am." Lovely hazel eyes, strawberry blonde hair, freckled cheeks and a welcoming grin looked back at Rachel. "And you must be Annie? Right?" Corrine reached a hand awkwardly over the seat and shook Annie's outstretched fingers.

"Yep, nice to meet you."

"OK gals, we're going to swing by my office to grab Rachel's file—which I inexplicably forgot this morning—and then we are meeting Greta at her home."

Rachel looked at Annie and started to cry, "Her name's Greta."

Annie slipped an arm around Rachel's shoulders and pulled her close. "It's a beautiful name, babe."

Thirty-seven

Physically Gwenn felt much better than she had expected. Walking was still a laborious task—but the pain was minimal and she was comfortably self-sufficient. Gramma Carlson had indeed stocked the cabin with ample food, instant cocoa and tea. She poured boiling water over the tea bag in her mug and inhaled the sharp peppermint aroma. She carefully made her way back to the sofa and found a comfortable position.

Cold air drifted in through the cracked window. Gwenn pulled a blanket around her shoulders. "Ow, crap. Frickin' stitches." She was tired of discovering things that she could not quite do for herself. Determined to get outside and walk in the fresh air for a few minutes, Gwenn sipped her tea and listened to the haunting cry of the loon couple somewhere across the grey, white-capped lake. Their cries pricked a long forgotten memory.

Gwenn could see a much younger Gramma Carlson steering the pontoon boat around the tiny island that gave her lake its name. "Loons mate for life, Gwenny. Did you know that?"

"No Gramma, we only learned about ducks and swans at school. What happens if one of 'em dies or gets lost? They can't remarry?"

"Oh no, sweetie, that's why their cry is so haunting. Those are the mournful wails of a loon who has lost its mate. It's a reminder to all of us to appreciate the people in our lives before it's too late."

Those words had forced Gwenn to create appreciation for some seriously unworthy folks over the years. All grown up and armed with the knowledge that loons find new mates whenever a mate dies or fails to return during mating season, she marveled at the effect of that childhood perception.

Maybe she had felt so shattered when Steven left because she thought she would be alone for the rest of her life. Maybe she hung on to Bruce, despite the red flags of his sexual orientation, out of fear rather than love. Maybe Jax... maybe it would be better to leave the skeletons in the closet and take a short walk.

She placed her half empty cup on the coffee table and made her way to the front door. Thankfully she had packed slip-on shoes. She planned to use the long dirt driveway as her measuring stick for healing. Today she would walk across the yard to the beginning of the drive and back. Each day she would push a little farther, until she could make a complete round trip, doorway to mailbox and back—pain free.

She zipped up her coat and opened the door, preparing for the brisk rush of frigid air and slight step down to the porch. She froze in mid stride and gasped.

There, in the middle of the "Gone Fishing" doormat was a beautifully folded, handmade parchment envelope with a wax seal. She looked in both directions to confirm that the summer-only neighboring cabins were empty. Confirmed. Now, to retrieve the vexing enticement.

Gwenn grasped the door handle with one hand and the doorjamb with the other. She lowered herself down to one knee and attempted to stretch her arm like a comic book superhero. In the end she had to bend a bit in the middle and her stitches protested with a barbed pinch. "Got it," she announced to the birch trees.

She flipped the item over and saw the salutation, "To: Miss Hutchinson." Gwenn could not imagine why Flora would leave her such an over-the-top note. She bit the envelope between her teeth and cautiously pulled herself upright.

She retrieved a knife from the drawer and slipped it under the wax seal. The wax was debossed with a symbol that looked vaguely like two letters intertwined: "YS." The letters made even less sense than the envelope. She slid the card out of the case and admired the intricately painted image...

Gwenn steadied herself on the counter. Image. Painted. This was from Daniel—maybe she hadn't burned as much of that bridge as she had imagined. The image depicted two women leaving a dance floor, and consisted of layers of tiny torn bits of paper and carefully added watercolor details. The women were clearly she and Rachel. The Gwenn character was leaning heavily on the Rachel character, which was holding something toward the foreground. A matchbook! *YS—Yellow Submarine.* The piece was entitled "Guardian Angel."

A rush of heat swept over her. She remembered the over-indulgence in sloe gin fizzes, the sexy dancing and the tingle of warmth she felt when she had noticed the patron she had dubbed the "Lion King" watching her with a slightly lascivious grin. Oh, that gorgeous mane of hair. She quivered with longing. The night had ended badly—a hellish hangover, vomiting and Rachel writing her number on a matchbook and handing it to a total fricking stranger, Lion King. She was prepared to embrace the regret swelling in her chest when she flipped the miniature work of art over and saw the poem.

> *Flickering*
>
> *My wounded heart aches with doubt, bravely I stumble on.*
> *My head swims with unnamed pain and I pray for the dawn.*
>
> *This newly found love is so fragile--tender and rare.*
> *Like a helpless babe, it shamelessly begs constant care.*
>
> *Some days I lack the strength to nurture this precious gift,*
> *But then I remember the emptiness of the rift.*
>
> *My mortal soul is bound to you by powers unseen.*
> *My body craves a union, the yin to my being.*
>
> *I yearn for the time when all second thoughts disappear*
> *And every fiber holds strong in the now and here.*
>
> *The flame is flickering from an invisible breeze.*
> *I do not want to put up walls for the flame's own ease.*
>
> *I will not deny the difficulty of our path,*
> *But I know, together, we have power to surpass.*
>
> *I will seek out the source of this unwelcome ill wind.*
> *I will bind it and banish it beyond the world's end.*
>
> *I will open my heart to rekindle the love that was offered,*
> *The flame will swell and re-ignite passions undiscovered.*
>
> *I am made for you, and you for me—a perfect match, a gift, a legend.*
> *~Daniel*

Gwenn dropped the card and wept shamelessly.

Thirty-eight

Corrine tucked the folder into the passenger seat and smiled over her shoulder at Rachel. "OK, that's the file I needed. Are you ready to meet your birth mother?"

"I'm dying to meet my real mom."

"Just a point of etiquette, Rachel," Corrine smiled into the rearview mirror and caught Rachel's eye, "Greta is your birth mother and Shirley is your adoptive mother, you will find the shortened terms 'bMom' and 'aMom' on most adoption support forums. The term 'real mom' can be hurtful to an adoptive parent, who most likely raised and loved you for decades."

Rachel nodded and looked at Annie. "Shirley definitely raised me—for better or for worse—but I don't think she loved me."

Corrine nodded in acknowledgement of the statement she had just overheard. "Based on some of the file notes, I think Shirley loved you, in her own way, but at some point the fear of her secret being uncovered pushed her a little off track." Corrine drove the busy streets of Chicago with one hand on the wheel and rifled through the manila folder in the passenger seat with the other. "Ah, here it is." She handed a photocopy to Rachel. "Here's the letter I was telling you about, the one that prevented Greta from contacting you."

Rachel took the document and held it out for Annie to read, along with her. They exchanged shocked, appalled glances as they made their way down the page.

"That is f'd up," Annie declared.

"Holy shit! This isn't even my handwriting, Corrine. Shirley must've faked this when I turned 18."

"After we spoke on the phone, I was fairly certain that was what happened. There weren't many documents in the original file that contained Shirley's handwriting—from the initial adoption papers—but I found a couple of telltale ligatures that confirmed your story. I guess we're lucky your...Shirley...isn't a computer whiz."

"I have some other words besides lucky..." Rachel let the words evaporate and turned to gaze out the window. "Wow, this is some serious soap-opera-deception shit."

"I didn't want to upset you, Rachel, I only shared that document because I wanted you to be able to tell Greta that you never wrote the letter. You can imagine how devastated she was when the previous Intermediary showed her the 'no contact' request."

"She must've been splintered," Annie volunteered.

"Yeah, totally," Rachel added.

Huge Lake Michigan waves crashed against the shoreline as they made their way to the northern suburb of Andersonville. Currently, Corrine told them, it was one of Chicago's "hot" suburbs, but originally Swedish farmers founded the community in the 1850s. Rachel was surprised to learn the area included one of Chicago's largest gay and lesbian communities.

"This is it." Corrine expertly parallel-parked in front of a two-story brick walk-up with a manicured lawn, potted-plants and a low wrought-iron fence.

"Damn, looks pretty posh. I think I'm underdressed." Rachel squeezed Annie's hand and grimaced.

"It's my understanding that this home has been in Greta's family for a generation or two," Corrine spoke with compassion and hoped the tone of her voice would aid Rachel in finding some way to calm down before the big meeting.

The trio made their way up the stone steps, past the huge potted plant carcasses guarding the entrance, and Rachel rang the doorbell. "Shit, I should've knocked. What if she has a kid takin' a nap, or a sick husband or an invalid dog—"

The rest of Rachel's insane ramblings lodged firmly in her throat as the door opened and revealed Greta. She knew instantly that it was Greta because, aside from the dishwater-blonde bob, the woman was the spitting image of Rachel.

No one spoke. Greta pressed her hand over her mouth and whispered something into her fingers, while the pupils in her grey-blue eyes rapidly dilated. Annie squeezed Rachel's hand and exhaled softly—but audibly. Rachel felt her legs shaking and desperately wanted to sit down.

The vastly more experienced Corrine leapt to everyone's rescue. "Greta, this is Rachel Hutchinson. Can we all come in?"

Greta's hand remained firmly over her slightly agape mouth, but she stepped back and gestured for the ladies to enter.

Annie steered Rachel toward a small diamond-pleated settee and gently pushed her to take a seat.

Corrine hung back and exchanged a few words with Greta. A series of furiously affirmative head nods, followed by a handshake and several pats to the shoulder resulted in Greta finding her voice.

"Rachel," Greta stopped and wiped a tear from her eye before she could continue, "I am so thrilled to meet you, finally. If you will excuse me for a couple minutes I think I just need to have a good solid cry—get it out of my system—and then I will be able to carry on a normal conversation." Her eyes glistened with love and pride and just a tiny bit of fear.

She could stand it no longer, Rachel launched herself off of the settee, swallowed the space between them in two strides and engulfed her mother in a signature rib-cracking hug. "You can cry right here—with me…Mom."

Annie smirked and wiped a few happy tears from her own eyes while the freshly united mother and daughter wept and smiled, wept and laughed, wept and hugged the stuffing out of each other.

Several minutes passed before Corrine found the right moment to invite Rachel and Greta to join her in the living room to go over some paperwork.

The pair locked their hands together and walked, as one, to the sofa.

"Here is the letter we discussed, Rachel." Corrine gestured to the "no contact request" and slid it across the coffee table.

Rachel's joyful tears stopped abruptly. "That," she pointed to the photocopy, refusing to pick it up, "that is the kind of thing Shirley has been doing to my sister and I our entire lives. I never wrote that letter. I couldn't have. I didn't even know I was adopted until we took the blood tests, less than two weeks ago, to see if we could donate a kidney to my M...Shirley."

Greta grasped both of Rachel's hands in hers and smiled through her tears. "Deep down...deep in my heart... somehow I knew you would never write that." More tears escaped and Corrine went to fetch a box of tissues from the bathroom.

In the silence, Rachel realized Annie was perched awkwardly on the settee and she was eyeing the door. "Greta, I mean Mom. Is it OK if I call you Mom? I don't have to if it makes you uncomfortable. I was...it's just that—"

"I would be honored to have you call me Mom." Greta was certain that her heart would swell right out of her chest. This beautiful, kind, amazing woman was her daughter—right here in her living room.

Rachel looked at Annie and raised her eyebrows questioningly.

Annie nodded her confirmation.

Keep breathing. Rachel forced air in and out of her lungs before she locked eyes with her birth mother. "Greta, this is my fiancée, Annie."

Greta looked back and forth from Rachel's tear-stained face to the determined set of Annie's jaw. A smile spread across her face like fresh butter on a warm baked potato. "Welcome to the family, Annie. I guess the good Lord saw fit to give me two daughters today." She squeezed and released Rachel's hand as she stood up to give Annie a motherly hug.

Rachel sat stark still on the sofa. Her eyes crept left to watch Annie stand up and return Greta's hug, but she pinched them closed. She was terrified that the whole scene would drift away like smoke in the wind if she dared to re-open them.

"Babe, whatcha doin'?" Annie teased.

She risked a quick peek and slammed the lids closed. "I don't want to wake up. I don't want to sit up in bed and discover that this whole magical reunion was a dream."

Greta plopped down on the couch next to Rachel and squeezed her tightly. "It is a dream, sweetie—a dream come true. I can't tell you how many times I've pictured this moment. I can assure you, my imagination is not this good." She released her hold on Rachel and chuckled. "Well, now that we have the first round of mushy stuff out of the way... what say we start at the beginning?" She turned toward the kitchen, "Mia, honey, can you bring out some snacks and see what everyone would like to drink?"

A cherubic face peeked around the polished oak pilaster. The stout older woman rubbed a hand through her close-cropped brown hair, tugged on her Chicago Bulls sweatshirt and gave a timid wave to the guests.

Rachel and Annie exchanged an awestruck glance. "Mom, are you gay?" She hadn't meant to blurt it out so bluntly, but the shock turned off all her social filters.

Greta laughed and slapped her leg. "If I had a dollar..." the rest of the sentence was swallowed in chuckles.

"I guess I'll have to introduce myself, I'm Mia. Your mother and I are roommates, actual roommates, it's not just a cover story as most of the neighborhood thinks." Mia shook Rachel's hand and then Annie's. She nodded politely to Corrine, a spectator to the proceedings.

Greta regained control of her voice and added, "It used to be scandalous but after nearly 20 years the gossip has died down. Now, Rachel, I really think I better get the scrapbooks and take you through this tale properly."

Corrine stood up to excuse herself. "I would have to say my 'Intermediary' services no longer appear to be necessary.

If you two will be all right I think I'll head back into the city. Rachel, you can call me when you're ready to be picked up."

"Oh, nonsense, Rachel can spend the night here...if she wants."

"Babe, I hate to rain on the parade but I have a sound check at 4:00."

"Oh shit, I...oops." Rachel covered her mouth and wondered if she should apologize or pretend it never happened. Before she could decide, Corrine came to her aid.

"How about this, I can give Annie a ride back to the city now, so she won't be late for her sound check and I'll come back later...I'm assuming you wanted to go to the concert, right Rachel?"

"Concert?" Greta smiled. "Annie, are you in a band?"

Annie opened her mouth, but Rachel beat her to the punch. "Omycrap! I can't believe I forgot to mention that Annie's band is on tour with Prince. They have a totally exclusive concert at the Aragon Ballroom tonight."

"Prince?" Mia lit up like a Christmas tree.

"Why don't we bring Rachel in for the concert?" Greta looked at Rachel and waited for her reply.

Rachel looked at Annie and made her famously irresistible pouty face. "Can you get us all tickets?"

"The floor is sold out. I might be able to get you VIP passes...I mean if you don't mind running into His Royal Badness backstage?" Annie made it sound like a boring game of shuffleboard.

"I'd swoon, but I may not be able to get back up," Mia joked.

"OK, that settles it. I'll take Annie back downtown and you three will meet her at the Aragon by 7:30. Sound good?"

Corrine looked around the room and everyone nodded in agreement.

Annie kissed Rachel and whispered in her ear, "You hit the mom jackpot, babe. I love you."

"I love you, too." Rachel smiled as Annie disappeared out the front door.

Just as the door was about to close, Annie poked her head back in, "You should probably call Gwenn..." she winked and closed the door.

Thirty-nine

Gwenn whipped open her laptop and confirmed that Chicago and Duluth were in the same time zone. She had expected a call from Rachel over an hour ago. The delay could mean things were going great or it could mean—

BUZZ BUZZ BUZZ!

She snatched her phone off the table and answered. "Rache? Is everything OK?"

"Is this Gwendolyn Hutchinson?" an official-sounding voice inquired.

This is it, this is the call Gwenn had been dreading. The meeting had not gone well and Rachel had done something drastic—she was either in the hospital or in jail.

"Miss Hutchinson?"

"Oh, sorry...yes, it's me. Is she OK? Does she need bail money?"

"I beg your pardon? Miss Hutchinson, this is the shift nurse at St. Luke's. I'm afraid I have some bad news."

Of course, how silly of Gwenn to think that something bad had happened to someone else. Bad things only happened to her. The surgeon probably left a clamp in her gut...or worse. "Is it about my surgery?"

"No ma'am, I'm afraid it's about your mother. There were complications, an infection. The doctor said she might not make it through the night. Your father asked me to call, he didn't want to leave her side."

The words hung around Gwenn like thick fog. She heard the words, but she could not comprehend the words.

"Ma'am?"

"She's dying?"

"I'm not qualified to make that diagnosis, ma'am. I'm told she is septic with a poor prognosis for recovery."

"Oh, OK."

"Is Rachel with you, ma'am? She's the next number on my list."

Gwenn snapped back to reality, and protective big sister, in a flash. "Yes, she's right here. I'll let her know. Thank you for the call." She ended the exchange before her lie could be discovered. There was no way in hell she would let Shirley's final act on this earth be to destroy Rachel's first meeting with her real mom.

She turned to slip on her shoes and realized she didn't have a car. *Shit.* She looked at Daniel's card and mentally slapped herself. *No, that is not happening.* Her fingers made the decision for her and less than 30 seconds later Steven was in full crisis-management mode, racing to her rescue.

She set her phone on the countertop and caught sight of her reflection in the warped hall tree mirror. *Fantastic.* She had thirty minutes and limited mobility. She thought about washing her hair in the kitchen sink, but when she attempted to raise her arms above waist level the home-of-her-former-kidney protested sharply.

One-handed hair washing would take an eternity. She quickly prioritized clean underwear and some semblance of makeup to the top of the list. If all else failed—and it would—she would settle for a stocking hat fashionably shoved over her greasy auburn tresses.

Steven, ahead of schedule as usual, arrived before she had managed her mane.

"Hi, I'm emotional and unwashed—please don't comment."

"You're gorgeous."

"Seriously, I'm in no mood. Can you help me put this stupid beanie on to hide this mess?" She gestured toward her head.

"I can do ya one better if you show me to your brush."

"Steven...oh fine, I'm too tired to argue." Gwenn went to retrieve her hairbrush.

"Grab a rubber band, too." He turned and leaned back against the counter, right next to Daniel's card. If he put one of his hands on the countertop he would most certainly feel it.

Gwenn slowly rounded the corner and saw the card directly behind Steven. She inhaled sharply.

"You OK? Where does it hurt?"

In my heart. She wanted to throw Daniel's card into the trash bin and focus on the wonderful, loving man right in front of her, but hearts can be bad listeners. "Oh, it's OK. I think I was just moving a little too fast," she covered.

"Here, sit down carefully and let me put your hair in a nice, classy ponytail. I used to help my sister out, when my mom was too busy."

She eased herself into the wooden chair beside the scratched dining room table. It felt good to let someone take care of her. Steven gently pulled the brush through her hair and scooped her locks up into a totally passable ponytail.

"There, perfect." He set the brush on the table and admired his work. "Where's your coat?"

She knew one of her coats was by the front door, but she also knew that if she sent him hunting for a coat in the bedroom she would have time to stash Daniel's card in a kitchen drawer. "Grab the grey North Face jacket from the bedroom closet. Thanks."

Steven walked toward the bedroom and Gwenn moved as fast as post-surgically possible toward the kitchen. She had barely shoved the card into the drawer when she heard him returning.

"Boy, I thought it would take a little longer than that to get into the bedroom."

She laughed nervously as she pushed the drawer closed behind her back. "No jokes, OK? Shirley might be in real trouble...I just...too rollercoaster-y, all right?"

"Whatever you need. Let me help you to the car."

They drove to St. Luke's in relative silence. He asked a couple questions about her recovery and she mumbled some monosyllabic answers.

BUZZ BUZZ BUZZ!

"Frick! It's Rachel. I didn't call her...it seemed..." she looked at Steven.

"Morbid?"

"Yeah."

"You better answer. She'll just keep calling."

Gwenn chuckled softly, "Yeah, you're right." She accepted the call and prepared to lie. "Hi, Rache. Did you meet her?"

A flurry of partial sentences, tears, giggles and exclamations of joy spilled through the phone.

Without any clear idea of what was said, Gwenn went with the general impression that Rachel was excited—in a good way. "I'm so happy for you, sweetie."

"I wish you were here, Gwenny." Rachel had stopped to take a breath and uttered a coherent sentence.

"I wish I was, too." Gwenn looked at Steven and he shook his head. "I better let you go, Rache. It sounds like you're in the middle of a party. I'll call you later, OK?"

"Call me in the morning. We're all going to Annie's concert tonight."

"Wow, Rache, that's awesome. I can't wait to hear all the details." The line went dead and Gwenn hung her head and exhaled, "I should've told her."

"No, you did the right thing. Rachel is having the best night of her life—nothing should interrupt that. I mean if Rachel and Shirley were close...well, that'd be different. You did the right thing, trust me." Steven patted Gwenn's knee and nodded supportively.

Forty

Rachel scooted back into the couch and laid half of the scrapbook in her lap. Greta paged through volume after volume of Tornquist memories. The family had lived in Andersonville since before it was Andersonville. Great-great-(and possibly a couple more greats)-grandpa Tornquist was one of the original Swedish farmers to move north and settle in this area. The solid brick home she was sitting in was built in 1904, after the Great Chicago Fire scared residents away from erecting wooden structures.

Time passed slowly and Rachel squeezed every detail out of each frame of the memories she was creating. She was on her sixth or seventh photo album before she noticed the absence of her father from all of Greta's stories.

"Mom, what happened to my dad...I mean my birth father?"

Greta exchanged a worried look with Mia.

Mia stood up quickly, "I'll get some wine. Rachel, do you like red or white?"

Rachel glanced at Greta's worried face and stumbled through a reply, "Um...red...I guess, or...whatever everyone else is having. I mean...I don't care..."

Greta patted Rachel's knee. "You have every right to ask, sweetheart. It's just...well, it's still hard for me to talk about it."

"Did he rape you? Is that why you never married?"

"Oh gosh, no, dear. Loukas was the kindest man I've ever known." Greta sniffled. "Better hand me the tissues," she chuckled. "I told you I got pregnant in high school, well here's 'The Rest of the Story...' as Paul Harvey used to say."

"Sorry, I don't get the reference." Rachel shrugged apologetically.

"Oh, it's not important to the story. Anyway, Loukas was a foreign exchange student from Greece. He was exotic and handsome—big brown eyes and jet black hair, just like yours." Greta stroked Rachel's amethyst-streaked locks and smiled wistfully. "Without the purple, of course."

Rachel blushed.

"In a town filled with blonde, blue-eyed, pale-skinned boys, Loukas was a delightful anomaly. I took to him like syrup to pancakes."

The food-related reference rang true for Rachel.

"We were both experiencing our sexual awakening. Sneaking out after curfew and experimenting up on the water tower became a regular thing. One night things went farther than usual. He told me he loved me, wanted me to come back to Greece...a young wide-eyed girl can really get swept away by talk like that...that was the night you were conceived."

"So, you were in love? You loved each other?"

"We were the sappiest couple in town. He walked me to school, I packed a lunch for us to share everyday, he walked me home, and every night I would sneak out to be with him."

"Sounds like he was perfect for you. Why didn't you go with him?"

"It was a different time, sweetheart, and I was a minor. When I revealed that I was pregnant my family panicked. The Tornquist name carried a lot of weight in this town and a scandal would damage more than just my reputation—long-standing family businesses would be destroyed."

"Let me guess, religion?"

"Mostly, but also the prejudice against outsiders, like Loukas." Greta paused and opened an old shoebox; she searched for a minute and retrieved a photo. "This is the only picture I have of your father."

Rachel carefully took the worn photo from Greta's hands. The edges were bent and one corner looked faded from tearstains. "I'm no expert, but he looks pretty handsome." She handed the photo back.

"No, you keep it. In fact, this whole box is for you." Greta passed the shoebox to Rachel. "There's a birthday card in there for every year of your life. I never forgot about you...never."

Rachel laid the photo of her father on the coffee table and accepted the gift. Her eyes glistened with tears of love as she opened the box and thumbed through the cards. She found the first card and opened it. A photo dropped to the floor. "Is that you?" she asked as she picked it up.

"Oh, my goodness. Mia, come and look at this photo. This would have been my senior year. Would you look at that tiny waist? Where have the years gone?"

Mia looked over Greta's shoulder and nodded. "I wish you would've come back."

"You never finished high school?" Rachel asked.

"No, my family was so humiliated by my actions that I was sent to live with a distant relative in Iowa. I came back several years later and eventually got my G.E.D. Fortunately you don't need a Bachelor's degree to bake cakes!" Greta chuckled and exchanged a high-five with Mia.

Rachel jumped up from the couch and spilled the box of cards and mementos. "Shut up!"

Greta looked alarmed and Mia shook her head in confusion.

"You're a baker?" Rachel was jumping up and down like a toddler demanding ice cream.

"Well, baker may be a little loose. I make wedding cakes, just wedding cakes, nothing else. So, techn—"

"I'm a baker! I bake everything. I own a bakery in Duluth. I inherited it earlier this year." Rachel was pacing around the living room now. Her hands were gesturing wildly and she was talking a mile a minute.

"Inherited? Are your adoptive parents dead?"

"What? Oh, no luck there," Rachel joked. "No, the lady I worked for left it to me before…oh it's too long of a story and I'd rather hear more about you and Loukas."

A pinched look grabbed Greta's face. "He died, Rachel. I'm so sorry."

"How? When? Did you ever see him again?"

Greta rubbed her hands over her face and took a deep breath. "When I told him I was pregnant he promised to marry me and bring me to Greece." She shook her head and patted her heart. "The foolhardy plans of young lovers."

"Did you say 'yes'?" Rachel interjected.

"Of course, of course. He was my prince charming, my ticket out of this one horse town, but fate had other plans. I was two months pregnant when he boarded his flight at O'Hare…I never heard from him again."

"Wait, what? Was he lying to you? Did he just take advantage of you?"

"Well, this was all pre-internet dear, so it wasn't that easy to solve a mystery at 16 years old. I started to show, and I had to tell my parents...they contacted the Ladies' group and planned to take you away from me the second you were born. I ended up in Iowa and the only part of you I ever saw, before today, was the back of your head."

Rachel threw her arms around Greta and cried. "I'm so glad I found you. I'm so sorry he ran out on you."

Greta extracted herself from Rachel's embrace and smiled. "Luckily I became a regular Sherlock Holmes in my thirties. Maybe it was Saturn's return or something...I just woke up one morning and decided to find him. I remembered one of his sister's names and I knew he was from Santorini...I wish I had better news." She dabbed at her eyes with a tissue.

"Did he pass away?"

"I made contact with his sister, Zahara, through Facebook, and once we confirmed each other's identities—she told me about his accident."

"When? Was it recently?" Rachel sat up straighter and leaned toward Greta.

"It was 28 years ago. He died in a boating accident on his way home—his ferry from Athens to Santorini was caught in a terrible storm and it sank. There were no survivors. He never got to tell his family about me." Greta's shoulders slumped.

"That's terrible. How awful for you."

"It was awful, and wonderful, to know the truth. I was heartbroken to hear of his death, but part of me was happy to know that he did not abandon me—by choice." She smiled wistfully at Rachel.

"So I really am Greek...and Swedish. I'm Greek-ish."

"You are perfect. I am just so amazed by your strength. It had to be difficult growing up gay in a religious household." She gently rubbed Rachel's shoulder.

Rachel looked down at her feet. "I tried to kill myself, twice," she mumbled.

Greta put her arm around Rachel and squeezed. "I'm so glad you didn't succeed."

"Gwenn found me. She's the one who saved me. She's the best sister in the entire world."

"I hope I get to meet her someday."

"Oh, you'll meet her at the wedding...I mean, if you want to come. It's not like Shirley will be there. Last year when I told her I was a lesbian she announced, 'Rachel Hutchinson I'm not havin' this nonsense. If you two are gettin' married er havin' a commitment ceremony, er whatever you people call it, I will not be there. And if anyone asks why I'm not there, ya know, ya can tell 'em I'm dead.'" Rachel was pleased with her impression of Shirley.

The look on Greta's face could only be described as horror. "That's unforgivable."

"I guess, but for her it's just par for the course. I barely even notice her judgment anymore. I was even going to donate a kidney to help her, but Gwenn jumped in and saved me from that, too."

"Oh, is Gwenn her biological daughter?"

"Nope, she's bought and paid for, like me." Rachel regretted the statement as soon as it came out of her mouth.

"Rachel, I hope you know I never received any money for you. The church ladies gave it all to their adoption program. My family didn't want any connection—that was their decision, not mine. The no-connection part, I mean." Greta shook her head and looked away from Rachel.

"I'm sorry for that comment. Once you get to know me better you'll see that I put my foot in my mouth several times a day." Rachel wanted to ease the tension with some of her patented humor.

"We are just getting to know each other. I know there will be ups and downs along the way, but I will never judge you, Rachel. Never. I want you to feel comfortable being your true self around me—foot in mouth and all."

"Thanks. Will you come to the wedding?" She smiled eagerly.

"I will do you one better than that, if you will agree. I will make your wedding cake."

"Holy shit, that's awesome." Rachel's eyes widened as she waited for the reproachful look that should follow her swearing.

Greta smiled and extended her hand, "Looks like you just hired a wedding cake designer."

Rachel grasped the outstretched hand and shook it repeatedly, "I did. That was easy. Maybe you should help me with all the wedding decisions."

They hugged, but part of Rachel worried about offending Gwenn by replacing her as the wedding planner.

Forty-one

By the time Gwenn and Steven reached the hospital, Shirley's condition had been upgraded from severe sepsis to septic shock.

"Dr. Murashige, how is she?"

"Hi, Gwenn. I'm afraid it does not look good. Her body is shutting down. The infection is progressing rapidly. We've reached the limit of what we can do with antibiotics and she is too weak for surgery. The vasodepressors are barely affecting her blood pressure and clots are forming throughout her body."

"How long until you see improvement?"

"We've done all we can. Your father went to the chapel to pray. I'm afraid it truly is in God's hands now."

"So, does she have weeks, or…?" Gwenn couldn't finish her question.

"Hours, and precious few of those. Septic shock is fatal in 50 percent of cases, and with a woman her age…the odds aren't in her favor. I'm so sorry." Dr. Murashige gave his compassionate look. A part of him could almost remember what it felt like to lose a loved one, but he had to close that part off in a tiny vault in his heart. Too many patients, too many years, and too many crying survivors—he had to focus on the ones he could save. He couldn't allow emotional attachments. "You may want to retrieve your father, I think he will want to be with her now."

Gwenn nodded in what looked like agreement. Inside her head a thousand thoughts were swirling around in a cyclone of confusion, disappointment, fear, regret, rage, sadness, hatred, love, pain and worry.

Steven touched her arm; she jumped and winced in pain.

"Sorry, Gwenny. I know this must be overwhelming. Do you want me to go get your dad?"

"No, he won't even remember you. He's bad with faces, and names—anything that has to do with my life, really." She could not keep the bitterness out of her voice. So, this was it. Shirley was just going to waltz out of her life without so much as a goodbye. She was going to escape the revelation of the adoptions, her lesbian daughter's wedding, her straight daughter marrying a Jew...

"Can I get you some coffee or anything?" Steven spoke quietly and didn't touch her this time. He could see the look in her eyes—the look that meant she was far away inside her mind.

She turned toward him slowly and blinked twice. "I'll have coffee." She stared deeply into his clear blue eyes. *Will I marry him? Will I speak at Shirley's funeral? Will I cry when she actually dies? Will she die, or is this just one of her theatrical ploys? Who thinks that about their dying mother?* "I'm going to find Ed and I'll meet you in Shirley's room. OK?"

"Copy that." Steven swung into gear. She was going to need him and he was going to make sure he did not disappoint her—this time.

Gwenn entered the hospital chapel and saw Ed kneeling down in the aisle, resting one elbow on a pew for support. She immediately flashed back to seventh grade. The junior high pastor had been organizing the nativity rehearsal. Gwenn had been chosen to play Mary, because her dad was the minister.

"Has anyone seen Gwenn Hutchinson?" Nameless Youth Pastor queried.

A sanctuary full of pre-teens shook their heads.

Gwenn was tucked up in the balcony with Joel Fraley, eagerly improving her French kissing skills. She planned to skip the whole stupid rehearsal and get replaced by Heidi, the goody-two-shoes that was always sucking up to Nameless Youth Pastor.

"Gwendolyn Hutchinson, ya have 60 seconds ta report ta the front of this sanctuary." Ed threw out his Easter-Sunday-people-come-to-Jesus voice and shook the rafters with his demand.

She cracked her forehead on the underside of the pew as the voice caused her to involuntarily lurch upward. "Ow." Despite the hand over her mouth—Joel's—her pain resounded through the church.

"Show yerself." Ed boomed out his command as though he were casting out a demon.

Gwenn's forlorn face popped up above the balcony railing and the clueless Joel, who missed his opportunity to escape, rose up beside her.

"The Lord Jesus Christ will not stand by while ya besmirch His name, young lady. Mary was a virgin, not a harlot. Go wait in the car." Ed hung his head and murmured an additional rebuke, just loud enough for the main stage audience, and promptly appointed the angelic Heidi to play the role of Mary.

"Amen." Present day Ed uttered the last word out loud and brought Gwenn back to the current crisis.

"Ed, the doctor said she might not have much time. We should be with her—"

Pastor Ed turned his fear into righteous indignation, aimed at his favorite target. "Dontcha question the Lord's will, Gwenn."

Well, at least he got my name right.

"Yer mother's life is in the Lord's hands now. His will be done."

"OK, Ed. I just wanted to give you the latest *medical* report." Gwenn rolled her eyes as she turned. "I'll be in Shirley's room...with Steven," she added. At this point it truly felt like she had nothing to lose.

Forty-two

The ethereal feeling of living inside a dream world continued. Rachel could not believe she was backstage at a rock concert with her...mom. Greta, Mia and Rachel were all crammed into the wing listening to The Spanking Machine killing it on stage.

"Annie's band is *really* good, Rachel. You must be so proud."

Honestly, Rachel had been so wrapped up in her bakery- and family-related dramas that she had forgotten just how amazing Annie could be. "Yeah, she fuckin' rocks." She cursed without hesitation.

"She's a fuckin' rock star," Mia chimed in.

The three gals giggled and shushed each other, simultaneously.

The set was nearing its end and the headliner's people came to clear out the wings. "You'll have to go back to the green room now. He doesn't allow anyone to stand in the wings when he plays."

Rachel exchanged a wink with Mia. "Oh, Annie's my wife...she actually arranged for us to meet him before he went on stage." The lie poured out of Rachel's mouth like a siren's sweet song.

The information was met with a flurry of headset touching and walkie-talkie communiqués. "Follow me," Hot Pink Hair announced.

Mia suppressed a squeal and Rachel smirked at her co-conspirators. She never expected the lie to work. She was fairly certain his royal bodyguards would stop them.

They approached a private dressing room door and Rachel heard Hot Pink Hair whisper to the bodyguard, "Yeah, the one she proposed to from the Hollywood Bowl..."

Rachel watched in awe as the portal to the kingdom opened and they were quickly ushered inside.

"Hey, Rachel. Nice to meet you." Prince was looking back at her from his reflection in the mirror. His face warmed by a shy grin.

"Oh...um, hi. This is my mom, Greta and her friend, Mia."

"Hey girls." He nodded into the mirror and his reflection nodded to them.

Mia squealed and muttered nonsense.

Greta nodded and blinked back tears of pride. Everything Rachel did made her the proudest woman on the planet.

"Thank you, ladies, he needs to prepare. I'll walk you back to the green room." Hot Pink Hair was not negotiating. Their audience with royalty was over.

The three of them turned and jostled toward the exit.

Rachel felt a hand on her shoulder. She jumped and turned to find herself face-to-face with a rock legend. Her pupils dilated so fast they swallowed her irises.

"Congratulations on the engagement." He nodded and smiled encouragingly.

"Thank you...Your Highness...I mean, Prince. Oh, shit."

The sound of his laughter followed them out of the dressing room and they giggled all the way to the green room. Hot Pink Hair was not amused.

The Spanking Machine poured into the green room and the cacophony of praises and hilarious anecdotes drowned out the buzzing of Rachel's phone.

***

Gwenn patted herself on the back for making the call and thanked a god she didn't believe in for keeping Rachel from answering. "No answer, I'll try again later," she reported to Steven.

Shirley was a sight. Gwenn knew in her heart this was the end. She thought she had seen the worst when she checked in on her after the transplant—but this...there was no piece of Shirley in the husk that Gwenn saw lying in the hospital bed.

Steven didn't know what to say or do. Making comments about how terrible Shirley looked would be severely counterproductive and he had already retrieved the cup of coffee that had constituted his entire "To Do" list. Sit quietly and wait for death—a familiar, painful pastime that threatened to let his prisoner-of-war memories seep into the present.

Pastor Ed finally relinquished his prayer vigil and returned to his wife's side. Even in his sorrow-filled state he minded his ministerial manners. "Good evening, I'm Pastor Ed Hutchinson, Gwenn's dad."

"I'm Steven Hays, we actually met—"

A firm pinch on the back of his arm ended his greeting—too late.

"Steven, Steven...that name rings a bell. Are ya that Jewish boy?"

"Yes, Ed. He's 'that Jewish boy'." Gwenn spat the retort across the room. "I can't believe you are going to sit here, at a time like this, and worry about shit like that." The curse tasted sweet in her mouth.

"Watch yer tongue, young lady."

"I'm no young lady, Ed. According to Shirley I'm a whore and according to you I'm not fit to play the imaginary character of a fictional god's mother in a fucking x-mas play!" She turned to storm out, but the stitches reduced the hurricane to a gentle breeze. Luckily the "F" word had temporarily gagged Ed and she was able to make an exit before he could reply.

"I'll go after her, sir." Steven ladled on the respect in a fruitless attempt to compensate for Gwenn's tirade.

Steven found her shuffling down the hallway. "That was quite an exit. You botched it a little with the post-surgical shuffle, but I'd say you stuck the landing."

Gwenn chuckled and turned into his body. Wet, salty puddles formed on his chest and she wiped her nose on her sleeve, like a street urchin. "Take me home, please."

"You don't want to be here...don't you...I don't think she's gonna..." Steven couldn't finish his thought. The memory of missing his father's funeral rose up in his throat and he swallowed several times, failing to banish the lump.

"Steven, I can't explain how I feel—or how I *don't* feel. That woman emotionally abused Rachel and I our entire lives. I understand she had a shitty childhood, but that didn't give her the right to take it out on me. I mean, for fuck's sake, I'm not some accident—some unwanted pregnancy. She chose to adopt kids and then just fucked us up. I have to break this chain. I'm not going to pretend shit just to make other people happy—not anymore. I don't feel sad and I'm not going to beat myself up for that." Gwenn's fists unconsciously clenched with anger and defiance.

"Are you sure? You might wish you had stayed."

"I wish I had grown a pair when she was still lucid. The only time I ever stood my ground with her was when she was in a coma, waiting for the transplant. It's not going to matter one bit to her if I'm in that room when she dies. The truth is it will just upset Ed to have a nonbeliever in there—he'd probably blame her death on my lack of faith." Gwenn wiped her eyes and smiled bravely at Steven. "Sorry for the tirade." She exhaled and reached for his hand. "Take me home. I'm sure."

***

Rachel and Annie drove back to Andersonville with Greta and Mia. They sat up most of the night talking and swapping stories. Greta made everyone scrambled eggs, Swedish pancakes and mimosas around 4:00 a.m.

Mia was the first to succumb to exhaustion. "All right ladies, I have to open the book store at 10:00 a.m. today so I better get a couple hours of shut eye.

After she left, Annie asked the question that had been burning in her mind since she left the previous afternoon. "So, what's her story?"

Rachel and Greta giggled impulsively at Annie's directness, but mostly because they were both punchy from lack of sleep and over-stimulation.

"Sorry, good gravy I'm silly." Greta took a minute to collect herself. "Seriously, though, Mia's husband was killed in a terrible farming accident the first year they were married. He was her one true love—like Loukas was for me—she and I ended up becoming friends through our shared heartbreak. Neither of us ever wanted to remarry or have kids—you know my reason," she patted Rachel's hand,

"I was devastated over the loss of my baby, and Mia miscarried during all the stress following her husband's grisly death. We just couldn't imagine experiencing any of that pain again. We became each other's support system." Her mind wandered off to long forgotten scenes. "Gee whiz, I better get some sleep."

"So you're like *Kate & Allie*...without the kids."

"Who is that now?" Greta furrowed her brow.

"I was raised by a single mom, so I watched a lot of TV after school. *Kate & Allie* was this cool 80s sitcom about these two women living together, raising their kids and sharing expenses. I kinda had the hots for Susan Saint James." Annie smirked.

"Holy shit. That is the longest sentence Annie has ever uttered. We have to go to sleep immediately, she's delusional." Rachel convulsed with laughter.

"OK, girls. Your room is at the top of the stairs, to the left, first door past the bathroom. I will see you when I see you, sleep as late as you want."

Rachel hugged Greta one more time before she went upstairs. She could not wait to introduce her mom to Gwenn.

 Forty-three

Steven helped Gwenn into the cabin, hung up her coat and helped her to the sofa.

"I'll get a fire going in the fireplace and make you some tea...is there anything else I can do before I head out?"

Gwenn's head lolled back onto the couch and she closed her eyes. She knew it would be best to let him go, but if she were alone she would have time to think. Thinking was highly overrated. "Could you stay?" She meant it to come out like a friendly request, but it escaped like a whispered wish meant only for the candles on a birthday cake.

"Are you asking me to spend the night with you, Gwenn? Isn't that against the rules?" Steven teased.

"I just don't want to be alone with my thoughts tonight. I'm barely mobile...nothing is gonna happen, OK?"

Steven chuckled wickedly, "You'd be surprised." He turned off the kettle and dragged a chair to the kitchen. He procured several pillows, a blanket and two bath towels.

Gwenn could stand the suspense no longer, "What in the hell are you doing?"

"I'm creating a safe space for you."

"Oh, for fuck's sake...what are you actually doing?"

"I'm going to wash your hair in the kitchen sink," he replied as he walked out of the bathroom holding shampoo and conditioner.

Her emotions were already shaken up into a dangerous cocktail. It took all her strength to blink fiercely until the tears were banished. "Thank you."

He guided her to the cushiony throne and carefully leaned her back. Her neck rested on a rolled up towel and her dodgy tresses filled the sink. "Damn, I'm good," he announced.

"Not bad, Sergeant. Let's see your scalp skills."

He ran the water in the adjoining side of the sink and slowly moved it over Gwenn's hair, after it reached optimum temperature.

The warm water on her head sent shivers down her spine.

He squeezed some shampoo into his palm, rubbed his hands together to distribute the silky liquid and gently grasped her hair.

His fingers felt like velvet. He massaged her scalp with the perfect amount of pressure. Tension dissolved. Guilt flooded in to fill the vacated space. She thought about the promise she had made to herself at the hospital. The promise not to pretend shit just to make other people happy. She had pretended so much, for so long—she had even fooled herself.

He grabbed a small bowl from the counter and filled it with water to help him rinse the soap from her hair. The old-fashioned faucet did not have a pull-out nozzle and he didn't want to jostle Gwenn.

Warm water flowed over her scalp. Hot tears leaked from her eyes.

"Hey, you OK? Am I hurting you?"

"Wrap that towel around my hair...we need to talk."

He was instantly on high alert. That phrase had never led to good things. He dutifully wrapped her hair in the towel and tipped the chair back onto all fours.

"Thank you..." the rest of her words were swallowed by a fresh onslaught of tears.

Steven silently helped her to the sofa. He feared the worst. He was sure he had done something wrong today and she was going to dump him. He could feel it.

She wanted to prolong the moment of truth. She stalled. "Can you make us some tea?"

"You bet." Steven quietly returned to the kitchen and put the kettle on the stove. He grabbed two mugs and searched for a spoon for the sugar. He opened and closed a few drawers and froze when he saw the poem lying on top of the flatware. He knew he shouldn't read it, but he did.

The silence concerned Gwenn. "Did you find everything all right?"

Steven's jealousy percolated. He held the letter aloft, like an enemy transmission, and burst into the living room. "Is this what we have to talk about?" His eyes were wild and his voice echoed loudly in the enclosed space.

Gwenn looked at the card and wished it could be the lifeboat in this angry sea. Before she could formulate an answer the whistle of the kettle pierced the silence.

He threw the card at Gwenn and stormed back into the kitchen. He flicked off the burner and returned, seconds later. "Are you gonna tell me what the hell is going on?"

She drew a ragged breath and looked down at her fingers anxiously dancing in her lap. "I wasn't completely honest with you—"

"Clearly," he angrily interrupted.

"Steven, calm the fuck down. It's not about this goddamn card." She waved it furiously at him. "This just appeared on my doorstep. I'm not secretly seeing Daniel, OK?"

His pulse was racing and he could feel the pressure building in his skull. "Give me a minute...I'll...just hold on." He spun on his heels and walked out the front door.

She sat in shocked silence. Maybe he would leave and never come back, just like before. Perhaps fate would spare her the pain of revealing the truth.

The front door opened and Steven returned.

She could hear how his breathing had slowed. He was back. Fate would spare no one.

A few moments passed and finally Steven walked in with two mugs of tea. He set his down on the coffee table and handed the second mug to Gwenn, handle first.

"Thanks."

"What do we need to talk about?"

"About the day you left...about the false alarm."

He breathed a sigh of relief. She just wanted assurances of his commitment. He could understand her having concerns that the past might repeat itself. He had gotten himself all worked up over nothing—again. "What do you want to know?"

"It's what I want you to know. I've never told another living soul what I'm about to tell you...please don't say anything until I finish. If you...I...please." She could feel her heart thudding just behind her ribs.

"Gwenn, you're scaring me."

"Promise."

"OK. I promise I'll let you finish." Steven leaned back in his chair and folded his hands.

"I wasn't completely honest with you in Mexico, when I told you about the false alarm. I was nervous and excited...

a little scared. I repeated the story I've been telling myself for 12 years. It's the story I've always told...the one that makes the pain go away."

He leaned forward and Gwenn silenced him with a quick gesture. She shook her head, swallowed and continued. "It wasn't a false alarm. I was pregnant and I was terrified. There was no way in hell I was ever going to let Ed and Shirley know what I had done. When you left I shut down, emotionally. I went into a mechanical survival mode. I drove over to Eau Claire and I had an abortion."

Steven's head dropped to his chest.

Gwenn fumbled to find her way back to her story. "Then I erased the whole horrible event from my mind, created the false alarm story and never—ever—let myself look back."

When Steven raised his head to look at Gwenn his eyes were red and tears spilled over. "We had a child?"

She nodded robotically, refusing to say the word aloud.

He scooted to the edge of his chair and looked at her pleadingly. "If I had stayed, could I have convinced you to keep the baby?"

"No," she whispered.

"No? Just like that, no?" He stood up and paced behind the chair. "I might've found a way to convince you. We could've gotten married..." His eyes drifted off to alternate pasts.

"Steven, I had been raised on a steady diet of fear and guilt. There is no universe where I would have listened to you, my humiliation was too deep."

"But—"

"There is no 'but', we were drifting apart. You knew I wouldn't convert to Judaism and I knew you wouldn't marry a gentile. We were at an impasse, Steven. Things ended up the way they did for a reason."

He walked over to the sofa and sat down next to Gwenn. He picked up her hand like a piece of fine bone china and placed it in his. He smiled and whispered, "We had a child."

She shook her head and a small sob escaped her throat. "No, Steven, we didn't."

His jaw tensed and released. "We have another chance. This time we can get it right. We'll get married—no conversion—and we'll start a family, together. We're ready to make it work now."

Gwenn thought the most painful secret she would share had already been spilled. She was terribly wrong. "I'm sorry, Steven, but I don't want a family. That's why I donated the kidney in place of Rachel. I wanted her to have the best possible chance to get pregnant, and I knew I never wanted to have kids."

"That's selfish, Gwenn."

"It's my body, Steven. I get to be selfish with it."

He stopped pacing and fixed her with an unreadable look. "That's not what I mean, and you know it. I sacrificed everything to have a second chance with you and you're going to throw it all away because of some old buried guilt—over an abortion."

The word had only recently made its appearance in her vocabulary and she already hated it. One word that could carry so much weight. Guilt. Shame. Selfishness. Freedom. Peace. Loss. Survival. Terror. Pain. Desperation. Renewal. "It's a lot to process, Steven. Let's table it—for now. Maybe after a few neurofeedback sessions you'll be in a better place to talk about everything.

"Yeah, I'm not doing that. I decided it's my body and I don't think it's a good idea." He crossed his arms tightly over his chest.

"I hope you will reconsider...I hope we can..." Gwenn let the tears flow freely.

"There's nothing to reconsider, Gwenn. You made all the decisions without me. There's nothing left for me...I was living in a fantasy world. Thanks for the reality check."

Gwenn swiped haphazardly at her tears, but she could think of nothing to say.

Steven put on his coat and walked out the door.

She put another small log on the fire and turned up the heater. She knew there would be no sleep for her tonight, so she turned off all the lights and watched the moon-dappled waves lap at the shore. The ice had all but disappeared on the lake. She pictured herself paddling the canoe out to the middle and tipping it over so the glacial waters could swallow her—secrets and all. The pain and sutures in her abdomen were just fate having another laugh at her expense. No paddling on this day, Gwendolyn.

The inconsiderate early-morning ring of a phone pulled Gwenn from the depths of dreamland. She had somehow dozed off on the couch and her neck had a sharp pain on the left side. Before she had time to think about the previous night's debacle, the phone rang again.

Gwenn pushed off the couch, wrapped herself in a spare blanket and tottered to her phone. It was *the* call—she could feel it.

"Hi, Ed, what's the news?"

"The Lord saw fit ta call her home last night, Trixie. Yer mom is gone home ta Jesus."

Well, not my mom. She kept that thought to herself and replied, "I'm sorry for your loss, Ed."

"Services will be next Saturday and we'll have ta wait fer the thaw ta lay her ta rest in the cemetery. We're still frozen a good four or five feet down."

"OK, I'll call Rachel."

"Oh, I already—"

The intrusive CLICK of call waiting harassed Gwenn's ear and cut off Ed's sentence. She glanced at her phone and saw the avatar of Rachel's goofy face smiling back at her. "I gotta go, it's Rache." She hung up on Pastor Ed and answered her sister's call.

"Gwenny? Is it true? Did Mom, I mean my other mom... my adoptive mom—"

"Rache, slow down, slow down. Yes, Shirley passed away last night from complications."

"Was she sick? Did you know? Why didn't you call me?" Rachel was pacing around Greta's house and babbling like an idiot.

"I tried to call you—once—and then I selfishly chose to let you have one night of bliss. If you hate me forever, it will still be worth it to me. I just could not let Shirley take that moment away from you." Gwenn wiped away an errant tear. "I'm sorry."

Rachel's muffled sobs filled the silence.

Gwenn could hear someone, probably Greta, comforting Rachel in the background. "Do you want to call me back later, Rache?"

"No, [sniffle] no, [mini-sob] just give me a sec." Rachel managed to dry her tears and return to the conversation with Gwenn. "Tell me what happened."

Gwenn relayed the story of the septic shock, the hospital chapel scene and the mammoth f-bomb dropped before her exit from Shirley's room.

"You're not sad? No regrets?"

"Shit, Rache, I have a mountain of regrets and Shirley only accounts for a few boulders at the foot of that edifice. I don't know how I feel. We never made any real headway with her…she didn't ever meet us halfway…she's gone. It all feels kinda factual. Maybe it will hit me ten years from now, or maybe it will hit me tomorrow. But the one thing I am not going to do is let that woman guilt trip me from beyond the grave."

"I love you, Gwenny. She gave me you and that is the one thing I'm gonna hold onto." Rachel sobbed and blew her nose.

Gwenn pressed her hand to her chest, "Yeah, I love you, too…"

They listened to each other breathe and found comfort in their shared history. Rachel was the first to break the mood, "When's the funeral?"

"The service is next Saturday, but they have to wait a few weeks, maybe longer, for the ground to thaw so we can bury her."

"So we have to go through this twice?"

"Yeah, leave it to Shirley to get an encore performance at her own funeral."

They laughed until they both cried. "I better let you go, Rache. You need to tell Annie and your real mom what happened."

"It's 'birth mom', although I guess there's no one's feelings to hurt anymore…"

"Will you be back for the service?"

"Oh, for sure. I have to be back tomorrow night. I own a bakery, remember?"

"I can't frickin' wait. I want to hear all about Greta, and Annie's concert, and Chicago and…everything. I miss you like crazy…freak."

"You're the freak. Holed up in a cabin, all by yourself, like a weird hermit…"

"I had some company last night, but it's a long story."

Rachel leaped, "Gwenny, you are a whore!" She squealed with laughter. "You're supposed to be recuperating and 'sorting things out.' Sounds like you got yourself sorted, eh?"

"Trust me, it's totally not what you're thinking. Steven took me to the hospital last night and he just made sure I got home safe." Gwenn could not keep the pain out of her voice.

"Sounds worse than you're sayin'." Rachel's voice filled with concern. "You can tell me the rest of the story when I see you tomorrow night. I'm coming straight up to the cabin—you gonna be OK?"

"I can't wait to see you, sweetie. I really missed you these last couple days. Nobody gets me like you...maybe it's our shared PTSD, right?"

"Definitely. See ya soon."

Forty-four

Rachel opened her eyes and rolled over to watch Annie sleep. The light creeping around the edges of the blinds was a bright golden yellow. The aroma of coffee and delicious pastries floated up the stairs and encouraged her to roll out of bed. She moved slowly and quietly.

"Are you sneakin' out on me like a bad one night stand?" Annie mumbled sleepily.

Rachel raced back to the bed, slipped under the duvet and planted a big wet kiss on Annie's sassy little mouth. "Can you believe we are makin' out in my mom's house? And she's totally OK with it?"

Annie chuckled and wrapped her arms around Rachel. "What time does your flight leave?"

"Don't spoil my moment."

"Oh, it's *your* moment?"

"I mean, *our* moment." Rachel nuzzled into Annie's neck and inhaled the scent of rock n' roll. "You still smell like your concert." Rachel inhaled deeply. "Mmmmm. Like sweat, adrenaline, sex and…is that cigarettes?"

Annie closed her eyes and scrunched up her face. She did not want to get into a fight this morning. She knew she would quit as soon as the tour ended, but Rachel could not understand someone having that kind of control over their obsessions. It was not the right time to point out that one of them had will power and one of them didn't. "Cass and Mika were smoking. I shoulda jumped in the shower last night. Sorry." It was a partial truth—Cass and Mika—and Annie, had been smoking.

Soft whimpering interrupted Annie's mental acrobatics.

"Babe, are you crying? About cigarettes?"

"No, I was thinkin' about lung cancer and Grampa Hutchinson…I can't process…Shirley's dead. The last thing I said to her was so snarky, 'If this is meeting us halfway, Shirley—don't bother.' Now she's dead. It was so bitchy."

Annie hugged Rachel tightly and kissed her forehead. "You did right by me, babe. You came clean. It's all good from your side."

"Yeah? You think so?"

"I know so." Annie teasingly bit Rachel's lower lip and let her hands wander. "You better make a run for those Swedish pancakes, now—while you still have a chance."

Rachel giggled and jumped out of bed. "First one downstairs gets an extra pancake."

"You're on." Annie was not going to be the one to point out that extra pancakes and complaining about extra pounds were at cross purposes—that was Gwenn's territory—thankfully.

"Good morning! How did you sleep?" Greta grinned happily as Rachel raced into the kitchen.

"Like a rock." Rachel crossed the hardwood floor and crushed Greta in a good morning hug. "Do I smell pancakes?"

"You seemed to enjoy them last night...or this morning...whenever that was, so I thought an encore was in order. How are you feeling this morning?"

"You mean about Shirley?"

"Yes. Are you OK?"

"I feel really guilty about our last conversation. I was pissed and kinda threw her words back in her face."

"You had no idea, Rachel. I'm sure she knew how much you loved her."

"Ever since I came out, we had drifted apart. Gwenn tried to build a bridge...Shirley just couldn't see beyond the judgment."

"I'm sorry you didn't have closure. Believe me, I know how that feels." Greta dabbed at her eyes and forced a smile.

The floor creaked under Annie's feet and both women turned their heads in surprise. "Everything OK in here?"

Rachel stepped over to Annie's side and slipped an arm around her waist. "Yeah, I was just talkin' about Shirley."

"Babe, I won't be able to make it to the funeral. The tour heads east from here."

"It's OK. Gwenny has got my back. If it wasn't for my dad, I don't even know if I would go."

"Really?" Greta's voice was filled with shock.

"I'm just in such a weird fuckin' place right now, ya know?" Annie kissed Rachel's cheek. "I know, babe. It's OK."

"But, tonight I get to see Gwenny." Rachel beamed with anticipation. "I wish she could've come with me..."

Greta served breakfast and they ate in relative silence. Rachel polished off several pancakes and at least three sausages. "These pancakes are the best. You have to give me the recipe, Mom." She nearly choked on a bit of pancake as the word caught in her throat. Rachel looked across the table at Greta and felt the emotion well up in her eyes.

"What is it, honey? What's wrong?" Greta pushed her chair back from the table and prepared to move to Rachel's side.

"I'm so happy I found you." Rachel rubbed her watery eyes. "I'm a basket case. Sorry."

"You have absolutely nothing to apologize for, dear. You are ten times the daughter I ever dreamed you would be. I feel like I just got a new lease on life." Greta walked over to her daughter's side and gave her a loving squeeze. "You're not a basket case. You're beautiful." She kissed the top of her head. "And I love you."

Annie slid her chair back from the table and collected the plates. Deep down she felt genuine happiness for Rachel, but right on the surface she felt like a third wheel. "Hey, babe, what time do you have to be at the airport?"

"I don't know? Maybe by 2:30?"

"We can share a cab."

"Oh, a cab ride all the way to the airport would cost a fortune. I can drive Rachel to O'Hare." Greta smiled and nodded.

There was no way to win this without coming off like an asshole, so Annie just accepted her fate. She would not get one last moment alone with Rachel, but she was a big girl. She'd get over it.

"Actually, Mom, I don't mind the cab ride. I won't get to see Annie for almost two months after today, and if you take me to the airport I will sob like a lost child when you drop me off. Hutchinson 101: Do not make a scene in public—it's kinda hard to shake that one."

Greta chuckled, "I understand. I'm just being greedy. I don't ever want you to leave, but I'll get over it. Now that I know I can call you anytime...that you're real...that you want me in your life—well, I can face angry dragons, armed with nothing more than a garden hose."

They all laughed and nodded.

Annie felt her heart jump with a little anticipatory excitement. *Alone with Rachel—yes!*

"Well, you kids better gather up your things and hit the road." Greta blinked back the tears that threatened to burst forth. "Rachel, honey, can you just make sure I have your phone number and email address...maybe your Skype name and Facebook...and your address?" She blinked harder and took big deep breaths.

Rachel smiled through her own tears and added, "If you have some ink I can leave you a full set of fingerprints, too."

Greta laughed out loud. "I'll be better next time, I promise. This first...well, actually the second, but regardless, this goodbye is hard for me."

"It's not goodbye, Mom. It's just the beginning. I'm sure we'll be talking on the phone everyday." Rachel's grin held love and promise.

"OK, that helps a little."

Rachel and Annie climbed back up the worn wooden stairs and retrieved their stuff.

"Thanks for givin' me the cab ride, babe."

Rachel slipped her arms around Annie and dragged her tongue across Annie's bottom lip. "I pity the cab driver." She pushed her tongue deeper into Annie's mouth and kissed her hungrily.

Greta had gathered up all the photos and mementos, and placed them back in the special keepsake box. She heard Rachel on the steps and called, "Do you want me to mail all this stuff to you so you don't have to check a bag?"

"Absolutely not. I'm not lettin' that stuff outta my sight." Rachel dropped down onto the floor, dumped out the contents of her backpack, shoved it all into her rolling suitcase and reached toward Greta for the box. "See, it will fit perfectly in my backpack."

Annie and Greta exchanged a smirk.

"OK, all set." Rachel zipped up her rucksack.

"The cab will be here any minute. I'd say that I won't cry, but we both know that's a lie." Greta laughed at herself. "By the way, I can't wait to help you plan the wedding. You should go onto my website and see some of the cakes...you can have anything you want."

The taxi honked as it pulled up to the curb.

As promised Greta immediately wept. She hugged Annie quickly and pulled Rachel in for one last squeeze. "Call me as soon as you land."

"I will." Rachel let the tears shamelessly flow down her freckled cheeks. "Thanks for everything, Mom."

HONK!

"We better hit the road, babe." Annie picked up Rachel's suitcase and walked to the cab.

Greta and Rachel exchanged a few more hugs and promises before Rachel managed to drag herself to the waiting taxi.

The ensuing cab ride was far less of a turn on than promised. The driver was an overly friendly chatterbox and all thoughts of backseat sexy times were squashed.

Rachel did manage to prolong the goodbye at the airport—racking up an extra $3.00 in cab fare worth of foreplay.

"Babe, you're gonna miss your flight."

"I don't care." Rachel clutched Annie like a junkie holding onto her last high. "Maybe I'll join the tour. I could ride the bus and—"

"And lose the bakery, and not plan the wedding, and send Gwenn into a tailspin." Annie kissed Rachel's full lips with tenderness and promise. "I love you, babe."

Rachel smiled through her tears. "I love you, too. I can't believe it's going to be two more months."

"You'll be so busy with all the plans...time will fly."

"Call me everyday?"

"Don't I always?"

Rachel took one last taste of Annie's sweet lips and tore herself away. "I miss you already."

"Ditto."

She watched the cab pull away from the curb and disappear into a sea of taxis circling O'Hare. As the distraction of Annie dissolved the reality of boarding an airplane loomed hideously. Rachel decided a couple shots of courage might be required before she could find the nerve to climb back into the shiny metal cocoon of death.

Forty-five

Gwenn was looking forward to hearing all about Rachel's trip to the Windy City, but she had ulterior motives for bending her recuperation rules and driving to the airport—slightly medicated.

"Gwenny!" Rachel jumped into the Jeep and lunged toward her sister.

"Easy, killer. I'm not actually supposed to be driving or getting the life squeezed out of me yet, so back it down a notch." Gwenn hugged Rachel, cautiously.

A long moment of silence hung in the air as Gwenn exited the airport. "I can't believe Shirley's dead."

"I'm sorry I wasn't here, Gwenny. I feel guilty about everything. I let you down and the last thing I said—"

Gwenn jumped in, "Trust me, there is no way that it could be worse than the last thing I said."

"Omycrap! I totally forgot you dropped the F-bomb on her deathbed."

"Well, not directly on it...I was talking to Ed...but, yeah, I win worst final words."

"Do you feel sad? Did you cry?"

"Nope. I don't feel anything...about Shirley." Gwenn looked out the driver's side window and swallowed hard.

"Gwenny, what is it? What happened?"

"Steven."

"Did he fuckin' disappear again? I'll kill him, I swear I will—"

"No, it's my fault. We had a fight and I..." Gwenn could not face the truth. She struggled to connect to her well-rehearsed story, but she couldn't ignore the truth seeping through the cracks like blood leaking out of a serial killer's trunk.

"Are you OK?"

The dam broke. Tears exploded.

"Gwenny, pull over and let me drive."

Rachel's recessive take-charge gene suddenly appeared and Gwenn instantly pulled the car off the road. They climbed out of the car, hugged in front of the headlights and got back in on opposite sides.

"Did you guys break up?"

Gwenn silently recited her new mantra about not pretending shit, took a ragged breath and spilled the whole sordid tale to her sister.

"I'm so sorry I wasn't there to help you, Gwenny. It must have been awful to get an abortion all alone...to keep that secret...I'm so sorry."

"It's not your fault, Rache, you don't need to apologize." Gwenn let her head fall back against the headrest. "You had already tried to kill yourself once. There was no way I was going to throw my baggage onto your back...you had so much to deal with..." she sighed.

"Does anyone else know?"

Gwenn chuckled, in spite of her pain. "Hutchinson 101, right? Assess the damage. Repair the façade."

"Gwenny, that's not what I meant." Rachel took a moment to feel sorry for herself and added, "Does Daniel know?"

"Seriously? That's your question? Why the hell would I tell Daniel something like that, huh? It's over between us. I fucked it up like I always do and ended up with no one."

"You don't think Steven will come back?"

"It wasn't just the lie, Rache. I told him I never wanna have kids and that was the real deal breaker."

"Are you sure? You'd be a great mom, you were to me."

Gwenn smiled and squeezed Rachel's knee. "We were there for each other, sweetie. You helped me as much as I helped you." She leaned back in the seat and pondered her decision for a moment. "Ya know, Rache, I think I made the choice a long time ago. I don't want the responsibility of trying not to completely fuck someone up. Look at what I've done to myself." She laughed bitterly.

"Well, you'll be the best goddamn aunt in the universe." Rachel pounded her fist on the steering wheel.

"You still gonna knock yourself up?"

"Yeah, I'm even more excited now that I have Greta in my life. She's the mom we both dreamed of, Gwenny."

"I'm happy for you, Rache. You deserve it." Gwenn fiddled with her seatbelt and told Rachel where to turn.

"Gwenn?"

"Yeah?"

"Is it OK if Greta helps plan the wedding?"

"Rache, sweetie, it's more than OK. This is going to be the second best day of your life and I want it to be exactly perfect...I mean exactly perfect for you."

"What was the first best?"

"The day you met her, I would guess," Gwenn chuckled.

"You're wrong, the first best day was the day you became my sister."

Rachel parked in front of the cabin and they both got out of the car and walked straight into a much-needed hug. Rachel squeezed a little too tight, but Gwenn wouldn't trade the pain for anything.

They had covered most of the major issues on the drive back and there was a general consensus of exhaustion. Rachel had already fallen asleep by the time Gwenn crawled into bed. She reached over and threaded her fingers through Rachel's. She fell asleep thinking of all the different places they had lived, all the beds they had shared and all the times their intertwined fingers had been the only safe place in the world.

The cool grey light of dawn pushed Rachel's eyelids open. She rolled over and pulled Gwenn's hair.

"Ow, brat!"

"Hey, I have to get down to the bakery. Nathan said he'd open for me, but William couldn't come in early...so I gotta go."

"OK, can I hobble out and make you some scrambled eggs? I don't want you filling up on scones." Gwenn cautiously rolled out of bed. "Wow, I feel pretty good today. I can almost walk at a regular speed." She twirled and added, "Look at me, I'm a real girl."

"Hey, Florence Nightingale. Those eggs aren't gonna make themselves." Rachel chuckled as she pulled on yesterday's clothes.

"Hey, Ken Jennings, Florence Nightingale was a nurse not a patient."

"Who the fuck is Ken Jennings?"

Gwenn rolled her eyes and shook her head, "I'm officially done missing you."

They made their way to the kitchen and Rachel brewed the coffee while Gwenn scrambled the eggs. The toast popped up just as Gwenn scooped the eggs onto the plates. "Perfect timing."

"Too bad you can't date as well as you scramble eggs." Rachel giggled and brought their coffees to the table.

Gwenn didn't respond, she took a quiet sip of her coffee and twirled her fork in her eggs. "Can I show you something?"

Rachel was busy shoveling eggs and gave a quick nod and a grunt.

Gwenn retrieved Daniel's card from the living room and set it down in front of Rachel. "What do you think?"

She read through the poem and dropped her fork with a clatter. "Gwenny, he's still in love with you! You didn't fuck it up. You've still got a chance." Rachel picked up the card and felt the texture on the back. She turned it over and let out a low whistle when she saw the intricate paper mosaic depicting her and Gwenn. "What did he say when you called him?"

"I didn't."

"What? Not even to say 'thanks'?"

"There was a lot of shit goin' down around here, Rache. I didn't exactly have a clear head."

"What are you gonna do now—now that you know?"

"I'm thinking I'll take the coward's way out and just wait. If he's serious he'll try again."

"Well, that's just stupid."

"Rache, don't...don't judge. I've got enough to handle right now. Shirley's funeral, my recovery and at some point I have to actually run my company."

"Don't forget about my wedding," Rachel teased.

"And most importantly, your wedding." Gwenn shook her head and laughed.

Rachel suddenly remembered her conversation with Daniel, right after Gwenn's surgery. So much had happened she had forgotten all about the Elena secret, but for once she realized that it wasn't her secret to tell. She was also a little worried about dropping a bomb like that and leaving Gwenn alone for the day. "Do you still have feelings for him?"

"Daniel?"

"Who the hell did you think we were talking about? Randy? Yeah, Daniel, ya freak."

"I never stopped having feelings for him, Rache. But everything got mixed up when Steven showed up. I got all wrapped up in having a second chance and righting past wrongs...clearly all bad reasons to start a relationship. I'm gonna make a pros and cons list—"

"Oh, for fuck's sake, Gwenn, unclench." Rachel scraped her chair back from the table and set her dishes in the sink. "I gotta get down to the bakery, but I'm coming back tonight and we're gonna pull that stick outta your ass."

"I can't be impulsive, Rache, it never works out for me. I just need a couple more days up here to sort out my feelings, don't push me, OK?"

"OK, but I can think of a couple times being impulsive paid off...New Zealand and Daniel. Just sayin'."

"Let me get your coat." Gwenn shoved Rachel out the door and handed her the Jeep keys. "Just take the Jeep, I'm not supposed to be driving anyway."

"You should call Daniel."

"You should mind your own business. Bye." Gwenn closed the door and shook her finger at Rachel.

Rachel stuck her tongue out at Gwenn, climbed into the Jeep and drove away.

Forty-six

"Good morning, Dr. Mountainside's office. How may I brighten your day?"

"You just did," Daniel joked. "I have a 10:00 appointment."

"I'll put you right through, sir."

Dr. Brenda Mountainside had been expecting Daniel's call, but it was after 10:00. "I thought I might not hear from you this week, Daniel."

The professional admonishment was not lost on him, "I apologize for the tardiness of the call Brenda. I was searching around for my courage."

She chuckled, "What seems to have happened?"

"Some talented, not-so-young artist seems to have created a small work of art, embellished it with an original poem and placed it on Gwenn's doorstep."

"Tell me, Daniel, are you proud of this not-so-young man?"

"I think I am."

"Sounds like you took that 'showing her your heart' advice…to heart." Brenda smoothed her gray wool skirt and re-crossed her legs to create a better lap-desk, before she made a few notes about Daniel's art project.

"I did."

"What was the result of your risk?"

"Nothing."

"Can you explain?"

"Sure, but there's nothing to explain. Nothing happened. She didn't call, or text or show up at my place…nothing."

"That must have hurt. You took the risk, you dared to be vulnerable and you weren't rewarded." She made an additional note and flipped back a few pages before she added, "Will you try again or will you close yourself off, like you did after Angeline was killed?"

Daniel bristled at the unexpected mention of his saintly departed wife. "Why would you mention her?"

"Do you see any connection?"

He took a deep breath and focused his mind. It was difficult to get past the defensiveness that always cropped up around Angeline. He had been down this road with Dr. Mountainside, he had done the right thing—he let Angeline live her dreams. No one is immune from tragedy. He searched for the connection. He found nothing.

"Daniel?"

"I'm still here, Brenda. I guess I don't see it."

"Hmmm. That surprises me, you're a fairly intuitive man," she said. "Think about what we worked through surrounding Angeline's death, and what you're feeling today."

"The risk isn't worth the reward?" He floated it out hesitantly.

"Do you honestly believe that, Daniel?"

"The risk is the reward?"

"Ah, there it is." She made several hasty notes and checked the small clock on her desk. "Relationships are about more than some other person returning your affection. Relationships are a venue for you to experiment and grow as an individual—bringing more to the union, or to a future union."

"So basically you're telling me to stop licking my wounds and man up?"

"I'm not sure that's the clinical terminology," she chuckled. "You found your way back after experiencing great loss. You said yourself that Gwenn was the first person who allowed you to love without the specter of Angeline floating over the relationship."

"It's true, that's why I was so sure she was the one."

"Maybe she's 'the one' or maybe she's the path to a new you. A 'you' that can truly find love again in this lifetime."

Daniel exhaled loudly and stood up to pace the hardwood floor in his wool socks. "I'm not paying you enough, Brenda. This is some serious Kwai-Chang-Caine-level stuff."

Brenda acknowledged his cloaked compliment and pushed him a little farther. "What will you do next?"

"As you pointed out, I still have all my fingers and toes, and I don't know what's going on with Gwenn. I mean, for all I know the damn card could've blown away and she never even read it."

"Perhaps not."

"So, I think I'll give the romance strategy one more chance. I don't really have anything to lose, do I?" The question came out a bit more plaintive than he had intended.

"On the contrary, Daniel. I think you have something to gain—for yourself."

"Or in spite of myself," he laughed.

"Are we still keeping this standing appointment?"

"For now…it's a good touchstone for me, ya know."
"Indeed. All right, until next week."
"Thanks, Brenda."
"You are welcome."

Forty-seven

Gwenn walked slowly down the dirt driveway; the mailbox was within her reach. Today was the day to make a fresh start. She touched the mailbox and cold seeped through her gloves. The memory of Shirley's icy hand under hers hit her like an uppercut. She jerked her hand back as frigid drops of pain flooded from her eyes.

Her not-mother was dead. She would never have the chance to convince Shirley to love her—to accept her, completely. Gwenn hugged her arms tightly around her own torso and let the tears fall. She was not going to waste her life regretting the mistakes and missed opportunities of her past. *What's done is done.* She could not get her childhood back, she could not have a different mother; she could not rewrite history.

She continued to put one foot in front of the other and before she realized it, she was back on the front porch. She opened the door and made a decision. Now it was simply the matter of making the call.

Gwenn chewed furiously on her lip as she listened to the phone ringing. Initially she had hoped he would answer, but now she was just hoping for voicemail and a quick getaway.

"Hello?"

"Hi, Ed, it's Gwenn."

Silence.

"I know we don't see eye to eye on most things, but I had no right to say those things to you at the hospital. We were all hurting and I lost my temper, I'm sorry."

"We've both made mistakes, Gwenn. I've had a lot of time ta think since yer mom passed. So, let's both give this another try, eh?"

"I'd like that Ed, I really would." Gwenn didn't know what "another try" would entail, but she was willing to find a sliver of common ground somewhere.

"Are ya gonna speak at yer mother's service?"

She wanted to scream "no fucking way," but opted for a compromise. "I tell you what, if you can remove the altar call from your funeral sermon—just this once—I can figure out a way to say something decent about the woman who raised me. Deal?"

Normally Ed wouldn't even entertain such a request, but his world had shattered all around him. His God had not answered his prayers to save Shirley and his daughters were slipping away. "Is this part a that there meetin' halfway stuff you and Rachel keep talkin' about?"

"Yeah, I guess it is." Gwenn paused to pour boiling water over her hot chocolate powder and stirred the mixture before she answered. "I don't expect you to change your beliefs for me, Ed. I just want you to take a long hard look at the phrase, 'We're all equal in His eyes' and consider loving Rachel and I as we are, instead of as you wish we were."

"I'm not a young man, Trixie. A leopard can't change his spots."

"Ed, that's a cop out. You were someone before you 'found the Lord' and then you changed. I'm just sayin' I think love can cross some boundaries that your faith can't."

"I love ya girls more than my own life."

"Enough to change up the funeral rhetoric?"

"Will ya both come?" Ed paused and cleared his throat, "And say somethin' nice about yer mom?"

"I can't speak for Rachel, but she is the nice one, remember?"

Ed chuckled, "I know ya don't wanna hear it, but ya get that quick wit from yer mom."

Gwenn didn't feel generous enough to accept that comparison, but she was willing to scrape though her memories and dredge up something semi-sweet about Shirley. How hard could that be? "All right, Ed. We'll see you at the service."

"Okey dokey, buh-bye."

Forty-eight

Rachel drove out to the cabin to pick up Gwenn after receiving permission to pierce the recuperation-head-sorting-out veil.

Gwenn was walking back from the mailbox at a nearly normal pace when she heard her Jeep turn onto the dirt road. She turned and waved as Rachel barreled into sight.

She pulled up next to Gwenn and put the window down. "You want a lift back?"

"Nah, this is my big outing for the day. You can head down to the cabin and begin the shutdown procedures—I'll be way behind you," she chuckled.

"10-4." Rachel bounced down the remainder of the driveway and parked.

She opened the door and inhaled the mildly musty smell of history. She thought back to all the summers she and Gwenn had spent out here swimming, climbing trees, building fires and canoeing out to the not-so-secret island. She understood why this place meant so much to Gwenn.

"Hey, freak, what the hell are you doing?" Gwenn poked Rachel's shoulder.

She jumped and turned. "Wow, I guess I 'Gwenned' out. I didn't even hear you come in."

"That's 'cuz you left the damn door open. Good thing it's not quite mosquito season," Gwenn joked. "OK, battle stations. You unload all the perishables from the fridge and put them in that cooler," she pointed to the green Coleman ice chest, "I'll double check all the windows and turn off the heater."

"Hey, remember to leave a faucet dripping, so the pipes don't freeze," Rachel yelled.

"Gramma Carlson had them double insulated and did some other crap under the house, so that's off the checklist, but brownie points for remembering."

They closed up the cabin, Rachel loaded the Jeep and Gwenn slipped Daniel's card inside her jacket.

Rachel was on top of her game today and instantly noticed the gesture. "Hey, whatcha hidin' in there by your boobies?"

"None of your business." Gwenn quickly zipped up her jacket.

"Whatever. Did you hear anything from Steven?"

"No, I'm afraid there will be no resurrection sequel."

"Are you gonna be OK with that?"

"I broke it and it can't be fixed...so there's that..."

Rachel started up the Jeep and reached over to rub Gwenn's shoulder before putting the car in gear. "I mean if you could fix it, would you?"

That was the question that Gwenn had wrestled with since Steven stormed out of the cabin. The last few days had given her some strange clarity on several things. "When he showed up in Mexico, I nearly exploded with happiness. It was like one of my crazy dreams came to life. He was back, he was still in love with me, he wanted to make things right...it was a fucking fairy tale, Rache."

"So what happened, Cinderella?"

"Hilarious." Gwenn shook her head in frustration. "Reality happened. I'm not a 19-year-old girl desperate to escape Shirley's clutches and find someone to validate my worthiness."

"You too, huh?"

"Shit, Rache, I can't even remember half the guys I dated trying to prove that woman wrong...I'm lucky to be alive." Gwenn leaned her head against the cold passenger window and exhaled a puff of hot breath. A circle of condensation appeared and Gwenn took her finger and wrote, "I ♥ me," in the opaque mist.

"Is that true, Gwenny?" Rachel looked hopefully at her sister. "Do you love yourself?"

Gwenn could not contain the tears that spilled from her twinkling hazel eyes. "I do. I finally do."

Rachel pulled over, whipped off her seatbelt and awkwardly hugged Gwenn across the center console. "Life's too short, right?"

"It really is, Rache." Gwenn untangled herself from Rachel and wiped her eyes with one of the many paper napkins strewn about the interior of her vehicle. "When Ed told me that Shirley had passed, I waited to feel sadness." Gwenn looked up and blinked back the building surge. "I thought I felt nothing, but the more I beat myself up for that, the more I realized I did feel something." She took Rachel's hand, "I felt relief."

Rachel exhaled and leaned back in her seat.

"I'm a terrible person, aren't I?" Gwenn squeezed Rachel's hand with both of her own and leaned toward her sister, begging for absolution with every inch of her body.

"I felt the same thing. I thought I was a monster," Rachel said.

They both took deep breaths and sat in silence.

Gwenn was the first to find her voice. "We spent our whole lives being told 'It's not my favorite' and railing against her—arguing, hiding, begging, crying, trying to pry out a moment of unconditional love…" Gwenn shook her head.

"Everyday felt like a struggle," Rachel added.

"When she was gone, there was nothing to push against. There was no love to fight for, and never get. It was just me. Me without Daniel. Me without Steven. Me." Gwenn turned toward Rachel, her eyes glistening with hope. "I finally realized, I could love me. I could love me, and no one could stop me. I'm finally my favorite."

Rachel pulled Gwenn into another hug, "I love you, Gwenny, and you're my favorite no matter what."

"I know, Rache, and I love you no matter what. Now I'm just gonna give myself that same kinda love—like you gave yourself when you finally came out to Ed and Shirley."

Rachel pulled back and smiled at Gwenn. "Here we are, warts and all—deal with it!"

Gwenn choked back a sob and chimed in, "Yeah, deal with it!"

Forty-nine

Daniel was hunkered down in his studio with strict orders not to be interrupted. A cold wind howled outside, but warm indirect light streamed through his north facing windows. He had spent the morning clearing all the paints, brushes and half-full vessels of water off his worktable and now he was ready to begin his project.

He planned to take the image '*Plunder*' from his mental archive and create a mosaic for Gwenn. He remembered her love of shells and had taken several days to sort through the containers of shells Sabina had ordered for him. She had eagerly filled in for Todd, in hopes of a permanent position as Daniel's personal assistant, but he had quickly dispelled her fantasy. Todd was still hard at work finding his replacement and Daniel was going to leave that to the expert—Todd.

He sorted the shells into groups by color. Within each group he arranged his finalists by shade and reflectivity. He had learned a great deal about meticulous preparation from Lorenzo during his time in Mexico. If he had been able to keep his hands off Elena, he certainly would have learned much more.

RING! RING! RING!

"Damn, I thought I turned that thing off." Daniel picked up his phone and saw that it was Todd calling. He knew Todd would never break the "Do Not Disturb," order on a whim. "Hey, Todd, what's up?"

"Sir, damnit, Daniel—it's a hard habit to break—I know you are sequestered, but Flora just shared a bit of news that could not wait."

"Did that Steven punk walk out on her, again?"

"I don't have that information, but it seems that Miss Hutchinson's mother passed away this past weekend."

"Oh shit, I wonder how Gwenn's taking it? Should I call her? Maybe I should drive up there and see if she's OK. What do you think?"

"Oh, is it my turn to talk now?" Todd chuckled teasingly.

"Excuse the word vomit, please continue."

"I don't think you should do anything. I just wanted to tell you because I know you did not receive the desired response from the card you had me deliver. I felt these circumstances might explain her distraction."

Every fiber of Daniel's being wanted to race up to Duluth and comfort Gwenn. He was devastated when his mother's illness finally took her life. "You don't think I should come up?"

"I think you should focus on finishing your next piece and if I hear any additional information—of note—I will call you immediately."

"All right. Thanks." Daniel found himself pacing across the studio and nearly tripped on a stack of unfinished canvasses. "By the way, how's the search for your replacement coming along?"

"Horribly. It turns out I am irreplaceable," Todd replied, in all seriousness.

"Don't I know it," Daniel chuckled.

"That was not a joke, sir. However, Flora and I have come up with an ingenious strategy."

"I would expect no less. What's the plan?"

"We're interviewing candidates together, under the guise of hiring them to work as the office assistant at *The Organizer*, that way we don't get any spotlight chasers." Todd stopped for acknowledgement that did not come. "Anyway, it kills two birds with one stone, because we're bound to find a great person for Flora's office, too."

"Sounds like the Wonder Twins have it all figured out. You'll be permanently relegated to the rank of friend before you know it," Daniel teased.

"I think the Wonder Twins were brother and sister, so let's not use that reference in the future, agreed?"

Daniel's deep, rich laughter filled the phone. "Agreed."

"It's good to hear you laugh."

"It feels like the worst is over, aside from the Steven obstacle, I like my chances with this current future."

Todd opted to ignore the insane space-time continuum foible of the term "current future" and plowed headlong into the real reason for his phone call. "Daniel, can I ask you something, as a friend?"

"Of course. What's on your mind, buddy?"

He rolled his eyes, but chose to ignore the vocative. "As you know, I don't have a significant amount of relationship data with the opposite sex—"

"Todd, just ask the question. We're all runnin' blind when it comes to women. What's going on?"

"It's been a few weeks since I moved into Flora's flat. The first oddity was her need to relocate everything I unpacked.

No matter where I set something she always had a better place. I wrote that off to her expertise in organization and let it go. But last night I decided to wash a few loads of laundry—including both our things—and when I was folding the towels...she kind of lost it."

"Lost it how?"

"It was subtle at first, she came over and started helping me fold. I was perfectly fine with the assistance. Then I noticed she was unfolding and refolding all the towels and washcloths that I had already folded. I confronted her and it blew up into a huge argument."

"Did you leave?"

"Of course not. I did say a few things I regret, though."

"Buy her some flowers and apologize—she'll forget about it in a couple days."

"Yes, I agree with your tactic, but the problem is, I won't forget. I think maybe she doesn't want me there."

Daniel leaned against the windowsill and nodded. "Yeah, I bet. Let me share a little of the high-priced knowledge I gained in therapy. There's always a bigger, truer reason beneath the surface. See if you can get her to talk about who taught her to fold laundry, or what it represents...I bet you'll find out it's not about you at all."

Todd was deeply pleased with the logic of Daniel's suggestion. "Tell Dr. Mountainside she's worth every penny...and thanks for the advice, buddy."

"Nice one," Daniel laughed.

"I better let you get back to your mosaic, and I need to decode the Da Vinci laundry. I'll let you know if I hear anything else useful on the Gwenn front."

"Thanks, and good luck with Flora."

"I'll need it. Goodbye, Daniel."

"Oh, hey, should I ask Sabina to send flowers to the funeral home, or is that crossing a line?"

Todd contemplated the etiquette for ex-boyfriends sending flowers to ex-never-mother-in-laws funerals for a moment. "I think it would be best if Flora and I included you on our card, rather than make an overpowering Gregory Gallery splash."

"Sabina does have a flare for the theatrical, doesn't she?"

"Indeed. All right, I'll take care of the card. Bye."

"Buh-bye." Daniel turned off his phone, slipped it in the pocket of his faded jeans and turned his full attention to creating the shell mosaic of Gwenn.

Fifty

First day back to work. Gwenn felt re-energized and ready to take on the world. She loved the way her Armani featherweight wool slacks could fill her need for both sexy and warm—at the same time. She fought her way into her charcoal grey boyfriend pullover and shrugged at herself in the mirror. Apparently she could handle boyfriend sweaters—but not actual boyfriends.

She stood still for a moment and looked herself up and down in the mirror. Her first instinct was to mentally point out all the obvious flaws, but she forced herself out of that rut. She reached one finger toward the mirror and traced, "I ♥ me."

She slipped her feet into her Comme de Garcons Mary Janes and headed into the office. No winter boots today, she felt brave.

She navigated the skyway system, opened the glass door to *The Organizer* and froze. Seated behind the reception desk was all kinds of tall, dark and handsome. His dark brown hair was slicked back on the sides and his windswept bangs drew her gaze straight into his intense espresso brown eyes.

The incredibly sexy, ridiculously young man sitting behind Flora's old desk jumped up and walked toward her. "Good morning. Do you have an appointment?"

Before Gwenn could find her tongue and successfully embarrass herself, Thea saved the day. "Back off, jailbait, that's the boss lady." She swept past him, towering on her heels, and gave Gwenn a quick kiss to each cheek. "Sorry to hear about Shirley...I mean if you want me to be." Thea winked as she stepped back.

"Thanks, it's complicated, as you know. So, who's the junior achiever?" Gwenn indicated the smoldering hot man-child.

"Erik, meet your boss and the owner of *The Organizer*, Gwenn Hutchinson." Thea stepped back and finished with a flourish of her hands.

Gwenn stepped forward to meet Erik's outstretched hand. "Hi Erik, nice to meet you. Flora must've hired you while I was out." His grip was warm and strong.

"Yes, it's Erik, with a 'k' not a 'c', it's unusual, so I wanted to point it out."

His hotness changed inversely to the duration of his speech. The more he talked the less hot he looked. Gwenn smiled, "Thanks for clearing that up, Erik. I'm going to get settled in my office. Can you bring me a cup of coffee? Thea can tell you how I like it."

"One and a half sugars, just a drizzle of cream." Thea called over her shoulder as she followed Gwenn to her office. "So, what do you think? He's totally bangable, right?"

"Thea I'm sure it is my *bossly* responsibility to point out that you are heading into sexual harassment territory... possibly statutory rape." Gwenn put the Clark and Mayfield tote Randy had given her into her chair and turned to pull out her laptop, as she added, "How old is he, anyway?"

"I'm 25, miss."

Gwenn's head shot up as she blushed profusely. Thea cracked up.

"Please call me Gwenn." She set her laptop down and came out from behind her desk to accept the coffee. She took a long sip, "Perfect. I think you're going to fit right in here."

"Thanks, Gwenn." He smiled warmly and his hotness factor shot right back up to the stratosphere.

So, he's one of those guys that's hotter with his mouth shut. Gwenn realized a moment too late that her gaze was drifting over his body like a hungry breeze on a damp summer night.

He shuffled uncomfortably, "Well, I better get back to my desk. Flora said we have a big day." He backed out of the room, clearly fearful of turning his back on the two predators in the room.

"He's all yours, Thea. I'm swearing off men for a few years."

"Wait, what happened to Steven?"

Gwenn stiffened at the question that struck too close to the dark secret she had so recently unearthed. Luckily her Hutchinson training kicked in. "Kids, he wants 'em and I don't. There wasn't really a compromise...plus he wanted me to convert, I don't know. It wasn't meant to be." She affected extreme nonchalance; her performance would never have fooled anyone but Thea.

Thea smiled hungrily, "So he's back on the market?"

"Thea!"

"I'm kidding, honestly—kidding. Nobody survives that long in captivity without losing a piece of their soul. I'm not deep enough to handle that crap." She spun expertly on her 5-inch heels and walked back to her office.

Gwenn leaned back on her desk and sipped her coffee. *Shirley taught me to be an expert liar...maybe I could say that at her funeral.*

"You're back!" Flora bustled into the room and carefully hugged Gwenn. "Are you OK? I know you weren't close to Shirley, but once someone's gone..." her voice faded.

"I'm actually doing really well. Everything healed up perfectly from the surgery. It will take awhile to get over the deeper wounds, but Rachel and I hugged it out, we're gonna be OK. Thanks for asking." Gwenn took another gulp of the caffeine wonder drug. "This coffee is really good. Did you make this?"

"Nope. It was the wunderkind, Erik. Todd talked me into hiring him, I hope I don't live to regret it." Flora smoothed her hair nervously and adjusted her color-coordinated headband.

The familiar gesture brought Gwenn's full attention to the moment. She noticed the dark blue pantsuit, the flats instead of heels...something was different. "Is everything OK with you?"

Flora glanced anxiously over her shoulder, "Can I close the door?"

Shit! If she's pregnant I will shoot myself. Gwenn pushed the thought from her mind and nodded affirmatively. "Sit down, tell me what's going on."

Flora collapsed into the chair opposite Gwenn's and gushed out the entire laundry drama story. She was wringing her hands incessantly by the end of the tale. "I think he wants to leave. He said he doesn't feel welcome." She fidgeted in her seat. "I just like things how I like them, you know how it is?"

Gwenn nodded supportively. She had spelunked through enough of her deep dark spaces, while out at the cabin, to know that there was more to the story. "Who taught you how to fold clothes, Laura?"

Her dearly departed sister's name bore sacred power. Flora held her breath for a minute. "Yes...but it's not...she only showed me how to do it so she could get rid of a chore."

"Yeah, that sounds like classic older sister manipulation." Gwenn twisted back and forth in her chair. "Did you like it though, the folding?"

"At first, but I got mad when I realized she had played me." Flora's mind drifted back to her childhood home, the basket of laundry...her mother. "My mom liked it."

"When you folded?"

"Yeah, she said my folding was perfection. She said I did it much better than Laura." Flora reached up to smooth her hair and stopped mid-gesture. "Come to think of it, it was the only thing my mom ever thought I did better than Laura." Flora looked at Gwenn like a curtain had just been opened in a dark corner of her mind.

Gwenn smiled and nodded, "So it's pretty important to you, right?"

"It really is. How silly...and strange."

"So you should probably tell Todd your dirty laundry secrets, pun intended."

Flora's whole face brightened and she laughed with Gwenn. "Are relationships always this complicated?"

"Don't ask me, I don't have one."

"Oh, Gwenn, did Steven have a breakdown?"

"Of sorts, I guess. We just hit an impasse on kids and conversion...even when I shared my real reasons, he couldn't see my side. He stormed out of the cabin five days ago and I haven't seen him since."

"I'm so sorry. Are you OK?"

"I'm fine. I'm just going to take men out of the equation for a few years and see if I can get my shit straight...and stop having people ask me if I'm OK."

"I hope Erik won't be a distraction..."

"He's spoken for already. Thea has him in her sights."

"He's a goner."

They both laughed and breathed a little easier.

"I'll send Erik in with the Hit List in about 30 minutes, sound good?"

"Everything is changing. No more Flora's perfectly prepared Hit List? I feel like Rip Van Winkle, I went to get my kidney out and when I woke up I didn't recognize anyone."

"He's good, Gwenn. You'll get used to it. By the way, Thea landed a huge account in Minneapolis. I was wondering if we could all go out to dinner and celebrate?"

"That's a fantastic idea. Make reservations for tonight, if everyone can make it...and invite Todd. Maybe a peace offering dinner will open the channels of communication."

"Good idea. Done." Flora got up to leave and turned back, "Thanks, Gwenn, and welcome back."

Fifty-one

Nathan walked into the back of the bakery to pull out a fresh tray of blueberry-lemon scones for the display case and was met with a most unfortunate spectacle.

Tucked in a corner, covered in powdered sugar and custard, stood Rachel with both hands in a box of donuts.

"Rachel!" Nathan could not think of what to say next. He approached her cautiously and reached a hand toward the nearly empty cardboard box.

She twisted away and glowered at him. A lioness protecting her kill could not have looked more menacing.

He decided to try a gentler approach. "Can I get you some coffee? Would you like that?"

She shook her head vigorously. Her cheeks were puffed out like a chipmunk and salty drops were creeping toward the precipice of her lids. "Call Gwenny," she helplessly uttered, through a puff of powdered sugar.

Nathan spun on a dime and called the memorized number.

"Hello, this is Gwenn." She was pleased to use her ultra-professional, "I'm in the office" voice.

"Gwenn, it's Nathan. I think you better get down here." He described the pathetic portrait that awaited her in the recesses of the bakery.

She flew into action like a trained fireman responding to a five-alarm fire. When Nathan mentioned donuts, Gwenn felt her heart stop beating. Rachel hadn't eaten donuts since her last failed suicide attempt, in high school. This was a code blue situation.

Erik stopped in his tracks, Hit List in hand, as Gwenn blew by him with a full head of steam. "Miss Hutchinson?"

"Emergency."

And she was gone.

Flora had warned him about the rollercoaster, he just wasn't expecting a ride so soon.

Gwenn raced to the bakery.

Nathan was waiting on a customer when she blew through the front door like an arctic blizzard. His eyes said HELP and his finger pointed to the back room.

Gwenn covered the ground in long, purposeful strides. She rounded the corner and didn't know whether to laugh or cry.

Rachel's cheeks were puffed out, her face a mess and her eyes darting like an escaped asylum patient.

Closing her eyes and connecting with her inner nerd, she used the *voice* and commanded, "Rachel Hutchinson, put the donuts down. This is not what you want to do."

Her eyes widened to saucers and Rachel was aware of the box in her hands and her sister in the room. She dropped the box to the floor and stepped back.

Gwenn closed the gap and looked down in horror. The box had easily held a family of two dozen. There was nothing left but the splatter evidence of strawberry filling and large pools of custard. No one had survived.

Gwenn kicked the box away and escorted Rachel to the large industrial sink in the dishwashing area. She turned on the water and gently pushed Rachel over the sink. She aimed the sprayer and hosed the sugary remains off her sister.

Rachel jumped as the water hit her face, but as she fully realized what she had done. She doubled over and cried, her tears swirling into the mélange of donut debris. "Thank you," she sputtered.

Gwenn grabbed a fresh dishtowel from the metal rack and wrapped up Rachel's dripping purple-streaked locks. She handed a second towel directly to her sister. "Let's get you dried off and then you can bring me up to speed."

They threw the wet towels into the hamper and walked to the desk in the corner.

Rachel sat in stoic silence. She stared straight ahead, refusing to make eye contact with Gwenn.

"Well, let's start with the easy question. Why the hell do you even have donuts here? You hate them. They are your nemesis and you said you would get rid of them as soon as you took over. What gives?"

Rachel turned toward Gwenn and hung her head like a puppy that just crapped on the sofa. "Mike's a good guy."

"Good for Mike. Who the hell is Mike?"

"He delivers the don..." she couldn't even say the word.

"The donuts? You're doing this for a guy? Did I miss a memo?"

In spite of her anguish, Rachel could not suppress a snicker. "Fuck you."

"Oh, fuck me is it? I'm the one who raced out of my office, right past the delectable Erik, to come to your rescue." Gwenn hardened her features and leaned toward her sister, "So you better loosen your lips and tell me what the fuck is going on before I have you arrested for pastry murder." Gwenn slammed her hand down on the desk like any bad cop in any interrogation scene she had ever watched on television.

Rachel grinned sheepishly and wiped her eyes. "Gwenny, do you love me?"

"Of course I love you, freak. Now, for the last time, what the hell is going on?"

"Annie is cheating on me." Rachel let her head drop onto the desk. Her skull made an ominous thump as it impacted the wood.

Years of experience with Rachel's penchant for exaggeration and self-pity led Gwenn to dig a little deeper. "Tell me exactly what happened."

Rachel's voice was barely above a whisper as it ferreted its way out from under the mound of thick wet hair draped over her face. "She never called."

Inhale. Exhale. "When you say never, exactly how many days has it been since you last talked to Annie?"

"Almost two." Rachel spat the words at Gwenn.

"That does sound serious." Gwenn bit her lip to keep from laughing.

Rachel looked up, desperate for an ally in her delusion. "I know, right?" She noticed the smirk too late.

Gwenn grabbed Rachel by the shoulders and shook her vigorously. "Snap out of it!"

"But—"

"But nothing. Basically Annie didn't call you last night and you lost your shit. Not cool Rache, not cool." Gwenn was about to launch into a full-blown tirade, but the ringing of Rachel's cell phone interrupted her flow.

Rachel scrambled to get her phone out. "It's Annie!"

Gwenn slumped back in her chair and shook her head. She openly eavesdropped on Rachel's side of the conversation and waited to get the rest of the details.

"OK. I'm so glad you're safe. Gwenny's here, so I better let you go…call me tonight…I love you, Annie…bye." Rachel set her phone down on the desk.

"So, why don't you fill me in, Rache?"

"Their bus broke down in 'the middle of Ga-bum-fuck nowhere', according to Annie. They were on their way to the next gig in Pittsburgh…anyway; it was some huge dead zone. She walked for almost a mile and still couldn't get reception. They waited over six hours for a huge tow truck and by the time they got back into cell reception it was too late to call me. She didn't want to wake me…" Rachel looked at the expression taking shape on Gwenn's face and her words dissolved. "Are you mad at me?"

"Rache, I was scared to death. I haven't seen you like this in a long, long time. You had me really worried." Gwenn got up and pulled Rachel in for a hug. "Sweetie, what's really going on?"

"I guess I overreacted, huh?"

"Ya think?"

They laughed and Rachel shook her head. "I think it might have something to do with Shirley's funeral tomorrow. I don't know if I can do it, Gwenny."

"Here's what we're gonna do. You're going to come to the office dinner tonight, with Thea, Flora, Todd and the breathtaking Erik, and then you're gonna spend the night at my place. We can take the whole night to find something for each of us to say at the service. Sound good?"

"It was too much, the weird feelings about Shirley, meeting my birth mom, being alone, thinking Annie was cheating." Rachel twisted her hair up and pulled it into a knotted bun. "Thanks for coming to my rescue, Gwenny."

"No problem, but I don't care how nice this Mike guy is, cancel the donut order."

"It's not just that, the customers are kinda used to them. You know how people are, they get in a routine."

"You mean rut?"

Rachel laughed, "Exactly."

"See ya tonight. I'll text you the details."

"Thanks, Gwenny."

Fifty-two

Steven was wretched with guilt. He had waited over a decade, building up his hopes, and in one argument he had thrown it all away. He wasn't that same boy that ran away from his problems. He was a man, a sergeant in the United States Marine Corps—he was going to give Gwenn, and himself, what they deserved.

He pressed her number on his phone and waited. "Hi, I didn't think you'd answer."

Gwenn rolled that around in her mind for a minute before she answered. "I didn't think you'd call—ever."

"Touché."

"I never meant to hurt you, Steven. I just thought it was best to be honest."

"It was." He rubbed his forehead and added, "I was wondering if we could meet for coffee?"

"Steven, I think the fates have body slammed us enough, don't you?"

"I'm processing the reality of what happened, Gwenn, but I wanted to give us both something we didn't get last time."

"And what would that be?" She didn't mean to sound snarky, but a bitter edge was finding its way into her voice.

"Closure."

She muffled an errant sob and nodded as she answered, "Yeah, I think that would be good."

"Tomorrow, OK?"

"Shirley's funeral is tomorrow." She said it without emotion of any kind.

"I'm so sorry, Gwenn, I lost track of time. Do you want me to be there?"

"No, thank you though, Rachel will be there with me."

"Sunday then?"

"How about right now. I managed to work almost an entire hour today. No sense in going back into the office now." Gwenn shook her head. "I can meet you at Jitters in 20 minutes, will that work?"

"Copy that. Coffee or hot chocolate?"

"I don't think my body can handle anymore straight caffeine today, better go with cocoa." Gwenn swallowed. "Steven?"

"Yes."

"Thanks for making this call, I know it wasn't easy. I'll see you soon."

"You bet." He ended the call before she could hear his voice crack. No, it wasn't easy, but Steven had accepted the painful difficulties of life a long time ago.

He arrived at Jitters before Gwenn, and secured a private seating area for two. He was delivering the coffee and hot chocolate when Gwenn walked in the door, raindrops beading on her hair and coat. "We're back in this corner, follow me."

Gwenn removed her coat and noticed his gaze wiping over her appreciatively. She sincerely hoped she hadn't fallen for a ruse.

"You look nice." He grinned hopelessly.

"Thanks."

He sipped his coffee and leaned back in his chair. "I did some serious soul searching after our big argument."

She nodded silently and crossed her arms over her chest.

"It's true that the thought of you kept me alive over there, Gwenny, but after years of captivity I turned you into a fantasy version of yourself. I projected all my needs and desires into that fantasy…I never bothered to think about the reality of how time was passing in your life."

She nodded, this time with compassion, and reached for her cocoa.

"I am sorry I left you all those years ago—pregnant and alone. You must have been terrified. I'm sorry."

Her bottom lip quivered, but she refused to allow herself to cry. "Thank you."

"Some part of me always knew the truth. When I was sitting in that P.O.W. camp in Afghanistan I would allow myself to believe that you had kept the baby and I would come home to a wife and son that had never given up on me."

"Wow."

"I know, but your mind will go to great lengths to keep you alive. Survival is truly instinctual." He put his coffee cup down and leaned toward Gwenn. "I don't agree with your decision to never have children, but I respect your right to make it. I wish we could've found some compromise… that's just the one thing…I want a family…I need a family."

"I understand, Steven, I guess it's better that we ended things now…that we can have this closure."

He looked into her eyes and grinned. "You'll always be the best sex I ever had, Gwenn, the best."

She exhaled and blushed. "Steven, that's so not appropriate."

"I know, I know. Sorry, I got off track."

"So, what will you do?"

"I'm actually going to take your advice. After I cooled down I realized I had to face the PTSD. I'm going to work for Wounded Warrior Project, as an Outreach Coordinator."

"Steven, that's awesome. I'm so happy for you. You'll be wonderful." Gwenn breathed a huge sigh of relief and finally enjoyed her cocoa.

"I have to complete the program first, but I'm a bit of a celebrity, so they're pretty anxious to start pimping me out." He chuckled and looked down at his coffee. "Thanks for being honest with me about the PTSD, you were right, I can't ignore it."

"You're going to make such a difference for so many vets," her voice caught in her throat, "you are a hero, Steven."

"Thanks, I don't feel like one, but I'm willing to learn."

Gwenn's phone vibrated in her pocket. "Sorry, I have to take this, it's the office."

Steven finished his coffee and took his cup to the dish bin. Gwenn was finished with her call when he returned.

"I should get going. Thanks for the closure, it was a generous gesture."

Steven scooped Gwenn into a friendly hug. As he released her he said, "Take care of yourself, Hutchinson. Don't answer the door for any Land Sharks."

Gwenn chuckled, "You bet, Hays. What if it's a Candygram, is that OK?"

"Take care of yourself."

"Yeah, you too." Gwenn buttoned her coat and walked out the door. She'd watched enough breakup movies to know it would be a mistake to look back. She exited Jitters, tucked her head down against the frigid drizzle of rain and let her last image of Steven fade to black.

Fifty-three

Gwenn was the last to arrive at Pickwick. The only seat left was sandwiched between Todd and Erik. *Yippee. I will kill Rachel later.* She took her seat graciously and launched an array of eyeball daggers at her sister.

Rachel smiled back playfully and winked. She had chosen the seat between Flora and Thea—suspiciously positioned closer to the latter.

Thea, on her second Cosmopolitan, lurched out of her chair to make a toast. "To Gwendolyn Hutchinson, the best goddamn boss in the Twin Ports...and beyond." She raised her glass and sloshed a little pink liquid over the edge as she over-eagerly clinked glasses with everyone around the table.

As the toast pandemonium died down, Todd turned toward Gwenn. "Good evening Miss Hutchinson, I was very sorry to hear about your mother. If there is anything you need, don't hesitate to ask." He nodded his condolences.

"Thank you, Todd. She was a real piece of work; her passing is a mixed bag. I almost wish you could've met her."

"Oh, I did. Last year at *The Organizer*, she stormed in demanding to see you. I offered her a cup of coffee."

For some inexplicable reason Todd's dry delivery of that line caught Gwenn off guard. She giggled until she snorted, covering her face in embarrassment.

Todd didn't know how to react. "I'm sorry. Did I say something funny?"

His question sent Gwenn into an encore fit of giggles, sans snort.

Rachel couldn't' help but notice the kerfuffle on the other side of the table. "Hey, you guys wanna share the joke?"

Gwenn gasped for air, waved her hand in surrender and succumbed to another fit of laughter.

Todd stepped in and replied, "I was offering my condolences and mentioned that I had the opportunity to meet your mother once at Gwenn's office. I had offered her coffee."

"Oh, shit!" Rachel and Thea joined in the laughter.

Flora leaned over and whispered to Todd. "You know how their mom was...well...people deal with death in different ways." She patted his thigh with the tiniest hint of pity.

He actually felt a bit of pride at bringing such jocularity to the table. He decided he might be on a roll and added, "She declined, of course, and asked me to help her on with her *coe-utt*." Todd emphasized the impression of Shirley's thick Minnesota accent pronouncing "coat" as a two-syllable word.

The girls laughed uproariously. Rachel smacked the table a few times and Gwenn wiped a little moisture from the corners of her eyes.

Erik sat dumbstruck. He felt like an alien experiencing a new culture.

The group finally settled down and ordered dinner. As the entrées arrived, Thea stumbled to her feet and made yet another toast.

"To all the single ladies! Just you and me, Gwenn. Cheers!" Glasses were dutifully clinked all around and Gwenn tucked into her Roasted Pear Salad with Seared Salmon.

Todd immediately perked up. Single? Gwenn? He leaned close to Flora and whispered, "Will you excuse me for a minute?"

"Of course. They're off to the side, there." Flora pointed to the restrooms, assuming that was Todd's reason for excusing himself.

Todd nodded appreciatively and scurried off to a private location.

Daniel answered on the first ring. "Gimme some good news, buddy."

"This is exquisite news, pal." Todd met Daniel's colloquialism tit for tat.

"Hit me."

"Gwenn is single."

"What? This better not be a cruel joke, Todd."

"You know me well enough to know that I do not joke." Todd hesitated, "Well, I did not joke. It would appear that Flora is bringing out a mildly jovial vein in my personality."

"Oh, I'd say it's mild all right." Daniel smiled. "Details, I need details."

"I regret to report that I have no further information at this time. Thea just made a toast to all the single ladies, and she included Gwenn—to no one's protest."

"That's not much to go on..." Daniel hesitated to hope.

"I'll get to the bottom of it. I just wanted to motivate you to complete the mosaic."

"Just to be clear, you don't have an ulterior motive, do you?"

"I have no idea what you mean." Todd most certainly had an ulterior motive. The more Daniel exercised his creative muscle the more prolific his works. There was an entire gallery to fill in Duluth—the sooner the better.

"I mean, this piece I'm working on for Gwenn is not for sale. Capisce?"

"Capisco."

"What?"

"You asked me 'do you understand', in Italian, and I responded 'I understand', also in Italian."

"Todd, you never cease to amaze me. Thanks for the good news. I would love some details, though." Daniel threw an unidentifiable frozen brick into the microwave and pushed a few buttons.

The beeping intrigued Todd. "That sounds like the microwave. Did Frankie let you off your regimen?"

Guilt consumed Daniel's face. "I'll give you a hundred bucks to keep your mouth shut."

Todd chuckled, "Done."

"I better get back, Flora will come looking—"

It was Todd's turn to be caught red-handed.

"Too late, bye." He hung up on Daniel and shoved the phone in his pocket.

Flora smirked. "Mr. Warner, if I didn't know better I'd think you were calling Daniel Gregory to inform him of Gwenn's singleness."

Todd pulled Flora tightly to his body and let his lips brush her skin as he whispered to her cheek, "Why, Miss Long, you wound me deeply." He kissed her lightly.

She giggled with embarrassment at the public display of affection. "Good, I've secretly been rooting for him."

He leaned back and smiled, "Me too."

They returned to the table, trading conspiratorial glances for the rest of the evening.

Thea insisted that Erik give her a ride home. Everyone at the table looked sympathetically at her prey and nodded.

"It probably would be best, Erik. Do you mind?" Gwenn felt a bit of sympathy for the young man, but Thea could not be resisted.

"No problem. Thank you for the dinner, Miss Hutchinson." He scooted back his chair and chivalrously offered his arm to Thea. She latched on like lamprey, looked back over her shoulder and winked at Gwenn.

Gwenn's hand shot up to cover her mouth in shock. "Was she totally faking? She's not drunk at all, is she?"

Rachel snickered, "From the looks of the tablecloth, I'd say most of her drinks did not make it into her mouth."

"She is quite the calculating vixen. Poor Erik doesn't stand a chance." Gwen shook her head in sympathy for the human sacrifice.

"I'm sure he could think of worse ways to go," Todd added.

Flora nudged him with her elbow and whispered, "Todd."

Gwenn and Rachel both laughed.

"You know, Todd, I think Flora is having a genuinely positive effect on your personality," Rachel added.

Todd smiled and swallowed his retort.

"Well, kids, I think we better call it a night. Rachel and I still have to plan our funeral speeches..." Gwenn's voice carried a depth of emotion that caught her off guard. "Ready, Rache?"

"Ready. G'night, 'Flodd', or is 'Tora' better?"

"Bye, Hutchinsons. We'll see you tomorrow." Flora blushed at the teasing couple names Rachel had thrown out. "Thanks, Gwenn. This was really fun."

"It was your fabulous idea, Flora, but you're welcome. Goodnight, guys."

Fifty-four

Gwenn rubbed at the sleep in her eyes, thought about opening them and remembered that today was Shirley's funeral service. She did not open her eyes. Instead she listened to Rachel's soft, even breathing and thought back to the bunk beds they had shared in a tiny single-wide trailer in a suburb of St. Paul.

She had been crouched on a folding chair next to the open window, blowing cigarette smoke out through the screen. Rachel had scolded her, using one of her plastic horses as a puppet.

Six-year-old Rachel galloped the pony up the rusted metal leg and onto the seat next to Gwenn. "Hey, Gwenny, that's stinky and it's made Wachel sick."

Gwenn smacked the horse to the ground and glared at her little sister. "Shut up, WAY-chel." She hated the way everyone at church thought Rachel's speech impediment was "so cute." "If you say one word about this," she waved the cigarette butt menacingly at Rachel, "I will burn all your stupid ponies in the vacant lot. Understand?" She scraped a match across the striking surface and held the flame close to Rachel's face.

Rachel was six and the only thing she understood was a deep abiding fear that her precious ponies would be destroyed. "Daddy! Daddy! Gwenny has fire!" she screamed.

Pastor Ed burst through the door and quickly assessed the situation. He smelled the cigarette smoke, saw the matches and grabbed Gwenn by the arm. He sat down on the bottom bunk, turned her over his knee and spanked her until her sobs echoed through the trailer and his hand burned red.

Rachel watched in horror and sobbed along with her sister.

Ed dropped Gwenn to the floor and rebuked her with some verse about "man cannot serve two masters." He confiscated the cigarette butt and matches, and slammed the door behind him.

That was the day Gwenn had decided Rachel would make a better ally than an enemy, and Rachel understood the wages of sin.

A distant feeling of discomfort crept through Gwenn's daydream and she reached for her phone to check the time. The screen was black. Unfortunately her phone had died during the night and the alarm she had set never alarmed anyone.

"Shit. Shit. Crap. Shit. Rachel, wake up." Gwenn jumped out of the bed and rifled through the pile of her sister's clothes on the floor. "Rache, seriously, wake up. Where's your phone?"

"I left it in your kitchen, I think."

"Why didn't you set an alarm?"

"Why would I set an alarm? That's your job."

Gwenn raced out of the bedroom and grabbed Rachel's phone off the counter. "Oh for fuck's sake! Rache, it is 10:45. The funeral starts at 11:00. Shit!"

Gwenn ran into the bathroom and looked in the mirror. She shook her head in disappointment. "No time for showers Rache, ponytail up and get your damn clothes on—we leave in five."

"I didn't bring anything. You said we'd have time to stop by my place—"

A blouse hit Rachel in the face. "Wear this with whatever pants you had on yesterday." Gwenn was simultaneously hopping into her pants and swishing mouthwash over her teeth.

Rachel combed her fingers through her hair and caught the thick mess in a low ponytail. The blouse strained across her ample, donut-enhanced bosom. "Gwenny, this shirt's too tight."

"No one fucking cares. Get your shoes on." Gwenn threw the deodorant at Rachel. "Put on a fresh coat of this, too."

Gwenn had also opted for yesterday's clothes. Her hair was secured in a smooth, if slightly greasy, ponytail and she had applied lipstick and mascara. "OK, that's it. Load up."

They raced to the church, thankful the roads were clear. Gwenn parked illegally at the curb in front of the walkway. Last ones in first ones out—she hoped. Gwenn jogged up the sidewalk and Rachel panted behind.

"You better get out your running gear, Rachel. Gwenn's boot camp starts Monday."

Rachel wanted to protest, but she was grateful that her sister cared enough to help her get back into shape. She wanted to look sexy in her wedding dress. And there it was, the decision had been made, somewhere deep in her subconscious—she was wearing a dress.

They stopped on the top step and calmed their breathing. Gwenn slowly opened the doors and they quietly crossed to the sanctuary. The interior doors were still open. Maybe they weren't as late as they thought...

Rachel leaned in and whispered, "Did we get the time wrong?"

Gwenn surveyed the room and counted, roughly, 30 people. If they were on time, Shirley was certainly looking down on this turnout with disappointment. "No, I know it was 11:00 because Ed said there would be a potluck luncheon in the church basement after the service." She turned to Rachel and added, "We are not staying."

"No argument here."

Rachel took Gwenn's elbow and they hurried up to the front pew and sat down with a nod to Pastor Ed.

He looked at his watch and walked ceremoniously to the pulpit. "Thank you all for coming today to honor my dear wife, Shirley, whom the Lord has seen fit to call home."

Rachel used her church-time-ventriloquist skills to whisper to Gwenn without moving her lips. "This place was packed for that Mrs. Lindstrom bitch."

Gwenn dug her fingernails into Rachel's arm. The decades old signal to "shut it before Dad sees."

"...my oldest daughter, Gwenn." Pastor Ed gestured toward the front pew.

Rachel elbowed her sister and said, "Go, freak. Go."

Dread flooded her stomach. Gwenn was not a fan of public speaking, and public lying was even less inviting. She trudged up to the pulpit and endured a stiff one-arm embrace from Ed. "Thank you, Pastor." She turned and faced the sprinkling of congregants and saw the pity in their faces. She steadied herself on the pulpit and pushed ahead. "Losing a parent is a difficult thing, for any child." She was pleased with the generically vague speech she and Rachel had crafted. Her mind wandered while the empty words trickled out. She lurched forward as she suddenly remembered this was the spot where she was supposed to fake a tear.

Rachel scooted to the edge of her seat, nervous for Gwenn's performance.

And then it finally happened. Gwenn felt the loss, the sadness, the emptiness of death—she bent her head over the polished wooden podium and wept.

Pastor Ed hurried to his daughter's side and awkwardly consoled her. He led her back to her seat and returned to the lectern to announce Rachel.

She shook off the shock at Gwenn's painfully authentic performance and struggled to remember her lines. "Good morning, thanks for coming." She couldn't decide if she should say anything about the empty sanctuary. When they had planned the speech they had assumed a full house—the humorous quip would not work in this echo chamber. Rachel shared a few enhanced memories of family trips and a completely fabricated "fun" birthday story. "It's a difficult day for all of us and we appreciate your support. Thank you." She cut the big finish from her bit and hurried back to her seat to put an arm around Gwenn.

Pastor Ed wrapped up the service, and honored his promise to omit the altar call, before he invited everyone to bow their heads in a final prayer.

Gwenn could not endure the strangers' pity and convinced Rachel to sneak out a side door behind the organ.

They drove directly to Perkins for breakfast and some much-needed coffee.

"So are you gonna tell me what happened up there?" Rachel cut into her thick slices of French toast and waited for Gwenn's response.

"I honestly don't know. I mean, it wasn't about Shirley... it was just...it hit me, ya know? We're all gonna die." Gwenn felt the emotions bubbling up and blinked rapidly to push the tears back from whence they came.

"But, that's not news, Gwenny. Why did it make you so sad?"

"I feel like my life is a waste. I haven't really done anything...I haven't made a difference, ya know."

"That's bullshit. You made a difference in my life. You're the reason I even have a life."

Gwenn leaned back in the booth and grimaced. "That's not what I mean."

"Then I don't get it."

"What's my legacy? In a hundred years how will my life have made any difference?"

"Who cares what happens a hundred years from now, Gwenny. You should be more worried about how you can enjoy shit right now."

"Oh, should I live in the moment or some crap?"

Rachel stared intensely at Gwenn and actually stopped eating. She did not put her fork down—but she stopped eating. "Yes."

"What?"

"I know it's hard for you to imagine, but your life could use a little spontaneity."

"Rache, I'm not going to run around doing whatever I want and ignoring all my responsibilities."

"That's not what I mean. I mean stop worrying about a legacy and put a little effort into finding happiness today."

Gwenn did not like the turn this discussion had taken—not one bit.

Fortunately Rachel's phone buzzed and put their debate on hold.

"It's Greta!" Rachel grabbed her phone excitedly. "Hello? Mom?"

Gwenn looked out the window at the huge grey waves rolling monotonously across Lake Superior. Her life had an unsettling predictability. Things happened all around her, but her trajectory barely waivered. She was a business owner. She was single. She had no hobbies. She had no pets. Her future contained business meetings, business luncheons and eventually retirement. She didn't want to live a predictable life—and more importantly she didn't want to die a predictable death.

"Gwenn? Gwenny, snap out of it, I'm talking to you." Rachel had one hand over her phone and was desperately working to get Gwenn's attention.

"Oh, sorry. What is it?"

"Greta wants to know if you think a chocolate ganache cake is too weird?"

"Weird for what?"

"For my wedding, freak. What the hell do you think we're talking about?"

Gwenn smiled. Maybe she could assuage her need for excitement by living vicariously through Rachel for a couple months. "Sounds delicious, ask her to send pictures."

"Can you send us a picture?" Rachel nodded and mumbled before ending the call. "OK, she said there are pics on her website…" She flicked and swiped at the screen of her smartphone. "Wow. This looks amazing." She turned the screen toward Gwenn.

The three-tiered square cake was covered with glossy ganache frosting. An intricate hand-cut henna design wrapped around each tier. It was gorgeous and it looked delicious. "Rache, that is beautiful. Greta made that?"

"She did. She's amazing. What do you think?"

"I say absolutely perfect. Build the decor around the henna theme and pick a gorgeous accent color…" Gwenn stopped and smiled at Rachel. "Sweetie, this is going to be so amazing. I am so happy for you and Annie."

Fifty-five

Daniel leaned back from his worktable to get a different perspective on Gwenn's leg. He was pleased with the bits of shell in shades of coral, peach, ivory and white that he had selected. His artist's eye filled in the rest and suddenly he was swept up in a vision of her smooth, porcelain legs wrapped around his waist...he shook his head to erase the image.

"I gotta eat something." He stood up and felt the shaking in his legs. He tried to remember the last time he had eaten. He drew a blank. As he scanned the half-finished mosaic he realized more than hours had passed.

He made his way to the kitchen and dropped a couple eggs into a skillet. His stomach growled painfully and he decided to throw a couple slices of bread in the toaster, too. He pulled out his phone, turned it on and called Todd.

"Daniel, its 6:00 a.m. Is everything all right?"

He glanced out the window and realized he was watching a sunrise, not a sunset. "Hey, sorry about that. I kinda lost track of time in there. I came out to grab some grub and thought I better check on the rest of the world."

Todd rolled out of bed, without disturbing Flora, and quietly descended the staircase. "I called Frankie yesterday and canceled your sessions for the next two weeks. He said he'll be checking your garbage, so you better lay off the frozen crap."

Daniel chuckled, "Don't worry. I would never push my luck with Frankie. Thanks for handling that for me."

"Speaking of handling things for you. I think I found a possible candidate for my replacement."

"Sounds impossible," Daniel teased.

"Indeed, but we'll see. I have to run it past Flora, because he currently works at *The Organizer*. However, he is a fish out of water over there. I am afraid Thea will devour him."

"Todd, is this some kind of rescue hire, like a wounded animal?"

"Not at all. He is talented, intelligent and emotionally stable. I simply think his assets are currently being mismanaged."

"You're the expert. When do I meet him?" Daniel paused for a moment to scoop a bit of egg onto his toast and stuff it into his mouth before he continued, "I could come up?"

"We both know that is a bad idea, sir." Todd reverted to protective manager at the mere mention of Daniel popping up to Duluth.

"Fine. Clear it with your 'boss' and bring him down here."

Todd kept his professional demeanor intact, ignored the jab at Flora and replied, "I will call you this afternoon with a date and time for the meeting."

"Sounds good. Buh-bye." Daniel dropped his phone on the counter and attacked his breakfast with two hands.

He filled a water bottle and carried it back to his studio. He closed the door and circled around his worktable—looking at '*Plunder*, seashell mosaic' from every angle. He was drifting off into a pleasant memory of Gwenn's exquisite lips...

Fifty-six

Gwenn chewed on the end of her pen and scrolled through her emails. Her decision "to start fresh on Monday" and throw herself into running her business had lasted for almost an entire hour.

"Good morning, Gwenn." Flora walked in and smiled warmly.

"Oh, thank god...I mean, please tell me you have an interesting distraction to share."

"I do have something to discuss with you." Flora reached up and smoothed her hair.

"Good something or bad something?"

"Good...I hope." Flora took a seat and paused to gather her thoughts. "Todd would like to hire Erik." There, it was out, and she felt better.

"Oh, would he." Gwenn leaned back in her chair and crossed her legs. "To work at the gallery, up here?"

"Not exactly..." Flora fidgeted and continued, "he thinks Erik would make a good replacement for him, as Daniel's assistant."

At the mention of Daniel's name Gwenn perked up—literally and figuratively. "Is Daniel in town?" She struggled to suppress the eagerness in her voice.

"Oh, no. Todd's handling everything. Daniel is working on an important mosaic piece." Flora looked down at her hands in her lap and avoided Gwenn's gaze.

"Oh." Gwenn slumped back in her chair. "What do you think—about Erik?"

"Me?"

"Yes, you. You are the manager. Do you think he's suited for this business?"

Flora smoothed her hair and shook her head. "I think he's a bright young man…he's just a little…I don't know how to say it."

"Overwhelmed by so much estrogen?" Gwenn prompted.

"Exactly," Flora giggled.

"Speaking of which, was Thea successful…never mind, I don't need to know."

Flora blushed a deep cherry and snickered.

"Message received." Gwenn nodded. "I think Erik would be much happier, and safer, working for the Gregory Gallery. Give Todd a call and let him know you are a master negotiator." Gwenn gave Flora an encouraging wink.

"OK, I'll take care of it." Flora stood up and smoothed her fitted plaid pencil skirt. "Of course now I have to start the interviewing process all over again." She threw up her hands and walked toward the office door.

"I have every faith in you, Flora. Let's see if we can find someone, male or female, with a few more years under their belt. The waters can get a bit treacherous around here."

Flora nodded and walked out.

Gwenn stared at her computer screen and honestly considered reading one of her exciting work emails, but her cell phone graciously spared her the trouble. "Hi Rache, what's up?"

"Are you busy?"

"Of course not. I'm just the owner of the company, I don't actually do anything." Gwenn meant it as a joke, but the truth of her words left a little sting. Flora and Thea were doing a bang up job—all by themselves.

"I'm taking off early. Can you meet me at my apartment and help me pick out a dress?"

"Wait, what? You're actually wearing a dress? What happened to the matching tuxedos?"

"I don't know. I just pictured myself standing next to Annie and I see me in a dress." She liked the image in her mind, mostly because fantasy Rachel was at least 15 pounds lighter. "Anyways, I told Greta and she sent a ton of pictures. I need help sorting through the puff-ball disasters and finding the one that's me."

"OK, what the hell. There's no point in me putting in a full day here and throwing everyone off their game." Gwenn doodled on her note pad. "I'll meet you around 1:00, and I'll bring salads for lunch. OK?"

"Salads, yummy." Rachel made a disgusted face, but agreed.

"See ya in a couple hours." Gwenn ended the call and read several of her emails, before her cursor wandered over the Google icon and she watched as she typed "Daniel Gregory" into the search bar.

The search results loaded and she clicked on "Images." She was entirely unprepared for the rush of tingles that raced to her nether regions when she saw those sexy eyes, one blue and one brown. She sighed and crossed her legs, tightly. She closed her eyes and brought back the feeling of her hands entwined in his long, caramel-brown mane.

"Excuse me, Miss Hutchinson?"

Gwenn opened her eyes and stared at Hot Erik's broad, man-boy chest and wondered if she had just moaned out loud. "Um...yes," she fidgeted in her chair. "What is it?"

"Flora just gave me the good news...I mean I guess it's good for me...I didn't know...well, I just wanted...thanks for approving my transfer." He shoved his hands into his pockets and bit the inside of his cheek.

Gwenn laughed. He was the perfect replacement for Todd and definitely part android. He needed to upgrade his human communication chip. His manufacturers had spent entirely too much time on the chassis and far too little time on the interior. She realized that Erik was staring at her, waiting for a response. "Oh, right, the new job. Yes, you're welcome, Erik. I think you will enjoy working for the Gregory Gallery. I wish you all the best." She forced herself to focus on the person standing in her office, and not drift off into additional Daniel-related daydreams.

"I've never left a position with less than two weeks notice...I wanted to be sure...I wasn't sure if you had a replacement. I mean, I can stay longer, if needed."

She smiled, "Thank you, Erik. You are leaving on the best of terms, don't worry about that. I'm sure they need you to get started at the gallery as soon as possible. I know how much Daniel relied on Todd." She savored each syllable of Daniel's name as it passed through her lips. Her cheeks flushed and she broke eye contact with Erik. "Well, back to work for today. I have some catching up to do."

"Of course, thank you." Erik turned and walked out of her office.

She watched him exit and marveled at the perfection of his ass. She had to admit, she was turning into a lecherous basket case.

The remainder of her morning flashed by without incident and she eagerly bid farewell to all at noon. Time to pick up the salads and get a look at those dresses Rachel might actually wear.

Fifty-seven

Gwenn trudged up the rickety wooden steps behind the bakery and mused, *always the bridesmaid never the bride.* She wasn't entirely sure she wanted to be a bride. She knew she didn't want to be a mother, and now this marriage-phobia—she was turning out to be the non-traditional sister.

Rachel opened the door before Gwenn had a chance to contemplate juggling the salads in one hand to accommodate a free fist for knocking.

"You're late, Gwenny." Rachel snatched one of the salads from her sister and made a beeline for her kitchen. "Do you want anything else with yours? Bread and butter, or toast?"

"The entire point of a salad is the salad." Gwenn gently pushed the refrigerator door closed. "We're having salad. Yum!" She forced excitement into her voice.

"Fine." Rachel plopped down in a chair and ripped the lid off her salad. "Can I at least have dressing?"

"Of course." Gwenn handed Rachel a packet of reduced calorie dressing from the condiment bag. "These, however, are going in the trash." She tossed the bags of croutons into the waste bin.

"Oh, lovely crunchy little beauties." Rachel's forlorn gaze followed the tasty bits into the can.

Gwenn saw the look on her sister's face, retrieved the packets, crushed the croutons and returned them to the trash. "Eyes up here, Rache."

They gobbled up their salads and moved to the sofa. Rachel placed her laptop on her knees and turned it so they could both view the slideshow of dresses from Greta.

"Too Disney-princess." Gwenn shook her head.

"Too third-trimester-waistline," Rachel giggled.

"Are you kidding me with that neckline?"

"Is there a person in there somewhere?"

They clicked through several more.

"Rache, are you sure about the dress idea?"

Rachel was wondering if she had made a mistake. None of these cotton candy creations felt like her wedding. She was clicking without looking, just wanting to get to the end so she could report back to Greta.

Gwenn grabbed her hand, "Wait. Stop. Go back...one more...one more...there. That's the one! That's the one." She wiped a trickle of happiness from the corner of her eye.

Rachel looked at the romantic strappy V-necked bohemian bridal gown, with flowy chiffon and lace scallop layers. She reached one finger toward the screen and stroked the image. It even had a slit on the front of the skirt to show off her best feature—her sexy legs.

"Do you like it?" Gwenn's eyes glistened with anticipation.

"It's perfect. It's exactly what I didn't know I was looking for...but wanted."

"Order it." Gwenn clapped her hands encouragingly.

"What size?" Rachel poked at her belly with one judgey finger.

"What size were you before…well, before that happened?"

"Pretty much a size 8, mostly."

"Are you going to start running again? For real, not just a fake promise?"

"I want to…" Rachel felt her conviction slipping away before she finished the sentence.

Gwenn grabbed the laptop and set it on the coffee table. "Rache, look at me." She waited for eye contact. "You found your mom, and she's wonderful. You are engaged to a completely awesome, kick-ass woman and you own the bakery. Give me one good reason you can't make your health a priority?"

Rachel searched the recesses of her mind for a good excuse and found nothing but a few dust bunnies. "Thanks, Gwenny." She pulled her computer back onto her lap, selected a size 8 and clicked "Add to Cart."

"So, what do you think for Annie?"

"She looks really hot in like a skinny leg tuxedo pant."

"Did you just say 'pant'?" Gwenn cracked up. "Who are you?"

They poured over pictures and finally found the perfect "pant" on the Bindle & Keep website. Tapered leg slacks paired with a waistcoat and a dickie bow tie. Gwenn pushed for a teal accent color, but Rachel had grown quite attached to her purple highlights and thought a crisp lavender might be better.

Hours slipped by as Rachel bookmarked pages and Gwenn made notes on her legal pad. "Oh shit, Rachel, I just realized we don't have a venue."

"What do you mean?"

"I mean WHERE are you going to wear this gorgeous dress? Where are you going to have the ceremony?"

"Oh, shit. I better call Annie." Rachel made the call while Gwenn paced anxiously.

Fifty-eight

Daniel walked back and forth in front of the nearly finished mosaic. Something was missing, He couldn't put his finger on it...but it wasn't quite—

"Daniel. Are you in there?"

"Todd, what are you doing here?"

"I texted you several times and left a voicemail with details on that exact topic. When you failed to respond I went out on a limb and assumed you had turned off your phone."

He reached into his pocket and pulled out his phone. Sure enough it was off. "Well, I'll be damned."

"Sir, can we come in?"

"Sure, why not. I'm stuck anyway. Might as well take a break. Come on in, Todd."

"...and Erik, remember?" The opening door revealed Todd and his sidekick.

Daniel stared blankly at the pair. Slowly the fog of creation lifted and he connected the dots. "Right, right. You're Todd's replacement." He stretched out his hand and gave Erik a welcoming handshake.

"Thank you, sir. A pleasure to meet you."

"Hits me with a 'sir' right outta the gate. Definitely cut from the same cloth as Todd."

Todd accepted the compliment and smiled. "How's the piece coming along?"

Daniel turned and surveyed the shimmering patchwork of shells. "I'm stuck. I know there's something missing, but I can't quite see it."

Erik stepped forward, "May I take a look?"

"Knock yourself out." Daniel exchanged a doubt-filled look with Todd.

The young applicant walked back and forth in front of the mosaic and tilted his head to the side. "See the line, here?" He pointed to the space between the leg and the folded sheet. "It needs more depth, and here," he gestured toward the receding room in the background of the mosaic, "These lines need to fall into darkness." He stepped back and nodded. "Overall the piece is filled with too much light, with out the contrast of the darker shells...it feels somewhat flat." Erik paused and turned toward Daniel. "That's just my opinion, sir."

Daniel smirked and looked at Todd. "Where'd you find this kid?"

Erik looked back and forth, from Daniel to Todd, and chewed the inside of his cheek.

"Don't worry Erik, if he thought you were wrong he would've walked out." Todd smiled and nodded. "He's right you know, Daniel."

"Oh, I know. I know." Daniel stared long and hard at the mosaic. "I was afraid to let the darkness in...but without it how can I appreciate the light." He spoke softly to himself.

"So, he's hired?" Todd enquired.

Daniel smiled at Todd's protégé and smacked him on the shoulder. "Welcome to the team, Erik."

"It will take us six months to transition, but his background check is clean and his credit score is remarkable."

Their boss had turned back to the mosaic and didn't catch a word of Todd's thorough investigatory report. "I will have this ready for delivery next week."

"All right. We'll make that Erik's first official duty." Todd nodded at Erik and gestured for him to exit the studio. "We'll leave you to it, sir."

Daniel bobbed his head absently as he pictured the final steps in completing this offering to Gwenn.

Fifty-nine

Gwenn could barely remember the faces, let alone the names, of the sea of interviewees Flora had paraded through the office in search of Erik's replacement. She was finding a sense of purpose in the new projects on her desk and she realized there was a smile on her face that could not be explained.

"Good morning. You look happy." Flora was pleased to see Gwenn throwing herself into projects again.

"I think I am happy." Gwenn's voice was laced with genuine shock. "I'm actually excited about this project Randy found for us. It sounds like this investor bought up two solid blocks of West End." Gwenn tapped her pen on the desk. "I mean, I'm sure we won't get to work with every vendor that buys into the renovation, but I can't wait to design the displays for the import/export store."

"I was hoping for the European deli project," Flora added. "Last night I dreamed of this great shelving system for olives," she giggled. "Oh dear, don't tell Todd."

"Organization porn. It'll be our dirty little secret," Gwenn laughed. "How's the admin search coming along?"

"Gosh, it's harder than I thought. I'm kind of sorry I let Erik go before I had a solid candidate. I have three more interviews this afternoon. Do you want to sit in?"

"I've already lost track of where we were at with the first batch. I trust your judgment. Just let me know when you narrow it down to the final three...or something."

"Gee, thanks Gwenn. I appreciate all the responsibility you're giving me." Flora self-consciously rubbed her fingers together.

Gwenn had mentally drifted away from the conversation. Her head was nodding affirmatively toward Flora, but her ears were not on the job. "Do you think I would look good in lavender?"

"Pardon?"

"Sorry, what were you saying?"

Flora glossed over the missed bits and pressed Gwenn for more details. "Lavender what?"

"Oh, bridesmaid dress, maid of honor, I think, for Rachel."

"I almost forgot. When is the wedding?"

"She's flip-flopping between the first day of summer and the Fourth of July; kind of a 'new beginnings' versus 'independence' thing." Gwenn secretly hoped for June—the anticipation was killing her.

"Have they picked a venue?" Flora had to admit, the thought of a wedding did make her heart flutter, ever so slightly.

"Good question. The very question I asked last time I talked to Rachel. She was supposed to call Annie, but I haven't heard the verdict yet."

Flora smoothed her hair and debated whether or not she should volunteer her insider knowledge. Her need to please quickly won out over propriety. "I don't know if I should mention this, but Daniel has a fairly large boat, or maybe it's a yacht...anyway, I'm sure Todd could get it for them. You know, if they wanted to get married in the harbor under the fireworks...or something."

Gwenn closed her eyes and tried to picture Rachel and Annie saying their vows under the colorful bursts of fireworks in the sky. Unfortunately, the only image that popped into her mind was Daniel's sexy smile and the reflection of fireworks in his eyes as he pulled her into a storybook embrace. "Sounds wonderful," she mumbled.

Flora sensed something shift and decided to take her leave. "Well, let me know if they're interested, after you talk to Rachel. I better get set up for the interviews."

"Thanks Flora, keep me posted on the candidates."

Rachel pulled out Annie's Purple Rain cassette and opened the case. There was a small piece of paper, folded twice, tucked under the edge. She unfolded the paper.

"I found it. Now what?"

Annie chuckled, "Now your treasure hunt begins."

"I thought you said *this* is where I would find out where we're going on our honeymoon?"

"Oh, it is...eventually." Annie snickered wickedly. "But you gotta earn it, babe."

Rachel stuck out her pouty lower lip and retorted, "That's just rude! If you were home right now...I would..."

"You know I'm on tour, babe. You'll just have to hold that thought for another month." Annie paused to listen to Rachel's breathing, "You got your first clue. Call me when you figure out the last one."

"Annie Nelson, you are gonna pay for this torture."

"A little light torture sounds perfect, babe."

Rachel pretended to fume, but deep down she was all hot and bothered. "I love you."

"Ditto." Annie hung up.

Rachel read her first clue.

> *Filled with over 80 kinds of fish,*
> *It's where you served me my first dish.*

"Filled with fish" had to be Lake Superior. "First dish?" The second line was a bit of a stumper. The *dinner cruise!* Rachel had been desperate to impress Annie and thought a romantic harbor cruise would do the trick. She could only afford the Pizza Cruise tickets, but she remembered every bite of pizza she fed to Annie.

Rachel grabbed her phone and decided she was going to need to call in some back up. "Hey Gwenny. Whatcha doin'?"

"I'm at work freak. Like a real person, for once. What do you need now?"

"You know what? If that's how you're gonna act I won't even invite you on the awesome treasure hunt Annie organized for me."

"What are you hunting for?"

"My honeymoon!"

"Come again?"

"That's what she said." Rachel burst out in snorting laughter.

Gwenn refused to laugh at the infantile quip. "Never mind. Come and get me. I'll figure it out on the way."

Rachel talked a mile a minute as they drove down to the cruise line office. "Do you think they'll let me on the boats? I mean, it's not like I remember which one we were on. I'll have to search them all."

"Easy, Kojak. Let's just go to the office and see what happens."

What happened was that Annie had everyone in on the hunt and the lady at the office smiled warmly at Rachel and handed her an envelope. "Here's your second clue."

"Thank you." Gwenn took the envelope for the dumbfounded Rachel and steered her back to the bakery van. "Well open it, ya nutter."

"Oh, right."

A foghorn booms, full steam ahead.
This is where I talked you into my bed.

"Wow, this is a tough one."

"You can't remember the first time you guys did it?"

"Oh, that makes more sense. I was thinkin'...I got distracted."

Gwenn chuckled, "Yeah, I'll bet."

"The first time was...wait no that was after...we met at her...no that wasn't actually a date. Oh, I got it!"

"Care to share?"

"We went down to Canal Park and made out under the Lift Bridge..."

"OK. Drive woman."

They parked and walked out to the bridge. Rachel stared up at the behemoth structure. "How am I gonna find a tiny envelope on that thing?"

"Why don't we ask him?" Gwenn pointed to the man in the pilothouse. She quickly regretted her brilliant idea as they crept up the narrow 25-stair steel staircase to the bridge operator.

The man saw them approaching and opened the door, handing them an envelope off his desk. He opened the door and smiled, "Hello ladies. I'd love to chat, but I've got a

1,000 footer comin' in for coal, so, ya know, I gotta keep a sharp eye."

"Oh, of course." Gwenn's stomach lurched a little as she stupidly looked down. "Do we have time to get off this thing?"

"You betcha. Just head straight back down those stairs and you've got nothin' to worry about."

They beat a hasty but cautious retreat to the waiting van. Rachel ripped open the envelope. "Here's the next clue."

You handed me your number, and with some classic quips.
But all I remember is the taste of your lips.

"Easy! Mr. D's on Grand." Rachel drove like Dale Earnhardt, Jr. as she explained her first meeting with Annie.

"So you were on a date with some other chick?"

"Yep."

"And you kissed Annie?"

"She kissed me! I just gave her my number and told her to call. She kissed me."

"Slut," Gwenn teased.

"Takes one to know one."

They arrived at Mr. D's in one piece, no thanks to Rachel's driving, and the hostess was giddy with delight.

"Oh my gosh. Are you Rachel? Annie's fiancée?"

Rachel smiled patiently. "Yes, I'm Rachel. Do you have something for me?"

"Holy crap. Yes, yes," she fumbled in the drawer behind the hostess counter, "Here it is." She handed the envelope to Rachel.

"Thank you so much." Rachel poured a little too much sweetness into her reply and Gwenn was forced to roll her eyes.

The hostess lit up like Vegas neon and blurted, "Tell Annie I love her music. Happy to help."

"I will. Thanks, you're such a sweetie."

They hustled back to the van in the parking lot and Gwenn could contain herself no longer. "Shit, Rache, you sounded like Shirley in there. It was a little scary."

"Yeah, I kinda scared myself, I guess I catered one too many of those singles nights at their church."

"Mini sweet rolls!" They shouted in unison.

"And, that's why we're going to hell, Rache."

"At least I'll be in good company." She smiled at Gwenn, winked and ripped open Clue #4.

This is the place where I made our love sing.
You watched, while in a Bowl I made it ring.

"That makes no sense, bowls don't ring?" Rachel handed the paper to Gwenn. "Help."

Gwenn took the piece of paper and grinned. "Notice how 'Bowl' is capitalized, Rache?"

"Yeah, so?"

"You cannot be this dense..." Gwenn nodded encouragingly. "Capitalized, maybe because it's a proper noun...as in Hollywood—"

"Omycrap! The proposal. She was at the Hollywood Bowl when she gave me the ring." Rachel put the van in gear. "To the Flame!"

It was still early enough to find a decent parking spot. Rachel parked the van haphazardly and raced up the stairs to the bar. She was out of breath and leaned heavily on the wooden surface.

The bartender walked over and smiled, "I might have to cut you off before you get started. Seriously, sweetie, what can I get for ya?"

Gwenn had arrived in time to catch Rachel's confused look. "Um, I'm Rachel Hutchinson. Don't you have an envelope for me?"

The bartender fixed her with an unreadable look. "Oh, I remember you. Hi, Rachel. Sorry, I can honestly say I do not have an envelope for you."

Rachel turned to Gwenn, "What the fuck? Did we get the clue wrong?"

Gwenn was too out of breath to answer and just shook her head.

Rachel was having none of this. "Is there anyone else here? Can you just ask around? I'm on a treasure hunt and I know this is where the next clue should be. Just check, OK?"

The bartender shrugged his shoulders and yelled to some unseen co-worker in the back, "There's a Rachel Hutchinson here. She seems to think we have something for her—you know anything about this?"

A server walked slowly out of the back. She stepped awkwardly, like someone had a gun in her back. When she reached the edge of the bar, she stopped and someone popped out from behind her.

"Is this what you're lookin' for?" A large manila envelope covered the speaker's face.

Rachel walked forward slowly, shaking her head, and broke into a run. "Annie!"

The large envelope dropped to the floor and Rachel crushed Annie against her.

Gwenn cried unabashedly. The bartender leaned across the bar and handed her a napkin.

"What the fuck?" Rachel was pawing at Annie as tears streamed down her cheeks.

"It was Greta's idea. She's a hopeless romantic."

Suddenly Rachel realized she still didn't know where they were going. She dropped down to retrieve the envelope and tore it open. Two airline tickets peeked out. She pulled them out and read, "Athens, Greece. We're going to Greece? Seriously?"

"Seriously, babe. Greta did it all. We're gonna meet your dad's family in Santorini."

Gwenn could control herself no longer; she ran over to the couple and pulled them both into a hug even Rachel could admire. "You guys are the most fucking adorable...I can't even...I love you guys."

Rachel hugged Gwenn tightly. "I'm going to Greece!"

Annie ordered a round of Manhattans and they toasted each other, Greta and the honeymoon.

After Gwenn took a healthy sip she asked, "I still don't know where you're getting married, though?"

"I got this," Annie put a hand on Rachel's arm. "Right here at the Flame. I worked it all out before the proposal. A Fourth of July Lesbian Independence Wedding."

Three glasses clinked, "Here, here!"

Sixty-one

Rachel was severely disappointed when Annie broke the news that she had to catch a red-eye to Boston at 11:00 p.m.

"Babe, I have to get back to the tour."

"But I miss you, I miss you so much." Rachel squeezed Annie tightly.

"I've got at least four hours before I have to be to the airport." Annie pressed her lips to Rachel's ear and breathed out her teasing words, "Maybe we can watch a movie?"

It occurred to Rachel that four hours of Annie was better than no hours of Annie. She hastily decided to make smart use of her time and to quit wasting minutes on lengthy conversation. Rachel unbuckled Annie's belt and barked out the command, "Shower, now."

Annie feigned a salute, pulled her belt out of the loops and snapped the leather together in a titillating crack. "Yes, sir."

Clothes dropped like snowflakes in a blizzard as they raced to the shower.

Rachel kissed Annie while the water temperature reached a tolerable warmth. They climbed in together and let the water cascade over their bodies.

"What happened here?" Annie flicked lightly at Rachel's hardened nipple.

She moaned and reached for the shower gel. "Let me get that jet lag off you, sweetie." Rachel worked up a lather in her bare hands and turned Annie around to face the wall. She started at Annie's neck and worked the soap slowly down her back and around to her breasts.

Annie arched her back and pushed against Rachel.

Hands wandered down Annie's abdomen and slowly Rachel massaged the warm soapy bubbles lower and lower.

The lonely nights on the tour bus had taken their toll. Annie didn't have the stamina for a lengthy foreplay. She spun around and put her foot up on the handy shaving pedestal suctioned to the shower wall.

Rachel didn't need an invitation, she slipped between Annie's legs. Fingers, thumb, tongue—all working in unison to reward Annie for the glorious surprise visit.

Annie braced herself against the side of the shower with one hand and pulled Rachel closer with the other. Moans of pleasure escaped from her throat.

Rachel pushed two fingers into Annie's honey pot.

Annie's breathing sounded rapid. "More, more."

Momentary confusion blocked Rachel's instincts. "More, like faster or more fingers?"

"Yes, oh both, yes."

Annie was grinding harder and faster. Rachel regained her rhythm and flicked her tongue at a strategic moment.

A moaning scream escaped Annie's lips and her thighs tightened around Rachel.

Rachel maintained her pace until Annie relaxed her grip.

Annie pulled Rachel up from her knees and pushed her against the wall. She pulled a nipple into her mouth as she turned off the water.

"Wait, why did you turn—"

"I gotta get you into the bed where I can get some leverage."

"Oh...oh." Rachel quickly toweled off and practically ran to the bed.

Annie had her way with Rachel at least twice before the indefatigable march of time forced her out of their bed and reluctantly back into her clothes.

"How long until I get to see you again—for good?" Rachel's wet ebony hair was strewn across the pillow like a velvet shawl. Her eyes followed Annie's every move. Her heartbeat had resumed its normal post-coital pace and she felt like she was floating in a sea of bliss.

"Just weeks, babe, just a few weeks." Annie cracked her belt one more time before she slipped it back through the loops.

Rachel shivered with delight. "I like it when you take charge."

"Really, I hadn't noticed." Annie stared at Rachel with an impeccable poker face.

Immediately up on one elbow, Rachel leaned in to protest.

Annie snickered and added, "You better go see if you broke any windows. That last scream was...epic."

Rachel hurled a pillow at Annie, and missed by a mile.

"I can see why you never played softball." Annie walked over and kissed Rachel's forehead, nose, lips, neck...

"Whoa, whoa. If you want to have any chance of escaping this apartment in time to catch your plane, you better stop right there," Rachel said in the sternest tone she could muster.

"I gotta go, babe. I'm sure that's the cab honking right now."

"I love you, to the bottom of Lake Superior and back."

"All I heard was bottom." Annie smiled and kissed Rachel's pouty lips. "Ditto."

Sixty-two

Gwenn was snuggled into her sofa, tucked under several blankets, watching *The Lake House*, for the third time and crying in a bout of self-pity. She had completely blown it with Steven. No one would ever love her as much as Annie loved Rachel. She reached for a tissue and saw Rachel's name light up her phone. Her first instinct was to ignore the call—and continue the pity party for a few more hours.

The call went to voicemail, or so she thought, but instead the phone buzzed anew. She grabbed it angrily. "What now?"

"Geez! What crawled up your butt and died?"

Gwenn blew her nose before she replied. "You interrupted my pity party. Ya got a problem with that?"

"Not really...but I think we need to go to Dad's."

"Why? What could possibly be so urgent that I would actually have to get off my couch?" Gwenn was in no mood for Hutchinson family drama.

"He's put the house up for sale."

"They move every five minutes. How does this constitute an emergency?"

Rachel sighed, "There is no 'they', Gwenny. It's just him now. He said he's going to sell everything and move into some tiny apartment over by the church."

"Are you fucking kidding me right now? Why would he sell the blessed mini-mansion?"

"He said if we want anything before the estate sale we should come by today and take it." Rachel stood up and walked to her refrigerator. The rubber molding made a slight sucking sound as the door popped open.

"Close the goddamn fridge, Rache." Gwenn threw off her covers and walked into her bathroom. She looked at herself in the mirror and shrugged. "Pick me up in 20."

Rachel looked at the phone to make sure she didn't have the video chat on, closed the fridge and shook her head suspiciously. "OK, psychic Gwenny. See ya soon."

Gwenn managed to splash cold water on her face, put on a pair of jeans and twist her hair into a large hair clip. It was going to have to be good enough, because she just wasn't in a space to give a shit today.

">here," Rachel texted.

She grabbed her Patagonia fleece pullover and let her door slam behind her as she stamped down the stairs to the waiting van.

Rachel let out a low half-whistle, "Wow, that must've been one hell of a pity party. You look like shit."

"Yeah? Well, maybe I don't give a fuck. Looking like 'not shit' hasn't worked out too great for me so far—so why bother."

"Everyone's entitled to have a bad day, Gwenny. Don't get down on yourself. You're a totally awesome person and you are going to find a perfect guy who doesn't want kids and is an atheist, or something like that."

"Did someone drop some Ecstasy in your pancakes, Pollyanna?"

"Did someone...eat a bowl...of...Bitch Biscuits for breakfast?" Rachel thumbed her nose at Gwenn.

The sheer foolishness of Rachel's retort breached Gwenn's stronghold of self-pity and she found herself chuckling involuntarily. "Bitch Biscuits! That is fucking funny, Rache. That should be on a T-shirt." She rubbed her hands vigorously over her face and moaned. "Why do I always do this?"

"Do what?"

"I create horrible scenarios of unhappiness in my mind. I waste energy worrying about bad shit happening and then I barely enjoy the good shit that actually happens."

"What horrible scenario sent you in a tailspin this time?"

Gwenn didn't want to answer. She didn't want to share her pitiful little secret with her ridiculously happy sister. However, the idea of shoving it back down inside and stewing over it for the rest of the weekend felt like a worse idea. So she took a deep breath and blurted out her current greatest fear, "I don't think anyone will ever love me as much as Annie loves you."

Rachel covered her mouth with one hand and a tear escaped from her shiny brown eyes. "Gwenny, I've been jealous of you my whole life."

"Why? My life is a cluster fuck. That was one of Steven's expressions, by the way. One of the many sad chapters of my existence."

"But you got to live out loud, Gwenny. You got to bring your dates home to meet Mom and Dad. You could make out in public. You could dream about marrying someone." Rachel swiped at the tears. "I never had any of that. It's only been legal for me to get married, in this state, since 2013. So yeah, I was hella jealous of you all of my life."

"I'm sorry, Rache."

"I'm not saying it to make you feel bad, Gwenny. I'm just saying it because I want you to put things in perspective. I get the pain of hitting a low point in the romance roulette, but you and I both know it will pass. You will find your 'Annie' and I promise to be your not-bridesmaid at your not-wedding, if that's what makes you happy." She pulled the van into Ed's driveway, put it in park and leaned over to hug Gwenn.

"Today, it's actually enough to see you happy. I indulged myself and it was nice to have a good pout, but I am ecstatic about your wedding and your kick-ass honeymoon."

"I know! Right?" Rachel pounded both fists on the steering wheel. "Greta is like a 1960s T.V. mom, but without the prejudice."

"I'm not exactly sure that analogy holds water, but it sounds plausible." Gwenn laughed and unclipped her seatbelt. "Are you ready for this?"

"What are we supposed to do? Run through the house with a pad of sticky notes and put our name on shit?"

"Oh, please tell me that's what we are doing. The imagery is too good."

They exited the van and trudged up to Ed's massive front door. Gwenn pushed the doorbell and their eyes shot open as they heard strains of *Gloria in Excelsis Deo* resounding through the door.

"Oh, hi ya girls. How ya doin' there?" Ed opened the door and waved them into the parlor.

"We're fine, Ed. What's this I hear about you selling the house?" Gwenn thought it would be best to confirm Rachel's message before proceeding.

"Oh, have a seat there." He gestured to the dark leather sofa.

They sat down next to each other, for support.

"It's too much fer me, ya know. Yer mom was the one who liked ta do all the entertaining and what not."

Gwenn could not remember her mother liking anything of the kind.

"So what are you going to do, Dad?" Rachel felt sad for him. He really only had the church to keep him going.

"I'm gonna put this place on the market and so, I figured I'd get a little apartment across from the church. I don't need much, ya know."

"Ed, it might be a good idea to wait a few months before making such a big decision. You're still grieving."

"I won't be any less lonely a couple months from now, Trixie. All this was fer yer mom. It doesn't mean anything, now…" His voice grew quiet and his eyes were wet with unshed tears.

Gwenn looked at Rachel and shrugged her shoulders. "How can we help, Ed?"

"Well, I just thought ya girls might want some of yer mom's things. I'm just takin' my books and such to the apartment, so…" He nodded his head and rubbed his chin thoughtfully.

Rachel took Gwenn's hand and squeezed it. "We'll have a look around, OK, Dad?"

"Sure, you betcha."

Rachel pulled Gwenn down the hallway and into one of the bathrooms. She quietly closed the door and whispered, "Is there anything you want?"

Gwenn looked up at the ceiling and searched the corners of her mind. "The photo albums, I guess. Is that weird?"

"No, no. That's a good one. I was thinking I could act like some of her baking stuff would be good for me…I don't need anything…but, Dad is…you saw him."

"Yeah, it's a little creepy. It's like this whole pile of crap was just to make her happy...except she never was happy, was she?"

"I don't think so...it's so strange."

"I don't want to end up like her Rachel. I don't want to die miserable and bitter."

"You won't, sweetie, you won't."

"I have to stand up to him. I can't just look down at the ground and pretend I agree with him."

"By 'him' do you mean Dad?"

"I'm going to invite him to your wedding." Gwenn squared her shoulders and reached for the doorknob.

"Don't."

"Why not? He should be there. He should put all this crap aside and support you."

"Maybe, maybe not. The bottom line is he has to get there on his own. I don't want to spoil my wonderful day by spending it worrying if he's uncomfortable, or if someone said a swear word in his presence."

"You're right. I'll think of something else." Gwenn hugged Rachel. "I don't want anything to spoil your day."

"My day, my way!"

"Shhhhhh. Don't push it."

"OK, let's get out there and pretend to want some shit."

Rachel walked out to the kitchen and poked around in the cupboards. Gwenn returned to the parlor to ask about the albums.

"Ya can have any photos ya want, Trixie. Just leave me the wedding album." Ed forced a smile.

Gwenn thought of her "something else." "Ed, I find the nickname 'Trixie' offensive. I know it seems like a little thing to you, and I should've mentioned it ages ago, but I really wish you would call me Gwenn."

Ed fixed her with a pondering gaze and rubbed the edge of his jaw. "Ya know, I can't fer the life of me remember how that got started. Well, I'll put what's left of my mind ta fixin' that there mistake—Gwenn." Ed smiled proudly at his success and patted Gwenn on the shoulder.

"Thanks, Ed." She felt a little more room in her chest. Her heart didn't feel so squeezed and the air slipped into her lungs with just a tiny bit more ease. "Where are the albums?"

"Yer mom kept 'em in a big trunk in her closet. Just walk straight to the back and you'll see it."

Gwenn found her way to the vast walk-in closet and suffered a severe pang of closet-envy. "Damn, I wonder if I can have the closet," she mumbled to the clothes. She stopped cold in the middle of her 360-degree turn of admiration. The clothes were all hung by color, from white to black, with a rainbow of organization in between. In each color band the shirts were arranged from sleeveless to long-sleeved. Pants, skirts and dresses all followed the same pattern. A barrage of images exploded from deep within Gwenn's memory stores. Glasses organized in cupboards. Socks laid neatly in drawers. Utensils separated by purpose and construction. Even in that shitty singlewide trailer Gwenn could still see the neatly organized kitchen cabinets, holding their meager possessions.

She walked over to a yellow section of blouses and caressed the fabric. "I guess I was wrong, Shirley. I did inherit something good from you." She shed a tear or two and decided to select one thing from the beautifully organized closet to represent this moment. Her eyes scanned the racks until she noticed a section of large garment bags. Unzipping a few revealed gowns, long fancy skirts and... Gwenn held her breath and reached into a silver bag. She stroked the collar of a gorgeous grey wool coat with a luxuriously soft blue-fox collar. "Come to mama." She slipped the coat off its sturdy wooden hanger, glided her arm into the silver-grey lining and wrapped the shawl collar close to her face.

"Uh oh, are we playing dress up?" Rachel teased.

Gwenn nearly jumped out of her skin. "Shit. You scared the crap out of me."

"Well, you're still luckier than that guy around your neck."

"Don't get all holier than thou with me, missy. I know very well that you would eat a blue fox if I wrapped it in a Swedish pancake."

Rachel feigned indignance and looked around the room-sized closet. "Did you notice how it looks exactly like your creepy closet?"

"Yeah, freak. I had a moment. It was good and now I'm takin' this coat. Deal with it."

"Hey, it's fine with me. Now there's no way you can say anything about the Kitchen Aid mixer, panini press and ice cream maker I grabbed."

"Let me put this thing back in its protective bag. I still have to go through the albums." Gwenn busied herself in the trunk of photos and Rachel browsed the shoes.

"Hey, do you think these would look good with my dress?"

Gwenn looked up hurriedly, "You're not wearing a dress."

"Not now, Gwenny. I mean my wedding dress."

She looked up at the low-heeled strappy sandals, which she had never seen Shirley wear, and nodded. "They're kinda perfect. Do they fit?"

"Gonna find out right now." Rachel plopped down onto the floor of the closet and kicked off her tennis shoes. She pulled off her thick sock and slipped her foot into the shoe. "Check this shit out, Gwenny. I'm Cinderella." Rachel jumped up and posed her foot this way and that.

Gwenn laughed loudly and covered her mouth. A flood of guilt washed over her. They had never had this much fun in their mother's house when she was alive.

Rachel read the mood instantly. "Don't feel bad. I think it's good that we can create something good out of all of this." She gestured to the walls of possessions.

"I guess." Gwenn smiled as she remembered the feel of the fur against her face. "Let's load this stuff up and hit the road."

Ed followed them out to the car. A genuine smile spread across his face. "Boy, I sure am glad ya girls found some stuff. It's good to keep some things in the family."

They each hugged him and loaded into the van. "Let us know if you need any help moving, OK?" Rachel called through Gwenn's open passenger window.

"Well now, I don't know about that, little missy. I lost my whole National Geographic collection last time I let you help out."

Rachel's eyes widened and her cheeks blushed.

Ed cracked a smile and then laughed whole-heartedly. "Gotcha."

"Dad!" Rachel squealed.

They waved until they couldn't see him any longer.

"It was good to hear him laugh."

Rachel nodded. "Yeah, I think this apartment idea might be really good for him."

"You hungry?"

"Not funny."

"No seriously, I didn't have time to eat. Wanna grab a burger at Grandma's before you take me home?"

"Um, yes." Rachel delivered them to the saloon and grill in record time.

They walked into the gift shop waiting area and Rachel went to put in their name. Gwenn let her gaze wander over the racks of souvenir clothing and chotskies. There were a few patrons leaning against walls, here and there.

In fact, across the room she noticed a tall drink of water leaned up against a window, gazing out toward the bridge. His hair—

She ran to Rachel. "Take our name out. Take our name out, now," she hissed.

The hostess overheard Gwenn's panic and scratched through the name Rachel had just given.

"Thanks." Gwenn nodded at the girl, grabbed Rachel by the arm and dragged her out into the dampness of the fog-enshrouded harbor. "Run. Don't ask until we're back in the van."

Unusually compliant, Rachel ran to the van in silence. However, once she closed the driver's door behind her that ended. "What the fuck?"

Gwenn was so agitated she could barely speak. "He's in... I saw a tall...he was leaning...those legs...his hair. He can't see me like this."

"Do these legs have a name?"

"Daniel."

Sixty-three

Inspired by Erik's insightful commentary on the mosaic, Daniel had worked for over 36 hours without sleep. He had finished the piece ahead of schedule and decided to bring it up to Duluth himself. He figured he could lay low at his cabin on Park Point, while Erik made the important delivery.

As he drove past Canal Park he could not resist the call of Grandma's Saloon & Grill. He decided to stop in for some chicken and wild rice soup. He leaned against the window in the gift shop and stared at the bridge. He felt unsettled. Before he could change his mind about lunch, the hostess called his name and took him to a table.

He pulled out his phone to let Erik know he had arrived safely, when Erik walked up to his table.

"Good afternoon, sir."

Daniel looked dazed as he stared at Erik. He looked down at the unsent text on his phone, back up at Erik and back down at his phone. "How in the...?"

"Todd mentioned you usually stop here on your way to your cabin on the Point. I calculated your arrival time within 10 minutes and checked the parking lot before proceeding."

"OK, sure. Let's go with that story."

"Do you want me to retrieve the piece from your car?"

"Sure. Do you need the delivery address?"

"Todd asked me to call him when I have the piece. He said he would give me further instructions."

"Wow, he may be pushing the cloak and dagger angle a bit."

"He said it was critical to maintain confidentiality."

"True, true." Daniel took a sip of his water and continued, "The panel is in the trunk, wrapped in bubble wrap and brown paper." Daniel looked up at Erik. "It's not to be opened." The last thing Daniel wanted was to have Todd or Erik reading the syrupy love poem he had affixed to the back of the mosaic.

"Understood. May I have your keys, sir?"

He handed Erik his keys and waved the server over. He ordered the soup he had been craving and added a deep fried pickle to the tab—for no good reason.

***

Rachel and Gwenn had grabbed a couple Big Dipper sandwiches to go from the Smokehaus and were making their way back to Gwenn's apartment to partake.

"Are you totally sure it was him?"

"Rache, seriously? Do you think there is more than one broad-shouldered, long-legged, nice-assed guy with a touchable mane of caramel brown hair...in Duluth?"

"I wouldn't know. I don't notice that kind of thing." Rachel could not maintain her deadpan expression and had a big laugh at Gwenn's expense. "You got it bad, geez, Gwenny."

"I will punch you later. Can you stop at Jitters for coffee?"

"Sure. Let's just take our sandwiches inside and eat them with *hot* coffee, instead of lukewarm coffee by the time we get back to your place."

"They probably frown on outside food—"

"Unclench, Gwenny."

Gwenn made a face at Rachel and refused to acknowledge the jab at her uppitiness. She had much more important things to worry about than offending a barista. *Why was Daniel in town?* She continued to ponder several Daniel-related mysteries until Rachel slammed on the brakes. "Ouch. The seatbelt smashed my boob, freak."

"Oh, good. I was wondering if you were ever going to come back to this planet." Rachel shook her head. "I asked if it was OK to park a couple blocks away. I can't find anything closer."

Gwenn blushed as she realized how deeply she had slipped down the rabbit hole. "Sorry, Rache. I guess I was distracted."

"Uh, yeah, just a tiny bit." Rachel grabbed the bag of sandwiches and climbed out of the van. "Be a good girl and unhook your seatbelt," she teased.

They walked into Jitters, ordered coffees and found a place to sit. Once the delicious sandwiches were open, they both found their hunger to be far more urgent than their need for discourse.

"Damn, that was delicious." Gwenn wiped a dribble off her chin.

Rachel answered, mouth partially full, "It's the sauce. It's spicy and sweet and…yum-tastic." She gathered up their trash and walked toward the exit.

"Hold up, Rache. I'm just gonna grab a refill." Gwenn got her refill, added the necessary amount of sweet and creamy, and followed Rachel to the van.

"Any more errands before I drive you home, Miss Hutchinson?"

Gwenn laughed and put on her poshest British accent, "I'm not wearing the fur, yet. Gwendolyn will be sufficient."

***

Daniel finished his soup, took one bite of the deep fried pickle and saw Frankie's face floating over him. A ferociously unhappy Frankie's face. He did not finish the pickle. He paid his bill and drove across the bridge.

The humming of the tires was like a welcome home song to his soul. He glanced down the canal as a huge wave crashed against the lighthouse. '*Nature's Power*, mosaic and watercolor.' His next piece was already taking shape.

He walked into the cabin and smiled. Flora had done an amazing job on the re-organization project. Somehow she had managed to keep the feel of the heart of this special oasis, while banishing all unnecessary clutter.

He tossed his duffle bag onto the bed and went back outside to bring in some firewood. He grabbed a mix of oak, pine and birch. He made a couple trips so he could keep the fire going without having to brave the cold evening winds—with chance of showers. He had a roaring fire up in no time. The pretense of distraction dissolved and he texted Erik.

">Package delivered?"

">Yes. No one was home, so I left it at the door as Todd instructed. Just getting back in my car now, sir."

">Any problems?"

">No, sir."

">OK, thanks."

">You are welcome."

It was good news, but not great news. The package had technically been delivered, but without Gwenn there to actually receive it—once again he found himself without any way to confirm receipt. He should have embedded a GPS tracking device in the mosaic. He wanted to know exactly when the package moved from *outside* her door to *inside* her door. He would have to remember to stop using any phrasing that included "inside her" because it greatly disoriented his focus on remaining calm.

***

Gwenn wasn't going to invite Rachel up, but she realized she couldn't carry all the photo albums by herself. She rounded the corner first and stopped right in the middle of the hallway. Rachel ran directly into her, and knocked a couple albums to the floor, which was more post-surgically frightening than actually painful.

"Ow! Shit, Rache. Watch where you're going. I only have one kidney left, I don't need you knocking it outta me."

"Why the hell did you stop right in front of me?"

Gwenn stepped to the side so Rachel could get a clear view of her apartment door. "What's that? What did you order? Is it for me—for my wedding?"

"I think it might have something to do with the hair I saw earlier," Gwenn whispered the wish, more to herself than Rachel.

"Well, let's get this shit into your apartment and open it." Rachel carried her load to the door and set it down. She returned for the fallen albums and followed Gwenn back.

Gwenn slid the paper-wrapped package to the right, opened her door and carried the mementos inside. She returned to the door and stared at the object.

"Bring it in."

No movement.

"Don't you want to see what it is?"

"I don't deserve—"

"Oh, shut up." Rachel pushed past Gwenn and picked up the mystery package. "It's pretty heavy. I bet it's expensive." She carried the item to Gwenn's kitchen table and laid it down. "Scissors?"

Gwenn mutely obeyed.

Rachel carefully cut the packing tape and lifted the corner of the paper.

"Wait." Gwenn stepped forward. "I'm ready now." She peeled back the paper and worked to see through the bubble wrap. "Give me the scissors."

Rachel responded like an O.R. nurse handing off a scalpel.

Gwenn gingerly sliced through the plastic padding, careful to leave the contents undisturbed. Once she had slit two of the sides she reached in and freed the object.

The mosaic was met with a collective gasp.

"It's breathtaking," Rachel whispered.

"It's...me," Gwenn breathed.

"Gwenny, you're gorgeous. This piece should be in a museum." Rachel leaned forward. "Can I touch it?"

"I guess...be careful."

Rachel gently feathered her fingers over the texture of the shells. "You have to touch it. It's...holy shit, Gwenny. He fucking loves you like crazy."

Gwenn stroked the shells and flashed back to the utter bliss she had felt on that beach in New Zealand. "Do you think so?"

"Oh no, not at all. I'm sure he sits around making museum quality mosaics of all the trollops he dumps."

"I broke up with him," Gwenn defensively retorted.

Rachel turned her devilish grin on her sister. "Exactly, freak."

Gwenn casually picked up the brown paper and bubble wrap and attempted to rifle through it inconspicuously as she carried it to the trash bin.

"What are you looking for, a receipt?" Rachel laughed.

A pinkish hue crept up Gwenn's cheeks. "Well, last time there was a poem, too."

Rachel immediately talked into her wrist like it was a secret service communication device. "We need all units to converge on the apartment. We are missing a poem. This is a Priority One situation." She proceeded to dig through the garbage, in case Gwenn had missed something.

Gwenn lifted up the mosaic panel and looked at the back. "Ah ha! See, smart ass," she turned the back toward her trash-digging sister, "a poem." As soon as she realized Rachel was trying to read the poem. Gwenn spun the piece back around. "Don't read it, brat."

"You are seriously losing it, Gwenny." Rachel picked up the paper and plastic debris and shoved it all back into the kitchen trash can. She helped herself to some orange juice and plunked down onto Gwenn's sofa.

Gwenn eagerly devoured the passionate words inscribed on the back of the panel. She could hear Daniel's voice in her mind.

> *Anticipation*
>
> *I feel your absence in my heart and my arms ache to hold you.*
> *I imagine the smell of your skin and the heat of your breath.*
>
> *You vanished into the glistening dawn, and I held my tongue.*
> *You are a voice in the ether and a name on my phone's screen.*
>
> *I think I hear footsteps in the hall, I wish for your laughter.*
> *I long for the warmth of your body next to mine in the dark.*

You are miles away, I dream of folding space to be near you.
You left with your belongings, but now you carry my whole heart.

I am awaiting my lover, preparing myself for reunion.
I stand in the shower, soap bubbles cascade over my chest.

You will be weary from your trials; my hands ache to pamper you.
You will need time to heal, and I will struggle to mind my hands.

I will dab sweet scents on your neck, wrist, navel and your inner thighs.
I will ready our sanctuary, filled with flickering candles.

You and I will bask in the glorious anticipation…

~Daniel

Rachel waited with her usual impatience. "Are you going to call him or what?"

Gwenn was flushed with heat. The words had woven a seductive spell and she had some longing and ache all her own. "Maybe I should wait until tomorrow…I don't want to jump to conclusions…or seem desperate."

"For fuck's sake." Rachel got up off the couch, walked up behind Gwenn and read the poem over her shoulder. "Gwenny, if Annie wrote me something like that I'd be on the next plane to wherever the fuck she was without a second thought."

"But, my hair…and I need to shave my legs…"

"Whoa tiger. I didn't say go jump his bones, or whatever you call it. I just think you should call him and say 'thank you' because he gave you an in-fucking-credible gift." Rachel grabbed Gwenn's phone out of her purse and thrust it at her. "Here."

Sixty-four

Daniel had poured himself one Maker's Mark on the rocks and forced a relaxed pose in the tattered lounge chair in front of the fireplace. A mortal man would have drifted off to sleep in the cozy warmth—enveloped in the smell of pine, serenaded by the crackling flames. He was tensed like a predator, ready to pounce on his phone at the first sign of life.

It was late and his hope faded. He wanted to make excuses, but he thought to himself, how many kidneys could one person donate? Another death in the family just isn't possible. He finished his drink, stoked up the fire and headed to his big empty bed.

He turned back to the living room as soon as he realized he had forgotten his phone by the chair.

RING. RING. RING.

He tripped over the end table. The lamp was forfeit. He snatched up the phone and didn't even bother to control his breathing before he answered the call and panted into the phone, "Hello?"

His heaving breathing sent her pulse racing and her stomach flip-flopping. "Hi, Daniel, it's Gwenn."

His attempt to remain casual arrived—too late. "Oh, hi. What have you been up to?"

The nervousness, anxiety, desire and fear sent her into a fit of giggles.

"What? What did I say?"

She struggled to regain her composure. "We are pathetic."

"That's what I love about us."

The call back sent her giggles into a wave of silent sobs.

"Gwenn, are you still there?"

"Thank you."

"You're welcome."

"I mean it, Daniel, that is the most beautiful, touching gift I have ever received in my entire life." She paused to put more feeling into her voice, "Thank you."

"Can we meet for breakfast?"

"I like the Grill, but I know Grandma's is closer…" She realized, too late, that she wasn't supposed to know he was in Duluth and her voice trailed off in embarrassment.

He chuckled, "Closer to what?"

"Never mind. I'll save all my embarrassing secrets for breakfast."

"How about Perkins, for old times' sake?"

"Oh, that will chap Adele's hide. She thinks I'm gay, now."

"Sounds like you have a lot to tell me, Miss Hutchinson." He laughed and collapsed onto his sofa. Relief flooded his body and hope seeped into the corners of his heart.

"I'm looking forward to catching up, Daniel. Thank you so much for the mosaic." Gwenn floated her fingers above the sea of shell fragments. "I'll see you at 10:00, OK?"

"I wouldn't miss it for anything, Gwenn."

"OK. Bye."

"Bye." He ended the call and smacked his hand down on the arm of the sofa. "Yes!"

Gwenn had migrated to the bedroom for a little privacy and almost smacked into the eavesdropping Rachel as she ran back to the living room. "Rache, oh crap. Sorry. You OK?"

"Yeah, I'm great. I didn't need that foot."

Gwenn ignored the breach of etiquette. "Can you spend the night?

"I have to open the bakery at Too Early o'clock. I gotta go home, so I can just stumble down the stairs in the dark without having to be fully awake."

"Yeah, it's OK. I'll be fine."

"Why wouldn't you be fine?" Rachel eyed Gwenn suspiciously.

"He's just right down there," Gwenn pointed toward the lake. "Right down on Park Point, all alone in his cabin."

"Get a good night's sleep and see how things go over breakfast."

"Stop acting sensible. It doesn't suit you." Gwenn pulled Rachel in for a hug. "You're right, though. I'll stop by tomorrow after breakfast and catch you up."

"OK. G'night Gwenny." Rachel pulled on her jacket and walked toward the door. "Stay strong," she giggled as she grabbed the door handle.

"Hilarious." She walked over and jokingly pushed Rachel out the door. "Thanks for nothin'." Gwenn closed the door and locked it.

Before her mind could trick her into unlocking the door, she decided to make smart use of her time by picking out tomorrow's outfit tonight. She convinced herself this step would save her loads of time in the morning.

#

Gwenn rubbed the sleep out of her eyes, took one look at the outfit she had selected last night, and shook her head. Back to the closet she shuffled. It was all too much. She opted for a quick shower to clear her head.

The hot shower and thoughts of Daniel proved a potent cocktail. The detachable hand-held showerhead released more than the dirt in her hair.

The extra endorphins racing around in Gwenn's bloodstream considerably elevated her mood. She immediately fell back in love with last night's wardrobe selection. She loved the way the jeans hugged her curves and made her ass look quite shapely. Not that she assumed he would be looking at her ass; it was simply a factual statement about the pants.

To say that she was having an absolutely perfect hair day would be completely true. She honestly could not believe the gorgeous waves and the movie-star shine that had blown out of her hair dryer. She kept waiting for a huge zit to appear on her forehead or for one of her teeth to fall out.

She finished applying her makeup and dared one last glance in the mirror. A sexy smile caught her attention. Her eyes widened when she realized it was her sexy smile. "Damn, I look pretty good." Turning, she tilted her ass toward the mirror. "Let's see what we can do," she said to her derrière.

She arrived at Perkins almost 15 minutes early. Waiting in the car was an option, but she was eager to stake out a good seat. As soon as her hand closed around the inner door of the two-stage entrance, she saw him. He hadn't spotted her yet, so she had several seconds to drink in the visual before getting busted.

He lunged toward the door, nearly pushing her off her feet as he attempted an assist. He grabbed her elbow and pulled her toward his body to keep her from falling. "I gotcha. Sorry about that. Sometimes I can be such a klutz."

Words escaped her as she soaked in the tantalizing tingles of his nearness.

"Are you OK? I didn't pop your stitches or something..." He waited for a reply. None came. He felt the energy surging from her in waves.

She tilted her head up toward his hypnotizing eyes.

He pulled her closer. There was no resistance.

The world faded into oblivion when her gaze slid to his succulent lips.

He leaned down slowly and watched in awe as her eyelids melted over her enchanting tawny irises.

Gently he pressed his lips to hers.

She parted her lips and welcomed his mouth home.

His grip tightened around her luscious body.

Her pelvis smashed against him. She felt his firm response.

As his tongue caressed the edge of her lip her knees buckled.

Whipping back to reality, Daniel steadied her with his arm.

The shock of his lips tearing away from her flesh brought a convulsion of self-consciousness. She wiped at her mouth and pretended to straighten her hair. "We should...get a...table." Her gaze found the floor.

Daniel refused to release her from his side. He turned to the shocked hostess and said, "Can we sit in Adele's section, sweetie?"

Her silent robotic nod confirmed his request. She picked up two menus and walked away.

His baritone chuckle stirred Gwenn's loins.

"You put her under a spell," she teased—still a bit out of breath.

"I have no idea..." he let the retort fizzle as he unhappily released his grip on Gwenn.

She slid into the booth and he scooched in right next to her.

"Daniel, people will—"

"Um, Miss Hutchinson, I think we're way past 'people' at this point." He smiled and brushed a hair from her cheek.

Electricity arced across her skin where his fingers had been.

"Just so we're clear," Daniel looked at her with stern intensity, "I didn't plan that entrance. I thought I was picking up on a signal...so I went for it."

She blushed.

Adele arrived at their table. She inhaled sharply when she recognized Daniel and noted he was hanging out with the "skinny one" again. "What can I getcha, honey?"

"Good morning, Adele." Daniel graced her with a devilish grin and a wink. "We'd like two coffees and another minute with the menu."

"Comin' right up." She scooted off to get the coffees, shaking her head as she went. What a guy like that was doing with a girl that couldn't even decide which team she was playing for—well, Adele had no words—and that was a distinct rarity.

Gwenn had regained her composure under Adele's subjective stare. "We have a lot to talk about, and I don't mean this the wrong way, but I can't think when you're this close to me." Gwenn gestured to the bench seat on the opposite side of the table. "Would you mind?"

Daniel laughed. "Damnit, I knew there was going to be talking." He slid out of the booth and let his fingers linger on Gwenn's neck as he pulled his arm from her shoulder.

She was grateful he couldn't see the goose bumps popping up on the skin beneath her coat.

Adele rounded the corner with two coffees and smirked. She could've predicted all of this. "Here ya go, kids." She expertly slid the coffees across the table and plunked a few creamers down in the middle. "Are ya ready ta order?"

Daniel looked at Gwenn and nodded for her to order first.

"I'll have two eggs scrambled, bacon, breakfast potatoes and rye toast."

"So, that's one All American for the lady. And how 'bout you, dear?" Adele produced a genuine smile for Daniel.

He grinned right back. "I think I'll have the Hearty Man's Combo, Adele. But I can't decide between the buttermilk pancakes and the muffin. What's your favorite?"

Gwenn actually saw Adele blush. She wanted to kick Daniel under the table, but smiled instead. He was a sweetheart. There were worse crimes.

"I think ya'd love those pancakes. I can heat up the syrup fer ya, if ya'd like."

"I would like that very much. Thanks."

"Anything else, honey?" Adele did not include Gwenn in her enquiry.

"Just a splash of coffee, when you get a minute." He closed with one last wink.

Gwenn waited for Adele to refill their cups before she launched into the talk. "So I guess you heard Steven and I broke up?"

"Yeah, I cried for days." Daniel pushed the painful topic away from his heart.

"Be nice."

"I was." He fixed Gwenn with an intense stare. "I know we can't pick up where we left off—that this is like a fresh start...so I want to keep it fresh. I don't want to have any secrets slowly rotting away in the dark corners." He looked down at the table and reached for her hand. "I have to tell you something."

Her heart sank. Every ounce of her being struggled to stay in the present and listen. Her mind wanted to race off to fantasyland and imagine the worst—to soften the blow—or take cover before it came.

"I kinda let my anger take over when you told me you had slept with Steven. Deep down I knew it was going to happen...mostly, I was angry with myself for letting it...I wasn't thinking clearly." He released her hand and took a drink of his coffee.

Her hand went cold at the loss of his touch. "What happened?"

"I slept with Elena."

"Who...oh, wait...was she—?"

"The trainer that you were so suspicious of, in Mexico—the luchador."

Gwenn balled up her hands into fists and shoved them into the pockets of her jacket. "I knew it."

"Then you knew it before I did. Honestly, nothing ever happened before that night. I was disgusted with myself and she threatened to have her father 'make me disappear', so I hopped on a plane that night and came back to Minnesota."

Gwenn opened her mouth to make a snide remark about Daniel using Elena, but Adele came whipping around the corner and slid plates onto the table with total disregard for the moment.

Daniel thanked Adele and picked up his fork.

Gwenn mimicked the action, but her appetite had disappeared.

He took a few bites and waited for Gwenn to speak. He lost his patience. "Are you mad at me?"

She looked up, a mixture of guilt and judgment swirling across her features. She pushed at her food with the fork, but ate nothing.

"That's a pretty weird double standard, Gwenn. You pick up and leave Mexico with some ex-boyfriend who just wants to be your friend. But somehow during our 'break' you manage to sleep with him and then you officially end things with me."

"I ended things first." The words shot out of her mouth before she could apply the appropriate apologetic filter. Her words were all defense and no remorse.

Daniel set down his fork. "Is that what we're arguing about? The sequence of events that led up to you breaking my heart?" He rubbed his forehead, shook his head a bit and leaned back against the booth.

"I'm sorry. I said I was sorry." The thought of him with Elena stirred up a jealous indignation. "Why the hell are you making me mosaics and writing me poems if you're so pissed at me for breaking things off?"

The muscles in Daniel's jaw flexed. "Honestly, right now...I'm not sure I know why."

"This was a mistake." Gwenn stood up, dug through her purse and threw some crumpled bills on the table.

He watched in silent rage. He made no effort to stop her from leaving. Maybe she was right, maybe it was a mistake.

Sixty-six

Gwenn furiously drove directly to the bakery. She parked in the alley and let herself in the back door.

Rachel jumped when she heard the door slam shut. "Hi, Gwenny. How was it?"

"He slept with Elena." Gwenn was stone-faced.

She had not had the pleasure of meeting Elena when she was in Mexico, but based on Gwenn's description the woman sounded quite tantalizing. Rachel did not react appropriately; she was anxious to hear Gwenn's version of the story so she could stop pretending she didn't already know. "Before or after?"

"Before or after what?" Gwenn threw up her hands.

"Before or after you dumped him for Steven?"

"That's no excuse, Rache. He didn't even apologize. He just wanted to be 'honest.'" Gwenn smacked her hand on the pastry counter. "Well, fuck honesty."

All the logical things rolling around in Rachel's head would have to wait a few days. Gwenn was in pain and she needed support—not logic. "I'm so sorry, sweetie." She pulled her sister into a hug and offered her a cranberry-orange scone.

"I am kinda hungry. I didn't touch my breakfast. When he told me...my appetite...I couldn't eat anything."

Rachel spanked her curvy ass and shook her head, "Sorry, can't relate."

"Yeah, gimme a scone. I think my blood sugar may be off."

"OK. We'll get your mind off this, just let me hand off the dough to Nathan." Rachel walked up to the front and asked Nathan to watch the dough that was proofing. "Just punch it down and divide it into the pans when the timer goes off. Got it?"

"Got it," Nathan replied.

Rachel piled fresh apple-cinnamon scones on a plate and led Gwenn back to the computer in the corner. "So, the color we decided on is called lilac. It's kind of a bluish purple, so it should look good with my hair." Rachel clicked away on the computer and turned the screen toward Gwenn. "What do you think of these paper lanterns?"

"I think they're adorable. But Rache, I just don't get how you can have a Fourth of July wedding and not go red, white and blue?"

The idea had clearly not occurred to Rachel. "But my hair..." She turned a confused look on Gwenn.

"Sweetie, you could get red or blue streaks in your hair and it would still look awesome."

"Omycrap! Can you imagine how great red streaks would look in my hair?"

Gwenn felt excitement pushing out the anger. "Maybe Greta could make a white chocolate ganache frosting with red and blue henna pattern decorations."

"That's brilliant. Gwenny, I can totally see it. We can put bunting all around the Flame, and my bouquet can be white calla lilies and red poppies...Annie can wear a red bow tie. Oh my god, she would look so adorable. Can you picture that sexy blonde hair and a red bow tie?"

"I can." Gwenn felt the morning's disappointment fade into the background. She didn't need a relationship hassle right now. She could throw herself into wedding planning and work—that should keep her busy 24/7.

Gwenn jumped on Rachel's email and fired off some ideas to Greta. She copied herself on the email and asked Greta to "reply all" so they could work together.

A minute had barely passed and Gwenn heard the ping of an incoming email. "Rache, she already responded."

"I told you she was excited." Rachel beamed with pride.

"She loves it. She's never done a cake like that, so she doesn't have pictures, but she says she can promise it will be amazing—just like you." Gwenn smiled at Rachel. "I love her and I haven't even met her. By the way, when do I get to meet her?"

"She's closing her bakery for three weeks from the end of June through the wedding. She's going to ship the pans and whatever else she needs and give herself enough time to get used to baking cakes in my bakery." Rachel jumped up and down in excitement. "My mom is going to bake my wedding cake in my bakery. It's unreal."

"Three weeks, during peak wedding season—can she afford to do that?"

"She said she hasn't taken a day off in twenty-some years, if people can't understand that she has to be at her own daughter's wedding then they can go screw themselves." Rachel giggled with delight.

"She said that? 'They can go screw themselves'?" Gwenn was shocked and a little bit impressed.

"She did!"

Gwenn smiled. She had almost forgotten Daniel's Elena-laden news. Almost.

Sixty-seven

Daniel put the to-go boxes in the refrigerator and instinctively called Todd.

"Good morning, Daniel."

The shocking absence of the word "sir" knocked Daniel in the head like a blunt object. Todd did not work for him anymore. Todd was simply his friend. "Hey, Todd, how's it going."

Todd hadn't been retired long enough to forget that tone in Daniel's voice. "I get the feeling you called for a specific reason," he prompted.

"Can I bore you with my sad story for a few minutes?"

"Anytime." Todd waved a hand at Flora, indicating she should continue to eat her breakfast without him and walked out to the living room. "What's going on?"

"I won't bore you with the details, let's just say things didn't go as planned when I met Gwenn for breakfast this morning."

Todd rapidly calculated the potential failures in the carefully constructed plan and could see only one possible flaw. "Elena?"

"Yeah, that floated over like a lead balloon."

He chose not to remind Daniel that he had counseled against needless sharing. "What's the damage?"

"We went from a she's-weak-in-the-knees kiss at the front door to her walking out without taking a bite of her food... in about...I'd say, 25 minutes." There was an acerbic edge to Daniel's voice.

"Unfortunately I think your old friends 'time' and 'space' are the only remedies."

"I hate them," Daniel mumbled.

"Maybe she'll recognize the double standard by tomorrow, but I wouldn't put all my chips on red, if you know what I mean." Todd mindlessly straightened the couch pillows while he talked.

"I think I might, but I'm going to guess you're not a gambler?"

"You would be correct."

Daniel permitted himself a brief chuckle. "So, back to the Twin Cities with my heart in my hand, eh?"

"The upside is you'll have plenty of time to get those two pieces finished for the Gregory North gallery."

He flashed back to the crashing wave. "I've got a third one in the wings, too.

Todd was deeply pleased to hear that today's setback had not crushed Daniel's creative spirit. Progress comes in many guises. "Do you need Erik to assist you in closing up the cabin?"

"Nope. I'll be out of here in about an hour." Daniel glanced at his still-packed duffle. "Maybe less. Hey, is he going to sublet your place in Minneapolis?"

"Yes, that worked out rather nicely." Todd nodded his self-approval. "I'll let you go, Daniel. Call if you need...I mean, call anytime." He ended the call and returned to find Flora re-warming his breakfast in the skillet.

He walked over behind her and slipped his arms around her waist. "I could've thrown that in the microwave."

"You hate microwaved eggs." She leaned back against him and crooked her head into his neck. "It's no trouble."

He smiled and released his grasp. "Aren't you going to ask what that was about?"

"You'll tell me, if you can." She flipped the strips of turkey bacon over and stirred the eggs.

"It sounds like things were fantastic until he dipped into the truth serum and told her about Elena."

"But that was after she dumped him and..." Flora blushed and stopped herself from completing the sentence.

"Yes, all of the onlookers would agree with you. Regrettably, she did not see it that way."

"Gwenn's always been a pretty fair-minded person, she'll come around."

Todd bobbed his head in agreement. "Exactly my counsel. It's the open-ended time frame that has Daniel upset."

Flora re-plated the breakfast and set the plate down in front of Todd, with a fresh cup of coffee.

"I could get used to this," he teased.

"Me too." She leaned down and kissed his cheek. "I can let you know if she says anything at work."

"We probably shouldn't meddle," Todd chided.

"You mean we shouldn't meddle—any *more*." Flora laughed at her own joke and took a seat across from Todd. "They're just so perfect together."

"You're an incurable romantic." Todd winked over his raised coffee cup.

She giggled. "Yes, I'm in love and it's fatal. 'Til death do us part." She meant it as a joke, but as soon as the words escaped her lips her heart skipped a beat and she bit her lip.

Todd took a long sip of his coffee. His expression a riddle wrapped in an enigma.

Sixty-eight

Gwenn was grateful for the distraction of Rachel's wedding plans. Weeks were flying by and all the details were falling into place like Tetris pieces in the only video game she had ever played—and won.

Rachel had finally settled on the Duluth Grill to cater the reception. The difficulty Gwenn was facing today was convincing Rachel to narrow her selections.

"But everything they make is to die for, Gwenny. Can't they just do a little bit of everything?"

"Let's start with time of day, OK?" Gwenn had helped Rachel send out the Save the Date cards, but those cards had not included a time, because Rachel was really bad at making decisions. "Do you want to get married at sunrise?"

"Yuck, no way. I have to get up before sunrise almost everyday. I'd like to sleep in on my wedding day."

"Good. Progress." Gwenn scratched out the breakfast menu items. "How do you feel about a sandwich tray?"

"Ew, sounds terrible. Did you ask me that before?"

"Several times." Gwenn rolled her eyes and crossed out sandwiches. "If we shoot for mid-afternoon, we could go with a selection of appetizers and maybe some dips and salads. How does that sound?"

Rachel was lying on Gwenn's bed, swiping through pictures of Annie on her phone. "What about breakfast for dinner? That way we could get married later in the day, but still have yummy breakfast foods."

Gwenn waved her notebook at Rachel. "Breakfast is off the list. See this," she pointed to the big "X" on the paper. "Breakfast is no longer an option."

"Fine!" Rachel rolled off the bed and stomped out of the room. She yelled over her shoulder, "Maybe we'll just elope on a boat and sail off into the sunset and save you the trouble."

Gwenn heard her sister crash down onto the sofa. The mention of a boat sent her thoughts racing off to Daniel. There had been radio silence since the incident at Perkins. She was waiting for him to apologize. He hadn't apologized. End of story.

She marched out to the living room to set Rachel straight. She found her curled up in the fetal position whimpering into her knees. "Rache, what's wrong?"

"It's supposed to be the happiest day of my life, and it's not. Everyone keeps telling me what to do and I can't have anything the way I want it." She snuffled and curled up more tightly.

Gwenn knew that Rachel's statement was ludicrous, but she also felt a little guilty about the secret she was keeping. "Rache, what if you could have your reception on a yacht, in the harbor, while the fireworks were blasting overhead?"

"Holy shit, Gwenny." Rachel sat up and gaped at Gwenn. "That would be the most amazing...shit, that would be awesome. Boats are so expensive, though. I can't afford it, never mind."

"What if we could get the boat for free?"

"Do not fuck with me. If you can get me a free boat I will let you serve whatever the hell you want on that free boat. I won't even look at the menu."

The temptation for control was too great. "Daniel has a 100-foot yacht that holds 70-80 passengers. Flora told me about it, but...well, then...you-know-what happened."

"Gwenn, this is probably the boat-lust talking, but it seems pretty shitty to kick Daniel to the curb for sleeping with someone, one time, after you dumped him for Steven. I mean, did you ever stop to think that the guy wrote you those poems even after you slept with Steven and crapped all over his heart?"

Gwenn recoiled from Rachel's blunt retort. "Fuck you. You want the goddamn boat you go make nice with him." She stood up and walked right back into her bedroom.

Rachel was furious at Gwenn for dangling the carrot and then shitting on it. "Maybe I will." She grabbed her coat and stomped out of the apartment, happily listening to the door slam behind her.

She pulled her phone out en route to the van. "Hello, Todd? I have a proposition for you."

Sixty-nine

Rachel paced back and forth in front of baggage claim. She searched every face as the escalator emptied onto the ground transport level.

Annie returned from the bathroom and put one arm around Rachel. "Babe, you have to breathe. She texted you. She's here. Chill."

"Mom! Mom! Over here." Rachel waved her arms wildly to catch Greta's attention.

"Rachel!" Greta left her bag severely unattended and ran to embrace her daughter. Fortuitously, the TSA agent patrolling the baggage claim had a shred of human compassion and allowed the women an uninterrupted reunion.

Eventually the mother/daughter team calmed down enough to find the rest of Greta's bags, acknowledge Annie's existence and move en masse to the parking structure.

Rachel allowed Annie to drive back to Duluth, but only if she promised to stop at Tobie's for pecan caramel rolls. Annie dared a brief protest, but Rachel hastily reminded her that she had lost 11 and a half pounds and she was back to running six days a week—thanks to coach Gwenn.

The trio arrived at the humble apartment above the bakery, on a rare sunny day in Duluth. The weather had thankfully warmed over the last few weeks and Rachel crossed her fingers that the pleasantness would last until July fifth.

Annie knew she would be invisible for the rest of the day, so she made up some story about a band meeting and slipped away, nearly unnoticed.

"Mom, all your baking stuff arrived yesterday. You have to come downstairs and meet Nathan and William." Rachel grabbed her mother's hand and pulled her down the stairs. "Do you want to bake a sample cake today?"

Greta rushed to the bottom of the stairs before she was able to catch her breath and get a word into Rachel's stream of consciousness flow. "I'm pretty exhausted from the flight. I was hoping I could take you and your sister out for dinner, Annie too, if she's finished with her band meeting."

"Gwenny!" Rachel smacked herself on the forehead. "I totally forgot that I invited her over to meet you." She dropped her mother's hand and whipped out her phone. Gwenn answered on the first ring. "What?" She cast a guilty look at Greta. "No, I did not go bonkers over showing Greta everything and forget about you." Rachel put one finger over her lips and winked at her mom. "OK. Come over as soon as you can. We're going out to dinner, too."

Greta smiled at Rachel, "It sounds like she knows you pretty well."

"Better than I know myself, most days." Rachel rubbed her hands along her waist. "She's the one who helped me slim down for the wedding."

"You always look fantastic," Greta gushed.

Rachel's phone buzzed in her pocket. "Gwenn must've forgotten something." She answered without looking at the screen. "What now?" Rachel made a face at Greta. "Oh, sorry, I thought it was Gwenn." She turned away and finished the conversation in whispery mumbles.

"Everything all right?" Greta looked genuinely concerned.

"I hate to put you in the middle, but I have to go meet with someone about some wedding stuff...and...well, Gwenn can't exactly know about it."

"Rachel, this sounds like a bad idea."

"It's not, I promise. But let me show you the bakery real quick, and then you can wait upstairs for Gwenn. I'll only be gone an hour—tops."

Nathan and William took turns hugging Greta and dishing about how happy Rachel had been since finding her birth mom. Greta thanked them and promised to need their help with the wedding cake. Love fest complete, Rachel shooed her mom back upstairs and raced out the door.

The tires hummed loudly as she sped across the Aerial Lift Bridge. She felt her heartbeat accelerate in time with the rhythm.

She knocked lightly on the door, filled with a sudden rush of guilt.

"Hello, Rachel." He stepped back and gestured for her to enter.

"Hi, Daniel." She hurried in, fearful of being seen.

"Sorry I wasn't able to see you sooner, but I kinda went off the grid after my last trip to Duluth." Daniel took a seat in one of the mid-century nautical maple wing chairs and waved Rachel to the sofa.

"Yeah, I can understand."

"Todd tells me you'd like to use my boat in July." Daniel kept his tone professional. He knew Rachel had been on his side "once upon a time," but she was Gwenn's sister and family loyalty could've trumped that brief alliance.

Rachel wrung her hands in her lap. "Daniel, you know I don't like to meddle...but, I think Gwenn made a big mistake."

"It seems we still have something in common." He smiled and felt his shoulders relax as he leaned back to listen to Rachel's proposal.

"I'm not saying I can change Gwenn's mind, I mean you know what a stubborn bitch she can be when she thinks she's right about—"

"Hang on, hang on. I'm going to plead the Fifth on all of that." Daniel stood up. "Can I get you something to drink? Water? Juice? Whiskey?"

A loud snort escaped as Rachel over-laughed at his joke. "I would actually love a whiskey. Is that a real option?"

"Maker's on the rocks?" He enquired as he walked toward the kitchen.

"Yes, please." Rachel looked around the cozy cabin and immediately fell in love with the retro decor and the enormous split-rock fireplace. "The fireplace is gorgeous."

"All Lake Superior granite, supposedly hand-hewn by my great-grandfather, but you know how family rumors get started."

"Uh, yeah. You're preachin' to the didn't-know-I-was-adopted-until-a-couple-months-ago choir."

"Right. I totally forgot about that. Did you find your real mom?"

"Well, you're supposed to say 'birth mom', but yeah, I did, and she is a-fucking-mazing."

Daniel returned and handed Rachel a healthy pour of hooch. "Here's to finding happiness anywhere ya can." He clinked glasses with her and lowered himself into the chair.

She took a healthy draw of the alcohol. It warmed her insides and boosted her courage. "So, Todd must've told you why I called?"

"He did." Daniel kicked his feet up on the coffee table, crossed his ankles and leaned back.

"And?"

He smirked at her. "I want to hear you say it."

A second gulp of fortitude was required before she could respond. "If you'll let me use your boat for my reception, I will actively help you knock Gwenn off her high horse and admit that she's still crazy about you." Rachel recited the line like a bored child parroting back memorized scripture verses at Bible camp.

She had piqued his interest and he swung his feet to the floor so he could lean forward. "She's crazy about me?"

Rachel saw the look in his eye. That unmistakable look she saw in Annie's eyes, every day—genuine love between souls, not genders. "She doesn't know it yet, she can be kinda stubborn, but I have my ways."

Until this exact moment he wasn't sure he could let hope back into his life. Hope was the soul-crusher. "Can we have codenames?"

Rachel spit a little bit of whiskey back into her glass. "What?" She wiped her chin and snickered.

"Like an undercover operation, you know...I might have to call you about something and if Gwenn's in the room... never mind, it was a stupid idea." Daniel shook his head and looked down at the ground.

"Lion King," Rachel blurted.

"The kids' movie?" Daniel tilted his head. "I don't get it."

She decided her loyalty had already been split, revealing this secret could hardly matter, on top of treason. "Remember that night I gave you the matchbook cover, with her number?"

"Like it was yesterday."

Rachel covered her face with her hands and took them away with a huge exhale, "Sorry, Gwenny." She hesitated and looked keenly at Daniel.

"Might as well, Rachel. We're in this deep." He gestured to their drinks and the general plotting and planning.

"She noticed you first. She called you 'Lion King' because of your hair, which she thought was gorgeous." Rachel covered her eyes in shame and looked up pleadingly.

"No harm done, Rachel. Just one more secret we have—for now." He leaned back in thought. "So how about 'L.K'?"

"Initials are too suspicious." Rachel took a sip of Maker's. "What about Leon?"

"I like it. OK, you better change it in your phone."

"Wow, Leon, it sounds like this might not be your first mission."

"Hey, I was an only child with a vivid imagination. I may or may not have played several thousand hours of solo spy missions." Daniel put up his hand to hold her potential questions at bay and had a laugh at his own expense.

Rachel, not to be outdone, leaned forward and slammed her glass down on the coffee table. "OK, Leon, let's get down to brass tacks." Her lips twitched to suppress the giggles.

Daniel smiled and leaned in, as he called up his most menacing whisper, "Nothing leaves this room, Baker."

Seventy

Gwenn woke up long before her scheduled alarm. Today was the day her baby sister was going to get married. Pride. Joy. Excitement. Nervousness. Anticipation. Somewhere peeking out from a dark corner, there was also a sliver of jealousy. She pushed that sliver back into the depths and reached over to poke Rachel.

"Wake up, Rache. It's your wedding day."

Rachel's big brown eyes popped open and sparkled with excitement. "I get the shower first." She rolled out of bed and ran to Gwenn's shower.

The sleepover had been Gwenn's idea. She was desperate to cover all the traditional bases, as well as the progressive check boxes. Bad luck for the bride to see the bride before the wedding. *Check.* The shoes Rachel had grabbed from Shirley's closet covered "old" and "borrowed." *Check.* The sexy lace panties from Annie checked off "blue" and "new." *Check.*

Gwenn grabbed her note pad and decided to check things off her actual list, instead of her mental list.

Commemorative glassware, inscribed on one side with "Annie & Rachel, Fourth of July" and on the opposite side with a big "=" symbol for marriage equality.

The signage for the ceremony, "Choose a seat not a side, either way it's for a bride." A Pinterest favorite for Rachel.

Rachel's calla lily and red poppy bouquet—with navy blue ribbon.

Annie's calla lily and red poppy boutonniere.

Blue anemone and white button mum boutonnieres for the rest of the wedding party.

Calla lily, red poppy and blue anemone corsages for the brides' mothers.

Gwenn traced anxious circles around the next item on her list, "Reception - Rachel's handling everything." The very thought made her stomach cramp.

"OK, all yours, Maid of Honor." Rachel rubbed the towel over her freshly washed crimson-streaked black hair. Gwenn had been absolutely right about the red streaks. They looked fantastic.

Gwenn dropped her notepad on the bed and walked off to the shower in a daze.

As soon as Rachel heard the water running in the bathroom she grabbed her phone and called Annie. "I love you, almost-wife."

"Ditto, babe." Annie had volunteered to stay at the apartment with Greta. Rachel had put up quite a fight about abandoning her mother, but Greta loved the idea of Rachel getting ready in secret.

"Have you seen the cake? Is it amazing?"

"I heard your mom get up hours ago, but I'm still trying to get some shut eye."

"What if she needs something?" Rachel paced. "I should come over there."

"Babe, it's fine. You were with her yesterday and all the hard stuff is done."

"OK. You're right." She slipped into the "something new" from Annie. "I love these fancy panties you gave me."

Annie sat up and swung her legs out of bed. "Are you telling me you are practically naked right now?"

Rachel giggled, "Yeah, think about that while you're in the shower."

"Oh, I will," assured Annie, her voice still raspy with sleep.

"Shit, the water stopped. Gwenn will catch me. Gotta go. Love you." She hung up before Annie could respond.

Rachel tugged a T-shirt over her damp hair and fired off a quick text to "Leon."

">we all set for tnite?" Her eyes shot to the bathroom door while she waited for the reply.

">shuttles will arrive at 6:30 to take your wristbanded (blame todd) guests to the place with no codename"

">who gets wristbands?"

">todd got a list...from annie?"

">lets hope – thx leon"

">naturally"

Rachel chuckled to herself as she slipped the phone in her backpack.

"What's so funny?" Gwenn asked suspiciously.

"Nothing." Rachel spun around. Guilt had drained the color from her face.

"You're up to something and I don't like it." Gwenn narrowed her gaze and studied Rachel.

"Calm down, Gwenny. It's wedding day jitters, I swear." Rachel's brain tripped over itself searching for a proper emergency. "You have to help me with my hair...it's a disaster." She crossed her fingers behind her back, hoping the ruse would be effective.

"You are kinda hopeless with this stuff. Grab that chair and have a seat in my beauty parlor." Gwenn waved a hand toward her bathroom.

They briefly argued about the hairdo, but in the end Gwenn convinced her that mostly down, with a little up and the red streaks curled in loose ringlets, would be divine. Rachel acquiesced and Gwenn hated herself for using the word "divine."

She was also not particularly fond of the white linen suit she would be wearing. Linen was one of Gwenn's "avoid" fabrics, due to its tendency to look good for five seconds after it was pressed and never again for the duration. However, it was not her wedding, it was Rachel's, so after she completed everything else on her checklist—she would put on the suit.

Rachel looked at the curlers in her hair and sighed. "I'm starving. What can we get delivered?"

"Let's go to the Grill. We have time and I think you should eat your favorite breakfast on your special day."

"Go out? In public?" Rachel pointed to her hair, "Like this?"

Gwen leaned down close to Rachel's ear and smiled. "Don't you want to tell everyone you're getting married today?"

Rachel slowly turned toward Gwenn. A blind man could've seen the light pop on inside her head. "I do." And the irony of that answer, on this day, sent her into a fit of giggles.

They threw on enough clothing to legally go out in public and drove to the Duluth Grill for Red Flannel Hash and the best coffee in town.

The waitress barely had the opportunity to look askance at Rachel's hairdo in progress, when Rachel blurted, "I'm getting married today. My hair's not done."

The server nodded, took the order and disappeared into the back.

Gwenn shrugged her shoulders and watched as Rachel wound up for a good pout. Thankfully she was headed off at the pass by the return of the server.

"Congratulations." She plunked a warm frosted cinnamon roll down in front of Rachel. "You must be the bride in the Hutchinson/Nelson nuptials. We're catering your reception. The roll is on the house, by the way."

The pout turned into a beaming smile. "That's me, Rachel Hutchinson. We're both brides though, Annie Nelson is my fiancée."

"Oh, that's nice." The server blinked nervously. "Your breakfasts will be out shortly." Again, she disappeared.

Rachel looked at Gwenn, "It's not like she has to come to the wedding."

"I think she just didn't know what to say, Rache. Some people are supportive but inexperienced and they don't want to say the wrong thing." Gwenn pointed to the cinnamon roll, "Just eat your prize and be happy. It's your day."

"My day, my way!" Rachel took a huge bite of the warm pastry and frosting got all over the end of her nose.

Gwenn snapped a picture.

"What the hell?"

"Just makin' memories. Today is going to be a magical blur. I don't want to miss anything." She grabbed Rachel's hand. "I love you, and I am bursting with happiness for you and Annie."

"I hope you still love me tomorrow." Rachel spoke without thinking. The sugary goodness was gumming up her super-spy senses.

"Why wouldn't I love you tomorrow?"

She wished she had spent less time chasing girls and more time learning to be a good liar, like Gwenn. *Think. Think. Think.* "Oh, I mean...I'll probably drink too much and make a dumb toast...or fall off...the dance floor."

"You really are nuts. How do you fall off a dance floor?"

When it's on a goddamn boat, Rachel thought. "I don't know what I'm saying. I have a sugar-rush. Let's just eat and get back to your place to finish prepping me."

Gwenn took a few bites of her scrambled eggs and fixed Rachel with a penetrating stare. Before she could scrutinize the situation her mind flashed to her unfinished list. Where the hell had she put all the little bags of rainbow confetti?

Seventy-one

Todd and Flora walked in circles around Daniel.

"It is more than satisfactory." Todd gave his unsolicited opinion and nodded.

"Flora, I need a woman's opinion. Do you think she'll recognize me?"

She stepped back, squinted a little and tilted her head. "Put on the dark sunglasses."

"I can't believe I'm doing this." Daniel's words protested but the captain's uniform straining over his broad chest uttered an unwavering commitment to the plan.

Flora nodded and then shook her head. "Yep, she'll never know it's you. Just be sure not to say anything, and stand behind the real captain. You'll be surprised how people ignore the hired help."

"Here, here." Todd raised an imaginary glass and toasted Flora's comment on the plight of the common man.

"Can I work on your hair one more time?" Flora was not pleased with the flyaways and stray pieces escaping from the confines of the white captain's hat. "I think I'll have to use a bit more product to really slick it down, for good."

Daniel slid his sunglasses down his nose and gave Todd a playful glower. "Product, Todd. More product."

Todd grinned and shook his head, "The things you'll do for love."

Flora pulled Daniel over to a chair. Once he was seated she removed the eyewear and the hat. She re-applied the styling gel and combed it through Daniel's thick, stubborn mane. "I'm afraid we are going to have to resort to the bobby pins I warned you about."

"Fantastic." Daniel hung his head in shame.

"If it's any consolation, Daniel, you look great in the uniform."

"It's really not, but I appreciate the gesture."

Flora finally got all of his hair under control and pressed the hat back into place. "Now, when you put on the sunglasses, be careful not to poke them into the hair. OK?"

"Whatever you say." Daniel walked over and looked at himself in the mirror in his entryway and chuckled. "Wow, I don't even recognize me."

Todd ended a call and turned back to his co-conspirators. "Captain Jeff, our actual captain, is ready for us to come aboard. We need to get down there ahead of the caterers, etcetera to establish Daniel's crew status. We don't want any blurters spoiling our efforts."

Flora pulled on a light coat and grabbed her purse. "We'll drop you off at the slip and get up to the Flame, to see if there's any last minute details that need handling."

Daniel slung his backpack over his shoulder and walked out to Todd's car. He opened the passenger door for Flora.

"Oh, no. I'll sit in the back, you'll never get in there with those legs."

He chuckled and helped her into the back.

Todd dropped Daniel at the dock and rattled off an endless series of instructions.

"Don't worry, Todd. You guys just go enjoy the wedding, text me some pics and I'll see you aboard at 7:00."

"Aye aye, Captain," Todd joked.

Seventy-two

Rachel sparkled like a woodland fairy. Greta dabbed at her eyes and cursed her mascara. Gwenn fussed with the satin ribbons on the antique halo in Rachel's hair and pretended her own eyes weren't watering.

"Greta, can you help her with the necklace and the shoes? I have to make a few calls." She clicked a quick pic of Rachel's hair on her way out.

"Of course, of course." Greta rushed to Rachel's side and carefully kissed her perfect hairdo. "I love the red ringlet curls…and the way she pulled this bit up…oh, sweetie, I'm just so proud to be your mama right now."

"Mom, stop it. You're gonna make me cry." Rachel brushed at the corners of her eyes with a pinky finger and worked to blink back the tears.

Gwenn stepped into the living room and called Flora. "Did you check in with Annie?"

"Yes, she's great. Everything fits perfectly and she said Cass, Mika and Bree look great in their linen suits. She did mention that Bree hated the blue silk shirts and wanted to get traded to the Red Team." Flora giggled.

The Red Team consisted of the Maid of Honor, Gwenn, and the #1 Bride's bridesmaids, Nathan and William. They had been given the nickname due to their silk shirts all being variations on the red theme. Annie's bridesmaids, her band mates, were decked out in the same linen suits, each wearing a different style of blue silk shirt underneath.

"Flowers?"

"We just got to the Flame and Todd counted everything," Flora lowered her voice, "twice, and he said we are all set."

"Perfect. Will you guys pin them on as the wedding party arrives? I'd like consistent placement for the photos and if we leave it to each person...well, you know."

"Consider it handled." Flora knew exactly what Gwenn meant.

"How do the decorations look?"

"Really good. It's very much with the red, white and blue theme, but without looking like a political rally."

"OK, I have a couple more calls. See you soon." Gwenn almost hung up. "Oh, and in case I forget to say it later, thank you—a million times, thank you."

Nathan and William were on their way to deliver the cake. They still held Rachel's tightly-kept secret about the location of the reception, but they assured Gwenn the caterer was completely aware of the new location and they would get changed into their suits and arrive at the Flame at least 30 minutes before the ceremony.

Gwenn saved the best for last. She could not believe it had been so easy for her to convince her best friend, Randy, to officiate. "Hello Randy, did you get your ordination?"

"I did! I have the wallet card, laminated, and all kinds of official paraphernalia. I bought the whole package. I can marry 'em, bury 'em, baptize 'em and I can even start my own church."

"Simply terrifying," she murmured. "OK, sweetie you were my last call. Promise me your outfit is appropriate. Please?"

"Gwendolyn Hutchinson, I am shocked at your insinuation." Randy straightened his red bow tie, smoothed his striped Uncle Sam trousers and grinned at his reflection. To his credit he had refused to don the top hat and white goatee. "See you on the stage, love."

"Indeed," Gwenn sighed. "OK, time to load up, ladies."

Rachel emerged from the bedroom and Greta was right behind her fussing with the back of the wedding dress and tripping over the hem of her own gown.

"Rachel...I...you are..." Gwenn took another picture with her phone.

Rachel gestured for Gwenn to stop. "Don't, don't say it, Gwenny. I will weep all over this beautiful dress and my never-as-waterproof-as-they-say mascara will ruin my face."

"Fine. But you are." Gwenn grabbed the hangar displaying her bridesmaid suit and opened the door for the procession.

Gwenn drove at an uncharacteristically reasonable speed all the way to the Flame.

"Gwenny, is something wrong?"

"Of course not, why?"

"You're driving so slow...I mean, for you it's slow."

She refused to let a shadow be cast upon Rachel and Annie's special day. If she was missing Daniel and wishing she could swallow her pride and apologize, that was her little secret. Today was all about her sister, so she forced a happy tone into her voice and played to her strengths. She lied. "I was just thinking how much I will miss you when you're on your amazing honeymoon...and I was a little jealous. I mean, Greece? You are going to have such an amazing time."

Eager to bask in the spotlight of her day, Rachel gobbled up the lie—hook, line and sinker. "I can't wait. Mom, I still think you should let Annie and I pay you back. Those tickets were so expensive...it's too much."

"Nonsense. I've wished for a chance to spoil you my whole life. Get used to it." Greta patted her chest and held her breath, "And if you have a baby, well, all bets are off, sweetie. I will be visiting once a month—at least."

Rachel laughed and reached back to squeeze her mother's hand. Deep down there was a tiny wave of uneasiness, though. Once a month, in their small apartment above the bakery, could get a little nuts. She pushed the thought away and focused all her energy on her big day. She could not wait to see Annie.

Gwenn parked directly in front of the entrance to the Flame. She pulled her suit from the hook above the backseat of the Jeep and let Greta assist Rachel with her dress. The picture-snapping obsession resulted in a series of vehicle exiting pics.

Flora, glistening in the July humidity, opened the Flame's entrance door and waved everyone in. "All clear. Annie's not here yet." When she saw the look on Rachel's face, she added, "She's ten minutes out."

"Can you *flower* them while I get into this contraption?" Gwenn pointed to her suit.

"Absolutely." Flora nodded to Gwenn. "Follow me, ladies." She led the way up the stairs, pinned on Greta's corsage and handed Rachel her bouquet.

Rachel looked around at the decorations and flowers and smiled from ear to ear. "Wow, Gwenny is really good at this stuff," she said to Flora.

"Gosh, it's time to get you in the back, Rachel. The guests will be arriving and Annie will be here any minute. We have an area all set up for you." Flora led them to the back.

Annie arrived minutes later with her mother and band mates. Flora led them to their separate waiting area and turned on the additional fan.

Todd was gleefully wrist-banding guests. He had selected a primo spot at the top of the stairs, entering the nightclub, and placed his special list next to the box of wristbands. Rachel and Annie had sent an open invitation to the wedding, when they posted their announcement in the newspaper, but Daniel's yacht only held 80 passengers plus crew. Todd had forced Annie to create an "A-List" of attendees who would get access to the exclusive after-party aboard Daniel's vessel.

"Name?" Todd held his list.

"Nathan and William, from the bakery."

"What's your last name, Nathan?"

Luckily Flora arrived to save the day. "Todd, honestly, they're in the wedding party." She grabbed two wristbands and handed them to the guys. "Put these on. When the shuttles arrive it will get serious." She smiled and pointed to the back, "Rachel's in the back with her mom."

Todd smiled at Flora. "Maybe you should stay and help me. I get a little…"

"Yes, you do." She leaned over and kissed his cheek.

Everyone got a little bag of rainbow confetti and some people got wristbands. The Flame filled up quickly and once Todd had crossed off every name on his list, he and Flora abandoned their post to check on the brides.

Randy strutted through the crowd and took his place up on the stage. The crowd quieted to a dull roar and he cued the DJ.

The deep techno organ strains of "Let's Go Crazy" drowned out the last murmurs of the audience and Randy intoned, "Dearly beloved, we are gathered here to day to get these two chicks hitched!"

The chorus swelled through the crowd and the DJ faded to the instrumental version of the song. Bree and Nathan were the first pair to make their way up the aisle, followed by Cass and William. Gwenn and Mika linked arms—the Maids of Honor finished the procession of attendants.

A brief silence brought the guests to their feet and some overwhelmed fangirl shouted, "Annie, I love you!"

To which Randy replied, "Too late, sweetie."

The traditional wedding march played and Annie emerged on her mother's arm, followed by Rachel, clutching Greta's arm and fiercely biting the inside of her cheek in a fruitless attempt to keep her tears at bay. The photographer flashed a rapid series of shots and the quartet proceeded to the dais. Rachel chuckled when she caught sight of Randy.

"Who gives these women to be married?"

The proud mothers, Greta and Fontella, replied in unison, "We do."

Rachel turned, took Annie's hand and willed herself to hold back the tears of joy.

The mothers of the brides returned to their places of honor in the front row.

The audience sat down and Randy began the ceremony. "Ladies, gentlemen, and everyone in between, in the words of Gieselle C. Viera, 'Once in a while, right in the middle of an ordinary life, love gives us a fairytale.'"

Thunderous applause broke out.

Randy's general excitement kept the ceremony moving. When he asked for the rings Gwenn's face turned ashen. She shot a horrified gaze at Mika. Randy looked back and forth between the two. Gwenn gulped and slowly reached for Rachel's shoulder. She could not believe all her careful planning had resulted in this disaster.

Mika looked at Gwenn's face, at Randy's outstretched hand and clapped her hand over her left boob. "Shit. I got 'em right here." She reached into her pocket and produced the two low-domed sterling silver bands imprinted with Rachel's thumbprint on one side and Annie's on the other—connected by an equal sign.

The sudden rush of blood back to Gwenn's face made her a little woozy. She almost tossed a scolding glare at Mika, but when she saw the love radiating between Rachel and Annie, all she could do was smile as they slipped the rings on each other's fingers.

The ceremony was finished before Rachel knew what had happened. Suddenly Annie was kissing her and the crowd was on their feet cheering. They turned toward their guests and Randy announced, "May I present Mrs. and Mrs. Nelson-Hutchinson."

Rainbow confetti fluttered down, ignited by the flashes from the official photographer's camera and at least a hundred personal phones.

The DJ cross-faded the traditional wedding march into a now-famous song by The Spanking Machine, "Fire Meets Earth." Over the long intro he announced, "The newlyweds will have a toast with everyone and then all wristbanded guests must proceed in an orderly fashion to the shuttles waiting out front. The Flame will stay open, so stick around and help us celebrate Rachel and Annie's big day. Drinks are half price for the next hour." The song kicked in and Bree grabbed the mic to sing along, live.

The healthy number of fans in the crowd raised their glasses, cheered and screamed.

Gwenn hugged Rachel tightly and kissed her on the cheek. "Congratulations, sweetie."

Todd swooped in to get them moving. "OK, guests of honor, down that champagne, it's time to load into the special limo and get to your after-party."

"Rache, are you gonna tell me what's going on?"

Rachel winked at Gwenn and purred, "Never." She grabbed Annie's hand and they hurried down the stairs, under a fresh shower of confetti, to the waiting limo.

Gwenn shepherded the brides' mothers down to the waiting transportation.

Todd helped the wedding party into the limousine, closed the door and knocked twice on the roof to signal the driver to depart.

Bree had popped a bottle of champagne from the mini bar and was passing it around. It was a short drive to the harbor and when Gwenn saw the boat, a fresh wave of guilt washed over her. She felt awful for fighting with Rachel and forcing her to plan her own reception. Of course, now Todd's involvement made perfect sense. Gwenn knew Rachel wouldn't have dealt directly with Daniel, she had simply whined to Flora and gotten help convincing Todd to set everything up. Daniel would be miles away, in Minneapolis, and Gwenn had no one but herself to blame.

Seventy-three

Somehow Todd had arrived ahead of the wedding party and was standing up on the second deck, directing guests as they came aboard.

Once the last shuttle had deposited its cargo, Todd gave the signal to get underway. "Welcome to the after-party, everyone. I will turn it over to our First Mate, Jeff. He has some important safety information for you followed by the food service in the stern."

"First Mate" and secret Captain, Jeff, informed everyone on the location of life vests and basic safety measures while on board. "The water temperature is barely 50°F, so we'd like to keep everyone on this side of the rails tonight. Enjoy the wine and champagne, and walk with a buddy." He indicated that Captain Leon would take good care of them and they would have a spectacular view of the fireworks show in the harbor.

Captain Leon (Daniel) waved to the passengers, and just as Flora had predicted no one noticed.

Once they were well underway and the harbor breeze had cooled the passengers, Todd brought plates of food up to the Captain and his First Mate in the wheelhouse. "So far so good, no one's the wiser down below."

"Let me know when it's safe to sneak below decks and into the forward cabin so I can get changed." Daniel indicated his costume.

"Women love a guy in uniform, Cap'n. You might wanna leave it on," Jeff teased.

"Probably true, but I gotta get this crap outta my hair, it's starting to itch." Daniel looked pleadingly at Todd.

"Let's wait till the music kicks in. Bree assures me she is a 'kick-ass' DJ," Todd said and rolled his eyes. "Anyhow, I'll come and get you when the coast is clear."

"Thanks, buddy." Daniel patted Todd on the shoulder.

Todd exhaled and climbed back down to the main deck.

Rachel and Annie were sitting with their mothers and enjoying the amazing spread from the Duluth Grill. "I could eat at least three more of these salmon cakes, but I have to save room for wedding cake." Rachel winked at Greta.

Gwenn was standing in the bow, sipping champagne and talking to Cass and Mika about the tour. She wasn't actually listening, she was watching the water curl away from the prow and wondering how long she would survive if she fell overboard. She also didn't like the way the creepy captain seemed to be watching her, but who could tell with those dictator-dark sunglasses. She downed the rest of her bubbly and grabbed another glass from the passing server.

Todd crept up to the wheelhouse and gave Daniel the all-clear.

Daniel covertly wound his way below deck and into the forward cabin. He closed the polished walnut door and quickly undressed. He loved the feel of the teak and ebony floor beneath his feet. He climbed into the shower and eagerly washed the "product" out of his hair.

Up on the main deck, forks and knives clinked on stemware and Rachel and Annie kissed, again. Cheers rang out.

Gwenn tipped the last drop of brut nectar into her mouth and stumbled down the narrow stairwell in search of the bathroom, or "the head" as one of the servers had schooled.

The lack of food in her stomach, paired with the plethora of champagne, resulted in a bit of wobble in her sea legs. She caught her toe on nothing and pitched against a beautiful wooden door. Had the door stood firm she would have managed to stay on her feet, but the hatch had other plans.

She found herself face to teak on the floorboards of one of the private cabins they had been warned to stay out of, during the First Mate's speech. She checked herself for injury and heard a low chuckle coming from somewhere above her.

She rolled over and blinked her bleary eyes.

***

Melissa Ferrick's song "Drive" poured from the speakers and Rachel was grinding closer and closer to Annie. "I love you, Mrs."

Annie nuzzled into Rachel's neck, "I love you, too, Mrs."

Actual Captain Jeff announced the fireworks were about to begin and urged everyone to find a comfortable spot on the bow or stern, to get the best view.

Todd realized he had not seen Gwenn for several minutes. His eyes darted through the faces in the crowd and his internal facial recognition software found no match. He turned to conduct a more thorough search, but Flora forbid him from any further official duties.

"I want you to kiss me under the fireworks, Mr. Warner. This is our first Fourth of July."

He looked into her twinkling eyes and all thought of duty disappeared. He had gotten Daniel this far; the rest was up to Mr. Gregory.

***

The backlit silhouette of a broad-shouldered, mostly naked man towered over her. She could make out a towel, slung low over his hips, and little drops of water were falling from his hair and sending shivers across her skin. Her champagne-soaked brain could not deduce why a naked, wet man was on this vessel. Another droplet fell from his hair. *That hair. That chuckle.*

"Fancy meeting you here, Miss Hutchinson." Daniel extended a hand down to retrieve Gwenn from the floor. He pulled her up and closed the door.

She stumbled back to the edge of the bed as the first round of independence-celebrating explosions burst overhead. She saw the sparkles dance in his eyes. Her heart thudded and her throat tightened. Words tumbled through her brain, but all she could think in that moment was, words are overrated. She wanted the wet, naked man—now.

***

Todd pulled Flora close and kissed her with all the emotion he had been holding in check.

Flora flushed and pressed her lips to his.

Bree faded the music out and let the wind, waves and fireworks serenade the guests.

Annie cleverly slipped a hand inside Rachel's dress and whispered in her ear, "When do I get to take this off of you and seal this deal?"

Rachel's nipples hardened with excruciating pleasure. "I say we send Greta back to the apartment in a cab and keep the limo for an extra hour."

"Now, that's the girl I married." Annie retracted her hand and Rachel sighed.

***

Gwenn launched herself at Daniel, pinning him against the shiny walnut door.

He did not wait for a second invitation. He pulled off her jacket, yanked her blouse over her head and popped the button off her lined linen slacks in his haste to have her.

"Sorry, I broke your pants," he mumbled into her lips.

"You did me a favor. I hate them." She bit his lip and tugged.

He moaned. "How do you feel about these?" He ripped her panties off and pushed her onto the bed.

"Oh, Daniel." She ached for him. "You won't be needing this," she whispered, as she pulled his towel from its precarious resting place and revealed the intensity of his need.

He hovered above her—one hand pressed into the small of her back and one hand supporting his heaving torso. "Slow?"

She wrapped her legs around him and gasped, "Now."

He was inside her before she finished the syllable. The bursts of patriotic sound and color outside the cabin paled in comparison to the rocketing explosions in the stateroom. He lifted her up and pressed her back against the porthole.

She dug her fingernails into his flesh. Her body sparked with electricity as she felt his muscles flex and push deeper with each stroke. The fireworks reflected off the sweat on his chest and his hot breath on her neck sent fire to her nether regions.

He pulled her back onto the bed; she straddled him and matched his increasing rhythm. He tugged her hair and brought her face to his. This mouth, these lips—this is the only kiss he ever wanted.

She licked the edge of his top lip, nibbled his bottom lip and drove her tongue into his mouth. She felt the heat of his kiss and her body detonated. Her muscles convulsed and a muffled scream escaped her.

The grand finale of the independence celebration shattered the night with a concussion of sound and light.

He erupted seconds later and swallowed her screams in his hungry kiss.

She collapsed on top of him and he squeezed her ass, pressing their wet bodies closer. "No more breaks, OK?"

She wanted to keep reality at bay a little longer. Talking and words could come later, for now she just wanted to inhale him and feel the rapid rise and fall of his chest.

The Fourth of July display faded into the vast waters of Lake Superior and the silent rocking of the boat lulled them into a moment of pure bliss. An incredibly brief moment.

KNOCK KNOCK KNOCK.

"Daniel, I mean Captain Leon, are you in there?" Todd grabbed the door handle.

Daniel reacted instantly, "Todd if you open that door you will never forgive yourself."

Gwenn giggled and made an attempt to squirm away from Daniel's iron grasp.

Todd, being a human super-computer calculated the odds of that giggle belonging to the missing Gwenn, and immediately removed his hand from the door handle. "I will see to the disembarking of passengers and ask Actual Captain Jeff to leave the stateroom off the crews' final checklist."

Hushed whispers, more giggles and a muffled scream seeped through the door.

Before the sounds were translated, Todd added, "I will also make the appropriate excuses for Miss Hutchinson, with the brides."

Gwenn remembered a time, in the not-too-distant past, when she would have been mortified. Tonight she felt happy, free and even a little bit safe—in spite of her wanton nakedness.

Seventy-four

Annie gently shook Rachel's shoulder. "Babe, wake up." She kissed her eyelid and her cheek. "Look out your window, there's the Acropolis."

Instantly awake, Rachel pressed her forehead to the small ovaloid window. There, in all their ancient glory, stood the Parthenon and the Temple of Athena Nike. The sun-bleached stones defied time and she felt her heart flutter as her DNA absorbed this undeniably Greek moment. She turned to Annie and whispered, "My people built that."

Annie chuckled, "Yeah, babe. Your people built everything we're gonna see for the next three weeks."

They would only have two days in Athens before they hopped on a puddle-jumping prop-plane to fly out to the isle of Santorini, to meet Rachel's paternal relatives. Many of their wedding guests had urged them to sail to the isle of Lesbos, but that Sapphic tribute would have to wait for a future visit.

After collecting their luggage they braved the exhaust fumes at the ground transport exit and hailed a taxicab. The driver was not familiar with their hotel, so Annie had to flag down a policeman to translate. He assured them the driver now knew the way, and they climbed into the cab.

They arrived safely at the Art Gallery Hotel, just below the Acropolis. The view from their balcony rivaled any postcard in town. There was a faint scent of salt air on the wind. Eager to stretch their legs after the lengthy flight, Annie and Rachel decided to go back downstairs and get the lay of the land. The helpful, grandmotherly woman at the front desk gave them a short list of Greek words to learn and directions to a nearby creperie.

Annie ran her finger down the list of words, found "thank you" and said, "Euxaristo," to the kind woman.

They were both eager to explore Athens and, a little hungry, they took to the streets with their water bottles in tow.

Rachel fell madly in love with Greek crepes, and again blamed her DNA.

They had booked tours of the Temple of Poseidon, the Acropolis and Athens for the next two days, so they spent the evening exploring the gift shops and local haunts.

"There are more cats than people," Rachel said after stopping to pet her one hundredth stray.

Annie snickered, "So it's fair to say they're 'pussy friendly'?"

Rachel punched Annie playfully on the arm and Annie pulled her in for a kiss. For a moment Rachel felt self-conscious, but as she looked around at the Greeks ambling down the narrow streets—she noticed that no one cared. No one even gave them a second look.

Breakfast at the Art Gallery Hotel was simple but delicious. They enjoyed hard-boiled eggs, toast, yoghurt, juice, coffee and an apple. When they finished eating, they had to rush over a few blocks to catch the tour bus at a fancier hotel nearby.

First stop the Temple of Zeus. This was a drive-by sight on the tour, but the guide kept them informed. "These are the highest standing Corinthian pillars in the world." Oddly there was a smattering of applause on the bus, which made Rachel giggle.

"Whom are they clapping for? The guys who built this are pretty dead."

"They're clapping for your people, babe," Annie teased.

At the Odeon of Herod Atticus everyone unloaded from the bus and walked around snapping selfies like ancient Kardashians. Rachel preferred to stare off into the distance beyond the crumbling walls and imagine what it would've been like to grow up in this world. She could almost hear her father's voice telling her the stories of her ancestors.

Back on the bus. Next stop the Acropolis.

Rachel squeezed Annie's hand tightly as they walked up the steps of the Parthenon. They strolled over to the edge of the historical outcropping and Rachel cried as she said, "I can't believe I'm in Greece. This is totally awesome!" Her tears fell to the ground and disappeared in the arid soil.

"It is, Mrs., it is." Annie kissed Rachel's cheek. "Look, there's the first olive tree." Annie looked down at her pamphlet, "It says here that it was a gift from the goddess Athena."

"I think I could get used to a culture that honors gods and goddesses."

"Right?" Annie concurred.

They continued to walk around the Acropolis and drink in the crisp white sunlight. They looked down onto the Theatre of Dionysus and the Argos, where Socrates spoke.

After the tour they had crepes, again, and went back to the Plaka to shop for a few more souvenirs.

The next day they boarded the tour bus for a three-hour trip out to the Temple of Poseidon. The journey had them winding along the coast all the way out to Sounion. The sparkling cerulean blue waters of the Aegean flooded into Rachel's heart.

The ruins of the temple towered over them. Rachel walked to the brink and peered into the glittering waters kissing the rocks far below. Annie stayed behind to learn about the effects of pollution on the once-spotless marble.

Rachel dozed off on Annie's shoulder on the wending trip back to Athens. Annie convinced Rachel to try something besides crepes for dinner, and they found a nice little restaurant that served them ouzo, on the house, and brought baklava for desert.

Tomorrow they would depart for Santorini. Rachel missed Athens already.

Annie woke up at three minutes past 5:00 a.m. and yelled, "We slept through the alarm!"

The pre-paid cab was supposed to arrive at 5:00 a.m. They raced around the room, throwing on clothes and grabbing their luggage. They were on the sidewalk in front of the hotel by 5:08.

No cab.

"Shit. Shit. Shit. Shit." Rachel was moaning about never getting to meet her relatives and a great deal of other nonsense, which left Annie to devise a plan.

She ran to a payphone at the end of the street and called the cab company.

No answer. Now it was 5:20 and their flight to Santorini left at 6:45.

Rachel eventually joined the struggle. "Hey, let's run to that fancy hotel three blocks over. I bet that bellman will help us."

Fortunately, they were not travelling with Gwenn. They were able to shoulder their bags and get to the Divani in minutes. The bellman immediately ordered them a cab and they were racing to the airport by 5:30.

As they de-planed and stumbled across the tarmac, Rachel realized she had no idea who was picking them up. When they came out the front door of the airport, they were accosted by at least 20 Greek gentlemen all waving hotel pamphlets, pointing to their respective taxis and promising the best deals.

Rachel looked at Annie and smiled. "It's been a while since I had so many guys fighting over me."

Annie put her arm around Rachel's shoulders and mumbled in her ear, "Don't be such a dyke."

"Rakkel! Rakkel!"

Somewhere above the din, Rachel's DNA picked up on the sound of her name being horribly mispronounced. She scanned the perimeter for the source of the voice. She saw a small group approaching, led by an older woman, an extremely old woman and two boys about her own age.

She waved her arms, "I'm Rakkel."

The women rushed forward and covered her in hugs and kisses. They were speaking Greek a mile a minute and Rachel nodded, smiled and returned the hugs. Then she heard someone say "Loukas"—her father's name.

"Loukas? Did you say Loukas? Do you speak English?" The pleading tone in Rachel's voice got the older woman's attention.

"Yes, Rakkel, yes, we speak English. Sorry, my mother, Nahi, was saying how much you look like her precious Loukas."

"Do I?"

"You really do. I should introduce everyone. I am Zahara, Loukas' younger sister, and these are my twin boys, Hadwin and Haluk." She paused while awkward handshakes were exchanged with the young men.

The sun-wrinkled woman stepped forward and grasped Rachel's hand tightly. Her onyx eyes bored into Rachel's and tears spilled freely.

"This is your grandmother, Nahi Papathanassiou."

Rachel smothered the woman in an iron embrace and was shocked to feel the hug returned just as tightly. She felt a little tap on her shoulder and turned to find Annie looking on like a spectator. "Oh, sorry." Rachel released her hold on her grandmother and pulled Annie up next to her. "This is my wife, Annie. We just got married on July fourth."

A series of questions and answers were fired back and forth in Greek. Rachel watched as the brothers took the lead in apparently explaining lesbians to Grandma Nahi. Eventually there was a chorus of head nodding and Nahi clapped her hands together.

Rachel didn't realize she had been holding her breath until she felt her knees wobble beneath her.

Zahara turned to Annie and Rachel, "Nahi says we must have a wedding feast."

Rachel turned her face into Annie's shoulder and let the tears wash all the old pain away. Everything was OK.

She had a family; they accepted her and she looked like her dad. She didn't think the day could get any better, until they crested the edge of the caldera in Oia, and she saw the view. Sunlight painting the ocean a thousand shades of blue and the mountainside dotted with azure-domed, whitewashed cubical houses. Paradise.

Seventy-five

It took several days to meet all of Loukas' extended family and after nearly a week, Rachel and Annie were ready to rent a car and explore the island on their own.

Hadwin offered to drive them to the rental outlet. "I used to fish with the guy's son. I can get you a good deal."

Hadwin's friend's father brought out the tiny car and showed the girls all the features. He flicked on the high-beam headlights and said, "Big." He laughed with Rachel and Annie. He didn't speak much English, but he knew that wasn't the right word.

After some quick suggestions from Hadwin and some general directions, Rachel and Annie drove off to Fira. They made a few wrong turns, but eventually parked near the city center and enquired about cruises out of Old Port. They purchased two tickets, got directions to the docks and walked off.

After winding through the labyrinthine streets and asking directions three more times, they came to the conclusion that Greeks don't really give directions to a final destination.

Each person they stopped would simply send them down to the corner and left or right. The girls mistakenly thought that at the end of the directions would be their destination.

After 45 minutes of wandering through town they finally discovered the Incline. Now they had to choose between a cable car or donkeys to get down the cliffside to the actual docks. Rachel was not having donkeys. Once aboard, the boat took them out to a tiny volcanic island for a quick hike, which was hot and not what Rachel had in mind.

They got back on the boat and the guide told them they were now going to a little cove to swim in the ocean. Annie thought that sounded fantastic.

The vessel rounded the point of land and backed into a small cove surrounded by a hillside covered with goats. The guide climbed up in the rigging and shouted, "You swim here. Thirty minutes."

Rachel watched in shock as the zombie-like tourists launched themselves over the side of the boat into the chilly ocean.

"Come on, babe. Once in a lifetime...let's do it." Annie tugged Rachel's hand.

"I hope I don't regret this." Rachel climbed up on the bench next to the railing and she and Annie jumped into the Aegean.

Every cell in her body tingled as the biting salt water enveloped her. She dropped Annie's hand and clawed her way to the surface. She came up sputtering and gasping.

Annie shot up right next to her. "Well, it's nice to know that you would drop me like dead weight if we were on the Titanic."

Rachel splashed water at Annie. "How rude!"

"I'll never let go, Jack," Annie taunted Rachel and dove under the water to tug on Rachel's legs.

As promised a ladder was thrown over the side in thirty minutes, and everyone climbed back onboard.

They walked around Fira, ate some apple, raisin and almond crepes, and when they dried off they drove out to Akrotiri. The interesting archaeological site had ruins from the Minoan era.

Rachel stopped and stared at one of the unearthed living spaces, filled with pottery and implements from other parts of the dig. "Isn't it weird to think that these people were here one minute and the next, POOF, disappeared. Their entire village covered in volcanic ash for thousands of years?"

"Makes you think. Every moment matters, ya know." Annie smiled and rubbed Rachel's hand.

"I don't want to take things for granted."

"You don't."

"I've taken Ed, my other dad, for granted. I should've asked him to come to the wedding. I know he would've said 'no', but that would be on him."

"Maybe we should have him over for dinner when we get back."

Rachel smiled wistfully at Annie. "Seriously, you would endure that for me?"

"In a heartbeat, babe."

"Thank you, Mrs." Rachel kissed Annie's nose. "Hey, we better get back and see if Grandma Nahi needs any help preparing for the wedding feast."

"You should offer to make some bread. I think it would impress the heck outta her."

"You are officially the best wife on the entire planet." Rachel kissed Annie.

"But not in the universe, huh. Guess I got some work to do."

"Rude." Rachel laughed and smacked Annie on the ass.

Epilogue

Rachel looked out her bedroom window, over the sapphire sea and smiled. She glanced down at the men scurrying around on the patio. "Annie, you have to see this."

Tables and chairs appeared from nowhere. The entire neighborhood must have been invited to Loukas' daughters' wedding feast.

They dressed and went downstairs to lend a hand. As soon as they hit the bottom step Nahi handed each of them a steaming mug of black coffee and a thick slice of bread slathered with Nutella. She immediately instructed, "Fae, fae."

Rachel took this to mean, "eat" and happily obliged.

The house was filled with hustle and bustle. Zahara smiled and threw up her hands. "This is what we do."

"Can we help?" Rachel took a sip of the surprisingly strong coffee while she waited for a reply.

"Most of Nahi's friends do not speak English. They can make spanakopita in their sleep. You would probably be in their way. Go find Haluk's girlfriend. She speaks perfect English and she's in charge of decorations."

Rachel and Annie raised their mugs in a salute to Zahara and walked out into the penetratingly bright Ionian light.

The day was a blur of activity. Haluk's girlfriend Kyra was a riot. She had actually heard of The Spanking Machine and spent 15 minutes texting selfies, of her and Annie, to all her friends. By the time the sun was slipping toward the sea, the patio was decked out with enough tables and chairs for the entire village. Fresh white linens billowed in the salty air and Kyra placed heavy glass hurricane lamps over each of the candles.

Zahara came out of the kitchen balancing a huge platter of dolmades. "Hey, you two better get changed. Nahi will want you right next to her for the first toast."

Annie and Rachel came back downstairs to find a packed house. The sun toyed with the horizon and the sky rippled with shapes of orange, pink and purple.

Zahara led them down to the seats of honor, next to Nahi. "You will not understand a word for the remainder of the evening, but rest assured it will all be good." She kissed each of them on the cheek and disappeared into the crowd.

Nahi raised her glass of ouzo and rambled on, as though time had no meaning.

Rachel heard her father's name mentioned a number of times and watched Nahi dab at her eyes with her sun-drenched hands. She didn't need to speak Greek to understand the love emitting from this woman. She drank when Nahi drank. She cheered when Nahi cheered. The parade of toasts continued.

She and Annie had stopped worrying about the language barrier and let themselves enjoy the spirit of the party. So when someone yelled, "I'd like to make a toast!" Rachel thought perhaps she had consumed enough ouzo to activate her deeply buried Greek speaking DNA. She looked at Annie, "Was that English? Did you hear that?"

Annie looked away and pretended it was too loud to make out what Rachel was saying.

Rachel prepared to scold Annie severely when a face she recognized popped up above the crowd. There in the middle of a sea of sunset-kissed ebony hair flashed a fiery redhead holding her ouzo aloft.

"I'd like to make a toast," she repeated. "To the most amazing, beautiful sister in the entire universe!" She adjusted her position on Daniel's shoulder and shouted, "Ya mas! To Rachel and Annie."

Cheers broke out across the terrace, and as the sun dipped into the Aegean, Rachel pushed her way through the crowd to embrace the one person who never ceased to amaze her. "Gwenny!"

Acknowledgments

As I wrote the final chapters in this series and watched the Hutchinson sisters revel in their hard-won happiness, I realized my own happily-ever-after would not be possible without the genuine love and support of my partner, Scott.

My wonderfully original sons have been understanding and supportive. Their stories are still unfolding. They listen to me babble on about plot twists and character's traits, as though it's perfectly normal to discuss characters like they're real people.

I am extremely grateful for all the summers I spent with my hilarious grandmother, Rita [pronounced *Right-a*]. She taught me everything I know about Scrabble and fishing!

I would have given up a hundred times without the honest encouragement of wonderful people like Rhonda (*world's best sister*), Anne, Jenn, Katherine, Carolyn, Debbie, Melinda, Amy, Topher, Jim, Natalia, Patrick, Ken, Maree, Cindy, Tony, Ania and Andrew.

Thank you (*again*) to my fabulous editor Jazmine Hale! I feel truly blessed to have found her and look forward to many more projects together.

Thank you to my Beta readers, who gave me invaluable insights and feedback: Kathy, Anne, Summer, Mesa and Scott. (*More than once!*)

I definitely want to thank all the wonderful bloggers who helped blog, blitz and reveal!

A special thank you to DeeJay Arens, an award-winning indie author, who is generous, kind and fantastic! *Thank you* for taking the time to share some wisdom with a fellow traveler.

I love reading, and the tale of the Hutchinson sisters owes a thanks to Colette, Frances Hodgson Burnett, Yann Martel, Dylan Landis and Marian Keyes, just to name a few.

Of course none of this would matter without you! I am grateful for every reader who takes the time to explore The Lake Effect Series. Thank *you* for your loyal support. If you are new to the series, I'm glad you joined us! I would like to ask a favor of you. If you can find a few minutes to review FINALLY MY FAVORITE on Amazon, Barnes and Noble and/or Goodreads, it would be extremely helpful. Reader support makes all the difference. Your reviews give this book a life of its own.

Thanks for reading!

Connect with me online!
Facebook
Twitter
Pinterest
Goodreads

Photo by Michele Bradley

RUE is an award-winning author who graduated from Pepperdine University in Malibu, California, with a degree in Journalism. Her intimate knowledge of the Midwestern United States, the inordinate amount of time she spent in its churches' pews and her unique parentage make her an expert on life after religion. Having moved 17 times by the time she graduated from high school, Rue has seen more than her share of the Great Plains. She never stayed in one place long enough to make lasting human friends. Her best friends were all characters from her beloved books; and the love of reading led to a lifelong passion for writing.

www.ruescorner.com

Q & A with Rue

Q: What do your fans mean to you?

A: Fan = Reader.

Fans are the most important part of the entire process! If no one reads (and enjoys) my books then the process would be far less rewarding. One of the best parts of writing about the characters in my head is to hear from a reader who enjoyed the book. I could write a stack of novels and put them on a shelf—but that's not really the point. I want to share all these stories with other people. For someone to be called a "fan" I think that means that they would have to like the work and look forward to future novels I write—that is priceless.

Q: Describe your desk.

A: My desk is my altar. A section of trinkets, mementos and inspirational sayings which help encourage and motivate me as I write. A copy of a special invocation to the Goddess of Skills—is part of my ritual of relaxing into my writing space and focusing on the day's project. I have my stack of notes, printouts, pictures and any other research pertaining to the current project on my right (and it sometimes spills onto my left). I cannot begin without a dish of peanuts or almonds and a dish of dark chocolate covered pomegranate seeds. My office supply addiction requires a healthy supply of pens and a Post-it note dispenser—stocked with notes for posting. However, I would have to say that the things NOT on my desk are even more important. I do not have bills, To Do lists, business cards or my cell phone. My writing space is sacred, and when I sit down to write I have to minimize all potential distractions.

Q: Where did you grow up, and how did this influence your writing?

A: I grew up everywhere—Minnesota, Kansas, Massachusetts, Georgia, California and finally Arizona. I sometimes even got to revisit places; in fact there were a few rounders in the Land of 10,000 Lakes (MN). I would have to say that the nomadic lifestyle was hell as a child, but looking back I can appreciate all the nuggets I was able to collect for future stories. The reason I write fiction is simply because my entire life has been crammed full of experiences that are just too unbelievable to be true. The characters I create all have threads pulled from real people whom I encountered in my travels—yes, every one.

Q: When did you first start writing?

A: I wrote my first manifesto at age three; a letter begging my grandfather to stop smoking; to the small pink piece of stationary, I taped two dimes and a nickel—his reward for quitting. The entreaty was successful and the power of the pen was instilled in my soul. Throughout my life I have written unceasingly: journals, poems, short stories, screenplays, and articles for newspapers and magazines. My love of ink led me to pursue a B.A. in Journalism from Pepperdine University in California. I also suffer from a slight obsession with office supplies—mostly pens and fine paper.

Q: What's the story behind your latest book?

A: At the time of this answer my latest book is Book 3 in The Lake Effect Series, FINALLY MY FAVORITE. The story of the Hutchinson sisters is close to my heart. I have two brothers and a sister—I love them all, but my sister and I have a deep connection that deserved to be memorialized in print (or "e"). Now, just to be clear, the story is a vehicle to explore the unbreakable bonds of a sibling relationship in the face of serious family drama—but it is not "about" my sister or my family. I drew on decades of school, work and uncomfortable church-related interactions to create the characters in The Lake Effect Series.

Q: What motivated you to become an indie author?

A: I was motivated to become an indie author because I love challenges. I started my own publishing company and forged ahead. I learned most of my publishing lessons the hard way, but I am also grateful to those who came before me and were kind enough to throw out a proverbial breadcrumb here or there. I write five to six days a week and I love it. I am not crazy about marketing, but I am told it is a necessary evil. :-) I plan to pay it forward whenever I can and to share the knowledge I glean along the way.

Q: What are you working on next?

A: At the time of this answer I am approximately half way finished with a new YA novel, "Fractured Lives." Three seemingly unconnected stories that weave toward a surprising conclusion. I'm excited to be exploring new regions of the country in this story—in addition to good old Minnesota!

Q: What inspires you to get out of bed each day?

A: Nothing. I hate getting out of bed. I am the human equivalent of Garfield. I hate mornings. Coffee is my avenging angel.

Q: When you're not writing, how do you spend your time?

A: I cook to relieve stress, and then I eat to forget about the stress I was trying to relieve. I also love movies, television and reading. I'm an old school book reader. I have an eReader, but I don't *love* it. I like the smell and feel of a solid, paper-filled book in my hands.

Q: Do you remember the first story you ever wrote?

A: Yes, it was a sad tale of a young girl hell bent on running away from home and going to the same school for two or three whole years. Tragically that epic piece of fiction was lost in one of my family's MANY moves.